OF Hope & Blight

SANCTUARY OF THE LOST BOOK 2

LOU WILHAM & CHRISTIS CHRISTIE

Copyright © 2024 by Christis Christie & Lou Wilham

All rights reserved.

No part of this book may be reproduced in any form or by any electronic or mechanical means, including information storage and retrieval systems, without written permission from the author, except for the use of brief quotations in a book review.

 Created with Vellum

This one is for the quiet ones.

Authors' Note

Please note that this book contains scenes mentioning rape, depicting child abuse and neglect, and violence. We have done our best to handle these elements in a sensitive way, but if these issues could be considered triggering for you, please take care of yourself.
 - Lou & Christis

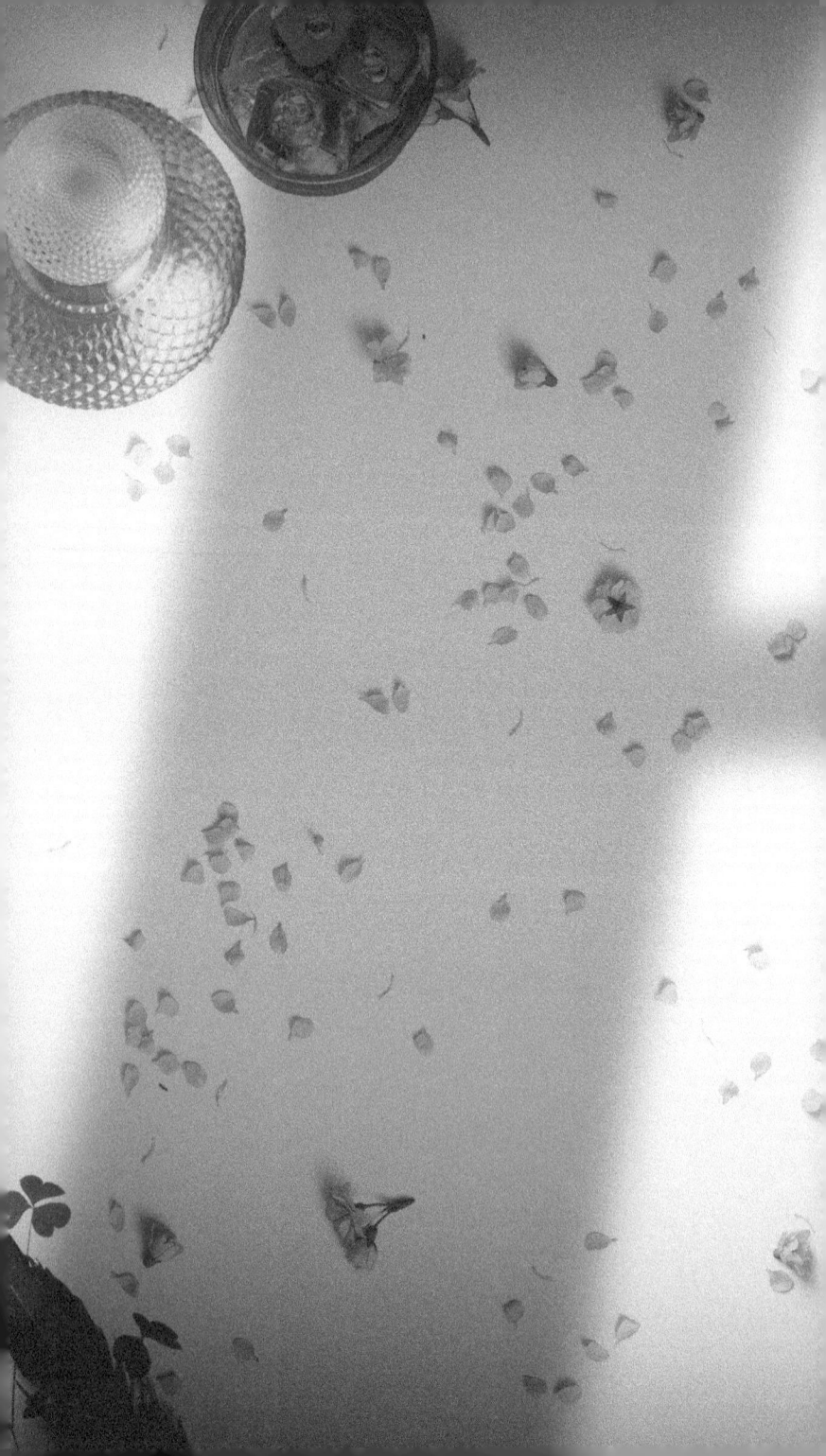

Prologue
456

Inanimi Fighting Camps, Syria - August 2005

Every part of him was cramped. 456 had long since outgrown the cage he was kept in between fights. His black wings took up so much space, and in order to keep them from bending in ways they should not, he had to scrunch his legs closer to his chest.

The heat of the day had faded to a chill that settled into his bones. His teeth chattered as his body struggled to warm his muscles up. The heat he could handle. The heat barely felt like enough to sustain him. But the cold was something altogether different. A type of torture all its own.

456 groaned, his legs beginning to spasm, the muscles and tendons clenching. With slow, careful motions, he gripped onto the bars to help his movement and rolled himself onto his back. He hated laying on his wings, his weight bearing down uncomfortably on the thin bones, pinching them between his torso and the stone below. But doing so gave him the ability to stick his legs out through the bars at the top of the cage and stretch out a little. He

wiggled his toes, looking at the rock ceiling of the cave above him.

It hid the encampment from the outside world, masking them from being found by anyone. A perfect little hidey-hole to cover the atrocities taking place in the desert.

The only time 456 saw the sky was when he was taken out to the ring.

There was always a brief moment of peace before the fight began when he was able to look up to the stars above him and dream of freedom in their vastness. When he could imagine opening his wings and soaring away from the hellish nightmare of his life.

But the metal anklet made sure they would find him. They *always* found anyone who escaped. When the escapees were brought back to the camp, all the fighters would be gathered into a group and made to watch as the prisoner who had attempted to flee was tortured then left to die in the desert. Either the heat of the sun or a vulture would eventually end their suffering.

456 had nightmares that would wake him screaming in the middle of the night, of vultures pecking out his eyes, leaving him wandering the desert, blind and helpless. He didn't know what was worse: being lost in a place he did not know or trapped here in this hell he did.

He made circles with his feet, his ankles stretching and popping. It was a momentary relief which did not last long as voices sounded from the opening of the cave. 456 tucked his knees in against his chest, wrapping his thin arms around them, attempting to make himself appear as small as possible.

"Who are we taking tonight?" asked one voice.

"Boss says he wants a good show. Some god is in attendance," responded the second. There was a snort from the first, then, "What'd the challenger bring with 'em?"

"Lamia, I think Shaki said," said the first.

A cold, hateful laugh echoed in the cave. It bounced around inside 456's head, and he curled himself more tightly, his wings tucking around his body like a shield.

"What's so funny?" asked the first.

"Lamia like children's hearts." He laughed again, and soon, the other male was joining in.

456 knew they were coming to his cage before the key scraped inside the hole, unlatching the lock with a *click* that made the chill in his body reach his core.

He didn't want to die.

When the door opened, 456 launched himself at the keeper, screaming in anger and shoving as hard as he could. While he was still just a child, he wasn't a human child and possessed more strength than most creatures his age.

The satyr staggered back, falling onto his ass in the sand. A cloud of dust rose into the air around him. 456 stretched out his wings, ignoring the bone-deep ache in them, and jumped into the air.

A calloused hand latched around his ankle and pulled him back down to the earth. Then a fist collided with the side of his face, and his head was spinning, a ringing sounding in his ears.

"Attempt that again and the lamia won't have a chance to get you," the second keeper spat, his hand now around 456's throat, squeezing tight. "You hear me?" He shook 456 roughly.

Growling, 456 glared up at the male with dark eyes and a hint of something other about him. He never showed his true form when he was here shoving the fighters around, but there was a strength beneath his human façade.

"You good?" he asked the satyr, who climbed to his feet, dusting himself off.

"Yeah." The satyr spat, glaring his hatred at 456. He leaned in close to his face. "I hope that lamia eats your heart out and makes you watch."

456 didn't allow them to see the terror seizing him at the thought. He kept his face blank and his lips sealed. There was safety in silence. Even if it wouldn't save him from what was to come, perhaps there would be less beatings along the way.

The second keeper with the dark eyes gripped the back of 456's neck and steered him along the long corridors of the cave until, at last, they emerged into the open arena.

A dirt floor lay before them, and seats that were carved into the stone surrounded it. Above, the moonlight was bright, and the stars shone, twinkling in the depths of the darkness.

456 looked up, staring at the bright specks. Maybe death would be better. To disappear and leave this all behind. To lift into the stars above. That's where he liked to imagine he would end up. Somewhere in the stars.

The second keeper put more pressure on the back of his neck and shoved him into the arena. 456 stumbled, almost toppling over. But the spread of his wings helped stabilize him and kept him upright.

The crowd roared, the sound almost deafening. Still, he could hear the announcer, loud over the speakers, talking in a language 456 did not understand. But it didn't matter; he knew what was to come.

The announcer would call out his words, the crowd would scream, clap, and demand blood. All those eyes staring down at him, watching as he faced off against another creature who wished to kill him. Eyes that were attached to angry faces. Jeers. Shouts. Cheers of pleasure as blood was shed on ground already so drenched with it, it should be red.

Across the arena, 456 saw a shadow emerging from the depths of a cave. A great beast that swayed back and forth. From the darkness, a tall woman with jet-black hair appeared. Her form was slender and pale, slim waist disappearing into the golden scales of a long tail that trailed behind her.

She slithered out of the cave and into the arena, and cheers of excitement roared up from the crowd. It was deafening, making 456 lift his hands to cover his ears.

If he could have, he would have curled into a ball and buried his face in his wings. But something wouldn't let him give up. Something kept him fighting even when the odds were all stacked against him.

He didn't want to meet the creature at the center of the arena, but prior experience told him if he didn't, he'd be prodded into place by a stick with sparks at the end of it. Those sparks hurt and caused pain to course through every part of his body. He would tense up, his world zeroing in on that one point of contact causing so much agony, until finally, the stick was pulled away.

His bare feet carried him slowly across the dirt, stepping over sharp stones that pricked into the soles, tenderizing flesh that barely felt the bruising anymore.

The lamia swayed side to side, coming to a stop just a few feet away from him. Her eyes were entirely black, no irises. They swept over him, stopping at his sternum, where she hissed, a forked tongue escaping her mouth as she scented the air.

"Haasssssa kaa yaaaasaa sssaaa basa," she hissed at him.

Though he didn't understand her, 456 knew she was threatening to kill him.

His skin crawled, prickles of warning making the hair on the back of his neck and along his arms stand on end. His heart tripped along at a rapid pace, frantically trying to encourage him to turn and flee. Instead, he unfurled his wings, letting the black feathers that glinted with hints of rainbow shuffle lightly in the evening breeze.

Neither of them moved until a horn sounded, then the lamia launched herself at him, fangs flashing as her mouth gaped open. Long black nails extended from spindly fingers that scraped at his arms and shoulders as he leaped back, just escaping her attack.

An *ooo* sounded from the stands.

Her long serpent tail slashed quickly across the soil, helping to right her from the fall forward when she hadn't collided with him, and she rose, preparing to strike once more.

456's knees shook beneath him. His stomach rumbled with hunger. And above, the bright lights of the fighting arena made his eyes ache in his head. He had no strength to fight. No strength to kill.

But if he didn't, he would die.

When the lamia shot for him again, barely giving him time to get to his feet after sidestepping her first attack, 456 forced what little strength he had into his wings. Flapping quickly, he lifted into the air.

The audience gasped.

He wasn't fast enough, and sharp black claws sank into the barely-there flesh of his calf. He squawked in dismay, reaching for the freedom of the stars above him, fingers scraping to catch on something that was not tangible.

The lamia yanked him down out of the air, and this

time, a loud cheer went up from half the crowd, while the other half booed.

456 swung at her face with his closed fists, catching her in the eye with one and across the cheek with the other. His blows were harsh, and her cheek split, dark red blood dripping from the gash.

She hissed at him and wrapped her hand around his throat, squeezing tightly.

"Ssya tssrana shhaaa," she growled lowly, dragging a sharp nail down his sternum, beginning to open the flesh of his chest.

456 didn't think, he simply listened to the instincts telling him to press his hands to her chest and push. A scream left his lips at the pain of the nails cutting him open, and heat welled up inside him. His hands began to glow, and as his scream intensified, fire erupted from his palms, quickly encasing the lamia.

She howled in agony and flung him away as she coiled and rolled up on herself, attempting to put out the magical fire now burning her alive.

456 tumbled over the ground, the wind knocked out of him.

And then the world around him seemed to explode. Smoke filled the entire arena and caught at his lungs, making him cough and his head feel woozy. Before he passed out, 456 saw beings just like him with large wings drop out of the sky to attack the creatures in the arena.

He awoke to bright lights and the steady beeping of something to the side of him. As his eyes blinked open, he found he was in an unfamiliar white room. His fingers lifted to brush over the bandage on his chest, and he looked down to see strange strings stuck to the skin around it and a tube going into his arm.

Terror gripped him, and he pulled the strings off his chest. A shrill noise ripped through the air as he did. Next, he pulled the tube out of his arm, which caused blood to spring up as a pointy metal piece withdrew from his skin. He leaped from the flat surface he was lying on to hide under the nearest thing he could: a small metal table with spindly legs. It was a tight fit, but he was used to that. And it was better than being out in the open in this strange room where anyone or anything could attack him.

Several people rushed into the room. Most of them looked like ordinary humans, but a couple had colorful wings. 456 stared at them from under the table, arms tight around his chest. What were they? Were they like him? Had they brought him here to hurt him?

One of them caught sight of him under the table and stepped forward, reaching beneath to grab him. 456 struck out at him, digging his nails into his arm until the male pulled back with a grunt of pain.

"Stop. He's frightened," a soft but stern voice spoke. "He doesn't know where he is right now."

456 watched as the man crouched down in front of the table and took a seat on the floor. He had dark, black hair and bright, blue eyes that were kind and gentle. A light smile formed on his lips.

"Hi there. My name is Colton Schields. What would you like me to call you?"

456 pulled his legs closer to his chest, unsure of what was going to happen.

"You're okay," the man continued when 456 didn't

respond. "You're never going to have to go back to that cave again, okay?"

456 just blinked. He only understood some of the words that were coming from the man.

The man looked up at one of the other people in the room and murmured softly for some food to be brought.

456 watched as the strangers continued to move around the room, then there was something meaty and delicious being slid on a plate across the floor to him. He stared down at it. His stomach rumbled as the smell hit his nose. He desperately wanted to eat it but didn't know if he should trust the food or the human who gave it to him.

"Go ahead," the man murmured softly. "It's okay. I won't let anything else hurt you."

456 reached out quickly and grabbed the hunk of meat, bringing it up to his mouth to bite into the juicy flesh, scooting farther back into the wall behind him as he did.

"Captain Hadrian explained to me that you don't have a name," the man named Colton Schields said.

456 simply blinked at him, swallowing the meat in his mouth to take another bite.

"What do you think of the name Quintus?"

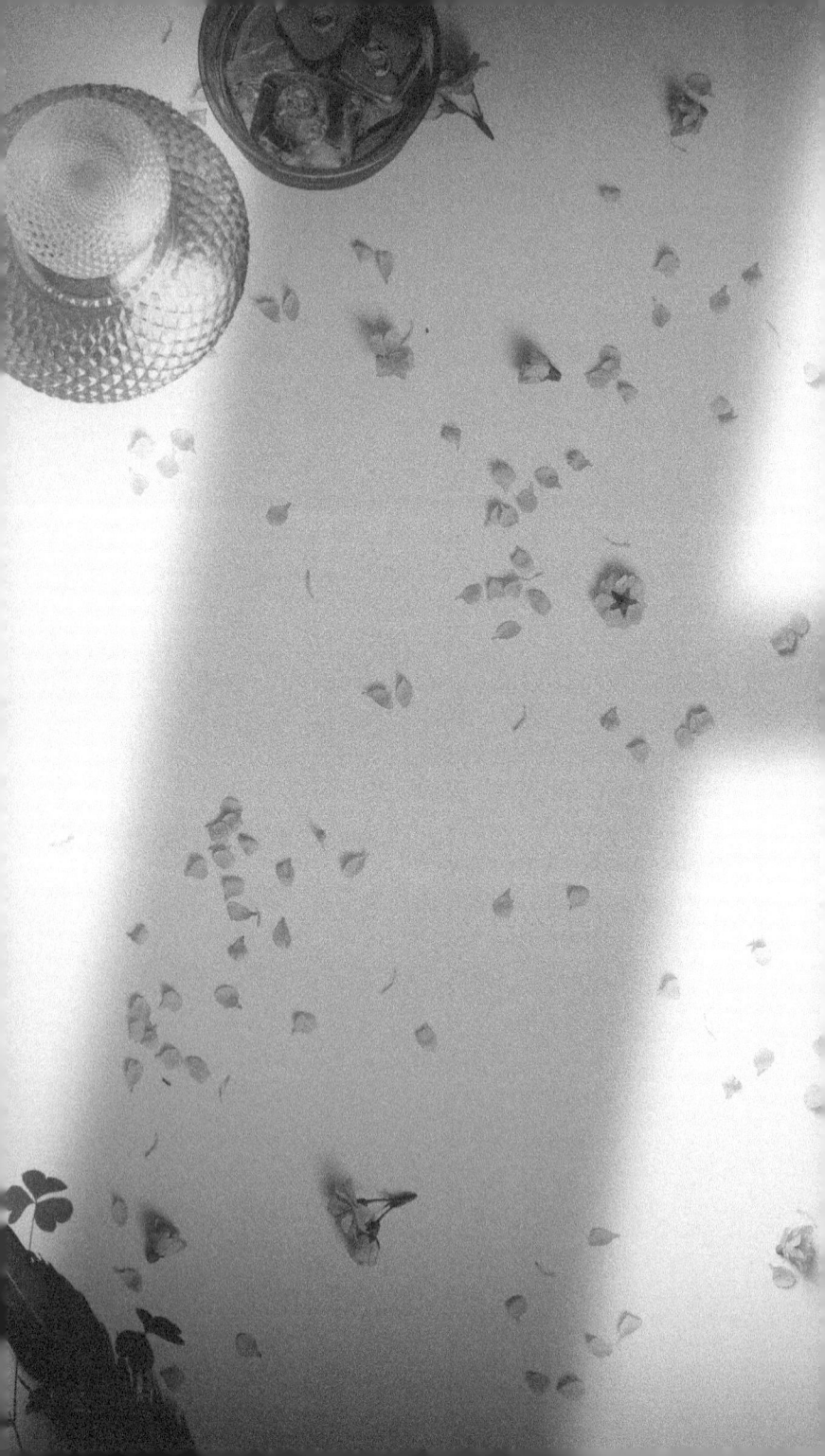

Chapter 1
Mab

Miami, Florida - 2018

Mab wasn't entirely sure why Ander had decided he needed to hold his housewarming party at *her* house. Hosting it at someone else's home seemed to go against the very nature of what a housewarming party was: a party held to celebrate one's new living arrangements, in which people were invited to poke around said abode like the nosey little shits they were.

Scratch that.

She knew *exactly* why he was making her hold the party at her house. It was so, one: he didn't have to clean up after everyone when things got out of hand, and two: he and Max could skulk away to do whatever it was they did—honestly, she didn't want to know—when they both decided they'd had enough of everyone. Not that she could blame them; it was a brilliant plan. She only wished she'd thought of it.

"You cannot invite Hazel and Willow," Mab said, marking them off the list Ander had provided, her free hand moving to brush a white curl back from her face. It was a long list. Far too long for a "small, intimate housewarming extravaganza, I swear, Mab." Further driving home the point that Ander wouldn't know small and intimate if they clocked him over the head. She supposed it was the word *extravaganza* that was throwing them off here. It didn't really fit with the description *small*.

"Why not?" Ander pouted. He was sitting on her couch, his arms crossed over his chest, his heels kicked up on the coffee table, even though she'd asked him repeatedly not to put his feet on her furniture. It was a lost cause, honestly. She was just glad he wasn't day-drinking. Maybe Wonderboy was doing him some good after all. He did look healthier, fuller around the cheeks. And he was definitely sleeping better. She'd send Max a thank you present if she didn't think he'd be completely confused by it and demand an explanation. The housewarming party would just have to do in its stead.

"Because the last time we invited them to something, there was a fire."

"A small one."

"They nearly burned down half the block, Andy!" Mab pinched the bridge of her nose, her other hand tightening around the notepad until the pages crinkled. This was not going well. Not well at all. And she wasn't really sure anymore how she'd thought it'd go any differently. "Look." She leaned forward, forcing Ander to meet her eyes. He'd dropped them to sulk, like a toddler, when she'd said no, she was not going to have Alfie and Tommy and their whole three-ring circus of fae folk at her house. Because the last time they'd shown up to one of her residences, all the silver had gone missing. It wasn't their fault, really, they had a penchant for shiny things, and in their defense, they were only "borrowing" them. But she wasn't doing that again. It had gotten prohibitively expensive to replace things. "We're going to have ignis at this party, Andy. A whole rack of them. Max and the frowny one—"

"Quin, Mab. His name is Quin."

"*And*," she pressed on ignoring him. She knew Quin's name. She just found it more fun to refer to him by increasingly ridiculous nicknames. "Their siblings, and a couple other friends they have from the sanctuary. They're literally magical law enforcement, Andy. We can't have any of the guests getting up to their usual shenanigans when we have literal *law enforcement* under my roof. Do you expect Max to just turn a blind eye to it? He's hopelessly in love with you, but he's not that stupid."

Ander huffed, looking petulant. "Fine. But we need to visit with them soon. We haven't seen them in ages, Mabbers, and we were in their wedding."

Mab decided not to remind him that they didn't have to stay in contact with every couple whose wedding they were in. Sometimes people drifted apart. That was normal. Normies did it all the time. Especially when the couple in question fought like cats and dogs and happened to be a will-o-wisp and a fire elemental who liked to set fire to things when they were bickering. But Ander had this need to stay not just in contact but friends with everyone over the years. She supposed maybe it spawned from the dark years, when Enrique had kept him locked away and unable to speak to anyone outside of Enrique's own circle.

She couldn't really fault him for that.

That didn't mean she wanted Hazel and Willow in her house, though. Especially with ignis on the guest list. She didn't need anyone getting arrested. It would spoil the mood.

"Fine. We'll reach out to them after the party and set up a date for drinks. The same with Tom and Alfie. But they aren't coming here." Mab put a little note next to their names and crossed them off the list.

"Fine."

Gods, she hoped he didn't sulk through this entire process. It probably would have been less painful if Max were there to help out, but alas, being Wonderboy was pretty much a full-time job it seemed. And with them only being two weeks out, they were still cleaning up the mess left by Enrique. Finding homes for the baby ignis. Paperwork. That kind of thing. Or at least she assumed that's what Max and Quin were doing, anyway.

"Now." She settled back into the arm of the couch again, tapping her pen on the legal pad in her lap. She'd gotten rid of the worst offenders among their friends. That didn't mean there wouldn't be an incident—that was impossible to prevent—but said incident was now much less likely to wind up with her house burned down, all her shit missing, or someone arrested, and Mab thought perhaps that was a job well done. There was just one couple left. "We need to talk about Juno and Indra."

"You can't keep vetoing everyone on my list, Mab," Ander grumbled, dramatic creature that he was. As if she'd said they couldn't invite literally any of his friends, when really, she'd only cut the list down by a third.

"I actually can. It's my house."

"It's my party."

"Still my house, babe." Mab shrugged. He wasn't going to win this one; they both knew it. But that didn't matter because she also knew—

"We can't just not invite them. They're the *king and queen of the gods*." He said that last bit less like Indra and Juno were royalty and more like they were the particularly annoying poodle his friends adopted instead of having children. It was funny. She wished Indra were there to hear it. "Not that it would keep Indra away, even if we didn't invite him."

Annoying. But true. Indra would show up, invitation or not. He never missed a party. And he'd been taking a special interest in Wonderboy as of late. Which was unnerving. Mab didn't think it was exactly a *good* thing that the king of the gods was paying extra attention to Ander and his ignis boyfriend. It could only end in disaster, in her experience. She didn't say that out loud. Ander had to know anyway. He wasn't stupid. But there wasn't exactly anything they could do about it, either. Indra would do whatever he wanted. He always did.

"Which is why we're going to." Mab's pen tapped furiously against the pad, the sound loud in her ears. She stopped it, holding it still where it hovered over the paper. Why was she so anxious about this party? It wasn't the first one she'd thrown. Actually, that wasn't true. It *was* the first one of its kind she'd thrown. It signified a dramatic shift in their relationship, a change in their lives. She knew she wasn't losing Ander to Max—that would be impossible. But their family was expanding. It hadn't done that in many years, not since Enrique. And although she knew Max wasn't like *him*, would never hurt Ander that way, she couldn't seem to get past the anxiety that crawled up her spine reminding her that the last time she trusted some guy with her best friend—her *brother*—the bastard she'd trusted him to nearly killed him. "I've already sent a formal message by way of Hermahas. Mum can't attend, but she said she'd send Seraphine to look after things. Hopefully that will be enough to keep Indra from getting out of hand. So you have nothing to worry about."

"Nothing?" He shifted in his seat, nail polish glinting as

he futzed with his soft, flowy tank top. Comfort wear. Because he was anxious about this party. Mab had seen it on him the moment he showed up in her kitchen about an hour ago.

This was the first big event he and Max would be hosting as a couple. He wanted things to go well.

He didn't have to say any of that out loud. Mab had known Ander Ruin for centuries at this point; she could read him like a book. Better, even.

"Nothing," she repeated, reaching out to take his hands as she scooted across the couch, pressing her shin into his thigh. "Andy, talk to me."

"I am talking to you."

She rolled her eyes, blowing out an annoyed breath. "How are things going with Max? How is living together working? I know it's only been a couple of weeks, but if you need me to come and kick him out . . . " She puffed out her chest and drew on the magic of the banshee, the wail. The air picked up in the room, making goosebumps rise all along her arms, and though she couldn't see it, she knew that her eyes had gone the washed-out white that terrified normies. "I will."

Ander blinked at her for a moment, perhaps stunned by the enormity of her love for him, then burst out laughing. Snickers jerked his shoulders and wracked his body as he flopped back against the opposite arm of the couch, almost throwing himself over it. Dramatic little shit.

"Well, it wasn't *that* funny," she mumbled, pulling her hands away from his so she could cross her arms. "Rude."

"I'm sorry, Mabbers. Mabinson Jones. Blight of my life." Ander was still laughing, but he pulled himself upright, straightening his shirt out again. "My darling. My first love. My—"

"Enough already, I get the picture." She swatted his hands away and pushed herself back to her end of the couch. She wouldn't say it out loud, but she missed him. Missed this. He'd been spending so much time with Max over the last few weeks, she'd hardly seen him outside of work. But she wouldn't begrudge him that. How could she? He'd found his soulmate. He was finally—*finally*—whole and happy. And after so many years living with the emptiness she knew sat like an ache in his bones, it was nice to see him like this. To notice how his cheeks were filling out. How his eyes didn't sometimes glaze over with want for something he couldn't quite name. She was also a little jealous, if she was honest. Which she wasn't going to be. Because she didn't have time for it.

No time to be honest. No time to be jealous. No time for a soulmate.

Ander's happiness would be enough.

"It's wonderful," Ander said when he finally got ahold of himself fully. "He's just . . . " He paused, seeming like he was searching for the words, like he couldn't even form sentences that would contain his joy. Good. That was good. He deserved that. "He's good. He's *so* good, Mab. So good. And he—he makes the world seem so much—so glittery. I don't think I've ever been so happy in all my life."

That stung more than she would ever let on, more than she would ever let him see. Because Mab had been there, for centuries, doing everything she could to keep Ander from falling apart at the seams. Pulling out every trick to make him happy. To bring him peace when he needed it and joy when he longed for it. But he had never smiled like this. Not in the many long years she'd known him. And Mab was struck suddenly by the jarring fact that she'd never been enough for him. That her love for him never filled that aching void. Had she ever been able to do that for someone? Had she ever been *enough*?

If Ander was too much, Mab wasn't enough.

She smiled. It wasn't even forced, not really. Because it was nice to see him happy. To know that someone loved him and filled him up. But she struggled to follow the flow of words from Ander as he fell into some story that involved Max, the packing boxes, and Monnie. She lost the thread of it, didn't even try to pick it back up. Just let his happiness wash over her in a slow, steady warmth.

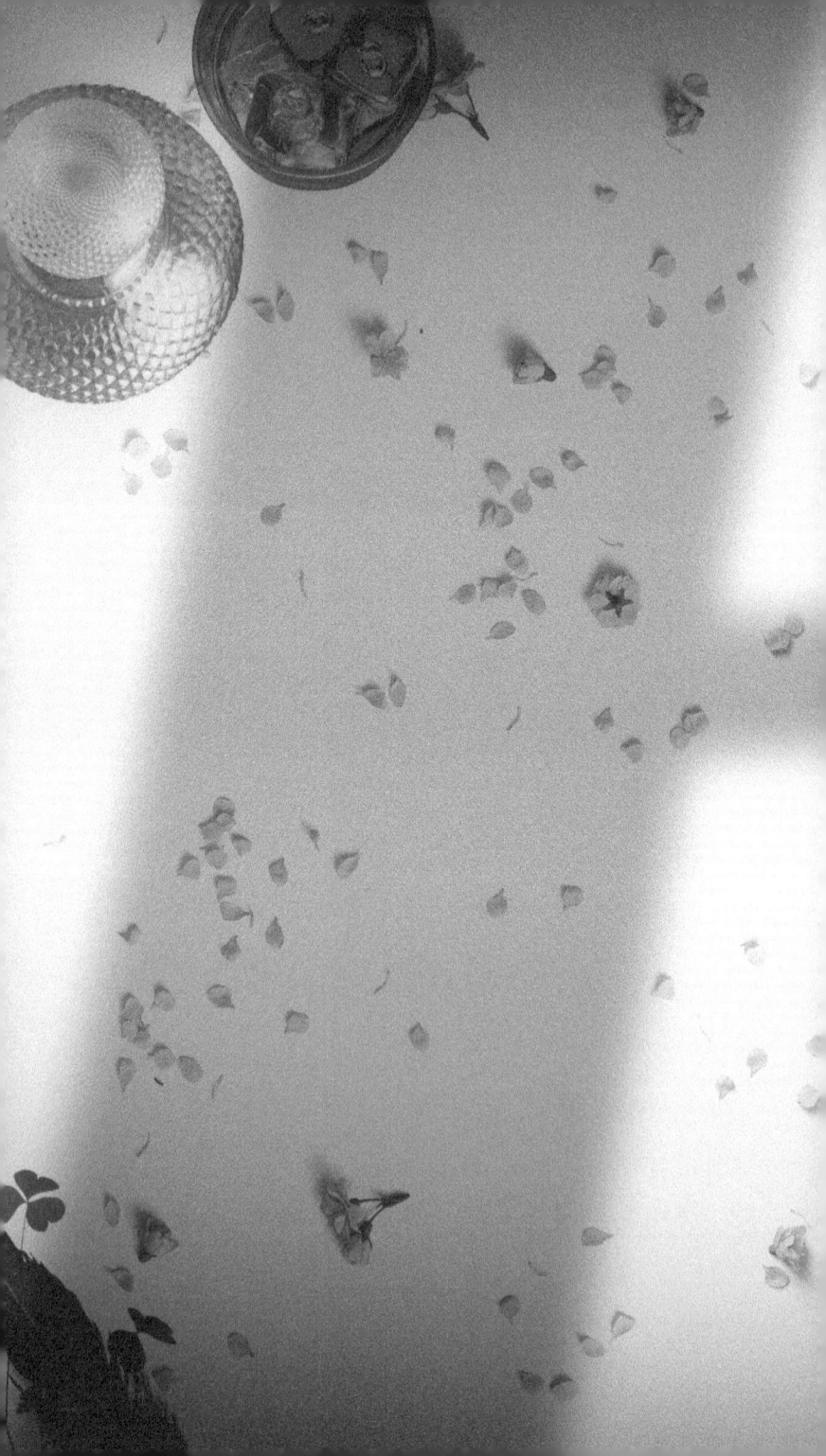

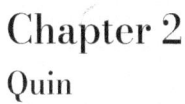

Chapter 2
Quin

A heel pressed into his eye socket, and an ankle rested across his throat, making breathing rather difficult.

Octavia. Tavi.

There had been no intention to keep the little youngling Quin discovered at the warehouse. He was supposed to take her back to the sanctuary and hand her over to available Guardians. But she wouldn't let him go. The only noise she'd made was to scream when her newly appointed Guardians attempted to pry her off of his chest.

Quin hadn't been able to force the separation on her. So instead, he'd phoned his parents and asked them both to come down to the sanctuary. Colton and Ezequiel Schields were listed as her official Guardians, but the tiny youngling clung to Quin as if he were her lifeline.

He remembered what that was like. Being in a good home for the first time, uncertain of anything that was going on. Knowing that things were better but still terrified that something bad was going to happen. Quin hadn't let Colt out of his sight for weeks. Not until Maximus managed to wheedle his way into his trust circle and take some of the pressure off of their dad.

A small squawk sounded, and the heel in his eye moved while the ankle across his throat only pressed more harshly. Quin slid gentle fingers around her foot to pull her leg off his throat and shifted it to his chest.

"Morning," he whispered.

Big brown eyes blinked up at him from her diagonal sprawl across the bed. Octavia had refused to sleep anywhere but in his bed last night. While she was doing really well with his parents, there were still times when the darkness of her own room became too much. When even the nightlight beside her bed was not enough.

Quin understood that feeling all too well. Could not fault her for the fears that still plagued her even though she was safe. It had only been a few weeks. The world was full of big, scary things and a lot of uncertainties. So he let her crawl into his bed, offering whatever comfort and solace he could.

Tavi, looking still half asleep, raised her hand—palm out—and brought it to her forehead then outward in a half-hearted salute, saying hello. Quin smiled, so proud to see how well she had taken to ASL. He understood the desire to remain silent and the level of pressure there was in speaking. So, as a family, they were working to teach her sign language.

"Let's go get breakfast." He signed as he spoke, watching her dark brown eyes follow his fingers as she connected what he said to the motions his hands made.

The small ignis rolled over onto her knees then raised up, holding her hands out. Quin sat up, threw off his covers, and plucked Tavi off the bed. He settled her on his hip as he climbed from the bed. Still in their pajamas—Quin in a sleeveless shirt and sweats, Tavi in a footed, unicorn-covered sleeper—they made their way down the hall to the kitchen.

It was early, so the only one in the kitchen was his dad. Colton Schields stood at the counter, a mug of steaming coffee on one side of him, a bowl of fresh fruit on the other. The steady chopping of strawberries filled the air, along with soft, slightly off-key singing.

"Good morning, Dad." Quin walked to the fridge and opened it in search of milk.

"Morning." Colt turned from the fruit he was chopping and grinned at them. "Good morning, Octavia." He nearly cooed as he said the words and leaned in to kiss her forehead.

Tavi beamed, shyly scrunching her shoulders up near her ears. She offered Colt a little wiggle of her fingers in greeting.

She allowed Quin to set her on the counter as he filled a sippy cup with milk. Her brown eyes followed his motions, the mess of dark curls on her head sticking out all over the place. He needed to take a pick to them soon, try to untangle them a little. Not that he really had any idea how to deal with the spring-like hair.

Part of him thought he should speak to Mab about how she dealt with hers. But the thought of starting that conversation filled him with dread. Not that Mab was likely to be upset by the question, but asking for help was the last thing he ever wanted to do. Maybe if he mentioned it to Max, it would get back to Ander, and Ander could speak to Mab for him.

Quin sighed heavily.

"Hey, what's so serious so early in the morning?" Colt asked.

"Just thinking about Tavi's hair," he admitted. There was no point trying to hide the truth from his dad; he'd get it out of him eventually.

"What about it?" Colt held out a whole strawberry to Tavi, who took it and happily chomped down on it.

"That I don't know how to take care of it." He hated being useless.

"Well, we can always stop at a hair salon that specializes in curly hair and ask for tips."

The thought made Quin want to vomit.

His father, being the intuitive man he was, saw it immediately and chuckled. "Don't worry, I think this is just the kind of task your Papa would love to do."

Quin sighed, relief washing through him, and he nodded. "Thanks. I'll mention it to him." He looked down as a small hand tapped his chest. Tavi motioned to the strawberries Colt was chopping and signed for more. Quin grinned at her. "Coco is almost done with the fruit salad. We can eat it soon. Do you want an egg as well?" he signed as he spoke, his hands moving slowly so that she had time to catch each movement with her keen sight.

Tavi nodded and motioned at him, wanting to be picked back up. He did, but only so he could carry her over to the table and sit her in the little booster seat strapped down to one of the chairs. Her little green wings fluttered quickly as she tried to pull herself from the buckle as he fastened it around her lap.

"No, no." Quin shook his head. "You have to sit there while I make your eggs, okay?"

Tavi stared up at him, eyes unblinking and a look of betrayal shining in their depths. He brushed his knuckles over her cheek.

"It'll just be a moment."

True to his word, preparing her egg took no time at all, and as he was tumbling the fluffy yellow scramble onto her plastic Minnie plate, Colt was there to add a scoop of fruit onto one ear. He nodded his thanks to his father and carried the plate, as well as Tavi's sippy cup, over to her.

She grinned brightly when she saw the food and pressed her fingertips to her chin, then motioned down and away from herself in thanks. Quin signed a quick "you're welcome" and patted her fluffy head of curls.

Tavi ignored the plastic fork he set beside her plate and instead picked up a strawberry slice, murmuring as she placed it on her tongue.

It was good to hear a noise out of her, whatever it might be. Quin knew from experience how difficult it could be to find your voice when you'd never been encouraged to use it. He wasn't sure what the cages in Orcus' warehouses had been like, but from the state the younglings had been found in, Quin knew Orcus wasn't worried about their mental well-being.

With Tavi distracted by eating, Quin moved around the kitchen, side-stepping his father and tucking his black wings in against his body to make sure he didn't knock something over as he prepared his own breakfast. Several eggs, three slices of ham, a big bowl of oatmeal, and two slices of toast.

The fire that burned inside each ignis also created a very high metabolism. It required a lot of food to sustain them, especially through physical activity.

As Quin sat down at the kitchen table, Tavi took one look at his breakfast and pointed at the oatmeal, kicking her feet. Quin lifted a brow. "Are you trying to ask for my breakfast too?"

Tavi's wings fluttered as well as they were able to with her seated in the booster seat, and she signed "more" rather aggressively, then pointed at the oatmeal. Quin laughed softly. "So it's the oatmeal you want."

"I'll grab her some!" his father trumpeted happily, sweeping around the kitchen to grab a bowl and spoon some from the large pot Quin made for the family.

When Colt appeared with the bowl of oatmeal, it had milk on it to cool it down as well as a scoop of brown sugar melting on top. "Here you go, peanut."

"Thanks, Dad."

Colt smiled at Quin. "No problem at all. We can't have our girl going hungry."

"I thought I was your girl." A very tussled looking Georgie padded into the kitchen.

Colt smiled and moved over to kiss his youngest daughter's forehead. At thirteen, she was nearly as tall as he was now. "Good morning to you too. And you will always be my girl."

Her bright pink wings were the only delightful thing about her this morning. There was a scowl on her face as she moved to the stove and looked into the pot. "Oatmeal? Ew."

"Don't eat it, then," Quin grunted and scooped up a big spoonful for himself.

Tavi, seeming to agree with him on it being tasty, scooped some of her own—actually using cutlery this time—and hummed once more as it settled on her tongue.

Georgie's only response to him was a grumble, which he ignored.

He had cleared his plate and bowl and put the dishes into the dishwasher before Nox and Nash even made their presence known. Both wore the evidence of their late night in the bags under their eyes, Nash looking exceptionally hard this morning. He almost nodded off over his cup of coffee, while Nox tickled Tavi's cheeks, winning giggles from the youngling.

With Tavi distracted, Quin took this as his chance to slip out of the kitchen and head back to his room to shower quickly and dress. Currently, the Schields team had no open cases, so he dressed in a pair of comfortable black cotton joggers with a tie waist and narrow cuffs at the ankles. These meant he could spar if Max wished to, and they'd easily slip into the tops of his combat boots without riding up his legs.

He pulled a black open-sided tank top over his head and tucked his wings through the slits in the back of it. Once everything was settled over his form the way he liked it, Quin shrugged on a slouchy leather jacket, tucked the back flap between his wings, and zipped it shut at their base.

Dressed, he finger-combed the pitch-black hair on top of his head, skimmed his black-painted nails along the shaved undercut beneath the shag, and scratched lightly at the scruff on his jaw. Tomorrow, he would have to trim it before it became an outright beard; today, he could get away with leaving it be.

Shrieks of terror drew Quin from his bedroom. He ran into the kitchen to see that Tavi had managed to pull herself and the chair into the air. They hovered about a foot from the floor, and her wings, with their base of green and long purplish-white primaries and light gray secondaries, flapped so fast that they were a blur, emitting a humming noise like a tiny motor.

A shrill wail came out of her, and her hands stretched toward the ceiling in her attempt to escape.

"Octavia!" Quin's voice was stern but not too sharp. It was forceful enough that her wings stopped flapping instantly, and her chair dropped to the floor. He was impressed she had kept herself and the chair in the air so long, given she didn't have the flying capacity a youngling her age should have due to the cages.

When he came around to the front of the chair, he found her rounded cheeks streaked with tears, her lips trembling with her sobs. The moment she saw him, her little body began to wiggle frantically at its confines, and she pushed at the booster seat, trying to get to him.

"Hey, hey," he said softly, moving to unbuckle her quickly and pluck her from the seat. "It's okay." The youngling flung her arms tightly around his neck and buried her face into the side of his.

Quin bounced her, rubbing her back, and looked at the startled faces of his three siblings seated around the table, then to his dad.

Colt lifted his hand as if to say, *What can you do?* "She was very troubled when she realized you weren't anywhere in the room."

"I think '*freaked*' is the word you're looking for, Dad," Georgie cut in.

Quin frowned and pulled Tavi back enough that he could look down at her. "Hey," he whispered. "You're okay here with Coco."

She chewed her lip, another tear slipping down her cheek. She pulled her arms back only so that she could sign "more" and point to his chest. Quin sighed.

"You have to spend the day with Coco and Zee. Okay?"

Tavi shook her head vigorously and tapped on his chest with her tiny brown fingers.

Quin looked up and over at his father, begging for help. Colt heaved his own sigh but came over to take Tavi from his arms, even though she began to wail once more. The sounds made Quin wince and rethink everything he was supposed to do today.

"Go," his father ordered.

"But—"

"Go," he cut him off. "She's going to protest for a while, and then she will get used to the fact that you're gone. Kids are terribly resilient."

"I know ... I just hate ... "

"You hate seeing her in distress and pain," Colt finished for him. "Trust me, I completely understand." He was looking at Quin with a tenderness in his eyes that transported Quin right back to the early days when he'd first arrived in the Schields home.

Quin nodded. "Okay, I'm going. If she doesn't settle, call me." He turned to the twins. "You're going to be late."

"Yeah, yeah . . . " Nox waved him off, and Nash groaned.

Quin stood behind the command station where Nox and Nash were set up, large steaming cups of coffee beside each of their monitors and the picture of an ignis up on their screens, his blue and teal wings bright against the relative darkness of the rest of the room.

Cyprian Ursus.

"Have you managed to finally track down his roots?" Max asked from beside Quin. He was dressed in a white shirt and a woolen sweater, tan slacks covering his long legs.

It was nice to see that moving in with his inanimi boyfriend, Ander Ruin, after only a few weeks of dating hadn't changed his brother's sense of style. It *had* changed the look in Max's eyes, though. There was a peace that had settled in them. For the moment, Quin was happy for the two of them.

"That's the thing." Nox clicked on the icon of a file and opened it up, showing a single link which was titled "Transfer." "He has none."

"What do you mean?" Quin asked, his shoulders tightening.

Cyprian had been directly involved in the suicide of a suspect Quin and Max brought in. A suspect with direct ties to an unsub the two of them were trying desperately to track down.

When human girls began to go missing from Ruin's nightclub, Inferno, two and a half months ago, it had looked like the half-muse was behind it. Max refused to accept that and hadn't stopped until they uncovered a sordid web of inanimi activity that stretched from human trafficking to drug production and sale to the kidnapping of ignis younglings for an assumed army.

All of it traced back to Ruin's ex-boyfriend, Enrique. Known in criminal rings as Timoros, and to those in Underworld as Orcus, god of punishment and Hades' right-hand man.

When they'd tracked Orcus down to one of his main warehouses in Sarasota, Cyprian had been a part of their mission. But instead of helping to take down Orcus and his crew, Cyprian joined in on the battle against the Sanctum tactical team.

Quin had fought against him. Watched him end his own life when Quin had taken him down, killing himself before there was a chance to get any more information out of him. The not knowing was driving Quin mad. He wanted answers.

"Well," Nash cut in. "Turns out all the information on his transfer paperwork was falsified. We contacted the L.A. sanctuary, and no one there has ever heard of Cyprian Ursus. So they weren't the ones who filed the transfer to Miami for him."

"It doesn't appear his Guardians ever existed either. Well, that's not entirely true. They did exist, but about a hundred years ago. We had to search through every database the Sanctum has, and it was only because of a kind normie working for the Roman sanctuary that we found their names at all. She came across them in some old written records they had stored away in the catacombs." Nox pulled up a scan of a yellowed piece of paper.

Quin's feathers ruffled as anger coursed through him. Cyprian's betrayal went deeper than they realized.

"So he was a sleeper agent for *Enrique*, then." Max nearly spat the name.

Quin understood his loathing. The god was not only behind one of the largest crime rings in the history of the sanctuary but was also the ex who had badly abused and confined Ruin for years in Acheron.

Max, currently head-over-heels for his new arrow-bound boyfriend, hated Orcus with a passion. Thankfully, they had captured Orcus, and he was currently locked away in a dungeon in Underworld's capital, Olympia, under the surveillance of the king of the gods, Indra.

"It looks like it." Nash nodded.

Quin and Max shared a look behind the twins' backs. *If Cyprian had been a sleeper for the god, did that mean there were more?*

Dread made its way down Quin's spine, causing waves of cold to slip through his nervous system. The chill spread to his fingers and his toes, numbing them.

Quin could see the same feelings in Max's eyes. *Who can we trust?*

"We need to pass this information on to the captain," Quin said, breaking the silent conversation passing between them.

Max nodded. "Let's go."

They left the twins without so much as a "see you later" and headed down the hall of the Miami-Fuego City sanctuary. They passed through a set of double doors into a round atrium that led from the command stations of their different ignis teams to the inner offices of the higher officials within the Sanctum.

Captain Galeo, head of active missions at the Fuego sanctuary, was not a fan of the Schields family, and he made that fact known any chance he got. They were deemed too soft, too sentimental, because they had been raised alongside human children by Guardians who believed in loving their children be they ignis or mortal.

As they arrived at the captain's door, Max rapped his knuckles on the doorframe. When Galeo's short, "Come in," sounded, he opened the door, and they both stepped in.

Galeo was a stoney looking ignis, slightly shorter than Quin and Max's nearly seven-foot height and with a set of deep-blue wings that would put a jay to shame. When his eyes lifted from the papers on his desk to the two of them, his lips pursed into a flat line.

"What is it?" he asked curtly.

"We have news on Cyprian, sir," Max said.

Quin folded his arms behind his back, just below his wings. As the head of their combat team, Max always took the lead with Galeo when on shift. Quin, while not needing to be here, preferred to show support for his brother and always attended the meetings when he could.

Galeo sat back in his high-backed chair. "Out with it, then."

"It appears, sir, that Cyprian was a sleeper agent for Orcus." Max stood up a little taller under the scrutiny, his voice dipping into a tone Quin recognized as something more "official." "All of his records were falsified. He was never a member of the Los Angeles sanctuary as we believed, nor did they transfer him here. The Guardians listed on his papers were names of those who died long before he was born."

Galeo frowned, clasping his hands before him as he listened. "So, you believe he was planted here by Orcus."

"He attacked me at the warehouse, sir," Quin finally added.

"I think he was one of the ignis trained by Orcus for his personal use." There was disgust in Max's tone; though it was carefully tucked away, Quin could hear it. "And if that is the case, I don't think Cyprian's involvement with Micah Brown's death was purely coincidental. It never seemed right that the demogorgon killed themselves when I had promised them protection if they talked."

"We've all seen the videos, Maximus. Cyprian only spoke briefly with it. He said nothing about suicide. How do you think he made Micah kill itself?" Galeo was watching him closely, a brow quirked in question.

Did he think this was another far-fetched assumption of Max's? Even if it were, Max's gut feelings had all proven correct as they unveiled the truth of this case.

Max frowned, his brows scrunching. "I don't know, sir. We haven't been able to figure that part out yet."

Galeo snorted. "Well, I wouldn't go spewing guesses until you have more proof. Not with the way the Princeps are watching you now."

Quin looked to Max, who was looking at him, then they both turned back to Galeo.

"The Princeps are watching me? What do you mean, sir?" Max asked.

The Princeps in Rome were the highest ranking ignis in all of the Sanctum. Their rule and law was akin to that of a king or queen's edict.

"They don't like that your key witness in the case against Orcus was an inanimi who was a known ex-boyfriend of the accused *and* a former suspect in the disappearance of the trafficked girls. They like even less how involved he was in this case. All of your *proof* damning Orcus came from him. How do we know that Ruin did not plant all of this evidence against the god of punishment in order to clear himself?"

Quin felt Max bristling beside him. His entire body stiffened, and the white feathers of his wings began to spread and fluff out. Max was going to say something to only further damn him in this situation.

"Captain," Quin said before Max had a chance to and stepped forward. "Crown Prince Ander of Helicon was cleared of all wrongdoing long before Orcus was brought into question. Orcus was apprehended on-site, where mermaids were being held captive and milked for venom. I, personally, along with several other ignis, found younglings in cages. They were preparing to move them to another location. There can be no doubt of Orcus' guilt in all of this."

He hadn't been a fan of Ander Ruin in the beginning. Not when all of the evidence was pointing to him and he thought Ruin was attempting to seduce Max in order to get out of trouble. But Ruin's innocence had been proven, and he'd seen the way the inanimi loved Max. Knew how Ruin put himself in immense danger to protect him.

Galeo spread his hands out at his sides, tone casual. "I am merely passing on the doubts that the Princeps had. So be aware and mindful. They are going to be keeping an eye on you both and your family. Perhaps take a moment to think before any more of you decide to shack up with an inanimi partner."

Max was practically stone, he had stiffened so much with all of his pent-up rage. Galeo, it would seem, was fully aware that Max had moved in with Ruin and was quite happily living with his boyfriend. Something that wasn't exactly forbidden but may as well have been. It just wasn't done. By any of them.

Ignis did not love.

And ignis did not date inanimi.

"Will do, Captain," Max bit out.

"You're both dismissed."

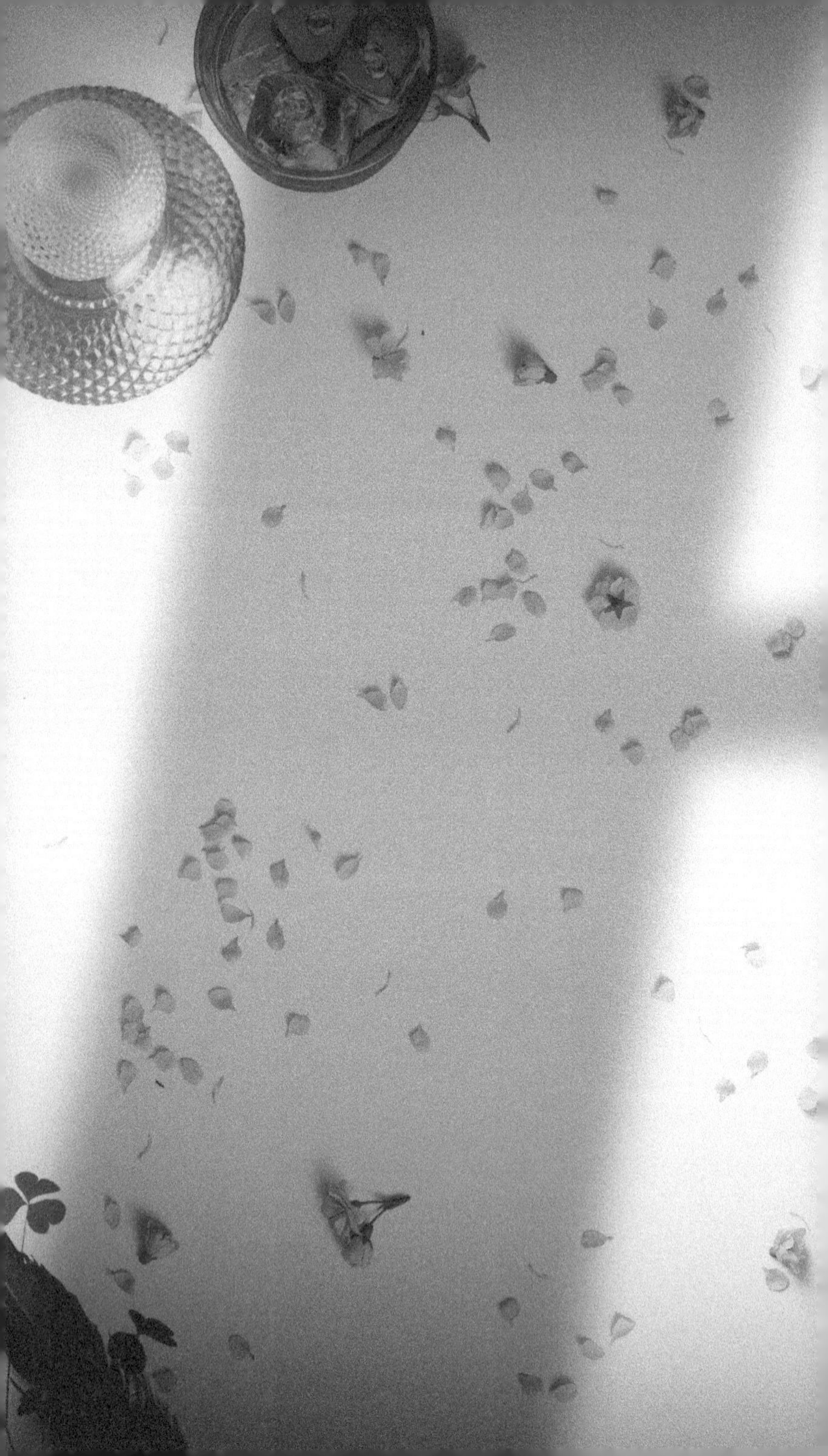

Chapter 3
Mab

They showed up anyway. The fucking fair folk showed up *anyway*. Without an invitation.

She supposed she should have seen that coming, even still...

"Indra told us you were having a little get-together for our dear Ander, Lady Duchan," Alfie said, smile bright, leaning back on his heels. He'd swept into a bow the moment she opened the front door, and Mab couldn't decide which made her eye twitch more: the bow or *Lady Duchan*. She hadn't been Lady Duchan for centuries, and Alfie damn well knew it.

"Funny we didn't get an invite," Tommy murmured from Alfie's side. They'd both stayed at the door to greet her while the rest of their ragtag group pushed past without so much as a word to "get set up." Set up for what? She didn't want to know, she was sure. She was just glad Ander said Gizmo—her pet rabbit—could stay with Monnie at his and Max's place during the party. She didn't want him getting underfoot and getting hurt.

"Probably an accident. An oversight." Alfie's smile

didn't fall, but Mab could tell he knew it hadn't been an accident as it seemed a little sharper than a moment ago. "Honest mistake."

Tommy hummed as if he didn't quite believe it but said nothing, and Mab refused to squirm under his ice-gray stare that felt like it could see down to her very soul. Gods, she hated dealing with the fair folk.

"Anyway," Alfie continued, ignoring the look Tommy was giving Mab, "Indra said you needed entertainment."

"Did he?" Nope. *That* was the thing that made her eye twitch the most. Indra and his godsforsaken meddling. She wondered what metal a knife had to be made from to skin a god. Maybe Ander knew. Or Juno. Scratch that, Juno *definitely* knew. She might even be willing to sharpen it for Mab. "Well, you're more than welcome to come in *for the evening.*" She felt that needed to be clarified. No one in their right mind would give an open invitation to the fair folk. Not if they ever wanted to sleep peacefully again and know where all their forks were. Especially fair folk like Tommy and Alfie.

Alfie nodded, his smile widening further to stretch across his face in a way that was inhuman, showing off far too many teeth, all of which *looked* blunt, but Mab could see the shimmer of a glamour hovering in the air around him. She hoped he left it up. She didn't particularly want any of the ignis or human guests getting the wrong idea. Although, normies were more likely to make stupid deals with inanimi when the inanimi in question looked human.

"This is for you, love," Alfie said, pushing a loaf of something into her hands and giving her wrist a warning squeeze before he went past her into the house. Leaving just Mab and Tommy standing on the stoop but calling over his shoulder, "Lovely home you've got here, Lady Duchan."

"Party ends at eleven," Mab said. She didn't look away from the glare Tommy was still cutting her. Like he knew this was a slight against them and he planned to make her pay for it. Damn it. She didn't need that. There wasn't time to deal with a fae vendetta. All she could hope was that whatever revenge Tommy planned to take against her would wait till after the party, when the ignis were gone. "And we have ignis guests."

Tommy inclined his head in understanding. "We'll be on our best behavior."

"I'm sure you will." She stepped back from the door and ushered him inside before shutting it behind them both. Her eyes scanned the little entryway to make sure there was nothing on the walls or the front table she was overly attached to lest the magpies she just let into her house take a fancy to those things and decide to "borrow" them. Bloody fairies and their borrowing. She rolled her eyes.

Between trying to tuck away anything with sentimental value and setting up, Mab didn't really have time to talk to anyone outside of greeting them at the door. A task which eventually fell to Ander because he wasn't doing anything *else* to help and Mab quickly grew tired of ushering him out of the way when she needed to move something. So she didn't even see when Indra and Juno joined them, but she sure as shit heard it about an hour later, once Indra had a few drinks in him. Not that gods could get drunk off what they were serving. He'd likely brought his own.

"Can I borrow Max for a minute?" Mab asked when she passed a wide-eyed Max, who looked like he'd do anything,

anything at all, to get out of the conversation he was in. Poor kid. He'd eventually learn how to deal with their friends. And where was Ander? Shouldn't he be the one doing the rescuing here?

"Oh, of course," Raine said, tilting their head back to grin up at Mab from their shorter stature. Mab didn't remember having a pwca on the list. How many others had Ander snuck invites to behind her back? Gods, she had a headache, and she was way too sober for this. "When you see Ander, would you please tell him that I have a gift for him?"

"Definitely." Max smiled back politely, and Mab ushered him away.

"Do not take anything from Raine," Mab said once they were out of earshot.

"Why not?"

"Because they're just as likely to pass off some cursed object they've picked up on the black market without realizing it as they are to give you something off your registry. They don't mean any harm by it, it's just . . . " She took a sip from her drink, wishing it was something stronger. "Well, cursed items don't affect their kind the same as they would yours. So just, don't. Okay?"

"Okay. Okay." Max held up his hands. "What did you need to talk to me about?"

Nothing really, she'd just been trying to save him. But now that she had him here, secluded and off to the side where no one could overhear . . . Well, she had been meaning to have a chat with him about Ander. Which had been impossible for the last few weeks because Ander and Max were attached at the bloody hip these days. A thought that made something sour turn over in her stomach. She swallowed past the feeling of it crawling up her throat and pushed on.

"I just want you to know that even if you're a trained warrior, crafted by the gods themselves to enact justice or whatever." Her fingers flexed around the glass in her hand. "I still have a few hundred years on you when it comes to experience, and I've spent the large part of them learning how to disassemble a man into such small pieces that no one would ever find a trace of him."

Max blinked at her for a moment, his full lips slightly parted, confusion drawing his brows together. Then he smiled, bright and happy. The glaring white wings behind his back fluttered a little, like a bird resettling. "This is a shovel talk."

"What? No, it's—"

"Yes it is!" Max crowed, brightening further. "You're warning me that if I hurt your brother, you'll hurt me!"

"Well, yeah, but—"

"Oh Mab," Max laughed, reaching out to take her wrists in his hands, the grip too warm from his ignis blood. "You have nothing to worry about."

"I'm not—"

"I'm going to take such good care of Ander. And he's going to take good care of me." He leaned forward, his words growing quieter and more hurried, like he'd been waiting for this conversation his whole life and couldn't believe he was finally getting to be a part of it. He probably had been, romantic bugger that he was. "I'd never do anything to hurt him."

"Right. Well." Mab straightened and lifted her chin to make herself appear bigger when compared to Max. It didn't really do much. The ignis was a bloody giant; add on his wings, and Mab looked tiny by comparison. But it made her feel a bit better. "If you did—"

"Then I'd be more than happy to die by your hand, Mab Duchan," Max said like a vow and lifted one hand to his chest to rest over his heart. Then he winked at her, smile bright again. "But you've got nothing to worry about."

"Good." Mab nodded and sniffed. Why were her eyes burning all of a sudden? Like she was passing the torch off to Max. Handing over something precious and begging him not to drop it. Then she deflated a little, pulling the hand he still had held in his away to scrub at the tip of her nose. "How'd I do as far as shovel talks go?"

"Oh, it was perfect. I was properly terrified." Max nodded happily. "Have you been practicing?"

"No." She laughed and gave his shoulder a little shove.

He laughed too, his hazel eyes bright as he leaned in to press a kiss to her cheek. "Thank you for welcoming me into your family, Mab."

"Go on, get back to your party, Wonderboy. I've got to refill the punch bowl. I think there might be a pixie swimming in it." She pulled away, hoping he didn't notice how her eyes had started to water.

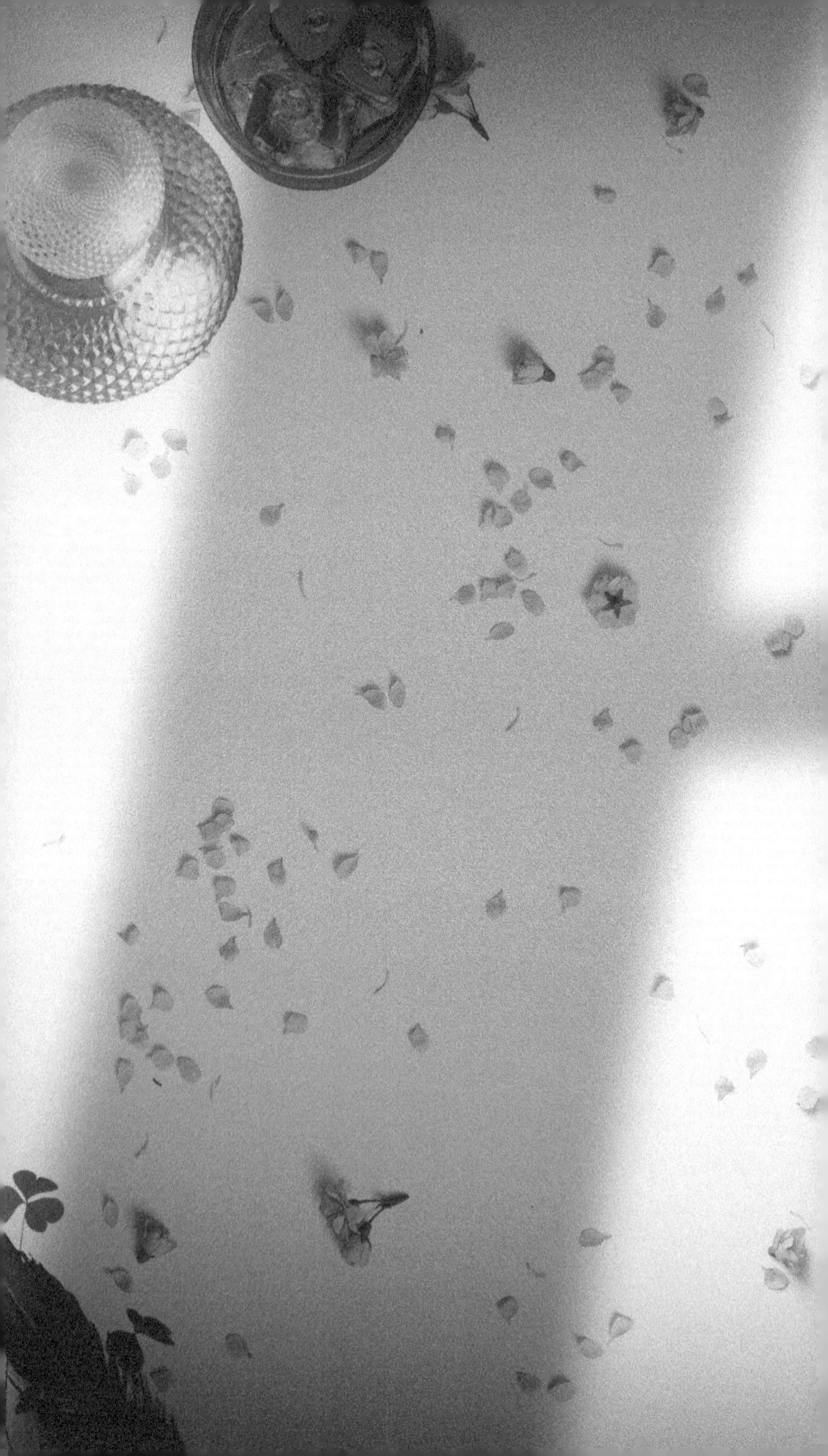

Chapter 4
Quin

The house was so *loud*, filled to the rafters with chatter, laughter, and music. Pair that with the overcrowding of guests and the colorful lights waving across the ceiling from the DJ's corner, and Quin could barely string two thoughts together.

He'd entered the house thirty minutes ago. Once inside, he found Max and Ander, gave his brother a hug and Ruin a nod, then excused himself to find a corner of the house to tuck himself away in.

That was where he'd remained ever since.

Quin was as sharp as a katana while in the midst of battle. Explosions, screams, gunfire, and more could be sounding off around him, and he would stay focused on his target. In those situations, however, he had a plan. He was in control. He knew what he was meant to do.

Here, in this travesty of an evening, there were too many people. Too many eyes. Too much chaos that was coming at him from all angles and none of it made sense.

Quin tugged at the collar of his black V-neck, which didn't cling to his chest exactly but definitely outlined the toned physique beneath it. Black stone-washed jeans with artfully placed frayed cuts and holes hugged his thick thighs and tucked into his combat boots. His black hair was mussed into a purposeful tussle on top of his head, and Quin had allowed his papa to talk him into lining his blue eyes in black to make them stand out.

Not that Quin wished to stand out. If he could physically melt into the wall and become one with it, he would do so. But it made Zeke smile to apply the eyeliner, and Quin found it difficult to deny his papa simple things that would bring such happiness to his face. Their father-son bonding had taken years, and Quin knew—though Zeke would never say it—it was something that still weighed on him to this day.

Quin sat perched on a small stool that may have also been an ottoman. His elbows were braced on his knees, leaving more room for his wings between him and the wall. He clasped a condensation-covered can of beer that someone had forced into his hand as he made his way across the living room. He hadn't even taken a sip.

A deep baritone of laughter drew Quin's attention from the floor—there was an interesting swirling shape in the marble—to King Indra, who stood with his arm around a petite green nymph who was most certainly not his wife, Juno. The nymph murmured something that Quin couldn't hear over the noise, and Indra's head fell back as he laughed heartily once more.

For a being who ruled over all of the kingdoms of Underworld and was in charge of the peace of all the inanimi who lived there, he seemed truly unconcerned and unfettered. He'd just found out his brother's right-hand man was building an ignis army to overthrow him and his rule, should he not be more serious? Quin didn't understand how he'd simply brushed all of that aside.

Why was the King of Olympia even here at a housewarming party for Ruin and Max to begin with?

Quin's eyes searched the crowd, and he found Max and Ruin, their arms twined around each other as Ruin leaned against Max's chest. They seemed entirely oblivious to everyone else in the room.

"What is he thinking?" a voice managed to filter through the noise to make it to Quin's ears.

"I heard he's arrow-bound to him. Some nonsense with Erotes shooting him with an arrow when Prometheus sent him to earth," another voice chimed in.

The first voice snorted deeply. "As if that is an excuse to ignore centuries of Sanctum training and go against everything we stand for. He's just going to be distracted with that inanimi and get someone killed."

Quin's belly burned with anger, the heat of his fire threatening to rise up and spill onto the offenders. Not that it would do any good against his own kind. But he let it lift him from the stool, his shoulders rolling and his wings shuffling in irritation.

A couple of quick strides took him to the two ignis, Ovid and Cicero, letting his shoulder collide roughly with that of Ovid. The deep-toned ignis winced at the impact and brought his hand to his shoulder as he spun, preparing to fight back.

Quin didn't give him time. Instead, he stepped into Ovid's circle so that there wasn't much space between them. "Even distracted, my brother still managed to take down a god and his entire crime ring. Maybe if you got your head out of your ass, you'd be able to get out of records and do something worthwhile too." Quin kept his tone even and calm but let all of his anger come out in his eyes.

Ovid kept his back straight and his head up. But the sneer on his face was all bravado. The corner of his eye twitched just a fraction as Ovid attempted not to blink in fear.

Quin didn't like to scare others. He knew the reputation he had among those at the sanctuary. The crazy youngling who'd been pulled out of a fighting ring with more inanimi kills to his name by the age of ten than most ignis twice his age.

Glasses crashed to the floor, breaking their eye contact. Quin looked over at the disturbance and saw that it was Nash, who had been in the process of stacking champagne saucers into a pyramid. Shaking his head at his younger sibling, Quin looked back at Ovid, saying nothing but glaring slightly. He then glanced at Cicero, who just nodded quickly, and Quin stepped back, returning to his spot in the corner.

He wasn't going to fight them, though there was a strong desire in him to do just that. To release the deep well of anger he kept buried inside him and take it out on someone who thought they could look down on his brother. No, ignis did not love. No, they did not form relationships with inanimi. But how dare anyone disparage Max simply because he'd found something no other ignis had. Max was different from the rest of them. He was filled with kindness and light. He deserved to be happy. He deserved to have love.

"Are you in time-out?" a throaty, slightly husky voice tinged with the hint of an Irish accent asked.

Quin glanced up and over to see that Mab had come to lean against the wall near him, a tumbler full of amber liquid with an orange peel along the rim clasped lazily in her hand.

"Time-out?" Quin asked, frowning.

Mab smirked at him. "For naughty kids who get sent to the corner to think about what they've done. Come on, Q-ball . . . this is a party, why are you alone in the corner?"

Quin just blinked up at her and shrugged.

Mab's brow lifted, and her lips twitched with something that might have been amusement. "Are you even drinking that beer?"

Quin gave a quick jerk of his head. "I don't drink alcohol."

"No? Is that an ignis thing?"

He shook his head again. "I don't find the notion of my faculties being impaired appealing."

Mab's expression changed a fraction. Quin didn't know her enough to understand what it meant, but there was something that flashed in her eyes for just a second before it disappeared.

"Well, put that down, then. I'll get you something else."

"It's fine, I'm not—" She disappeared before he could finish. "Thirsty."

Quin looked around the room, unsure of where the banshee had slipped off to. Ignis couldn't do that, disappear into a room full of people. With the tips of their wings, most of them stood close to eight feet tall. They were head and shoulders above most normies. Inanimi . . . now some of those were just as huge, if not bigger.

When Mab returned, she carried a green glass bottle with a lemon wedge stuck in the top of it. She held it out to him, and he took it apprehensively.

"Don't look at me like that," she grumbled. "It's just sparkling water."

Quin turned the bottle over in his hand and read the label, confirming that was exactly what it was. He nodded and looked back up at her. "Thanks."

"Sure."

Silence fell between them, and Quin took a sip of his water. The citrus was the first thing to hit his tongue with a sour little punch, then the bubbles from the water tickled his nose and made his eyes threaten to water.

It was tasty, but he would have been just as fine with a normal bottle of water.

"They're actually in love, aren't they?" Mab muttered.

Quin followed her gaze to where it lay on Max and Ruin, no longer facing each other so that they could talk to their guests but with their hands clasped. It was like they couldn't bear to be separated from each other.

He had to wonder what that was like. To feel so attached to someone you needed to be touching them at all times. Quin couldn't imagine that. He wasn't fond of touching anyone, really. His family and Tavi now being the only exceptions, and even that had its limitations.

"Max adores him," Quin said simply.

"I've never seen Ander look at someone the way he looks at Max." Was it just something he was hearing or was there a fraction of wistfulness in Mab's voice?

"Do you want that?" he asked, not sure why he did.

Mab snorted, took a gulp from her tumbler, and looked down at him. "Are you serious? No."

Before he could say anything back, a large cheer rose in the room, and suddenly, Indra was on the dining room table, hands on his hips as he dropped into a squat and began to dance, kicking his feet out before him.

"Oh, hell no!" Mab roared.

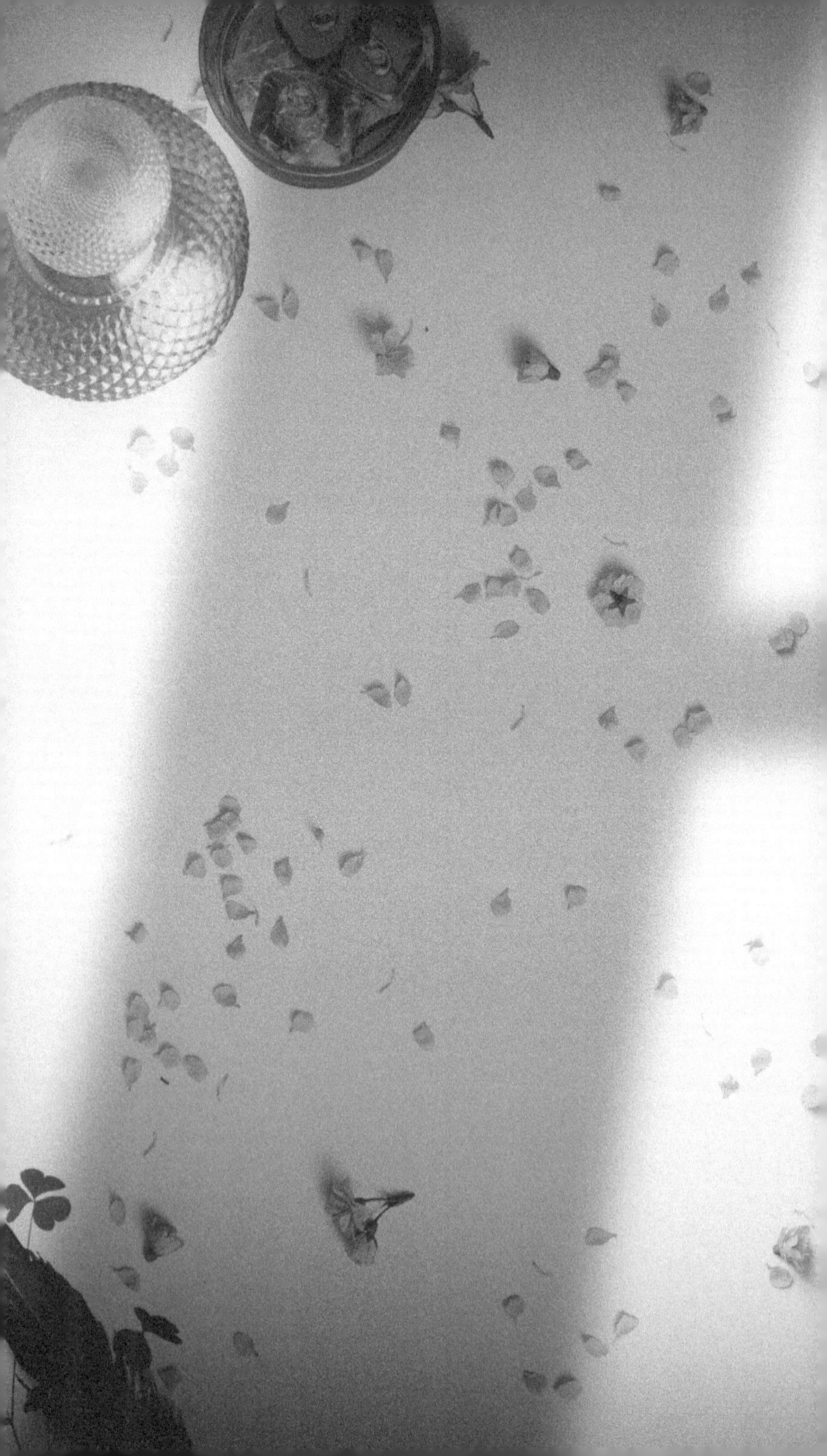

Chapter 5
Max

"You'll never believe what just happened," Max said when he finally tracked Ander to the kitchen where he'd gone to refill his drink. The glass of champagne in his hand seemed to never be empty for long. Either because he was magically refilling it or because someone was keeping it full for him. Maybe a combination of both. So it was a little strange that Ander had excused himself to refill his own glass. "Are you all right?"

Ander looked up from the glass in his hand to smile at Max, his eyes bright and glittering. "Right as rain, my love. Why would I be any different?"

There were half a dozen reasons why Ander might not be "right as rain." Max knew Ander was happy that they had moved in together. He knew that Ander was excited for this party. But maybe someone had said something to upset him. Or maybe someone reminded him of Enrique. There were so many little things that could dredge up his trauma, and Max just wanted to shield him from all of them. To tuck Ander in against his chest and curl his wings around him so nothing could touch him ever again. But Max knew well enough that wasn't a possibility. He'd always felt that way about his family too. Like if he could just hold them close enough, he could shield them from the worst things in life. It never worked.

Instead of pressing for answers, Max moved to hug Ander from behind, his arms wrapped around his waist, his chin resting on Ander's shoulder. A reminder that he was there. That he would support Ander no matter what. He didn't have to say what was wrong, not now, not ever if he didn't want. But Max would always be there, a safe space for him, when he was ready.

Ander sighed, leaning back into his hold, his glass forgotten on the counter, and they stayed that way for a moment, enjoying the closeness. Max felt the soft hum of Ander's contentment buzz against his skin. It was nice to be like this. To not need words for a moment. To just be.

The noise of the party eventually invaded their bubble again, and Ander lifted his glass to turn in Max's embrace and meet his gaze once more. "So, what was it you came to tell me?"

Max thought for a moment, then laughed when he remembered. "Mab gave me a shovel talk! It was adorable. I wish you'd heard it."

"Adorable," Ander repeated, taking a sip from his glass before he offered it to Max. "Did she threaten you with dismemberment?"

"She did, in fact." Max chuckled softly, taking a sip.

"Are you scared of her now? Do I need to protect you from the big bad banshee?" Ander cooed, leaning in closer and moving onto his toes to even out their height. The lights shimmered in his eyes, his smile spread so far across his cheeks that it looked like it might hurt. Gods, he was beautiful. Max knew he was, objectively, but it was like every time he looked away, he forgot a little bit. And then he was faced with Ander again, bright and shining like the morning sun, and he remembered, and it set his heart to racing all over again.

With the racing came the pang of regret at his luck. That he had won the love lottery in being arrow-bound to someone like Ander, in being arrow-bound at all, really. Ignis didn't fall in love, not like this. They were meant to dedicate their entire existence to their cause, leaving room for nothing else. And yet, by some divine twist of fate, Erotes had chosen him out of all the ignis that fell to earth to bind to Ander Ruin. It was like magic.

"Absolutely terrified," Max teased in turn, handing back the glass and pulling Ander in closer by his hips. "Your sister is perhaps the scariest thing I've ever faced."

Ander threw his head back and laughed, delighted. It was the best sound Max had ever heard in his life. Freedom ringing through every happy chuckle. Gods, did Ander even know what his happiness gave to Max? Probably not. "So did she scare you away, then? Will you be leaving me and our poor sweet Monnie?"

"Never," Max swore and leaned in to brush a kiss to Ander's lips, a happy murmur passing between them. If only all of Max's siblings could find this. If only they could know the soaring feeling swooping through him, making him feel lighter than air. It didn't seem fair that he was the only one. But he was a greedy man it seemed, selfish in his own way, and he'd take this as long as he was allowed to have it.

"Well, well, well. If it isn't the two lovebirds," a deep

voice said from behind them, making them both come up for air.

Max wasn't sure how long they had been kissing, but his chest felt tight with the lack of oxygen when he was finally able to take a deep breath again. He tilted his head to see around Ander's horns and offered Indra a grin.

"Am I interrupting?"

"I'd have thought that was obvious," Ander said, spinning in Max's arms so he could face Indra, but he didn't move out of Max's hold, just leaned back against his chest again, head tipped to the side so he didn't impale Max on the tip of his horns. They hadn't been away from each other much since the party began. Max wasn't complaining; it was nice having contact with Ander for hours at a time. Especially with how their schedules seemed to keep them both so busy.

"Is there something we can help you with, Your Highness?" Max asked, ducking his head out of respect. Ander and Mab may have been comfortable enough to treat Indra like he was a bit of a nuisance, but he was still Max's superior, so he wasn't about to let show his frustration at being interrupted mid-kiss. They probably shouldn't make out in Mab's kitchen anyway. She was likely to be a little pissed by that.

"I just wanted to check in on the happy couple." Indra shrugged his broad shoulders and tilted his head to look at them as if he were inspecting them. Maybe looking for some indication that they weren't quite as happy as they seemed.

Max wasn't sure. But he didn't think he liked being so closely examined by the king of the gods. He shifted a little, tightening his hold on Ander to comfort himself. Ander's hand fell to brush against his forearm, touch warm and soothing, and Max eased off a bit.

"Happy as can be." Ander held up his glass in a toast and waited until Indra mirrored the motion, then they both drank.

"Of course. Of course." Indra smiled, but the expression was a little sharper than usual, more akin to how he'd smiled at Enrique a few weeks back.

Max straightened his posture. The inspection wasn't over, it seemed.

"I do hope it stays that way," Indra continued, his tone almost conversational, but Max felt the underlying threat beneath the words. It lingered there, waiting to cut. "I'd hate for our dear, sweet Prince Ander to be heartbroken again." Indra leaned forward to pinch Ander's cheeks playfully, and Ander allowed it for a moment before he hissed and brushed him away.

"What are you getting at, Indra?" Ander's tone was guarded, careful. Max didn't like it. He didn't like anything about this interaction at all. It felt off. Just slightly to the left. Like there was a conversation happening within a conversation, and neither he nor Ander understood the smaller, deeper one.

"Oh, nothing." Indra shrugged again, pulling back to his side of the counter. "Just that it'd be a shame if this lovely ignis here did something to make you unhappy and something were to happen to him. Right, Maximus?"

"Yes, sir." Max nodded tightly. He wasn't sure, but he thought maybe he was being threatened by the king of the gods. Why *was* he being threatened by the king of the gods?

"So long as we understand each other." Indra lifted his glass in a salute and took another sip. "Now . . . must dash. It looks like my wife is coming this way."

Then Indra promptly spun around and disappeared into the crowd.

"So ... I, uh ... " Max shifted awkwardly. "I think the king of the gods also just gave me a shovel talk? What was that about?"

Ander shrugged. "Who knows with him. Come along, darling, we have more people to meet."

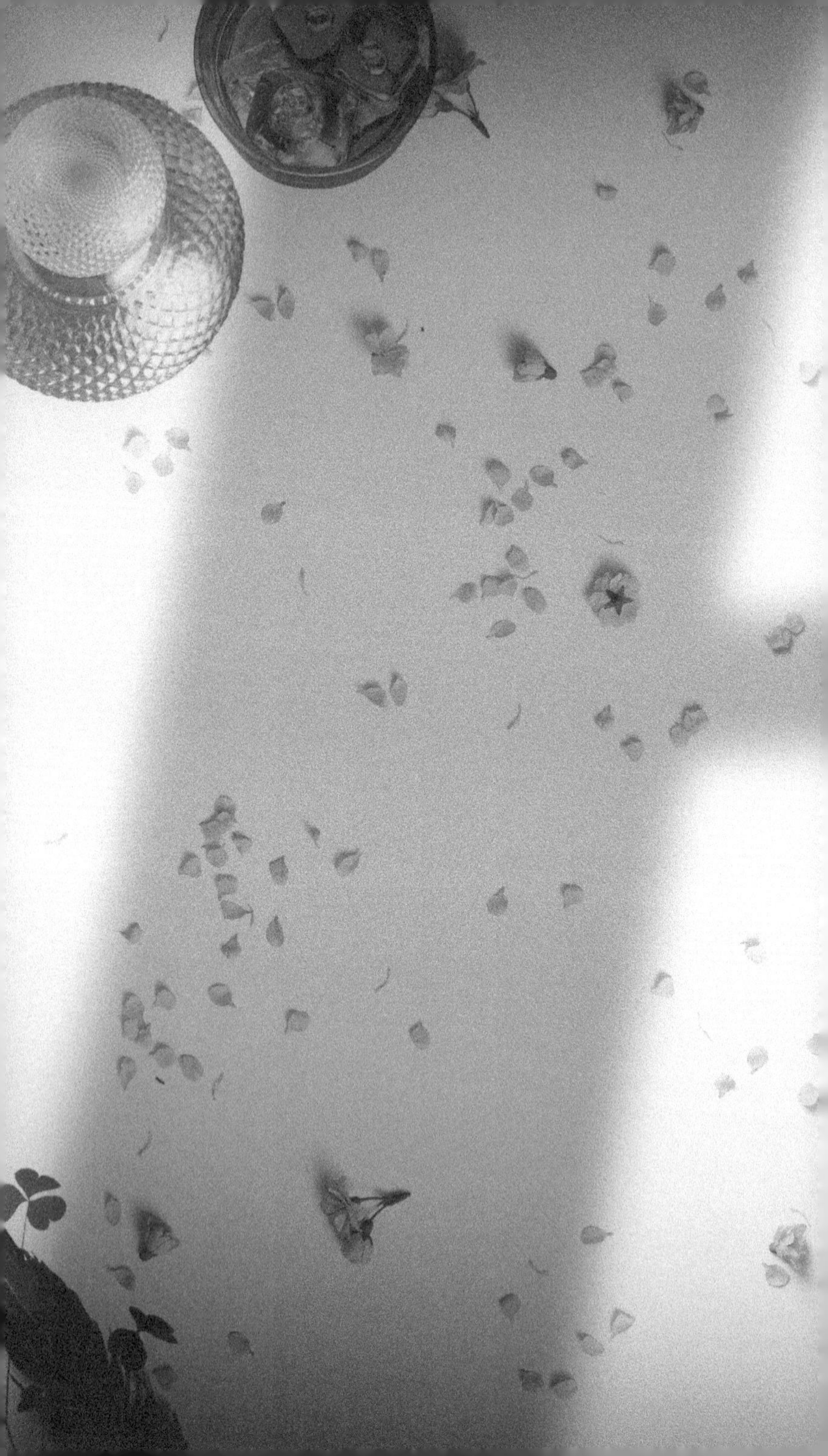

Chapter 6
Ander

Things were going well. Things were going *so* well that Ander was terrified. Living with Max was like living in a dream. Going to bed in his arms and waking up each morning to the sight of the beautiful ignis was everything and more than Ander could have ever hoped for.

So when was the other shoe going to drop?

This couldn't last. There was no way it could last. Ander was so terrified of when it was going to all go away that he was having a hard time focusing on just how good it really was.

Max's arm slid around his waist, and the ignis pressed warm lips to his ear, sending a shiver coursing through Ander's body. He murmured, unable to stop himself, and tipped his head up to kiss Max. He'd done that a lot lately. Kissed him at every opportunity he got. He simply couldn't stop himself. Didn't *want* to stop himself.

"Have I introduced you to Seraphine yet?" Ander asked Max.

Max shook his head. "Nope."

"She's one of the few muses I can actually stand. Come, let me introduce you to a spot of Helicon." Max's hand in his, Ander tugged the ignis through the crowd of guests and to the tall, slender muse, whose lithe frame was draped in cream satin. It just barely covered her breasts and swathed around her waist in loving folds that seemed made for her.

Seraphine, sipping a glass of champagne, smiled when she saw Ander approaching. "Your Highness!" she cooed happily and dipped into a curtsey before stepping into Ander's welcoming embrace.

"Hello, darling." Ander wrapped his free arm around her, giving her a tight squeeze, and kissed her cheek. "Also, no titles here."

"Ah yes, I forgot. In the mortal realm, you're simply Ander." Seraphine stepped back, smiling warmly at him, then her dark eyes lifted to take in Max. "Oh, I can see what our prince sees in you."

Max, to his credit, took the compliment better than Ander anticipated, though there was a faint hint of pink at the tips of his ears to bely his embarrassment.

"Thank you," Max said and stuck out his hand. Seraphine accepted, and they shook quickly. "So, you're a friend from Helicon? Ander hasn't taken me there yet."

Max cut Ander a look, and Ander simply smiled back at him. No, he had not. Helicon meant introducing Max to the place that had never truly accepted Ander because his half-muse blood meant there was an imperfection in him. His long, graceful horns, reminiscent of a gazelle, were not something any other muse had. And though his mother, Aemiliana—Queen of Helicon—had never admitted who his father was, many assumed he was a satyr. That had been enough to disapprove of Ander.

It had been enough to want him dead.

The thought that his grandson may have servant blood in him had been enough for Aemiliana's father to attempt to kill Ander not once but *three times* before his thirtieth birthday.

"Yes, I am a friend from Helicon, and I'm sure Ander will eventually right that wrong and bring you home to his kingdom." Seraphine looked at Ander for a moment, then returned her gaze to Max. "It is a beautiful place, one which you would enjoy, I believe. Warm. Sunny. Filled with music, art, dance, and theatre. You haven't experienced a truly brilliant, emotionally moving society until you have spent time in Helicon."

Max's eyes widened a little, and he nodded. Ander sighed, watching him, and squeezed his hand. "I really do want to see where you come from, Ander." Max turned to look at him with a feverish expression.

Ander smiled softly. "I know, sweetheart. And Seraphine is right, I will right the wrong. I know my mum wants to meet you as well."

"Oh . . . your mom." Some trepidation made its way into Max's eyes. Ander wondered if it was because he didn't know if he would live up to her expectations or if it was because Aemiliana was a queen.

"Yes, after that surprise breakfast with both your parents, one of which wanted to boil me alive . . . I do owe you a parental visit."

Seraphine's face lit up with interest. "Oh, please do tell me about this breakfast."

Ander chuckled. "Well—"

"Of all the egotistical things to do!" a shrill voice sounded above all the noise, making all chatter halt so that nothing could be heard in the room besides the heavy house music playing in the background.

Ander turned toward the voice to see Juno, Queen of Olympia and wife of Indra, standing with her hands on her hips and glaring daggers at the green nymph straddling her husband's lap.

Indra, with little to no self-preservation, lifted his hands from the nymph's ass cheeks to hold them up in an act of innocence. "Accident, my love, I thought she was you."

If it were possible, the daggers in Juno's eyes seemed to grow sharper and more lethal. Ander swore and began heading toward them. A fight between the king and queen of the gods was never good.

Just as Ander reached them, Juno grasped a fistful of the nymph's leafy hair and yanked her back off of Indra with enough force that she toppled to the floor. A cry of pain rose over the music.

"My queen!" Ander called, hands lifting.

Juno's head whipped around to face him, and Ander stopped in his steps as icy-cold dread swept through him. "Do. Not. Defend him," she spat out.

"Absolutely not!" Ander rushed to say. "Merely . . . perhaps no bloodshed on Mab's new rug?" He smiled weakly, eyes drifting down to the beautiful Persian he'd bought Mab a few months ago. The room had been lacking a little something and needed a pick-me-up.

Several of the ignis in attendance stepped forward, uncertainty painted on their faces. They clearly had no idea what to make of this situation. It was their job as part of the Sanctum to interfere in violence such as this. But the king and queen were the heads of the Sanctum. Ignis would not even exist if Indra hadn't ordered Prometheus to create them.

Juno's head tipped to the side, her hand still tight in the nymph's hair. The nymph, face streaked with tears, clutched onto her queen's wrist, trying desperately to ease the pain of her hair being pulled out by its roots.

"P-please, Your M-majesty," the nymph begged.

Juno only snarled at this. "Don't beg me for mercy, you ill-bred trollop." Juno shook her head, causing the nymph to wobble on her knees and cry out.

"May I—" Ander halted as Juno's eyes snapped back up to him. "Just as a house-warming present," Ander continued gently, "ask that her punishment—very deserved, might I add." He shook his head, tsking and frowning down at the nymph, though he knew the one who actually deserved punishment was Indra. "—be a smidgen more lenient than normal. Just, you know, for the sake of the party." Ander twirled his finger in the air.

Juno released her hold on the nymph, who sobbed in relief and fell to her hands on the floor. "Very well." The queen of the gods lifted her hand, swirled it slightly, and snapped her fingers.

The nymph, who'd been in the process of wiping the tears from her face, gasped, arched her back, then quickly transformed into a small, potted lemon tree.

"Clio!" Another green nymph, dressed in nothing but a few spare leaves on key parts, flung herself into the midst of the circle. "My sister! You can't do this, you callous *wench*!"

Ander winced. That was not the best decision she could have made.

Juno's face darkened, and Indra himself finally stood up. "Excuse me?" the king boomed. "What did you say to my wife?!"

"She can't do this to my sister!" the nymph shrieked and raised her hands. They began to glow with forest magic.

Before the spell could be released on the king and queen of the gods, one of the ignis stepped forward and wrapped an arm around her waist, then thrust her hands up into the air.

The spell, which was a wave of icy water, sprayed against the ceiling then fell in ice droplets down onto the guests. A minotaur who had not been paying attention, presumably thinking someone behind him had dumped ice cubes down his back, let out a bellow of fury. He spun and punched the unsuspecting griffin behind him in the back of the head.

And then all hell broke loose.

Ander wasn't sure what happened next except that violence erupted like a volcano through the party guests. A chair went flying, someone was suddenly hanging from the pendant light in the ceiling, and an enormous flash of fire exploded and blew out the side of the dining room.

It could have been worse, *much* worse, but there were six ignis in attendance, Max and Quin being two of them. They swiftly put an end to the chaos, pinning the worst perpetrators to the floor, while others were backed against the wall. Ander saw that Nox and Nash had even stepped in to help prevent the situation from getting worse.

When all was said and done, the drapes in the windows were all singed, Mab's Persian rug bore a large stain that looked suspiciously like blood, and the waves on the beach could be heard through the giant hole in Mab's wall.

Not even panting but looking a little mussed, Max slipped up beside Ander. "Are you okay?" he asked, concern pinching his brows.

Ander threw his arms around Max's neck and leaned into him, grinning up at him. "Are you kidding? I'm fabulous! We've just had the party of the year!"

Of Hope & Blight

Laughing and shaking his head, Max dipped his head down to kiss Ander roughly. Ander clung onto Max, kissing him back for all he was worth. Losing himself to the taste and feel of his boyfriend. To the heady emotions that washed through him at Max's touch.

Ander lived for these moments. Thrived on them.

"I love you," they both whispered at the same time.

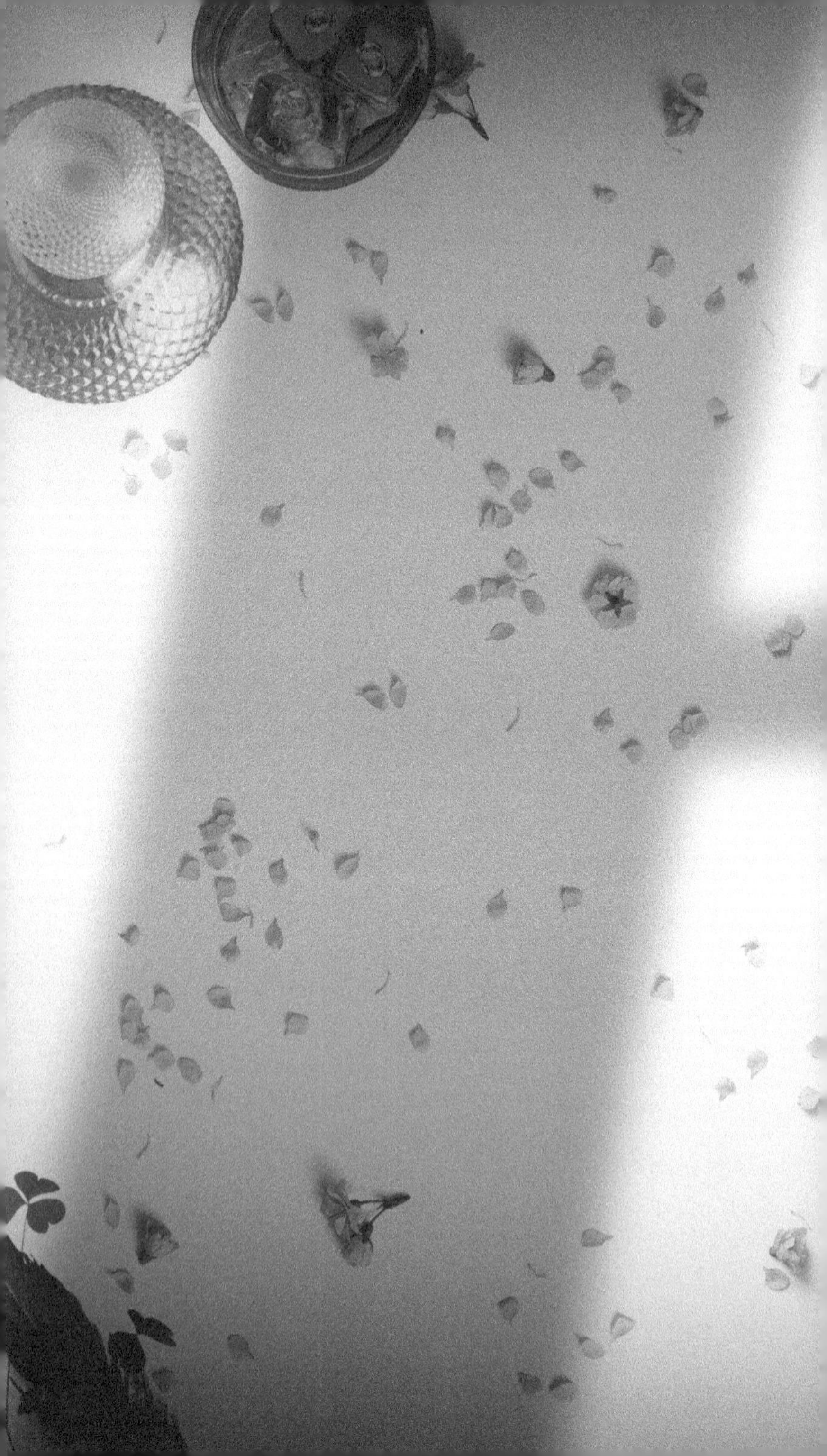

Chapter 7
Mab

"I am *never* inviting Indra and Juno to another party," Mab said, brushing the back of her hand across her brow as if to wipe away sweat.

Really it was just because her forehead was itching from the dust in the stockroom. They needed to take a minute to clean that up, but that would require life to slow down for about half a second so they could think about the dust and cobwebs lingering there, and it hadn't. For months. Between the case of the missing girls, the amare bond issue, and Ander falling ass over teakettle in love with the man who was investigating him *for* the case of the missing girls . . . Well, some things had to fall to the wayside. Maybe they'd have time now that Max and Ander were living together and settled, and life could slow down at least for a couple of months. Mab could dream.

"*Ever* again," Mab emphasized, clinking the bottles perhaps a little too loudly as she loaded them onto the shelf behind the bar.

"Oh, come on, Mabbers, it wasn't that bad." Ander didn't even bother to look up from the paperwork he had sprawled across the bar. He'd gotten behind on things like scheduling and ordering as of late with everything going on. So at least Mab wasn't the only one of them who was distracted. But this was good, she decided, the way things had quieted. Ander happier than he'd ever been in his entire life, and her content with the way things were. This was so good. She couldn't ask for more. "I mean, remember that time in Cairo when they—"

"I think my new lemon tree would beg to differ." The poor nymph had really gotten the raw end of the deal as far as things were concerned with Juno and Indra. Of course, she should have known better, but it wasn't exactly her fault. Mab imagined people found it hard to say no to the king of the gods. Not her, of course, but she seemed to be a special case since Ander was Indra's favorite little half-muse, and she was by extension his . . . Gods, she hoped she wasn't his favorite *anything*. That would be much worse than bland indifference. Either way, she seemed off limits as far as most things went. Indra didn't flirt with her unless it was in jest, and Juno was comfortable enough with her to not be too surprised when she found Indra on Mab's couch sleeping one off. Mab had only been threatened with being turned into a house plant once or twice. That was a lot more than most could say who interacted with the volatile couple. "By the by, when do you think they'll turn her back? And should I feel weird about using the lemons to make lemonade? I mean . . . they're there. But what part of her is lemons? Is it—"

"Don't overthink it."

Mab hummed her agreement and put the last bottle of liquor among the ones behind the bar before turning to look at Ander, one pale brow raised. "So. Other than the citrus-related consequences, I'd say that went rather well, all things considered. Certainly better than expected."

Ander lifted his head to meet her gaze with a smile. "I think so. Max seemed to have a good time too."

"Good. That's good." She wondered if that meant Ander was going to host more parties. Hopefully, he wouldn't decide to try hosting them at her place. Her little house on the water might not survive, and to be honest, the cleanup was a nuisance. Even with a best friend with magic. Although it did help not having to explain to a contractor why there was a hole in the dining room wall that looked as if it'd been blasted there by dynamite. Ander had even been kind enough to clean the rug before he left. "It was strange having ignis and inanimi all in the same place, though."

"Strange, but kind of awesome, right?" Ander dropped his pen on top of the papers and gave Mab his full attention. He perked up a little, his smile stretching across his face. There was excitement there that Mab didn't think was entirely warranted but that she also couldn't find it within herself to quash. "They didn't even cause a fight."

"They didn't." Mab wasn't exactly sure how to feel about the blending of Ander's two families. The ignis and inanimi hadn't fought, no, but they hadn't exactly mingled either, aside from Max's family. The others who were invited kept to themselves, secluded off in corners, and Mab wondered if it was because they were all awkward or because they saw themselves as above the rest of the guests. She wished she'd had more time to talk to some of them. Quin, especially, could have given her some good insight into what the other ignis were thinking. Where Max seemed to be off in his own head most of the time, too busy curling his body around Ander to notice that there was any lingering tension, Quin sat off to the side and watched. She imagined he saw a fair bit more than he ever let on. Still, sometimes Ander needed her optimism more than her realism, so she said, "Maybe that's a sign they can all coexist more peacefully soon."

"I think it is. I'm thinking of having a night at Inferno where we invite some ignis to mingle with inanimi. Maybe we should start off human-free at first? Then there will be no issues of the ignis feeling that the inanimi are preying on the normies. I'd have to put in some new wards, but I think it'd be nice to have a safe space where they could interact." Ander's eyes danced with this new idea, his back straighter as he spoke, fingers tapping on the bar top. "It would go a long way toward the ignis seeing us as something more than just monsters."

Mab shifted on her feet, the floorboards groaning beneath her weight. She didn't want to kill this new spark in Ander. She didn't want to tell him that it was probably not the best idea. That Inferno might not survive it. But she also didn't want to support this wholeheartedly. It wasn't a bad idea, not necessarily. Just . . . "Maybe we should start smaller?" Mab offered diplomatically. "Have Max and his family come for a couple of nights. Let the regulars get used to seeing them around for something other than investigating, then we can move on to inviting more ignis that Max trusts."

Ander frowned a little as if disheartened, and Mab hated herself a little bit for killing this new dream of his before it'd properly gotten off the ground.

"We don't want Inferno to go down in flames, literally." Mab knew Ander hated it when she was reasonable, especially about things he was excited about. But one of them had to be the pragmatic one who thought things through, and it sure as shit wasn't going to be Ander. He was a good businessman—she'd never say that he wasn't. But sometimes he got ahead of himself and needed her to bring him back down to earth. "It's a good idea, and I like the thought of Inferno becoming the place where all the creatures of Underworld can come and just hang out without having to worry about being arrested for something trivial. But we have to think about how our existing customer base would feel about a bunch of ignis showing up to the bar."

They wouldn't like it, she knew that for certain. Especially with the ignis' habit of detaining inanimi with little evidence or provocation. The Schields family was different, she'd seen that for herself, but the vast majority of the ignis weren't like that. They seemed determined to think all inanimi preyed on humans any chance they got. Never mind that the vast majority of them, the Mabs and the Anders of their world, wanted very little to do with normies at all, much less eating them or sucking them dry or whatever the others liked to do. They weren't all demogorgons and lamia.

Ander huffed and opened his mouth like he meant to argue his point further, and Mab decided to change the subject.

"So, I heard you talking to Seraphine about taking Max home to meet Mum." She braced her elbows on the bar so she was more of a height with him and shot him a knowing smile. "When are you planning to do that?"

The bar stool creaked under Ander's weight as he shifted, seeming to try to get as far away from Mab and her questioning gaze as he could manage, but she had him pinned down; he wasn't going anywhere. "I saw you talking to Quin while—"

"Nope. We've already had one subject change, we can't

have another for at least five minutes. Rules are rules." Mab looked down at her watch. "You'll just have to wait till 1:37 to ask me that. So, Aemiliana and Max, when are they going to meet? You know she'll love him to bits, what are you waiting for?"

"I just ... " Ander shifted again, glancing at the clock over the bar as if he could stall long enough to reach the allotted five minutes, but they both knew he couldn't. Not that Mab was going to let him anyway. "I feel weird about taking him back to Helicon when the muses were never overly accepting of my ... you know."

She did know. His horns. His lack of perfection. His otherness. She understood it perhaps better than anyone else in their world. She didn't fit in with the sirens and the banshee either. Too human for them, and not human enough for the normies. It put them in a weird place. A place where they bonded perhaps better than they ever would have without that.

"Then why don't you invite her here? I'm sure she'd like to see Miami again, it's been a while. She does love the beach." Mab shrugged and stood up to grab the crate she'd brought from the back and started stacking the empty bottles inside. "She can stay in my guest room if she feels like she's encroaching on your space at the condo."

"I don't know ... "

When Mab turned back, Ander was chewing on the inside of his cheek, his eyes flicking from one thing to the next, unsettled. She hated seeing him like this. Her best friend was always sure of himself almost to a fault. Most might call him arrogant, but Mab knew him well enough to know that the confidence he displayed to the world hid a deep well of insecurity. About his looks. About his weight. About his family. Ander Ruin was a mess of contradictions.

Startlingly loud and ostentatious when he was hiding something, but more than happy to burn the world for the people he loved. And gods, Mab loved him so deeply it ached sometimes. He was her best friend. Her savior. Her family. And she'd do anything, absolutely anything, to make it so he didn't have to feel this way ever again. Even if that meant letting Aemiliana stay at her place, which would probably lead to a fair amount of probing into her own personal life she didn't really care for.

"The worst thing she can say is no, Andy." Mab leaned forward again, bracing the crate between her hips and the bar so she could take his hands and give them a squeeze. "And we both know she won't say no. So just reach out and invite her. I think it'd be good for her to meet Max. And once that's done, then you can think about taking Max back to Helicon later, when you're ready. But at least this way he won't think you're trying to hide him from your mother."

"He doesn't think that." Ander scoffed, then his brows drew together. "You don't think he thinks that, do you?"

Mab huffed a laugh. "Who knows with that one. But either way, you're living with him, he's your soulmate, and Mum will want to meet him. I'll even sit in if you need me to act as a buffer. We can drag grumpy cat into it too, make it a real family affair."

"Eventually, you're going to run out of weird nicknames for Quin, you know that, right?"

"Not any time soon." Mab shrugged and headed back toward the stockroom. "Call your mother, or I will."

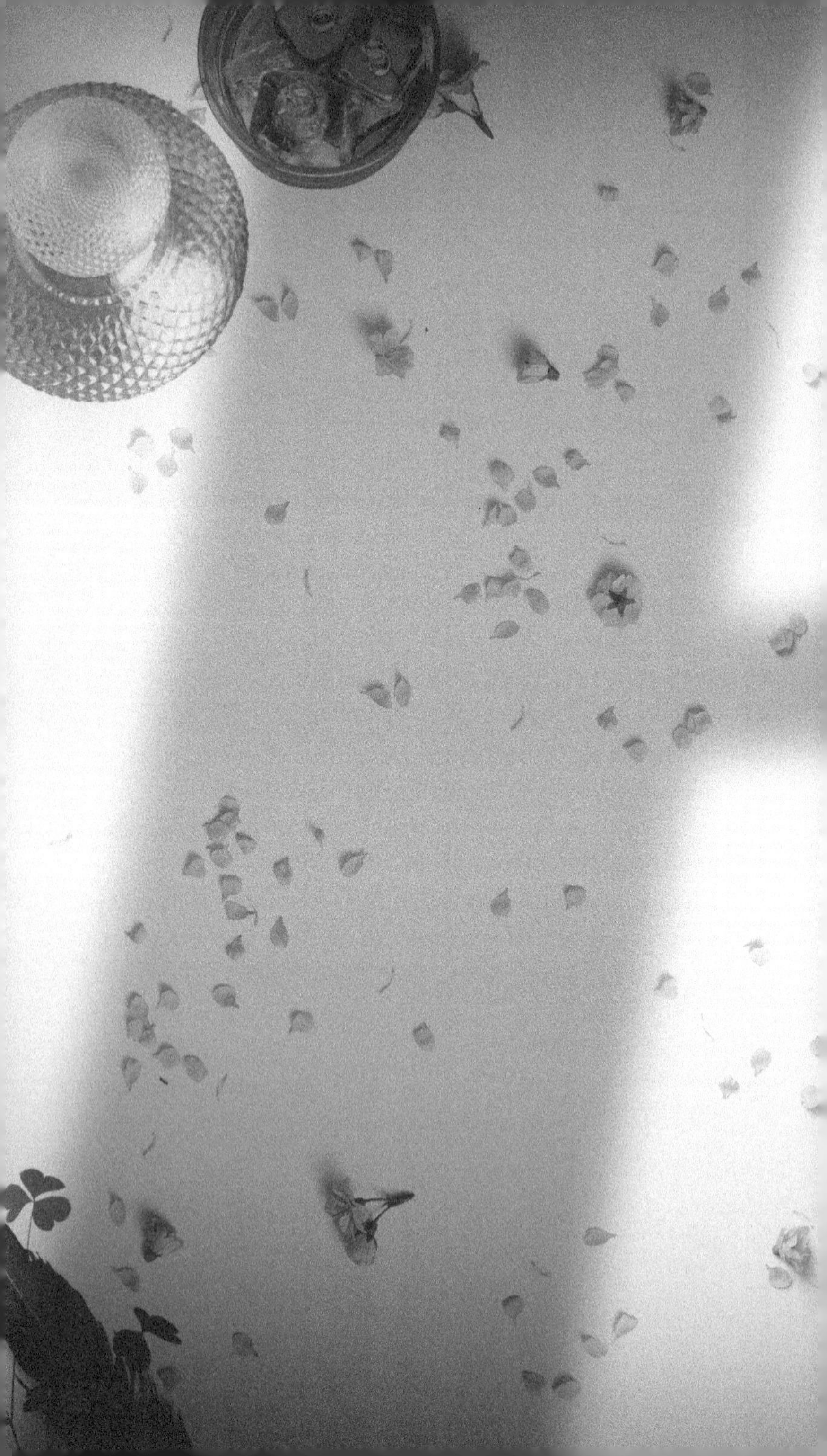

Chapter 8
Quin

The charcoal pencil moved quickly over the canvas, the face of an elderly gentleman taking shape. Quin hummed softly along with Mozart's "Symphony No. 25" in G minor. The orchestral arrangement, while high tempo, filled him with a sense of peace.

There was something about the passionate sounds of a string instrument that soothed the wild part of Quin that was never settled. The trauma-riddled portion that had melded into part of his very being and wouldn't go away.

When he listened to classical music, the noise of the day, all of his worries and responsibilities, melted away, and he was able to focus on the creative portion of his brain that was silenced far too often.

He finished the slope of the cheek and brushed over it with his thumb, smudging the charcoal to add shading. Quin stopped humming as he heard loud giggles coming from the corner. Turning slightly, he looked over at Tavi and Max.

Tavi was covered nearly head to toe in finger paints, her dark brown curls spotted with red, yellow, and blue. Her dress, which had been picked out for her by his papa, was now smeared in a mix of the three, blending into green, purple, and orange where they touched.

The small youngling stomped over paper with her bare feet, leaving behind colorful footprints. She seemed to love it, and took large, heavy steps that slapped against her canvas.

Max, who was most assuredly hungover from the housewarming party the night before, looked on with as much interest as he could muster. He clapped along to Tavi's movements, but even those were only half-hearted. He squinted from the bright lights above, his face scrunching.

"That's very pretty, Tavi." Max laughed, then winced, his fingers rubbing at his temples.

Tavi hopped up and down, clapping her hands at Max's encouragement.

"Oh . . . you're splashing it everywhere!" Max looked over at Quin, making a face. "Is this okay?" He pointed to the splatters on the cement floor.

Quin nodded. "Let her play," he called back. He'd spilled worse.

He turned away from the sight of Tavi and his brother and returned to the portrait of the elderly man. His eyes drifted to the photo of him taped to the top of the canvas for reference, then he lifted the charcoal once more and started lightly shaping the eyes. The portrait had come from a trip to the park, when Quin had seen the man sitting alone on a bench feeding ducks by the water.

It was a simple sight, and yet beautiful to Quin. The man looked peaceful, completely at ease in his solitary endeavor. A soft light in his eyes as he gazed at the ducks, like there was nowhere else in the world he wanted to be.

The sentiment echoed by the slight hint of a smile on his lips.

Quin couldn't help but wonder what that was like. To feel so at peace with your own thoughts. Quin certainly didn't have that. Not when he was in the silence of the outdoors. He should have been able to find it there, but the open sky only reminded him of those nights in his childhood. The openness taunting him with what he could not have.

Quin's fingers tightened around the charcoal, threatening to snap it in half. Realizing he was tensing up, Quin relaxed his hand and rolled his shoulders. He closed his eyes, listening to the music. Letting "Symphony No. 25" rush over him once more. Trying to let his mind be swept away by it.

This time, it didn't work.

Instead, his mind wandered to the party the night before. It had ended in chaos, which shouldn't have surprised anyone. That was what happened when you placed ignis and inanimi in the same house and threw in the king and queen of the gods to top it off.

Things had been going well, Quin was forced to admit, until that nymph took up residence on Indra's lap.

If Indra hadn't been there, and Juno hadn't lost her temper, perhaps the evening would have continued fine. Remained uneventful.

But the ignis still wouldn't have enjoyed themselves or changed their opinion of the inanimi. Ovid and Cicero were proof of that. Their opinions of Max caused the blood to heat in Quin's veins. He hated that they thought ill of Max simply because he had fallen in love. Because he had been able to do something that the rest of them were unable to.

Connect with someone.

Quin glanced quickly back at Max, who was now dragging his finger through paint, to Tavi's excitement.

"Look at the pretty swirls!" Max encouraged Tavi, who stomped on them playfully. "Hey! My painting!"

Tavi squealed delightedly.

How had Max done it? What part of himself had opened up so that he could not only connect but love that way? Quin didn't even know what it was like to feel attraction for another being. He'd never had the desire to be intimate with someone else. He could look at a being and find them beautiful, but it went no further.

Sometimes, he wondered if he was broken. Other ignis took pleasure in physical relationships, but Quin had no desire. No need. Felt no draw.

Was it something caused by the trauma of the fighting ring? Had his captors beat it out of him?

Quin pushed his fingers through his hair, brushing his bangs out of his eyes.

He hated how distracted he was today. Typically, he could focus on his art. Drown out the rest of the world: all the horrors that he saw, the viciousness of the inanimi underworld, the relentless feeling of not fitting in.

But not today.

There was something about today.

The phone in his back pocket began to vibrate, pulling him out of the tailspin of his thoughts. Setting down his charcoal pencil, Quin wiped his smudged fingers on the cloth tucked into the front pocket of his black jeans and pulled out his cell.

Nox's face, scrunched into a wink with a stuck-out tongue, flashed on his screen. He hit the green Accept button and pressed the phone to his ear.

"Yeah?" he greeted his little sister.

"Quin." There was a momentary hesitation over his name before the rest of her words tumbled out of her. "You and Max need to come to the sanctuary right now."

Quin frowned. "What's going on, Nox?"

"Just get here, *please*!" Nox almost shouted and hung up.

Quin stared down at the now black screen of his phone, not sure what was going on. He turned to Max, who was trying to fend off a paint-covered Tavi.

"Max!" he called loudly over the music, reaching for the remote to turn it off. The warehouse filled suddenly with silence, and both Max and Tavi froze and turned to him, their eyes widened in surprise. "Something has come up, we have to get to the sanctuary, now."

"What is—" Max began.

"Nox didn't say, we just have to go." Stooping a little, he scooped up Tavi. "Come on, Button, we have to get you cleaned up."

There hadn't been time to do anything with Tavi; the concern that filled both him and Max was too overwhelming to swing by and drop her off with their parents. So she had come with them.

Tavi sat on his hip, one of his arms around her waist and his hand on her thigh to keep her held up, as they walked into the Schields command center.

Nox and Nash, the only biological twins in the family, both looked pale and anxious. Nash's dark hair stood up all over the place, evidence that he'd run his fingers through it too many times. As Quin and Max entered, they both stood.

Nox, wringing her hands and looking at Max apologetically, stepped forward slightly. "Max . . . " she started, but her words trailed off. Almost like she couldn't bear to say it.

Quin looked quickly between her and Nash. "Spit it out," he demanded. The hesitation and suspense were only making this worse.

"What is it, Nox?" Max's tone was far gentler than Quin's.

"Enriqueescapedhiscell," Nash cut in, spitting the words all at once. His bright blue eyes, which he had gotten from their dad, stared back at Max with apprehension.

Quin froze, feeling like he needed to shake his head. Because he was sure he hadn't just heard what Nash said correctly.

"What do you mean?" Max asked. Quin could tell by the sound of confusion and lack of emotion in his tone that Max was also having an issue comprehending what he was hearing.

"We just got word from the Rome-Olympia sanctuary. Enrique escaped from his cell last night. It's believed he had inside help." Nox looked between Max and Quin, searching both of their faces.

"*What do you mean?!*" Max shouted this time, both anger and terror in his exclamation. "How could they let this *happen*? How could someone *help* him?" Max's hands went to his hair, fisting it and pulling at the dark strands until his knuckles turned white.

Quin frowned and looked down at Tavi, who was shrinking in fear at the shouting. He rubbed her back gently and pressed a kiss to her forehead. "It's okay. You're okay."

Her eyes filled with unshed tears, but she seemed to

ease a little at the calmness in his voice and buried her head in his shoulder.

Quin looked at Max, who was now pacing. He could tell that his brother was trying hard to reel himself back in. Quin wasn't used to seeing Max explode like this—but then, he'd never seen Max desperate to protect the man he loved before, either.

"Do they know who helped him?" Max asked.

"No, the cameras in his wing were turned off." Nox bit her lip.

That didn't make sense. The cameras were never turned off, especially in an area of the prisons where they were keeping someone as powerful as a god. Quin's stomach knotted with dread.

How many more sleeper agents were there?

How far did Enrique's corruption go?

"Where is he now?" Max growled and turned on his heel to face them all once more, his expression dark and clouded.

"They don't know." Nox's voice was soft, like she was hesitant to add more fuel to the fire.

Quin wanted to give her a hug and reassure her that this was not her fault. That Max wasn't upset with her, it was the situation. It was the terror he was feeling, knowing that one of the worst kidnappers of ignis younglings in history and the largest crime lord they'd ever brought down—along with being his boyfriend's abusive ex—was now free once more.

"How is this *possible*?!" Max shouted, his arms flying into the air along with his wings, knocking aside the nearest office chair. He reached out to catch the chair before it could knock into the opposite desk. "Sorry. Sorry," he muttered.

Tavi let out a scared little *eep* and shuddered, curling into Quin more. "Max ..." Quin started.

Max's face whipped in his direction, ready to growl at him too, but then his eyes landed on Tavi's huddled figure, and the fury visibly drained out of his body. His entire form seemed to shrink, and instead of anger, what was left was the underlying terror. "He's going to kill him," Max whispered.

"No Max, he's not. We would never let that happen," Quin said, quick to reassure him. Although he could understand his fear. As well as his rage. Orcus should never have been allowed to escape, and King Indra should have seen to that by having him executed.

But the deaths and kidnapping of some ignis weren't important. Because they were nothing but soldiers built to die for the cause. The well of anger that Quin kept buried deep inside him bubbled up, threatening to flow over. He pushed it down, focused on calming Max instead.

Better to think of his brother than those unresolved issues.

"Exactly!" Nash rushed to add. "We've caught him once, we can catch him again."

"We're the Schields, we're not afraid to kick a god's ass," Nox proclaimed.

Max's lips twitched slightly, and his eyes softened as he looked at them all. "Thank you, guys." He met Quin's gaze head on. "We need to go talk to the captain."

Quin nodded and looked down at Tavi, who was peeking out from his shoulder tentatively. "I need you to go to Nashy and Nox, okay?"

She blinked at him, trying to shrink up more, but Quin shook his head.

Nash stepped over to them and held out his hands. "Come to Nashy, he's got candy!"

This did attract her attention, and though she was obviously still hesitant, Tavi reached out and let Nash take her.

"Come on," Quin said to Max. "Let's go see what the plan is to deal with this, and then you call Ander and make sure he's safe."

Max nodded, and together, they headed down the hall to Captain Galeo's office.

It was like he had been expecting them. The light-haired ignis barely lifted his head when they knocked on the frame of the open door and waved them in.

"I suppose you're here about Orcus," he said when he deigned to speak, sitting back in his chair.

"Yes, sir, we are." Max stood straight, head up, hands behind his back. The perfect little soldier. He always had been. And yet, they hated him for his kindness. For the fact that he could feel. Could love.

Quin kept his own back straight, but his hands rested in fists at his sides.

"As I'm certain your ops team has shared, he escaped from his cell sometime during the night, the cameras were malfunctioning at the time so we have no way of knowing who aided him." Galeo's tone was neutral, showing no concern, like he was discussing what he was planning to have for lunch.

Max nodded, impatience twitching at the corner of his lips. "We can leave at once to help in the search and re-capture."

"No."

From the corner of his eye, Quin watched Max's head dip down a little, no longer standing straight at attention.

"We have no current ca—"

"I said no." Galeo was firm. "Orcus was in the custody of the Rome-Olympia sanctuary, the Princeps are well aware of the activities that led up to his arrest. Their officers will handle the escape. We will be focusing on Miami, as is our duty."

Max's entire form stiffened, and Quin knew that his brother was ready to explode. He wasn't sure what to do or say to stop him.

"Sir, you know I have a personal stake in this. You have to understand that Orcus will be coming to Miami, he will want to take revenge on the ones who put him away and took down his operation." The words rushed out of Max, as if he was afraid if he didn't say them quick enough, they would disappear. "We don't even know where his ignis army is yet! We can't just sit back and—"

"We can, and we *will*." Galeo's face hardened, his eyes darkening in a threatening manner. "You are to have no involvement in this case, is that understood? *Any* of you." His eyes moved to take in Quin, making sure that he was aware this included him as well. "And if I hear even the faintest whisper that you have put your noses into places they don't belong, I will strip both of you of your ranks and disband your entire team. Am I clear?"

Quin and Max both straightened, nodding in unison. "Yes, sir," they said together.

"You're dismissed."

Outside the office, Max took a swing at the wall. His punch didn't land only because Quin stuck his hand out to capture it quickly, taking the impact himself.

Max's eyes flew to his face, his fury there once more. "Qu ..."

"I know," Quin said softly, keeping his tone firm but soft.

"I have to protect Ander."

"I know," he said again. "And we will. We'll find a way to do this without Galeo finding out." And they would, because Quin knew Max would never sleep again if they didn't. But also because the god deserved to be locked up. To be punished for what he had done. Caged for his crimes against their kind. For the younglings, like Tavi, who couldn't fight for herself.

Max's eyes widened a little, as if he were surprised his brother was so ready to defy direct orders. "You don't have to risk it. I can do this on my own."

Quin shook his head. "No, Ander is family now. We don't abandon family."

Max suddenly embraced Quin, his arms tight around him. Grunting, he hugged him back, then pushed his brother away.

"Go call Ander. Make sure he's okay."

Concern filled Max's hazel eyes. "Oh gods, he doesn't even know yet."

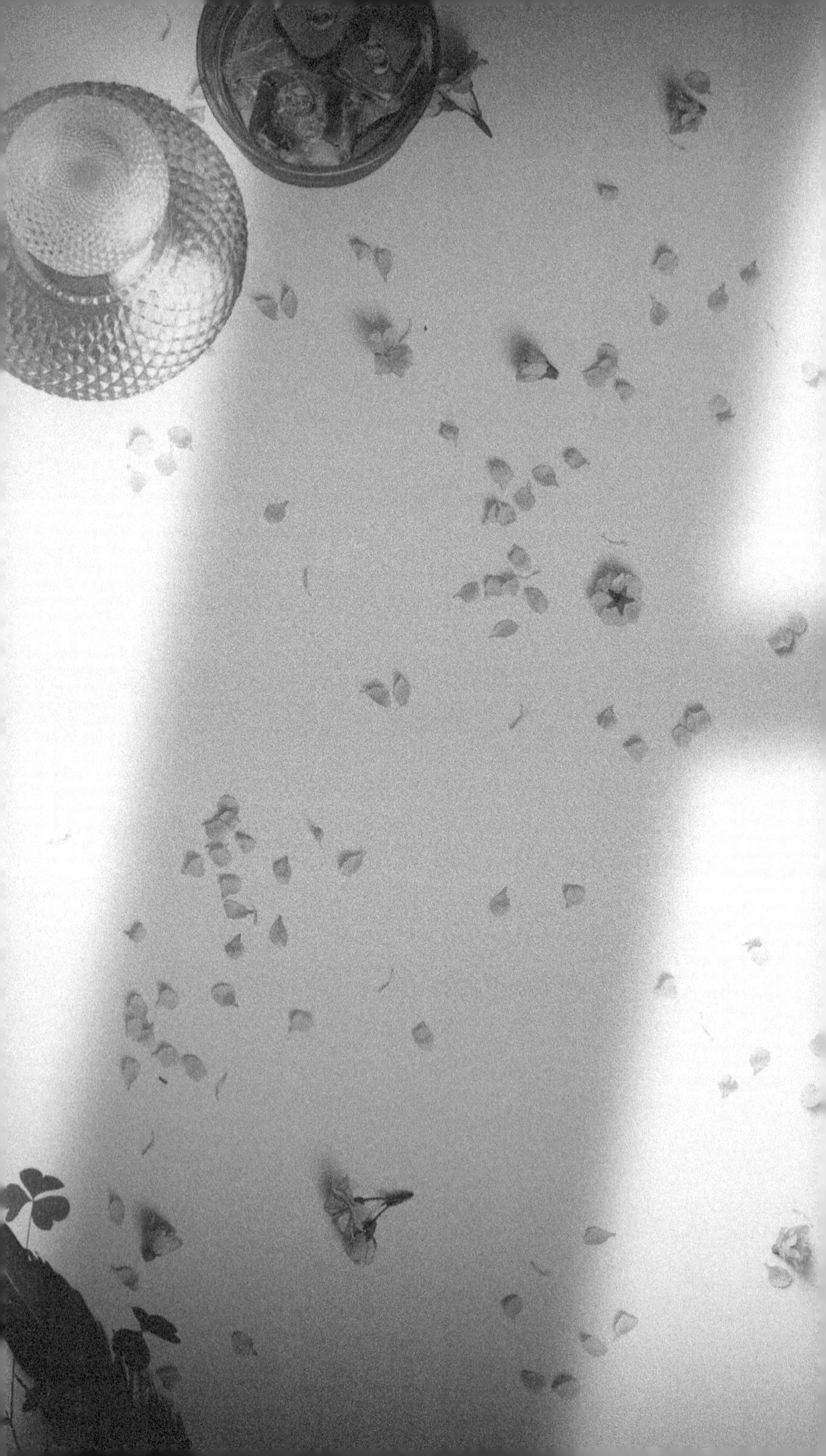

Chapter 9
Mab

Inferno was more packed than usual. As if all their regulars had decided to take the previous night off right along with Mab and Ander. Which was just impossible because no one knew their schedule, but still, it was crowded. Wall-to-wall people at the bar. The music thumped against Mab's eardrums so hard, she wished she'd brought earplugs. It wasn't a normal occurrence that the music got to be too much for her, but sometimes. Well . . . sometimes, she just needed a break.

That combined with this feeling that had been growing in her gut all night . . . a twisted sort of nausea that didn't really make any sense. She wasn't hungover. After so many years partying with Ander, it was near impossible to get hungover. And she wasn't due for her cycle for another couple of weeks. Why was the feeling sneaking up on her slowly like this? Why hadn't it hit her all at once? It seemed to grow worse with every passing hour. Could she have caught some weird paranormal bug? That didn't seem possible. She'd spent the last few hundred years not getting even a sniffle. As far as she knew, inanimi couldn't get sick at all, but she'd been wrong about things like that before. A cold sweat had started up at her hairline about a half hour ago, and it didn't seem to be going away.

"I'm gonna grab some air and some refills," Mab shouted over the music to Parker, who was working the bar with her, and held up two empty bottles of vodka. They nodded, and Mab slipped through the door behind the bar into a corridor that was mostly soundproof. There were two doors off the short hall, one that led to the stockroom and one to the back alley where the dumpsters were. Both should have been closed and locked, as only Mab and Ander had keys, but the stockroom door was cracked. A sliver of light leaked out into the hall, and the feeling of something being wrong crawled along Mab's spine, threatening to make her slouch under the weight of it.

She crept forward, gripping the neck of the bottle in her hand more firmly in preparation for using it to bludgeon whoever had broken into their stockroom, and nudged the door open further. What she found on the other side made her drop the bottles. They thunked hard against the floor, not shattering but chipping off enough pieces that she'd have to bring the vacuum in to make sure no one cut themselves later.

"Andy . . . " Mab's voice got caught in her throat, her accent thick as emotion threatened to choke her. "Ander. What's wrong? What happened?"

He was curled up on one of the big crates in the back corner, his knees pulled up to his chest. There was an empty look in his eyes when he lifted his head to look at her. But at the sight of Mab, he pulled himself upright and smoothed out his clothes, pretending as if nothing at all had happened. As if she hadn't just found him curled in the fetal position in their stockroom like Max had broken up with him. Shit. Was that what happened? Did Max—

"Enrique escaped," Ander said in a detached sort of way. Like it didn't matter. Like it was fine. It wasn't *fine*.

"Excuse me?" Whatever Mab thought was happening could not have been worse than those words, and could not have lessened the blow of them, either. Dread rolled her stomach. Her dinner crawled up her throat, and she was dangerously close to vomiting all of it onto the cement floor, which would mean more cleaning. But she swallowed it down, the bile burning the whole way. "He . . . he escaped? How? When? Why didn't they tell us sooner? We've got to—"

Ander shrugged. "Max just called. He said he'd be home early tonight, to make sure I was all right."

"Well of course you're not *all right*." How could he be? Enrique was his worst fucking nightmare. Hers too, if she were being honest. There wasn't much in this world that scared Mab so much as the god who would love to wipe her best friend off the face of the earth. "We've got to get you somewhere safe. I can have Jennifer cover for me, and I can take you back to my place. Indra put up those wards that'll—"

"No."

"No? Ander, what do you mean no? It's the safest place for you in all of Miami. You have a perfectly serviceable room there, and Max can stay too. I really don't mind. I just need to know that you're safe."

"I'm fine." There was a hard edge to his tone now, more clipped than Mab thought she'd ever heard before. And she knew what this was; logically, she did. It was Ander masking. Hiding away what he was feeling.

"You aren't. And you don't have to be." Why had she

thought he was done doing that with her? Enrique really brought out the worst in both of them, Mab knew that well enough. He had made her jealous and spiteful at one point in her life; she wouldn't allow him to rip them apart again. "Come on, Andy, I'll call Max and let him know you're—"

"I will not hide like some coward." Ander spat the words, ripping his arm away from where Mab had been reaching for him. "I won't go tuck myself away while Max faces this alone."

"He's not facing this alone. He's got his siblings, and the whole bloody *Sanctum*. Max will be fine. It's you I'm worried about!" It was Ander that Mab would *always* be worried about. He was the only family she had. He was the person who had saved her when she thought everyone had forgotten about her. And that was before he even knew her, when he was drunk on his own grief and liquor so strong it would now likely be illegal. The memory of her prophecy flashed through her mind: Ander burning alive while Enrique looked on. She'd saved him from that, she could save him from this too.

"Enrique is a god. Max can't stand against—"

"He already *has*! Max is a warrior, and he already stood against Enrique once. Remember? It was him who brought Enrique in in the first place. He'll be—"

"I am not going into hiding Mab! Drop it!" Ander snipped, his eyes flickering with magic as his irritation with her warred with his fear.

"Yes. You are. I will not let—"

"Let me?" Ander laughed, the sound cold and empty. A chill swept down Mab's spine, cooling the sweat that had settled in the dip at the small of her back. "Like you've ever been able to *stop* me." He lifted his hand, his fingers prepared for a snap.

"Ander. Don't you fucking dare. You will not—"
Snap.

And he was gone. Leaving her alone in the storeroom with the sinking nausea of dread turning her belly.

Oh. Dread.

That was why she'd been sick all day. Some sixth sense had tried to tell her this was coming. That she needed to prepare for the worst. And she hadn't listened because she'd thought she had a stomach bug like a normie.

"Okay." She breathed, brushing her fingers through her hair, hoping it hadn't started to frizz from her sweat. "Okay. I just need to get through tonight, and then I can drag him home by his ear."

Probably. Maybe. Hopefully.

Well. She was going to try, anyway.

Closing time rolled around, and Ander was nowhere to be found.

"What a jackass." Mab rubbed at her face. Her stomach had only grown more upset over the ensuing hours, and now she had a headache that was steadily approaching a migraine to go with it. She'd be lucky if she made it through the night without throwing up. Not that she'd sleep anyway, knowing that Enrique was out there somewhere plotting against them and Ander wasn't within sight.

Even if she did try to sleep, it'd probably be riddled with nightmares. There really was no use in trying, except for the fact that a lack of sleep would only make her feel sicker.

At least she was home now. She could take off the corset required for working behind the bar at Inferno and change into a pair of baggy sweats and a T-shirt that went down to her knees. Maybe she'd even forgo the sweats, just to keep there from being any pressure on her stomach.

She nodded to herself, moving through the house to put away her purse, check Gizmo, and change. It wasn't until she was standing in her bedroom, sipping a cup of tea and looking out at the water behind her house, that she saw the strange lump on the private beach out back.

"Damn it. What washed up there now?" Mab huffed, setting down her mug and grabbing her phone in case she had to call animal control again. She hoped it wasn't another dolphin. She knew they were little assholes but couldn't really help feeling bad for them when they got turned around in the canal and run over by boaters. It wasn't their fault they had a natural inclination toward mischief. And honestly, Mab seemed to have a soft spot for creatures of that variety. Ander included.

The sand was cool under her toes. The moon was full enough to light her steps. Not that she needed it; she'd walked this path so many times, it was practically muscle memory. Drunk at night with Ander to sit by the water and talk. Early in the morning to head out to wakeboard. The beach had become her sanctuary since coming to Miami in a way the cliffs of Ireland never were. She tried not to think too hard about why that was, and how it could be connected to Ireland being the place she'd lost her family, and Miami being the place she'd come with the family she found.

Shaking herself, Mab pushed her satin bonnet up a little more when it threatened to slide down her forehead.

It was too small to be a dolphin she decided as she got closer. But too big to be a tuna or a marlin. A swordfish maybe? No, there was no pointed—

A body. It was a body.

Her stomach lurched, and Mab stumbled back away from the pale face of a creature the light of her phone revealed. Their eyes and mouth were hanging open. Their hair was tangled but not full of seaweed or grass like it should have been if the body had washed up out of the water. And there was—There was something dark staining the pale sands beneath their shoulders, trailing down by the person's legs. Legs that were too long to be human. Too slender. Bent backward at the knee, like a fawn or a gazelle. Inanimi. Satyr? No. There were no horns.

She—

She needed to call someone. She needed to report this. She needed—

Ander?

Mab shook herself. Ander would just snap the body away for fear of it incriminating Mab herself.

Max?

He'd tell Ander, then Ander would snap the body away, and Mab would be right back to the place where no one would know the poor creature had even died. Much less allow anyone to investigate it. And yeah, sure, it would be better if the death weren't directly linked to her. But if this was the scene of the crime? Or even if they'd washed up here? There could be evidence! Max and his brother would need—

His brother. Quin! She could call Quin.

They'd exchanged numbers at some point to coordinate Max moving in with Ander. In fact, he was the only other Schields whose number she had. So she scrolled quickly through her contacts, found Q, and hit call.

Quin picked up on the third ring, and before he even had the chance to say anything, she blurted, "It's Mab. I need your help. Can you—Can you come to my house? I just—" Gods, she couldn't even get the words out. Her hands were trembling. She was going to drop her phone. And she was definitely going to be sick now. There was no question about it. "Please."

"Give me ten minutes," Quin said, his voice somehow steady and not groggy from sleep. Maybe the steadiest thing Mab had ever experienced in her life. And then he asked, "You'll be okay for that long?" in a tone so different from the Quin she knew thus far that Mab felt herself calm for the first time in hours.

Quin was steady, and he was sure, and he would be there in ten minutes.

"Yeah. I'll be okay for that long."

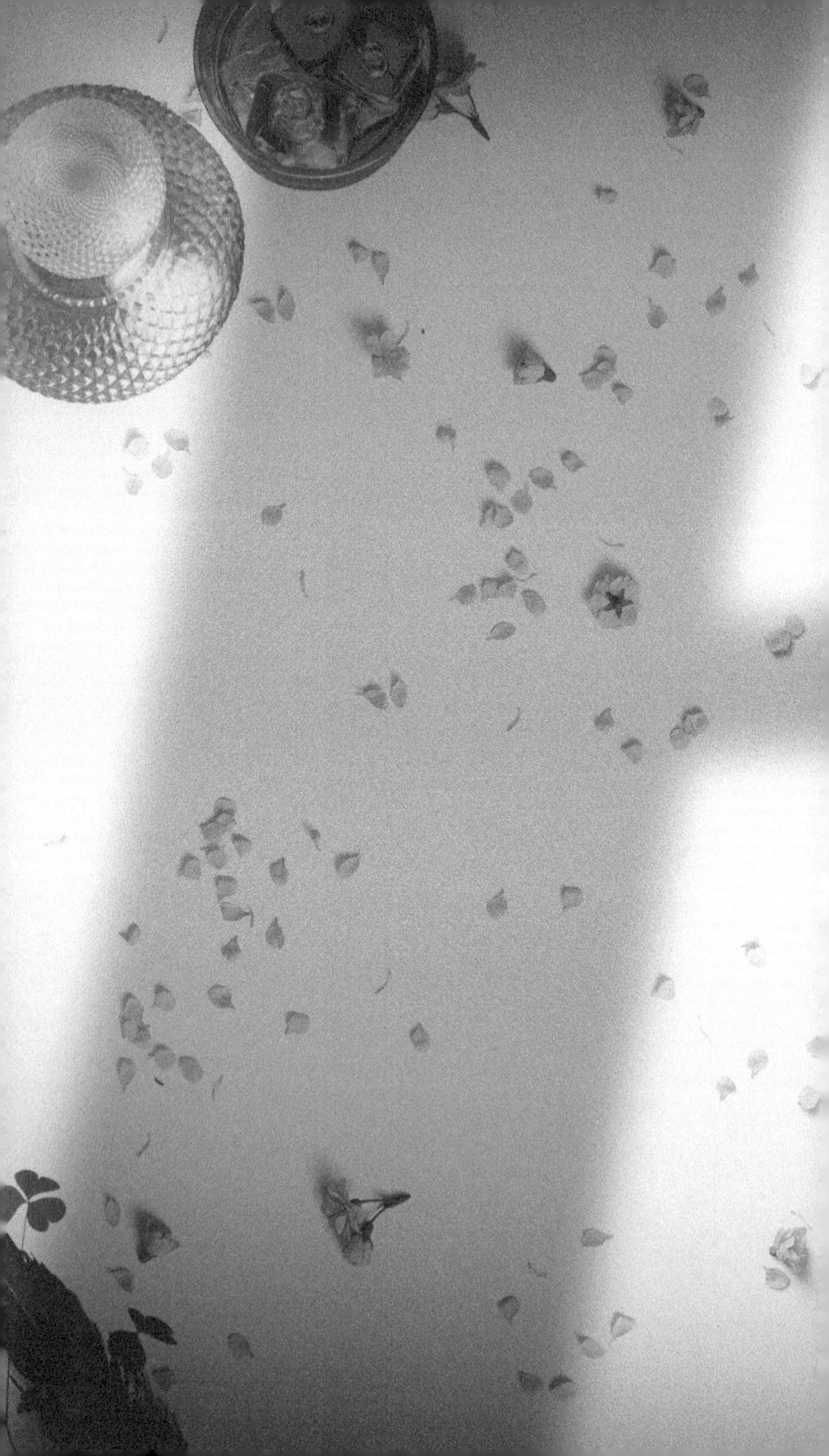

Chapter 10
Quin

His phone woke him from a deep sleep, one that he had just managed to get into after a long night of discussing the Enrique/Orcus case with the twins. Letting Max know what they were planning, the searches they were doing, and trying his best to console his troubled brother.

He hadn't expected it to be Mab Duchan on the other end of the line. And even more unexpected, for it to be a Mab who sounded very scared and who needed him to come to her place immediately.

Quin wasn't sure what was wrong, but Mab hadn't sounded well, and so he didn't press her for information. Instead, he dressed quickly, strapped a dagger to his thigh, and tucked his bo staff into his back holster.

He stopped long enough to wake his dad and let him know he'd been called out in case Tavi woke up, then took to the dark Miami night sky. The flight to Mab's house took him just under eight minutes, Quin pushing himself to the point of straining his muscles so that he would be there in the time he told her. When he landed, Quin found Mab ready and waiting. He didn't even get a chance to knock on the door before it opened.

Mab looked relieved to see him, a little of the tension in her face slipping away.

"Come around back," she said hurriedly. There were worry lines at the corners of her eyes and hesitation in her movements.

Quin wondered if she was questioning whether or not she had chosen right in calling him. He nodded at her command and followed her through to the back of her property. She led him past the pool, and down the stone steps to the beach beyond.

Even in the dark, he could see the prone figure of someone on the sand.

Quin stopped and looked at Mab, who halted when she realized he had stopped moving.

"Did you do this?"

Mab's brows shot up, and her mouth fell slack for just a moment before she shook her head. "No! Of course not!" Her arms crossed defensively across her chest, like she was blocking herself off from him and his accusations.

He hadn't meant it as an attack, he merely needed to know what he was dealing with.

"What happened?"

Mab took a deep breath and looked away from him. Her dark brown eyes filled with an emotion Quin couldn't quite read. "I got home from work. Was getting ready for bed when I looked out the back window and saw something on the beach. I thought another dolphin had washed up. It happens sometimes." She swallowed and shifted on her feet. "I came down to check. I usually just call Ander when it happens, and he snaps it away for me. But . . ."

"But it wasn't a dolphin," Quin finished for her.

Mab shook her head and finally looked at him once more. "No. It was not."

"Did you touch anything?"

She shook her head again.

"And they were already dead when you got down here?"

"Yeah." Her throaty voice was strained, coming out softly. He did notice that her Irish accent was thicker with the stress and worry surrounding her now.

"Okay. You stay here. I'm going down to look around." Quin turned back to the beach and pulled his phone out. Quickly, he hit Nash's number in his Favorites list.

It took a minute, but finally, Nash picked up. "Whaaaat?" he groaned, voice thick with sleep.

"A body has shown up on Mab's beach. Grab your tech kit and get here right away. I need your forensic opinion on this."

Nash seemed to wake up at the mention of a body. "Oh shit. Okay, I'll be right there."

Hanging up, Quin turned the phone's flashlight on and began looking around the beach for any signs of where the body had come from or who had dumped it there.

Long drag marks trailed from up the beach, leading in the direction of Mab's house, and around the body, there were several small footprints which, by a quick glance to Mab, Quin could tell were hers. That didn't mean she had been the one to drag the body down here—some were certainly from when she had come to investigate. But it didn't help her case any.

Because he would need to, he snapped a couple of pictures of the prints, then knelt down closer to the body. The form was long and garish, knees bent at different angles than a human's and fingers curled into spindles of death that tapered into sharp claws. The large yellow eyes with their big round pupils stared lifelessly up at the night sky. Eyes that were perfect for seeing prey at night but no longer saw anything, a gray film coating their brightness. A fury, not fully matured, as her sharp fangs were not protruding over her bottom lip yet.

The creature's head had fallen to the side, and from her long, tapered ears, blood had poured out to cover a portion of her face, neck, and the sand below. She had bled out so badly, the blood soaked the sand beneath her and pooled around her legs.

She hadn't been dead when she was brought down there. The blood proved that. No . . . the fury died on the beach, bleeding from massive head trauma.

"Have you noticed anything strange around your property lately?" He looked up at Mab from where he crouched near the creature. "Any large paw prints? Scratches on your doors or near your windowpanes?"

"No," Mab muttered. "Ander and I did a full refinish and clean of everything before the housewarming party. Plus, with my wards, no one can get up to the house."

So the fury hadn't been here prior to her death, scoping out the area for prey, which was their typical habit. A fury would track its latest victim, lured by their scent. Scope out their home or work and mark the area with its own scent to warn off any other furies or creatures who might be thinking of taking the prey for themselves.

This fury had not been in the area hunting. Someone had brought it here to leave it.

"Your wards, they don't include the beach?"

Mab shook her head. "The sand shifts too much, changes with the tides and rain, the wind. There's nothing to anchor the magic to. So they end at the steps." She pointed to the stone steps that led from her upper deck and down her property to the beach.

"Top of the steps or the bottom?"

"About mid-way, I think. In case of erosion."

Quin nodded and eyed her property line. So whoever killed the fury wasn't able to leave the body in her house, but there was enough room where the wards ended for them to drag the unconscious fury from the small cluster of trees and avoid the sand until they got to Mab's staircase.

Carefully, Quin looked over the creature's body again, examining it for any other signs of brutality or violence. She didn't seem to have any other wounds, only the blood that trickled out of her ears. But she also didn't have defensive wounds. So how had they knocked her out before leaving her on the beach? Had she been coherent right until the grass line, and that was where they'd killed her? Or had the killing happened elsewhere and she was dragged here to bleed out?

The only scrap of clothing on her was a small set of shorts on her lower half. While furies ran hot, it still seemed strange to Quin. Going topless wouldn't help her blend in with the normies. Even other inanimi would notice. Where had this fury come from?

He snapped a few more pictures until his phone rang. Quin was relieved to see it was Nash.

"Hey, I'm here," Nash said.

"We're down by the beach, come around back of the house."

"Sure thing, boss."

Quin rolled his eyes. The twins loved to bug Max by calling him that, knowing that Max hated it, even though he was the leader of their team. Whenever Max wasn't around, the twins passed the title on to Quin.

Nash wasn't long meeting up with them, a bag slung over his shoulder that appeared heavy and full of gear. "Hey Mab, great party the other night," he said on his way by her.

Once on the beach, he gave a little wave to Quin and tugged on a pair of latex gloves, letting out a low whistle. His brows lifted in surprise. "A fury?"

Quin nodded, standing up and stepping back from the body so that Nash could step in and do his work. "Yeah, it would appear so."

"I didn't think we had any fury packs in Miami right now," he said, walking toward Quin.

"We don't."

"They took off her shirt," Nash said bluntly. "Why would someone take off her shirt?" He looked from the corpse, then back up to Quin, as if he might have answers.

Quin stared back at him. "Why would I know?" he signed quickly with irritation.

Nash shrugged, then set his bag down to pull out a tripod and light, switching it on to illuminate the body better.

Above them, Mab looked on, her arms tightening around herself even more as her teeth worried her bottom lip. Quin wondered what he could say to reassure her that this was going to be okay. He really had nothing for her. He didn't know that this was going to be okay because he wasn't even sure what this *was*.

Nash had begun to snap pictures of the body—taking far more than Quin—from every angle. As he knelt down near her head and took pictures of the bleeding ears and the blood pools on the ground, he paused to look up at Quin.

"I hate to say this . . . " he muttered softly so that his voice wouldn't carry up to Mab. "But this looks exactly like a textbook banshee kill if you ask me."

Quin was thinking the same thing. There were few mystical beings whose abilities could cause harm in such a way. "I know."

His eyes flicked from Nash to Mab. She looked so scared. She should have Ruin here; he was her family. Quin moved away from Nash and stepped up to Mab. "I can call Ruin for you if you'd like. He should be here with—"

"No!"

Quin's brow lifted a little. He hadn't expected that. "No?"

"No." Her tone was definitive. "Ander would want to snap the body away. Make it disappear so that any trouble that might come from this would disappear with it. That won't help me. I know it won't."

Quin shook his head. "No, it won't help."

It would only make her seem guiltier. Make Ruin look guilty as well. And in turn, all of that would reflect back on Max, who was living with him.

"Quin," Nash called from farther down the beach.

"Yes?" Quin looked down at his little brother.

"I have to call in the rest of the forensic team to make sure we don't miss anything."

Quin nodded.

"Um . . . " Mab began.

"We have to," he said softly, turning to face her. "It will look suspicious if we don't."

And the Princeps were already scrutinizing them since the capture of Orcus. As if somehow, one of them had managed to frame a powerful god of Underworld. One especially with a reputation for being a bit of an asshole to begin with.

Orcus.

A chill went through Quin's body, which had nothing to

do with the bit of night breeze that was coming in off the water and making his overly warm ignis body cool and everything to do with the thought of the recently escaped god.

How much of a coincidence could it be, that Orcus had recently escaped from imprisonment and now there was a dead inanimi on a property belonging to Ruin's sister? An inanimi who appeared to have been killed in a manner that could be done by such a banshee as she.

Quin's stomach knotted. He was going to have to tell Max, and Max was going to lose his mind even more than he already was.

"I don't like this," Mab muttered.

Neither did Quin.

It was the sound of ignis wings from above that drew Quin out of his own thoughts. When the other Sanctum soldier landed not far from them, Quin's frown deepened. *That was quick.*

"Marius? What are you doing here?"

Marius adjusted the holster wrapped around his waist, bringing the large dagger that was strapped to it around to his hip rather than behind. "I'm taking over this investigation."

"What are you talking about? I was first on scene." Quin's body tensed, his shoulders stiffening and his back tightening.

"And your brother is involved with her business partner. You're too close to this, so I am taking over."

Quin wanted to curse. He wanted to say a lot of things. Instead, his features hardened, and his lips pressed together. Of course they were taking over. Amazing how quickly word had spread with one small phone call from Nash. Who on the forensics team had squealed to Galeo? How did they even have time to wake him up and make this decision?

Gods, he wanted to protest this so bad. But what point was there in trying when it would get him no further ahead?

Marius moved down to examine the body, walking around Nash, who continued to map out the crime scene.

"Hey Q . . . " Mab pulled Quin's attention away from the scene before them. "What does this mean for me?"

"I'm going to stay involved with this. I won't bow out so easily." Quin knew Max would want them to stay a part of the investigation, and so he would do this in his brother's stead.

"Mab Duchan, you're under arrest for the murder of our unnamed vic." Marius stepped forward, pulling out a pair of cuffs.

The banshee's mouth fell open, but before she could say anything, Quin did. "What's going on, Marius?"

"We have a dead fury on her property who was obviously killed by a banshee. Mab Duchan is the only registered banshee on the entire east coast of the United States. I'm taking her in."

Before Quin could protest further, Marius slapped the set of cuffs onto Mab's wrists and led her to the front of the house. She looked over her shoulder, her brown eyes wide with shock and the beginning of fear, the faint scar lines on her cheek glowing pale beneath the moonlight.

Quin stomped after them, noticing that the forensic team had shown up but that there was a suspect wagon pulling into the driveway as well. He cursed under his breath, his fingers itching to pull out his phone to call Max.

But he would wait. For now.

As they loaded her into the back of the wagon, Quin

stepped up to the open door. "I'll be there when they book you."

Mab nodded, her lips pressed together, concern pinching at the corners of her eyes.

"Don't say anything until I show up, okay?"

The last thing Quin saw was Mab nodding her head as the wagon doors closed.

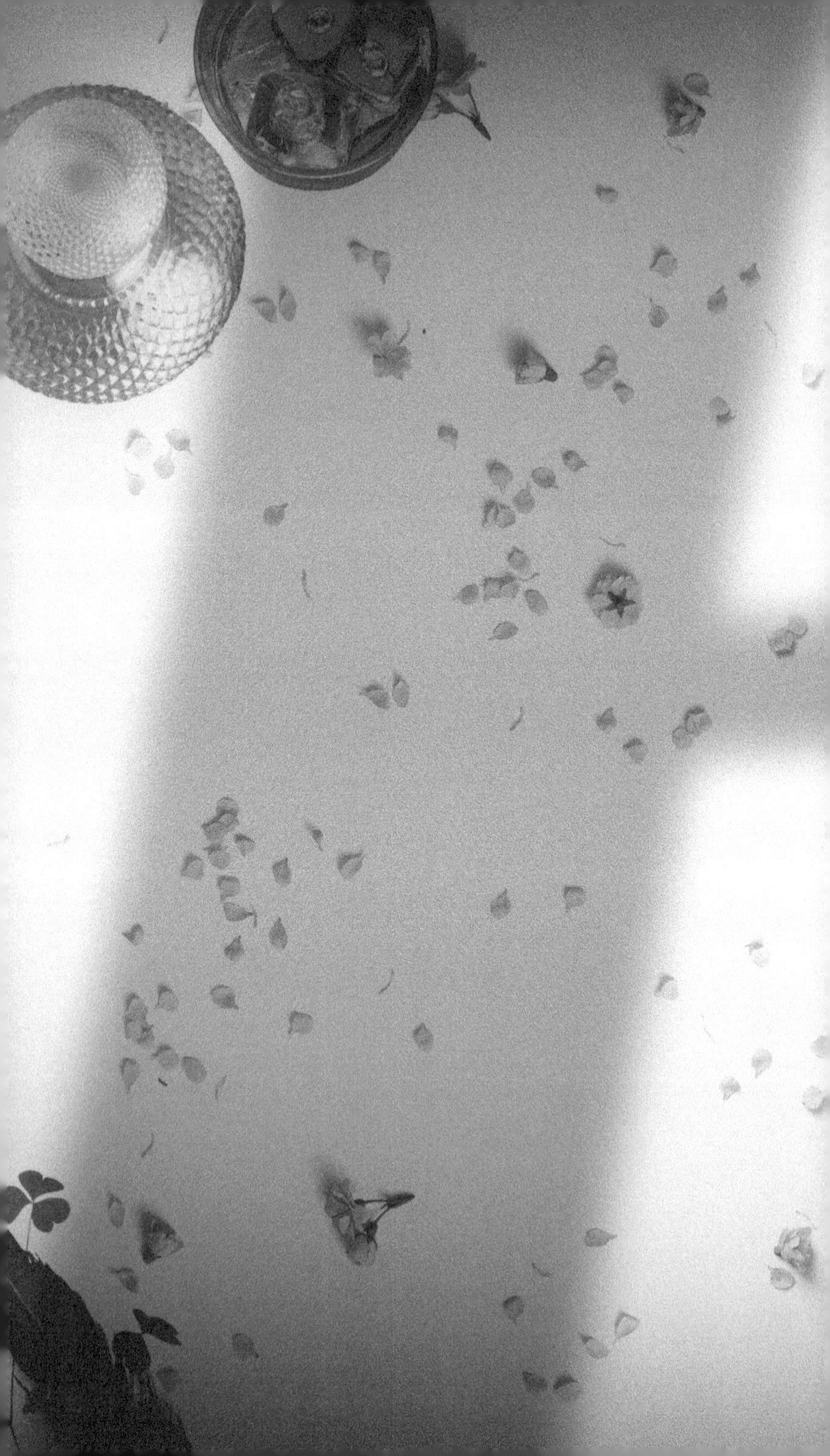

Chapter 11
Mab

This was fine.

Everything was fine.

Quin and Nash would find something to prove that Mab wasn't guilty of this soon, and she'd be out of there before Inferno opened the following day. Ander wouldn't even have to *know* what happened. She had complete faith in the Schields family to get her out of trouble.

That didn't mean she was having a good time sitting in the hard metal chair under the bright lights of the interrogation room. Because she was not, in fact, having a good time. She was tired and cold, and the metal dug into her legs in a way that she was sure would leave marks. She hadn't slept yet, and nausea still rolled through her belly, making her clammy all over. No one had even bothered to bring her a cup of water. They just locked her in this fucking room and left her, for gods knew how long. There wasn't even a *clock*.

Had it been minutes or hours? She couldn't tell.

She was tempted to call out and see if someone would answer. But maybe it would be better if they forgot about her? At least she wasn't chained to the table. And it felt less like she was trapped since there was a door and a window to the hall on the other side. This was less cell and more waiting room.

How long would that last? She didn't know.

She didn't have long to wonder, though, as the door creaked open. Quin walked through the door, and Mab relaxed a little, her mouth opening to greet him. Her jaw clacked shut a second later when she saw the ignis who entered behind him.

It wasn't Max.

"Where's Max?" Mab asked before she could stop herself. Only belatedly did she realize that probably wasn't the best question to ask at that exact moment.

She was proven right when Quin subtly shook his head and the other ignis fixed her with a cold, hard stare. Like she was . . . like she was a *murderer*. Oh gods. He really thought she'd done this, didn't he? He thought she'd killed that inanimi on the beach.

It was all right. It was okay. Quin didn't think she'd done it. None of the Schields did. They knew her. They knew she wasn't capable of this. Right? *Right?!*

"Mab Duchan," the other ignis said after he settled into his chair across from her.

"Yeah?" Mab fidgeted. Why wasn't Quin saying anything? If he wasn't going to be a part of the interrogation, why had he been allowed in at all? Her eyes flicked back to Quin, but she didn't know him well enough to read his facial expressions the way she might have with Ander or was beginning to be able to with Max.

"You called Quintus Schields this morning at 3:30 a.m. to report a body on your private beach. Is that correct?"

"Yes."

"Are you aware that the victim showed signs of a banshee attack?"

"I . . . No. I didn't know that." Mab frowned, her fingers flexing in her lap under the table.

"Can you tell me what happened? For the record." The other ignis leaned forward, his pen held at the ready.

Mab took a breath, forcing herself to remain calm when it felt like the lights above were burning the back of her neck. "Like I told Quin—" She paused when the ignis interrogating her narrowed his eyes. Had she fucked up? Was she being too familiar? "Like I told Quintus," she corrected, then continued to relay the events once more. "When I saw it wasn't a dolphin but was a dead inanimi, I called Quintus. I know him from when he worked on Ander's case and figured . . ."

What had she figured? That he'd come and take a couple of pictures, remove the body, then she could just go to bed? She'd known better than that. There had been a dead body on her beach. There was no way that could have happened.

"You figured what, Duchan?"

Mab didn't like the way the ignis said her last name. The same way some people said its meaning: blight. Like she was nothing more than a piece of trash he'd stepped in and would very much like to rub on the rug. Quin visibly stiffened as well but didn't say anything.

"I figured he'd be able to report it to the people who needed to know about it." That was the truth of what happened.

"Why didn't you call your business partner?"

Business partner. Like Ander wasn't family. Like he wasn't her brother. Mab didn't know much about the ignis, but she knew enough to know they didn't do attachments.

The Schields family was an anomaly, their connection so abnormal that Mab almost wondered if the other ignis looked down on them for it. Max never let on, at least not in front of her, but she got an inkling now.

She also knew she couldn't tell him the truth. It would incriminate Ander. Of what, she didn't know, but she wasn't willing to chance dragging him into this. And besides, if the ignis didn't understand that Ander was her brother, how could he possibly understand the lengths Ander would go to for her?

"I didn't want to bother him." Mab lifted one shoulder in a shrug. She was still in the thin T-shirt she'd been prepared to wear to bed, but thankfully, she'd managed to put pants on before Quin arrived.

The ignis hummed like he maybe didn't quite believe her, but Mab didn't so much as shift. She had at least a couple hundred years on him. He was a child in the face of all she had lived through. She could do this.

"She told me as much, Cedaloin," Quin said, not blinking.

Mab wanted to raise her brows in question, to ask why he was lying for her, but she didn't. Instead, she kept her gaze focused on Cedaloin, waiting for his next question.

"Right." Cedaloin scribbled something on the pad in front of him. "And where were you at about eleven last night?"

"Behind the bar at Inferno. If you don't believe me, you can check the security cameras." Surely that would earn her freedom, right? There was no way that—

"We've already acquired that footage." Cedaloin tapped his pen against his pad, clearly impatient with something. "The hour surrounding our victim's time of death is missing."

"Missing?" That wasn't right. How could it be missing? "Like someone erased it? Why would they—"

Oh. She understood now. They assumed *she* had erased it. Or Ander had. To cover for her. To hide the fact that she wasn't there at the time.

"Fine. Then you can talk to Parker. I was on bar with them tonight. They'll tell you."

Cedaloin hummed again.

"We spoke to them," Quin said. "They confirmed you were there all night."

"Okay." Mab nodded, relaxing a little more. So there was no reason why they should think that she was lying about her whereabouts. She had someone to vouch for her. She had . . . an *employee* to vouch for her. Shit.

"Do you recognize the deceased?" Cedaloin asked, sliding a picture across for Mab to examine. It was a crime scene photo, the fury's normally burnished skin washed pale with death and the flash of a camera. Blood trickled from her ears and from the corners of her eyes like tears. Mab had seen those kinds of injuries only once before. On the men who were trying to burn her at the stake the night her banshee abilities fully manifested. The night Ander saved her. The night they met.

"No. I don't know who she is." But she couldn't look away from the fury's face. She was young still, Mab realized, now that she could see the face in something more than moonlight. A veritable child by fury standards. Not more than a few decades old maybe, if that.

Cedaloin didn't seem to believe that either. "She had a photo of you on her."

She'd been marked by a fury? Why? She'd never done anything to hurt anyone. Why would a fury mark her for death?

"Are you aware of the recent marking and killing of a banshee by a fury pack in Seattle, Washington?" Cedaloin watched her intently, waiting for a reaction.

Mab froze, the chill spreading through her body. "No." She swallowed roughly.

"You're a banshee, you're sure none of your siren friends filled you in?" His eyes narrowed on her.

"Yes, I'm sure. I don't have any siren friends."

"You don't need friends to want revenge for your kind." Cedaloin tapped his fingers on the tabletop.

"Cedaloin," Quin growled in warning. "Stick to the facts of this case."

Cedaloin shifted in his chair, then continued. "In addition, we noticed there are extensive wards around your property."

"Yes, there are." Mab cleared her throat, sitting up a little straighter. "When I knew it was getting close to the end of Orcus's punishment, I hired someone to ward all of my residences. I wanted to provide a safe place for Ander should he need it, where Orcus couldn't get in." "Hired" was perhaps a little bit of a lie. She'd browbeat and annoyed Indra until he'd done her the favor under the condition that he, too, could use it as a place to hide from his wife. But . . . well. she didn't think bringing the king of the gods into this was a good idea. Mostly because she just didn't have the energy to deal with Indra at that moment. Plus, she knew for a fact he wouldn't be able to keep it to himself; he'd call Ander and Aemiliana too.

"So no one but yourself or Ander can get on the property?"

"No one can get up to the house," she corrected. "Or the pool area. The beach, although it's private by mortal standards, isn't warded. Anyone can access it by boat if they want to."

"I see."

What did he see?

"Well. That's all the questions we have for you right now." Cedaloin rose from his seat.

"So I can go home?" Hope bubbled up in her chest, warming her chilled fingers.

"No." Something like a smile flashed across the ignis' face for the first time since he entered the room, but it lacked all the warmth a smile should have. "You'll be escorted to a holding cell while we look into this further. You're too much of a flight risk."

"Why? I didn't do this."

"We have no proof of that yet."

"You have no proof I did, either!" Mab rushed, her heart jackhammering in her chest, her breaths already coming too short and too fast. A cell. They were going to take her to a cell. "Quin. Quin. Do something."

Cedaloin shrugged, and when he went into the hall, he nodded to two other ignis. "Take her down to holding."

Mab scrambled from her chair and tried to put as much space between herself and the approaching ignis as she could. She didn't want to be locked up. She couldn't be locked up. They couldn't tuck her away in a cell somewhere. They couldn't shut the door and throw away the key. She wouldn't make it. She wouldn't survive. She'd go insane. She'd lose it.

She opened her mouth to wail, but before she could, someone clapped a thick, iron shackle onto her arm, and it was like they'd put a clamp on a vein, cut off the flow of her magic so that when the scream finally ripped from her throat, it was just that of a woman, a mortal, shouting. It hurt. It cut her throat open, leaving it raw like her wail might have. But it didn't do anything to the two ignis who already had her arms pinned behind her back so hard, she felt like they might pop out of the sockets.

Mab lost track of where they were going. She couldn't see faces. She couldn't make out her surroundings. All she could do was struggle. Kick and twist. Add to the bruises the ignis were leaving on her arms. Something wrenched in her shoulder, and her right arm went numb, the fingertips tingling. She screamed again, coughing around the sound, a mouth full of metal.

Now was *then*. *Then* was now.

Two people bigger than her, stronger than her, held her so tight, she was sure they'd leave permanent marks.

They dragged her down a hallway. She thought. Maybe. But her vision had gone dark.

The door to the cell creaked, echoing through her mind, off the stone walls of the asylum.

And she was thrown inside, landing hard on her injured arm with a sob.

Then they left her there in the dark. Whimpering against the pain in her throat, her arm. The hard ground seeping cold into her very bones. She'd never get out. She'd be here forever. Years and years. Until everyone forgot about her. Until she was nothing, not even a fond memory, not even a name. And the screams of the other women in the asylum, their mournful cries, would deafen her to all else.

"Mab," a voice called to her. She thought maybe it had repeated that word over and over again, trying to get her attention. But she was still sobbing. Blood coated her tongue. Every breath through her mouth sliced all the way down to her lungs.

She didn't answer. She just laid there, staring at the wall. It wasn't the same color or the same kind of stone as all those years ago. But she swore she heard dripping from somewhere far off, could see a trail of water slowly eroding the stone the way this place would chip away at her.

"Mab. Come on, Mab. Look at me," the voice continued, soft and calm. Soothing in a way it hadn't any right to be when her heart was still slamming painfully in her chest and bile rose in her throat so hot, it burned. "Come on, Mab."

Mab let a breath out through her nose and opened her eyes. The light burned, causing them to tear up, and she groaned, squeezing her eyes shut again. Then she shook her head. She couldn't move.

"Okay. I'm coming to you."

There was a loud screech. Mab hissed at the way it settled into her ears, sharp and grating. But then someone was touching her, and she kicked out, scrambling away, forcing her eyes open even as the light burned them.

"Don't *touch* me!" she hissed from where she'd backed herself into the corner.

"Okay." The blurry shape that must have been a man— No, wait. There were big dark blurs behind him. Were those . . . wings? An ignis, then. Quin? He held up his hands. "Okay. I won't touch you. But I need you to breathe with me before you pass out, okay?"

"What're—I'm not going—" But her breathing was shallow and ragged in her chest, and her vision had started to dance with little stars.

"In," he coached, and Mab inhaled deeply, despite thinking she didn't need the help. Then she held it for a moment until he said, "Out. Good. That's good. Again."

They continued like that for a while, until he'd gotten

her breathing to something normal, and Mab was finally able to see Quin clearly through the haze of her panic.

"How do you feel?"

"Don't—" She stopped, wanting to bite through her tongue to keep the words crawling up her throat inside of it where they belonged. She was pitiful. Absolutely pitiful. She wouldn't beg him to stay. She wasn't that pathetic. "I'm better."

"Okay." Quin nodded. He still hadn't gotten any closer to her, wasn't touching her. But he'd crouched on the floor in front of where she'd wedged herself into the corner so hard, her shoulder was throbbing. "I'm going to call a medic in to look at you. I'll tell them not to touch you without permission. Is that okay?"

Mab didn't want anyone anywhere near her. Least of all someone she didn't know. But her shoulder wasn't going to stop throbbing, and she couldn't tell by feeling alone what she'd done to it. So, she nodded.

"All right." Quin scooted back to settle onto his bottom. "I'll sit with you while they look you over."

"Thanks," Mab croaked.

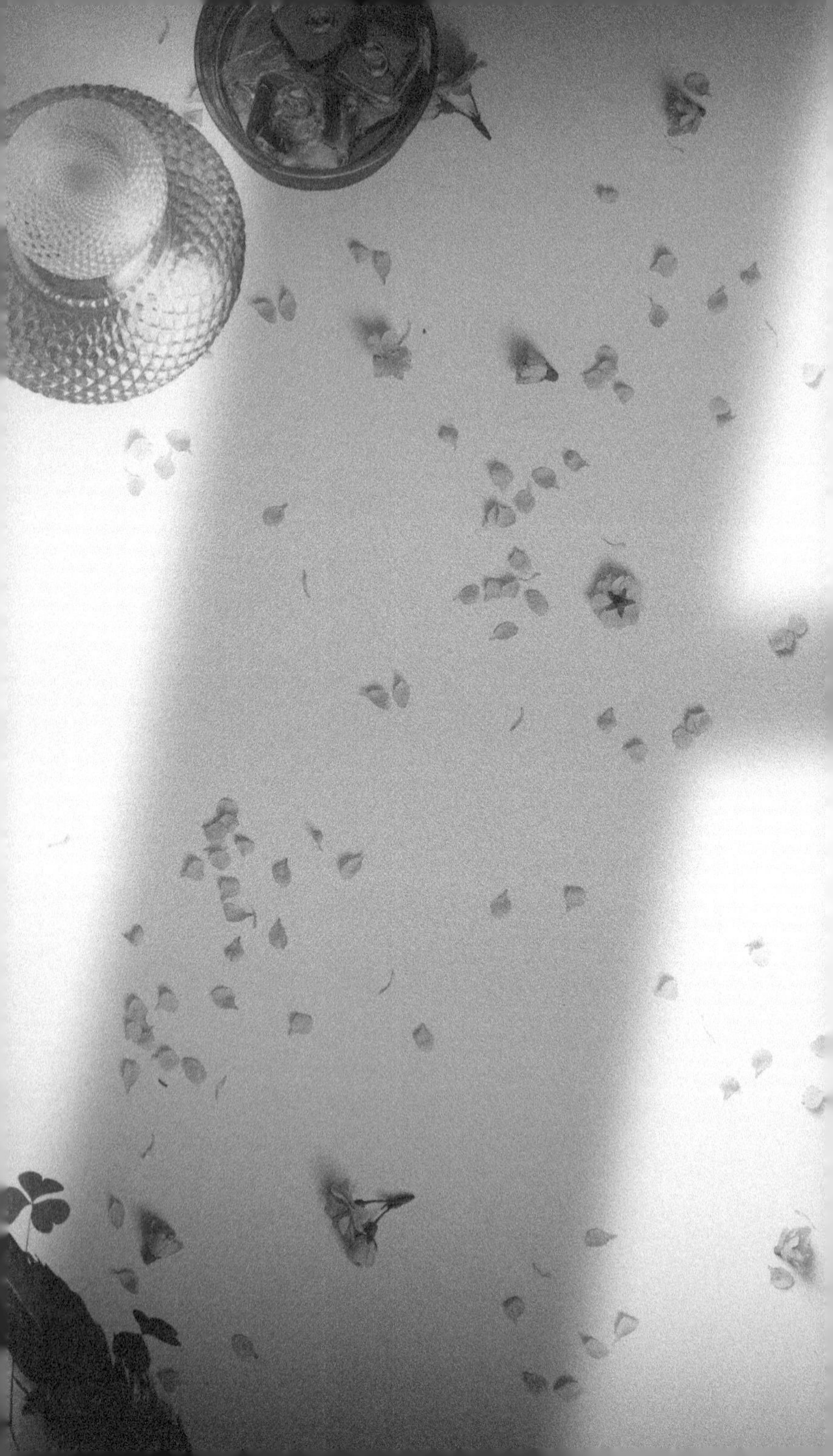

Chapter 12
Quin

Quin waited until Mab seemed calm and she had been taken care of by the medic team. Once he was sure she wasn't going to black out from a panic attack, he excused himself from the cell.

He didn't know Mab well, but Quin didn't like seeing her in such a state. He knew firsthand what it was like to sink into a panic attack brought on by trauma. What it was like to lose yourself in the horrible memories. Mab had been taken by something dark, and it didn't seem right that such a strong, self-assured woman had been driven into the arms of misery because of them.

He wanted to call Max and have him send Ruin, but she was still refusing to have her brother involved. So for now, Quin would do what he could to help her.

The forensic team was still at her home, and knowing he would never be able to just go home and sleep, Quin flew back there. He didn't trust Marius' team to take care of it. While they weren't the type to frame someone, they were looking for things that would prove her guilt, not for the things that would help set her free. And Quin knew that

Max would feel better knowing Quin had been there to oversee things.

When he arrived at the beach house, Nash and Nox were inside. They were both busy dusting the kitchen for prints.

"Hey," Nash said as he spotted him. "What are you doing back here?"

Quin cast a glance around them. There were several other forensic team members milling about, working, so he chose to quickly sign to his younger brother. "Thought I should come and keep an eye on things here."

Nash nodded, his eyes shifting to look at the others. "Yeah, that makes sense," he signed back just as quickly, then went back to dusting.

Nox wiggled her fingers at him in greeting. "How is she doing?" she asked softly. Quin only frowned, and Nox winced. "That bad huh?"

"It's not great."

"Have you phoned to tell Ander yet?"

Quin shook his head. "I think evidence gathering needs to be over first. She's worried he'll interfere." His hands moved swiftly as he detailed Mab's concerns.

Nash snorted. "Yeah . . . just a snap of his fingers."

Quin sighed. He didn't like that Ruin and Max were in the dark about this. It felt like too great a thing to keep from such important people in both his and Mab's lives. But he would adhere to Mab's request for now. She was the one locked up, after all.

"I'm going to look around."

"We'll be here," Nox replied.

Quin left them in the kitchen to begin a slow circle around the living room. The house looked so different now that it wasn't filled with party guests.

Toby, another human investigator, was busy rifling through some magazines that were on the end table by the sofa. It irritated Quin to see someone so aloof in Mab's house. She was a private person, and now there were so many strangers invading her space. It made his own skin crawl, and it wasn't even his home being exposed to others.

But he understood all too well what it felt like to have no control of your own space and body.

Quin left the living room and headed down the hall. Another forensics tech was going through the hall closet, pulling out her jackets and shuffling around in her pockets. When the tech reached for her purse, Quin stepped forward.

"Let me finish the closet."

Sari looked up, her brows lifting. "I'm fine."

"I said I would finish it." He didn't raise his voice, but there was a sternness to it, a quality he'd learned from his dad, that made Sari instantly take a step back.

She nodded and let the purse swing back into place on its hook. "Okay." She stepped back and went down the hall to go into what looked like a spare bedroom.

With her gone, Quin pulled a pair of black gloves from his pocket, tugged them on, and moved into the closet. He reached for the purse, feeling terrible as he began to go through it. He'd never had to search through the belongings of someone he knew before; it added an entire depth to this that he wasn't used to. Suddenly, the investigation felt like a violation, and he didn't like it. However, he knew it was better him than someone else.

Carefully, he searched through the first pocket, finding nothing out of the ordinary. A packet of tissues, and ChapStick with sunscreen included. In the next, there was a small switchblade. Quin snorted. He was surprised and yet not. Because of course Mab Duchan carried a knife on her at all times. He knew he'd have to confiscate it since it was a weapon.

"I need a bag over here," he called out.

A passing forensic tech stepped up, pulling out a small plastic evidence bag. Quin placed the switchblade into it. Next, he moved on to the larger pocket, which was the main part of the purse. Sticking his fingers into the side pocket on the inside, he found what felt like a napkin. Carefully, he pulled it out of the purse, and there was the sketch he had done of Mab weeks ago at Inferno.

Quin blinked, staring down at the scrap of paper in his hand. A flurry of questions rushed through him, but at the top of his mind was, why?

Why hadn't this just been thrown out? But better yet, why had she kept it?

It wasn't even that good of a portrait. Just something he'd sketched quickly to pass the time. Something Quin hadn't even deemed good enough to keep for his scrapbook and build on later. But for some reason, Mab thought it was. Mab had kept it.

It didn't mean anything. Except that she liked it. At least, it shouldn't have meant anything. And yet, Quin felt a warm, fuzzy sensation buzz along his neck and over his scalp. Scratching lightly at his temple, Quin slid the napkin carefully back into its pocket and moved away from the purse.

Focusing on the jackets and sweaters, he made his way through them quickly, seeing nothing else that needed to be booked for evidence. There also was nothing in the closet that would help clear her name.

Quin stepped out of the closet, shutting the door behind him, and made his way down the hall. He stopped at the entrance to her bedroom, feeling like he was on the brink of yet another very personal invasion of her privacy.

There were two techs in the bedroom. Her bed had been torn apart to show that there was nothing hidden under it. One of them was in Mab's walk-in closet sorting through her clothes. A number of small boxes from the shelf were spread out on the floor around the closet, their tops off and contents rifled through.

Quin stepped around the items, scanning the contents quickly: old keys with tags tied to them that read things like "our first townhouse" or "baby's first t-bird", polaroids, seashells, and other things that seemed random to him but obviously meant something to Mab. He moved into her ensuite bathroom. Inside was nothing but typical bathroom toiletries. He crouched down in front of the vanity, opening up the doors. Inside were cleaning products, a hair dryer, straightener, and some towels.

As he stood back up, Quin caught sight of himself in the mirror and winced. He was snooping in Mab's life. Rifling through her stuff. This wasn't right.

With the toe of his shoe, Quin shut the doors to the vanity and turned to look around the toilet and shower. Nothing stood out of the ordinary.

A tech knocked on the doorframe. "If you're done in here, we have to check for blood residue."

Quin nodded. "Come in."

Once the tech moved into the bathroom, Quin turned sideways and slipped back into the main bedroom.

Everywhere he looked, someone was going through Mab's things, dusting surfaces, gliding a black light over a wall or piece of furniture.

After having seen her in that cell, reacting to being locked up, this felt like too much. Quin was suddenly overcome with the need to be outside breathing fresh air, so he walked out the back glass sliding doors to the cement patio surrounding the pool. The water reflected the LED lamp lights being used by the tech teams, only emphasizing that no matter where he went on the property, there would be someone taking samples.

The team on the beach was extensive. Someone was gathering tubes of sand while another was checking down by the waterline with a black light, and three more searched the grass leading down to the beach.

Quin had teased Max about it before, but he truly could feel it in his gut that something about all of this wasn't right. Why would Mab leave Inferno just to come home and kill a fury? He didn't for one second believe what Cedaloin was trying to insinuate, that Mab had revenge-killed a fury for some unnamed banshee murder on the other side of the country.

"Marius!" he shouted down to the other ignis still overseeing the forensic team.

Marius looked up, a brow arched. "You're back," he stated blankly.

"Have we spoken to any of Duchan's neighbors yet to see if a banshee scream was heard?"

"None of the local normies seem to be awake. There is no reason to believe any of them has heard anything."

Quin frowned and turned away, walking back into the kitchen to speak with Nash and Nox.

"I need you to search the mortal police reports," he said quietly.

Nash and Nox shared a look between them. "For?" Nox pressed.

"To see if anyone reported hearing a high-pitched scream. If the fury was killed by a banshee, someone around here had to have heard it. Even across the water. It would have echoed out to the boats out there."

The twins nodded. "You're right. It's too loud for *no one* to have heard and reported it," Nox said.

"Even if they thought it was a siren or a car alarm of some kind going off," Nash added.

"Let me know as soon as you find something, or better yet, if you don't."

They nodded again, and Quin turned on his heel and left them. Once back outside, he moved to the one area not overrun by the forensics team and pulled out his cell. Carefully, his thumb opened his favorites list, and he pressed Max's name.

"Yeah?" Max croaked.

"Sorry to wake you, but you and Ander need to get to the sanctuary."

"What? What's going on?" Max's voice was more alert, and if Quin had to guess, he would say he had sat up in bed.

Over the water, the sky was beginning to lighten along the horizon. Morning was coming. He had waited long enough to tell Max what was going on.

"Mab is in custody."

"What?" Max's voice pitched up in surprise, and through the phone, Quin could hear Ruin murmuring to him. "I've got you on speakerphone, Quin, so Ander can hear too. What happened?"

Quin sighed. "Mab phoned me around 3 a.m. She found a dead fury on her beach. They look like they were killed by a banshee scream, and Marius has taken her into custody. She's in a holding cell at the sanctuary."

"What?! You've got to be shitting me!" Ander went off, cursing and swearing more. Raving that this was not something Mab would do, that they had to know her better than that, and they couldn't keep her in a cell. That she wouldn't *last* in a cell.

Quin pulled the phone away from his ear to protect his hearing as he waited for Max to calm his boyfriend down.

"We know. We know, Ander. We'll get this sorted out. Okay?" Max murmured to him before his voice grew louder, clearly speaking to Quin once more. "We're going to get dressed and be right there."

"Why wouldn't she call me?" Ander wailed in the background, his voice leading away from the phone.

"Okay," Quin said, then hung up.

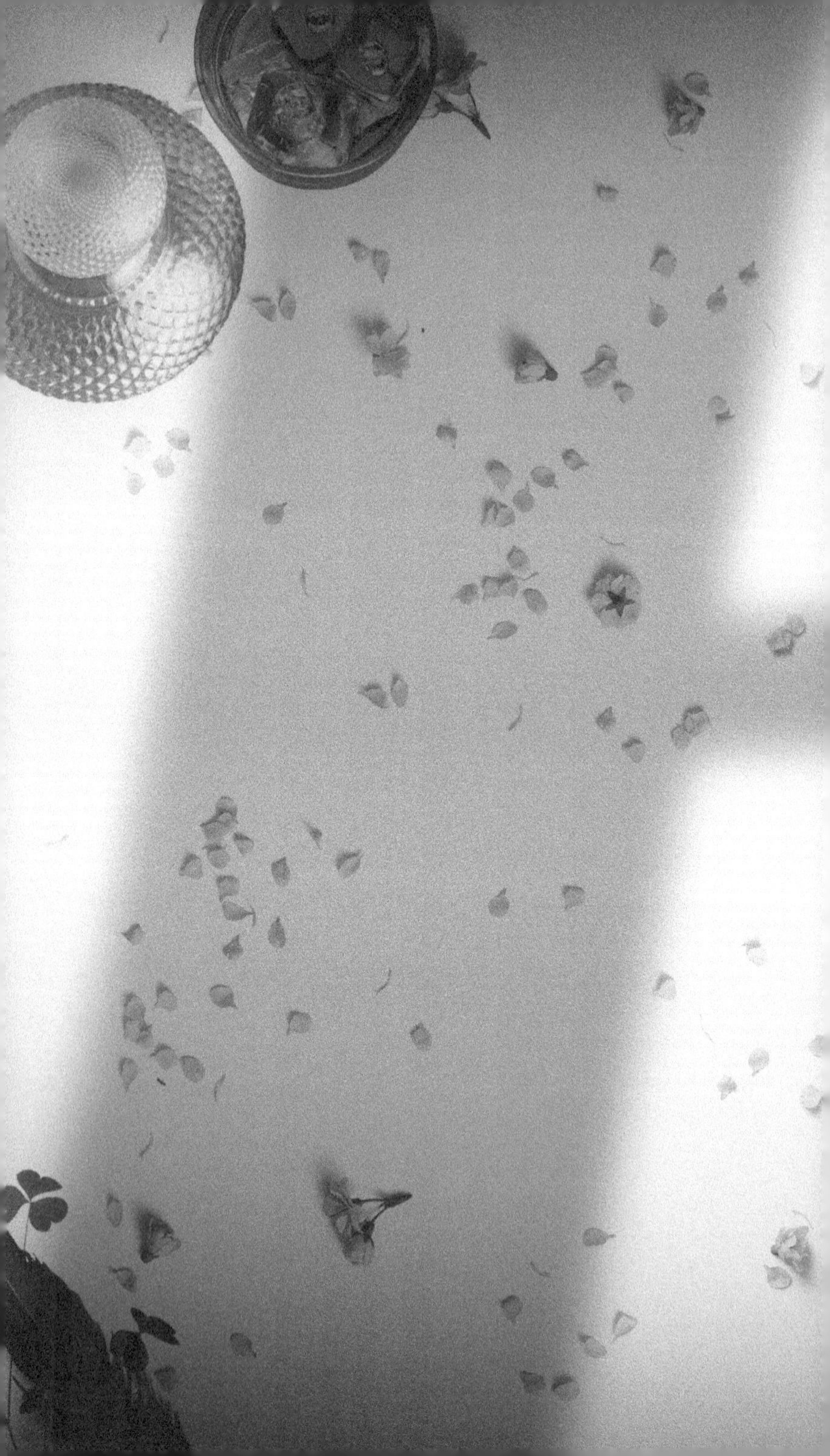

Chapter 13
Ander

Ander barely stopped long enough to change out of his silken pajama bottoms into jeans and a T-shirt—that turned out to be Max's—and put on a pair of shoes. Max was taking too long to dress, and so Ander simply waved his hand in his general direction, and Max's clothes snapped into place.

Max yelped in surprise.

"We have go!" was all Ander said in return before yanking his tall, beautiful, ignis boyfriend into him and snapping them directly into the middle of the Miami-Feugo City sanctuary.

All around them, startled ignis drew swords and moved into a fighting stance.

Max waved his hands, wings spreading to show them it was just him. The ignis relaxed a little, though their eyes traveled to Ander in a wary fashion.

"I am here to see Mab Duchan," Ander said to the ignis working reception. "Take me to her now."

The ignis blinked. Looked from Ander to Max, then back to Ander again. "It's not visiting hours. You'll have to come back later."

Ander felt the itching, crawling sensation of his anxiety rear its ugly head, scuttling beneath the surface of his skin, threatening to burst out and consume him and everyone else.

His sister was in a cell. They had locked her up for something she had not done. *Again*. While he had not known her inside of the asylum, Ander had held her through the nights after. When her night terrors were so bad, she would scream and kick out at ghosts of the past. Ander had held her through those nights, when she was too scared to go back to sleep after waking from the horrors relived in her dreams. The thought of her back inside another cell made him want to tear the entire sanctuary down.

"Come. Back. *Later?*" Ander bit out. Burning rage ate through his anxiety and filled him with something altogether different. "Do you have any idea who I am?" he snapped.

"Um . . . " The ignis looked to Max once more, who had moved up to press his hand to Ander's lower back.

"Don't look at him when I am speaking to you," Ander growled. Was it possible to physically see the color red when you were pissed? "I am the Crown Prince of Helicon," he continued. "And none of your silly little wards can keep me out of any part of this sanctuary. You've already tested that and failed. My *asking* was a mere pleasantry on my part." Ander narrowed his eyes on the ignis. "If I want, I can be in her cell with the snap of a finger. So, you either open those doors for me, or I will force my way in. Up to you, honey."

He was being petty, and he was being bitchy, and Max had never been fully exposed to this side of him. All Ander could hope was that when this was through, Max wasn't entirely disgusted by his behavior. But the ignis managed to lose Enrique after Ander had exposed himself to his abusive ex time and time again just so they could lock him up, and now his sister was being held by them for something she hadn't done. He had no patience for any of them standing in his way.

The ignis cleared his throat, clearly surprised and not quite sure what to think or to say.

"I'm taking him in," Max said at last. He pressed his hand more firmly on Ander's lower back and guided him toward the main doors leading deeper into the sanctuary.

Ander cast one last, spiteful glare at the ignis behind reception, then walked through the doors into the back halls.

"I'm sorry," he breathed out, looking up at Max.

Max did not appear to be disgusted. If anything, there was a heat in his eyes that surprised Ander. "There's nothing to be sorry for. You're fighting for your sister. Come on, she'll be down here."

Together, they walked past a few offices and through another locked area that Max had to use a key card to get into, then they were in the holding area with all the cells. Mab, when Ander spotted her, was curled up on her side on the hard bed at the back of the cell, her hands covering her ears and fresh blood staining her cheek.

Ander's heart fell out of his chest, hitting his feet as it sank with mortification and horror. "Mabbers!" He pulled away from Max and hurried to the cell, his hands grabbing onto the bars as he leaned into it. "Mab! I'm here."

When Mab didn't respond, Ander snapped his fingers and transported himself into the cell. He rushed to her side, dropped to his knees, and wrapped his fingers gently around her wrists to carefully pull her hands away. She jumped, eyes shooting open in shock and fear. She struggled for a moment, sitting up and trying to pull away, then recognition dawned.

Realizing it was him, Mab's eyes filled with tears, and she threw herself into his arms. Ander stood, pulling her to her feet so that he could better wrap his arms around her, tucking her into his chest. He held her tightly, just rocking her. His face pressed into her curls as Mab clung tightly to him, nearly cutting off his oxygen.

He didn't care. Let him pass out. He would never tell her to loosen her hold.

"Darling," Ander murmured at last. "What have you done to yourself?"

Mab sniffled and lifted her head. The scars on her cheek had reopened from where she'd dragged her nails along them once more. It made him sick to see it. Not because they could ever tarnish her beauty in any way but because she had been in so much turmoil, she had done this to herself.

"Why didn't you call me?" he whispered, his voice cracking with emotion. "I would have taken care of this. I would have protected you from this."

Mab seemed to come back to herself at last and swiped the back of her hand across her cheek, pulling away slightly as she snorted. "Like that would have helped me. That would have only made things worse."

"Why?! Because I could have gotten rid of that body and made sure you didn't end up here in prison?!" His desperation and anger were getting away from him.

"Yes," Max said from outside the cell.

Ander whipped his head around to glare at him for a moment. "Why? Because your people need another innocent inanimi to lay blame on?"

Max sighed, his face showing his guilt once more. "No, because that dead fury deserves justice, and if you'd disposed of the body, it would have made you both look even more guilty."

Ander's eyes narrowed, and a dark smirk tilted his lips. "Oh, sweetheart, they would never have found the body once I was involved."

"Ander." This time, Max did look a little aghast. As if he wasn't sure if Ander was being serious and he should be concerned or if Ander was simply being protective and over-exaggerating what he would do.

Ander was being one hundred and fifty percent serious.

Had Mab called him, he would have snapped that body into pieces. Into such fine dust that no amount of forensic technology would have ever been able to find it. Did the fury deserve justice? Definitely. Did he care more about Mab's freedom and innocence? Abso-fucking-lutely.

"And this is why I didn't call you." Mab dropped back down onto the hard bed, leaning against the stone wall, and looked at him in a mildly-perturbed manner, her lips pursed, her nose curled.

He was happy to see it.

"Well, you should have!" he snapped. "I have an entire kingdom at my disposal, Mab! I could have taken you home to Mum until this was all figured out. We have an entire army that would have been able to protect you. Why wouldn't you let me protect you?!"

"Because of all of that! None of it would have helped me, Ander. Except for making me look even more guilty than they apparently already think I am. And I'm not bringing that kind of trouble to Aemiliana's court. It's not her responsibility to clean up all my messes."

Ander snorted. "As if my mother cares! She would want

to be here for you. She *should* be here for you. Hell, you don't even *need* to be here. I'll just snap you out." He raised his hand, fingers ready to snap.

"No!" Max and Mab cried at the same time.

"Why not?" he shouted, his hand swiping out in front of him so hard that one of his large, stoned rings went flying across the cell, through the bars, and *tink*ed off a wall sconce, cracking the glass.

Max winced, but Ander merely huffed.

"It won't help, Andy!" Mab cried out, frustrated, body taut with agitation. Her hands came up to cover her face.

It made Ander instantly crumble. The anger slipped out of him like air out of a leaky balloon, and soon, he was as deflated as she was. He moved to sit down beside her, reaching to take her hand. "I just hate seeing you in here."

"I know." Her voice was squeaky, belying her personal torment.

"Here, let me heal these." Turning her face toward him, Ander brushed his fingers lightly over her cheek, healing the fresh wounds she'd given herself. "I'll stay in here with you," he murmured.

Her brows lifted. "What? No, you won't."

"Yes, I will. They can't stop me."

Mab sighed. "Andy . . . "

"What?"

"You can't stay in here with me. Please . . . don't do anything that's going to make this worse."

"I don't know how that would make things worse. It would make them *better* for you." She shot him a look, and Ander grumbled, hating all of this. "Fine, but I'm snapping you a blanket and your pillow and some of your books and things. There is no reason why you can't have some comfort while you're in this horrible place."

Mab smiled slightly, peering back at him with all the patience in the world, a sister toward her problematic brother.

Ander slid his arm around her waist and pulled her into his side. As her head came to rest on his shoulder, he placed his chin on top of her curls and gave her a squeeze. "I won't let them keep you in here, Mabbers, I swear it."

"I know," she whispered back.

Across the cell, Max met Ander's gaze, and Ander did the best he could to tell Max with just his eyes that they were going to get Mab out of here the legal way, and soon, or he was going to burn the entire sanctuary down around everyone's heads.

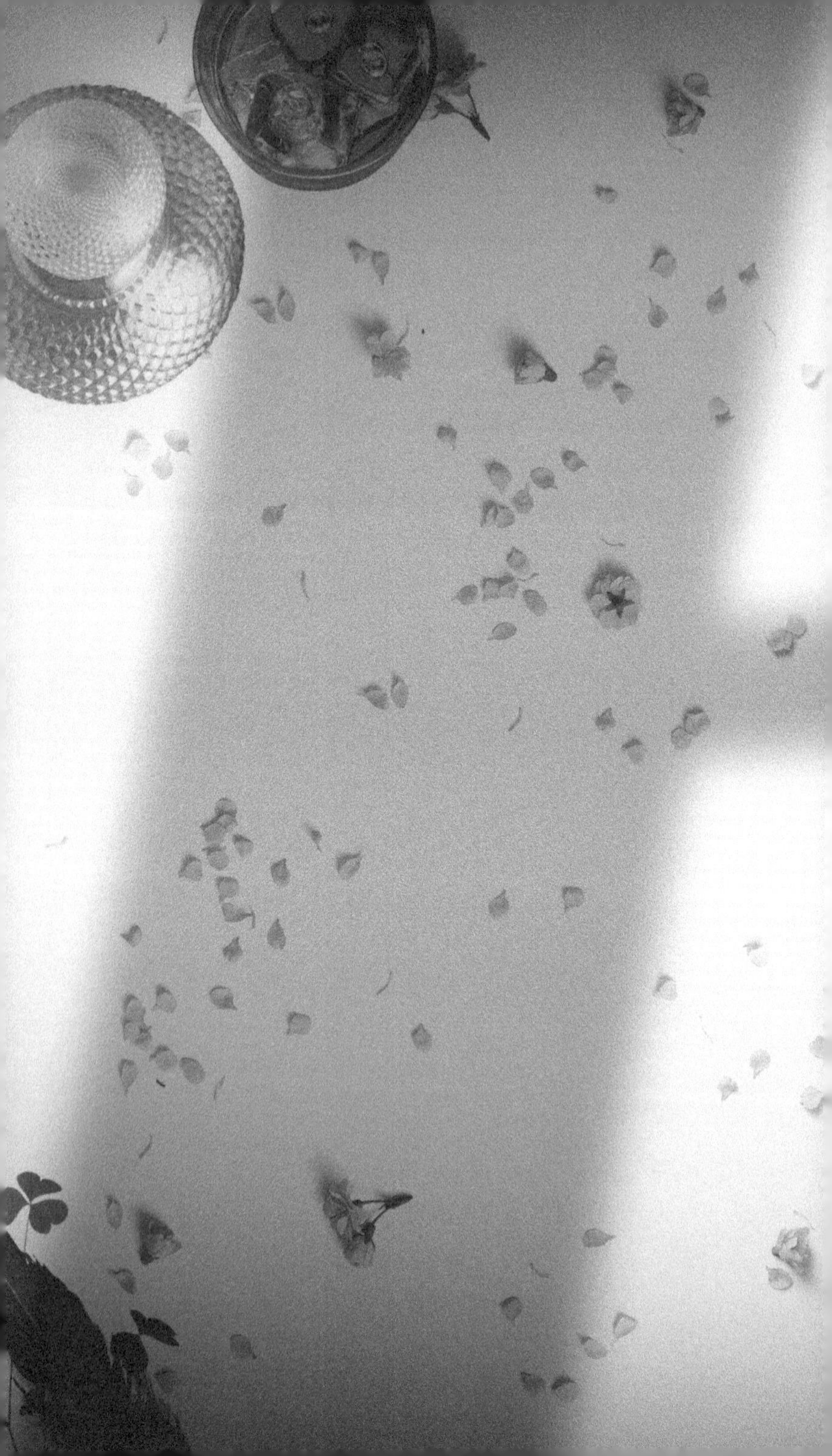

Chapter 14
Mab

Gods, she loved Ander. She didn't tell him that enough.

As often as Mab made it clear to everyone within shouting distance that she would take a bullet for Ander if she had to, sometimes she forgot that the devotion went both ways. Ander was just as likely to throw himself on a blade for her as she was for him. He was her brother in more than words, more than blood. He was her family in every action he took to protect her. Which included being an absolute idiot who would definitely snap away a body lest it incriminate her.

She loved him so fucking much.

"Darling, why don't you go get us some drinks?" Ander said, tilting his head toward the hall in an indication for Max to go on.

Max shifted as if unsure, then nodded and disappeared the way they'd come.

Ander waited until his footsteps completely retreated, then he took Mab's face in his hands, his grip firm but gentle. "Tell me what's really going on."

"I don't—I don't know, Andy." Mab swallowed against a

throat still raw from her screaming. Gods, she hoped she hadn't accidentally hurt someone in her distress. If she had, it would only make her look worse. Quin would have told her, right? And he would be hurt. He was standing right there ... "I just found the fury there."

"Not that, Mab. I don't care about that." Ander shook his head, the motion tugging at her still healing face, but she didn't even wince. She was used to the pull and drag of the skin there. It wasn't the first time she'd reopened those scars in a fit of terror, and she doubted it would be the last. Not now that this cell had opened up that can of worms for her. "What's going on with you? Where is your head at?"

"It's—" Mab squeezed her eyes shut, needing a moment away from his searching gaze. "It's not in a good place, Andy, if I'm being honest. I don't—I don't even remember them putting me in here. I didn't really—I was in a daze until you showed up." Her throat clicked on another painfully dry swallow. "And all I can think is ... did I do this somehow? I've had blackouts before—"

"Night terrors, not blackouts. Those aren't the same thing, Mabbers."

"No, I know. But what if it's the stress of everything going on? What if, with all the changes, and the news about Enrique? What if I lost it? I mean ... it was probably in self-defense, either way. But what if I did hurt someone with my wail? It's been—It's been so long since I've even used it." She shook her head, his hold on her making the motion a little clumsy.

Ander stilled her movements with the press of his hands, forcing her to meet his gaze again. Brown and liquid, and so, *so* comforting. "You didn't do this, Mab. You've never killed anyone with your wail."

"I hurt the—"

"Hurt. Not killed," Ander insisted. "Those bastards trying to burn you were still alive when I got there. I'm the one who scared the living shit out of them and made them trample themselves."

Mab's eyes widened, fear making her gaze jerk from his to the corners of the cell. "Ander," she hissed. "You can't say shit like that here. What if they're listening? You shouldn't —You shouldn't even *be* here. They'll think you were a part of it."

"I shouldn't be here." Ander scoffed. "Of course I'm going to be here! And fuck them if they think they can pin this on either of us. We've done nothing wrong. We've just run our little club and tried to create a safe space for inanimi like us." He turned from her, then narrowed his eyes at the camera across from her cell. "Do you hear me? We've done nothing wrong! Stupid. Bigoted. Useless—"

"Ander. Enough." She pulled his face back to hers, her hands tight on his chin. Fear was making her pulse jitter in her veins, anxiety making her skin feel too small for her bones. "You need to go. Check on the club. Keep things going normally. If we let this slow us down, we're just playing into the hands of whoever this was." She didn't say that maybe they already had. Maybe whoever planted that body on Mab's beach or sent the fury after her so she had no choice but to defend herself—she still wasn't entirely ruling that out—wanted her and Ander out of the way. Wanted to punish them for something. "And if you could? Go by and pick up Gizmo. I'm sure he's scared with all those ignis at my place. And he doesn't like being locked up in his pen for too long."

Ander let out a long, slow breath, the warmth of it tickling her cheeks in his closeness. It was nice having him here like this. Knowing that he'd raced down here without a second thought, as evidenced by the fact that she'd never once in hundreds of years seen him wearing an off-brand T-shirt—it must have been Max's. A not-so-subtle reminder that he loved her. "I'm sure your rabbit is fine, but Max and I will pick him up and bring him home with us. Is his food still in the crisper?"

"Yeah." Relief made her sag against Ander, leaning forward to press her forehead to his. The fate of her pet was one less thing she had to worry about.

"And I'll be back—"

"No." She stopped him, shaking her head, his horns getting caught a little in her wild curls. "Don't come right back here. You heard me. Go to the club. Do your normal thing. Do not show weakness."

"Maaaaab," Ander grumbled, banging his head lightly against hers. "You know if you want me safe from Enrique, this is the perfect—"

"You heard me. Whoever did this wants to throw us off. Or maybe they want you here so they know exactly where you are and how to get to you." She pulled her hands away from his face and sat with her back to the wall. It was nice to have something behind her, but she'd have preferred the corner. There, she knew the only way someone could get her was by coming straight at her. She'd have to move the cot once Ander was gone. "And besides"—her gaze flicked to Max over Ander's shoulder—"you might overhear something while you're there that can help me. Right, Max?"

"She's got a point." Max stopped outside of the cell, two bottles of water in his hand. "The best way we can help Mab is by trying to find answers. You aren't going to find those by sitting in—*here* with her."

Mab noted that he had carefully not used the word

"cell," and she wondered why. Had Ander told him about the history that came with that? Or did Max just dislike the reminder of the time Ander had been locked away in this very block? Although . . . not so deep in the sanctuary. There wasn't even a window. At least her cell at the asylum had a window. A place for natural light to come in. For her to watch as she lost yet another day to the cruelty of a man who couldn't take no for an answer. Watch as her life slipped—

"Did you hear me, Mabbers?" Ander asked, breaking her from where she'd been staring at one of the hard, cement walls.

"Hmm?"

Ander looked at her hard, his mouth pinched into a disapproving line. She could tell there was another argument on his tongue as to why he couldn't leave her here alone. Why he needed to stay. She couldn't let him say it, whatever it was. Her tenuous control holding back the begging to not be left alone was already on the verge of snapping.

"I'm all right, Andy. Really." She patted the pillow he'd snapped her a bit ago. "I've got everything I need, right?" She motioned to the stack of blankets, the little pile of books, everything he'd snapped from her house to keep her occupied. "I'll finally get caught up on my never-ending TBR." She forced a smile.

Ander didn't seem wholly convinced.

"You two should head out," Quin said by way of hello. Not that Mab would have expected any less of him. He'd been kind to her, but that didn't make her think he liked her. Even if there was some inkling at the back of her mind that said he was her arrow-bound, he'd shown no signs of it so far. "Galeo is . . . " He made a couple of motions with his hands that Mab couldn't decipher, and Max grunted in annoyance.

"He's right, Ander. We don't want to overstay our welcome." There was a warning note in Max's tone Mab didn't like. She wondered what Quin had said to him. And who was Galeo? Maybe now that she had all this free time, she'd dedicate some of it to learning ASL, then she could know when the Schields family was talking shit about people.

"But Max—" Ander stopped at whatever expression he must have read on Max's face and nodded. "All right. But I'll be back for lunch tomorrow. And no one will be standing in my way. Am I clear?"

"I'll make sure of it." Max nodded his agreement and held his hand out to Ander, waiting for him to snap himself out of the cell and back into the hall beyond.

"I'll see you later, Mabbers." Ander hugged her tightly, her bones shifting under the force of his love. She closed her eyes, wanting to imprint the feeling of someone who actually cared about her into her skin before she was alone in this fucking cell again. Then she pulled back and gave him a sharp nod. He returned the nod and snapped himself to Max's side.

"I'll stop in and see you soon too," Max promised before he turned to lead Ander down the hall.

When they were gone, it was just her and Quin. Mab saw him look around at the room full of stuff Ander snapped her in the name of comfort and raise his brows.

"This is *exactly* why I told you not to call him," Mab groaned, brushing her hair back from her face. "He doesn't do anything by halves."

"I can see that." Quin moved to the door and unlocked it before he stepped through and shut it behind him. "It would have been worse had I not told him, though."

"If you hadn't told him, the only one he would have been pissed at was me. And I can take that." Mab shrugged. "The sanctuary, on the other hand, might not survive his temper."

Quin hummed a response. "They asked me to come in and hold everything up to the camera. Just to make sure none of it is dangerous."

"Be my guest. Not like I can really stop you." Mab pulled one of the fluffy blankets from the end of the cot to spread across her shoulders and tried not to watch Quin as he lifted every book, shaking it for the cameras and flipping through the pages. Then he picked up all the blankets to shake out and rifled through everything else. She didn't look back until he was close to finished and was surprised to find he'd put everything back to the best of his abilities. The blankets were refolded, albeit not exactly as they had been, and the books stacked in the exact same order. It was nice. "Have they found anything?"

"Nothing." Quin shook his head and shifted a little, like he wanted to sit next to her on the cot but wasn't sure if he was allowed, so instead, he stood in the center of the small space, his wings taking up a good portion of it.

"What do you mean *nothing*? Like, nothing to say I did it? Or nothing to say I didn't?"

Quin's lips pursed, as if he didn't want to say anything more. Because he was afraid of hurting her feelings? Or because he knew he shouldn't? "I mean nothing either way."

"Well, that's unfortunate." Mab reached for one of the water bottles Max had brought, cracking it open and taking a deep drink that didn't soothe the scrape of her throat. And then, after a moment, something clicked with his tone, his words, and the way he wasn't making eye contact. "Wait. Are you saying *you* think it's me? You think *I* did this?"

Quin frowned and pulled a pad from his pocket. "Can you write everything down for me that you have in here?" But even as he said the words, he scrawled something across the page. When he handed the pad to her, the words, "I know it wasn't you. I think it's Orcus." were there in a neat and loopy hand.

"Yeah sure," Mab mumbled, hoping the volume would hide how her breath caught in her throat a little. Then she wrote, "If this is him, he'll be after Ander next. Look after him for me."

When Quin took the pad back, he gave her a curt nod. Which might have been in thanks to anyone else on the outside, but she recognized it as an agreement, and a promise. His family would look after Ander while she couldn't. They would all keep each other safe while she was locked away. That, at least, she could find relief in. "Try to get some rest," Quin said as he turned for the door. "Sleep well, Mab."

"You do the same, Batman." Mab grinned a little to herself, hiding it in the blanket she had wrapped around her shoulders as he slipped out.

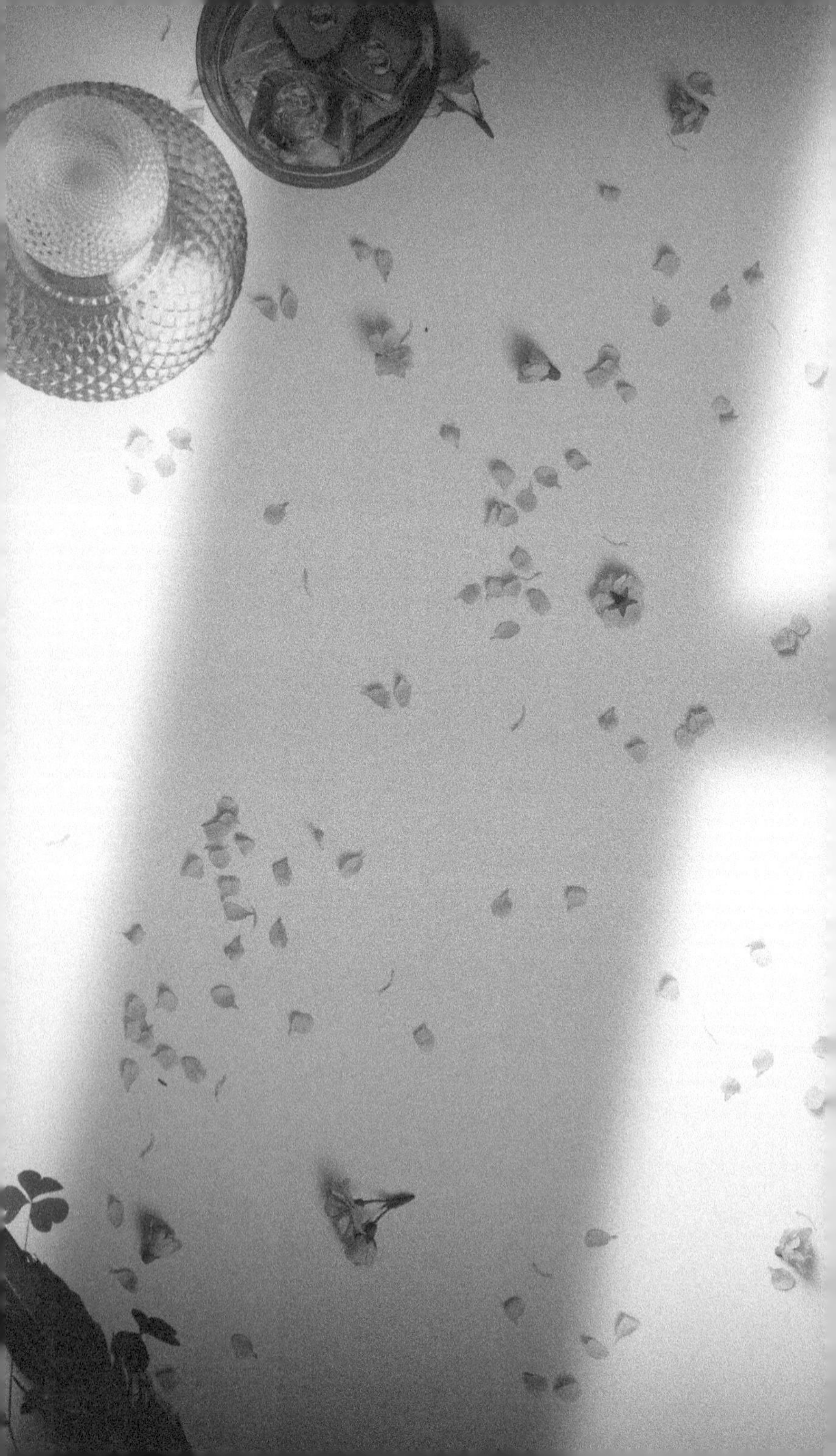

Chapter 15
Quin

"How is Ander?" Quin asked Max when they met in the Schields command center.

A part of him felt terrible leaving Mab in that cell last night, but at least she seemed to have calmed down. Something he attributed to the visit from Ruin. A visit that caused *quite* the stir amongst the rest of the Sanctum.

Quin hoped that her loneliness did not get to her once the dullness of the day settled in. He had seen the open wounds on her cheek. If harming herself was how she soothed the fear and torment in her mind, she would need to be checked on.

"Really broken up and worried about Mab, and add that to his worry about where Enrique is . . . He's a mess, but he'll be okay. We just have to get her out of there so we can focus on finding that asshat."

"Well, we will do whatever we can to get her out quickly."

"And in the meantime," Nox cut in, "we've got every possible search out there on the net that we can think of to track down Enrique. Hopefully he'll do something stupid that will alert us to his whereabouts."

Quin nodded. "Exactly, and then we can put him back where—"

A knock on the doorframe interrupted their conversation. Quin and Max turned at the same time to see Marius standing there.

"Captain wants to see you in his office."

"Thanks, we'll be right there," Max said.

Marius nodded and left.

"What does he want?" Quin signed quickly to his brother.

"Who knows?" Max signed back with a shrug, then nodded his head to the door, and together, they headed into the hall.

It was a quick walk to Galeo's office. Their captain was standing to the side of his desk, flipping through paperwork. When they appeared, he looked up and motioned them in.

"Good, you're here. I have a case for your team."

"A case?" Max asked. "But we have—"

"Yes," Galeo was quick to cut in. "A case. I am taking Quin off the Duchan case, and the rest of the team along with him."

"What?" The question burst out of Quin before he could stop himself. "That makes no sense. I was first on site. This is *my* case." His shoulders bunched, and his wings shuddered with agitation.

Galeo narrowed his eyes on Quin, his lips thinning in his displeasure. "Yes, you were first on site because the suspect called you for help. Now that we have Duchan's DNA on the corpse, it's looking even more likely that she is the culprit."

"How can that be? She didn't touch the body." Quin frowned. Mab's DNA should have been nowhere on the fury.

"That question is exactly why you are no longer on this case. There is usually only one reason a suspect's DNA is on the deceased, Schields, and since that isn't at the forefront of your mind, I am making the right decision taking you off. And that decision is final." He said it firmly, leaving no room for protest. "I want you to track down this diaboli fruit trafficker." Galeo held out a folder, which Max stepped forward to take, then slipped around to the other side of the desk and sat down.

Quin sputtered, and beside him, Max stiffened. Galeo was taking a murder case from him and making him take over a pitiful fruit trafficking case? Quin felt the slap of the insult that it was meant to be. Gazing from the corner of his eye at Max, he could see from his brother's pinched lips that he felt it too.

"But sir," Max said, holding the folder in his hands. "We need to keep an eye on Mab, we've promised."

"No," Galeo said in a clipped tone. "You do *not* need to keep an eye on her. Marius and Cedaloin will be handling the banshee-fury murder. You two will be focusing on the three humans who were killed by diaboli fruit. Find out where they were acquired and get them off the human market before we lose more mortals." He looked between them as he spoke, his eyes narrowed as if daring them to challenge him. "The normie police got their hands on this before we did because there was no actual magic used in the killings. They have them listed as poisonings. The coroner's reports pinged a tag the tech team had on police records for suspicious poisonings and flagged it for review. Forensics recognized heavy amounts of diaboli in each victim's system."

"Do the normies have any suspects?" Quin asked.

"No. The diaboli is a completely foreign substance to them. And as long as they can't place it, they hopefully won't be able to trace it back to the magical community. You need to get ahead of this, find the perpetrator, and get it taken care of before the police stumble on something they shouldn't."

"Of course, sir. We're on it." Max straightened his shoulders.

"And keep away from the Duchan case. Your involvement with that entitled inanimi prince is a conflict of interest."

Max's face hardened when Galeo called Ruin entitled. Quin knew that Max responding right now was not a good idea, so he nodded to Galeo. "Aye, captain." He nudged Max and got him to follow him out of the captain's office.

In the hall, Max's eyes filled with a stormy intensity that only appeared when Max felt protective of someone he loved, and his dark brows drew together to wrinkle the skin in the center.

"He's just upset about yesterday," Quin murmured, trying to soothe him.

"Ander has done *nothing* but help us take down someone dangerous to not only inanimi but ignis alike and risk his own life in the process," Max hissed, venom lining every word. "Yet all they do is insult him and treat him like a criminal."

Quin sighed and patted Max's shoulder. "Come on, we're not going to be able to change his mind standing around here. Let's go deal with this case."

Max's fingers tightened on the folder, but he nodded, and together, they headed back to their command station.

"What's going on?" Nox asked.

"I've been taken off Mab's case entirely," Quin growled.

"And we've got a diaboli trafficking case instead." Max waved the folder.

"What?" Nash's voice raised. "What the *hell*?"

"They found some of Mab's DNA on the body." Quin stepped toward Nash. "But she didn't touch the fury. I made sure of it when I first arrived."

Nash frowned. "I looked the body over myself . . . took my own samples."

"Did you find anything?"

"I haven't had a chance to run everything, not since they shoved us off the case and handed it over to Marius and Cedaloin's team."

"Start running them now," Quin ordered. "We need to prove that there was no DNA from Mab on that body when we were there initially. If something came up, someone had to have planted it. I want to know how." He didn't want to think that someone here in the sanctuary would have done it. But if Enrique was behind this, there could be another double agent they weren't aware of yet.

The door to the apartment was cordoned off with yellow crime scene tape. Quin took the knife strapped to his thigh and cut through it. With a slight push of his fingers, the wooden door swung open.

"Won't the humans notice we did that?" Nash asked from behind him.

Quin and Max had split up, each taking a twin so that they could cover more ground faster.

"We'll be gone by the time they do." He didn't have time to waste, or to worry about what the normie cops would think when they came back to the crime scene. As long as he and Nash found ties to the fruit in this apartment before the cops did, they could be long gone before they had time to figure anything out. And all traces to the magical community would be removed. "Just make sure you don't leave any DNA around."

Quin stepped into the apartment but still heard Nash snort behind him and snap on a pair of gloves.

"I am legitimately insulted."

Quin turned slightly to look back at him, brows furrowing in question. He dragged his pointer finger across the fingers of his left hand, palm up.

"Don't *what* me," Nash grumbled. "You act as if I don't *literally* do forensics for a living."

Nash pushed past him into the apartment, and Quin blinked after him in surprise. Was he actually upset? Quin hadn't meant anything by it beyond them needing to be cautious.

He watched as Nash went for the living room and began to open up her electronics, searching for something he could get into. Feeling guilty, Quin stepped up to him, tapped him on the shoulder, and waited until his brother was looking at him before he very solemnly signed that he was sorry.

Nash stared back at him, then sighed. "It's fine. I'm sorry I'm touchy."

While Nash could be dramatic just like their papa, he wasn't one to get overly sensitive most of the time. "You okay?" he signed carefully, wanting Nash to know he meant it.

"It's nothing."

They had a lot of work to do, but Quin knew when something was troubling his brother. He could see it there in the lines of his brows. Nash went to turn away, but Quin tapped him on the shoulder again. When their eyes met, Quin spelled out a name.

"Licia?"

"Ugh!" Nash threw up his arms. "Is it that obvious?!" He scrubbed his hands down over his face, making another frustrated sound. "I think she has a boyfriend. Some normie doofus! What am I supposed to do about that?"

His vivid blue eyes, the exact shade of their dad's, peered back at Quin in need.

Quin had no answers. He had never even dated, let alone been absolutely infatuated with someone. But he tried to think of what their dad would say. "Wait," he said softly.

"Wait?" Nash's brows shot up. His face grew slack, and he stared blankly back at him. "That's what you've got for me."

"Yes. If she's worth it, wait. If she's worth it, be her friend. If she's worth it, stand by her side no matter what. Not everything is about you, Nash." Quin turned away then and stepped into the kitchen that was off the living room/entry area.

"Huh," Nash mused out loud. "The virgin has a point."

Quin rolled his eyes and began to rifle through the stack of mail on the counter. There was nothing there but opened bills and one unopened invitation to apply for a Capital One credit card. Pushing the stack away, Quin opened drawers, finding nothing but cutlery and utensils until he came to the junk drawer.

Tape, batteries, elastics, and a packet of ketchup were all he saw at first, but then he noticed the wad of receipts trapped in the upper part of the cabinet as he pulled the drawer out. Shuffling his fingers around inside, he managed to work them under the bundle of papers and pull it out.

On top was a receipt for groceries. Just one of the local standard shops. But beneath that was a handwritten receipt from a market. Quin scanned it quickly. All that was listed was fruit, and nothing as diaboli. But it gave him a stand number and name to go by. A possible lead.

He looked at the bottom of the receipt. The date fell within the time period.

"I think I've found something," he called out.

Nash looked up from the computer he had hacked into and was searching through. "Oh?"

Quin held up the receipt. "She bought fruit the day before she died at a local market. At a stand called Donovan's. Can you check her bank records and see if she purchased there often?"

Nash nodded. "Can do."

Quin pulled his phone out of his back pocket and quickly sent Max a text.

> Check for receipts from a local fruit vendor called Donovan's.

It didn't take long for Max to text back.

> Thanks for the heads-up. I'll check.

He wasn't finished with his search, so he tucked the receipt into his pocket, then dug through the trash.

"Okay, quick search through Danielle's history says that

this was the first time she bought anything from that fruit stand," Nash called out from the living room.

Quin stood up from the trash, peeling off his gloves to stuff in his pocket, and looked to Nash. "So we need to figure out if she just happened upon the stand or if someone or something drew her in."

"Did you find anything?" Quin asked as he stepped into the command center.

Max looked up from the computer, where he stood looking over Nox's shoulder. "Yeah. Michelle had two receipts from Donovan's fruit stand." He plucked them from the desktop and held them up.

Quin pulled the receipt from his own pocket. "Then I guess we know where we have to check."

Max nodded. "Nox is searching for them online right now, seeing if we can track down the owners."

"I'll help." Nash popped into the command center behind Quin and moved to drop into the rolly chair in front of the empty computer.

As the twins clicked away at their keyboards, Max turned to Quin. "Ander is really not happy that we've been taken off Mab's case."

"We've been taken off a lot of cases lately." Quin folded his arms across his chest.

Max frowned, worry lines returning to his face that had been there for a couple of days now. "I hate it. Galeo won't let us near anything that actually means protecting the people we love."

"I've been thinking . . ."

Max's brown quirked up. "About?"

"What are the chances that Orcus escapes from the Rome-Olympia sanctuary, and the next day there's a body on Mab's beach?" Quin's brow shot up in question as he looked at his brother.

Max's frown deepened. "You think it's connected."

"I think there's a chance it is. I mean . . . wouldn't he want revenge? You're there to protect Ander, and when you're not, he's in a club full of witnesses, so he can't get to him—"

"So Mab is the obvious next choice," Max finished.

The sound of fingers on keyboards had stopped, and when Quin and Max looked to the twins, they found them both turned around and staring at them.

Quin raised a brow, fingertip sliding over his opposite hand once more, "What?" he signed.

"So, we're going to look for him, right?" Nash asked.

"Galeo told us to stay away from him," Max muttered.

"So?"

"We can't just hang Mab out to dry, you guys!" Nox added.

"And we can't just leave that asshat out there doing as he pleases. He needs to be in a cell!" Nash exclaimed.

Quin glanced over at Max. "They have a point."

"If Galeo finds out—" Max began.

"We know, we know. We all get separated, and he'll treat us like trash. Who cares?" Nox said loudly, her green eyes bright with conviction, which had both Quin and Max looking at the door to make sure she hadn't been overheard.

"We'd have to do this all completely on the down-low so he can't find out," Max continued.

Nash rolled his eyes and looked at his twin. "He talks to us like we know nothing."

"He always underestimates us," Nox agreed, then looked at Max and Quin. "We have all our programs duplicated on our personal computers at home. Don't worry, we can run this operation from anywhere in the world."

"Galeo never has to know." Nash steepled his fingers before him.

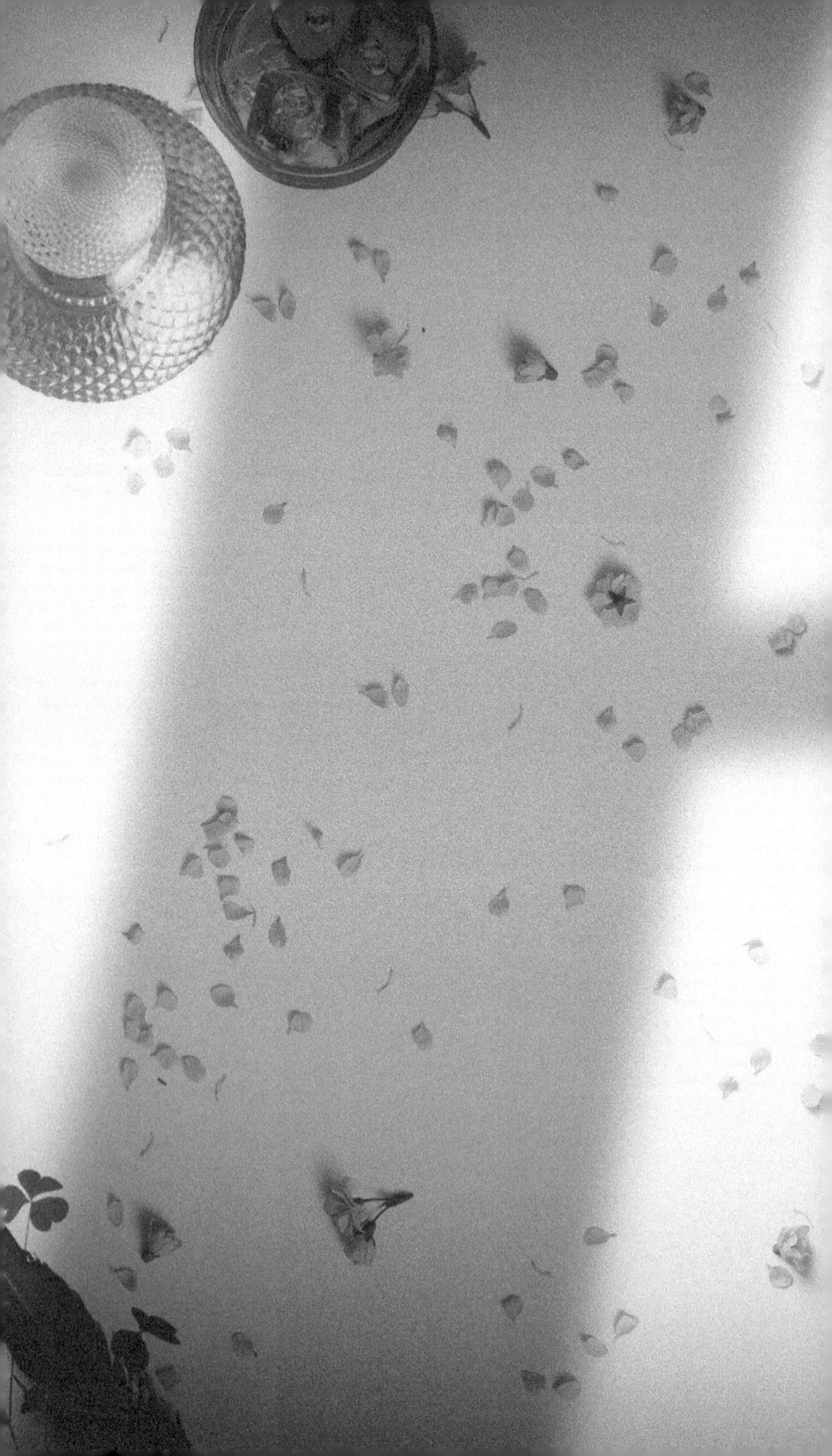

Chapter 16
Mab

This wasn't so bad. This was ... manageable. She could do this. She could *definitely* do this.

The main light switched off overhead, leaving only the dim glow of the nighttime lighting in its place, likely signifying the setting of the sun, and Mab jerked, her back hitting the wall so hard, the cement scraped her skin through her shirt.

She couldn't do this.

Logically, she knew the holding cells were silent. There was no one down there but her, but with the lights off and her back pressed to a cold hard wall, she could hear screams and moans. Whimpers and sobs. Prayers to a god who clearly wasn't listening. The women of the asylum never slept. Never found any escape from the torment of their captors and their madness apart from death.

The *drip drip drip* of moisture carved a ridge into the stone, the sound carving away at her, somehow louder than the screams.

I'm not there anymore. I got out. I'm safe. I'm not—

Another scream of anguish rent the air, and she sobbed.

Maybe it would be better if she were mad, like them. Maybe it would be better if Mab let go of the last shred of herself she clung to. Then she wouldn't be mentally there anymore. Physically, there was no escape. But mentally? Mentally, she could be anywhere. On a beach. On the cliffs. In Helicon.

She tried that. Tried to close her eyes and visualize somewhere else, *anywhere* else. Ander's condo. The beach behind her house. The rooms Aemiliana set up for her in Helicon, like she was her child as much as Ander. But none of the images stuck, and the screams grew louder with every passing second until she couldn't even hear herself think over them.

Mab curled in on herself, covering her ears, hoping to blot them out. But it didn't work. She pulled the pillow over her head, practically stuffing the filling down into her ears, and that didn't block them out either. Nothing did. They grew louder still. The sound split her head in fucking two as she tried, and failed, and tried, and failed to find peace, to find silence, to find rest.

And when it did seem like she'd blotted most of them out, her mind conjured up the image of a darkened alleyway with uneven cobbles beneath her feet and a man, his face still seared into her memories, chasing her.

She had to be faster. Her heart pounded in her ears, her muscles burning. She had to be faster. He'd catch her. She knew he'd catch her. And when he did ...

The lights finally, blessedly, came back on to full brightness, but it was only so that one of the ignis could drop a tray onto the floor just inside the door.

"Eat up, *banshee*," they said, the last word dripping like venom from their tongue.

Mab flinched back from it and pulled the blanket over

her head to block out the hate and the scorn. Why even bother coming down to give her food if they were just going to be nasty to her? Why couldn't they just leave her the fuck alone?

Gods she was tired. How long had she been in this bloody cell? How much longer would they keep her here? Forever. They'd keep her here forever. She was never getting out.

A whimper ripped itself out of her raw throat, and she curled further in on herself.

"Fine. Don't eat." They snorted, but Mab wasn't sure anymore if that was the ignis on the other side of the door or if it was one of the men from the asylum. For as soon as they were gone, the screams started up again. The unintelligible moans cut through her mind, worming their way through her in a way that was sure to make her mad.

"Good night, Lady Duchan," they said, but the voice wasn't the ignis anymore. It was another one. One that was deep and hollow. A voice that had haunted her for centuries. A voice she'd never be able to shake because it lived in her mind even hundreds of years later.

The lights went off again, plunging her into dimness, into her memories. And *he* was there again. Bartlett.

Moving in the shadows of the room.

In the corner.

Advancing on her.

Chasing her.

The cobbles were uneven under her bare feet, scraping against the skin, leaving behind deep gouges that burned from the dirt of the alley and slowed her down.

He was going to catch her.

He was going to catch her.

He was going to catch her.

And then he was on top of her. Pinning her down. His hands on her wrists, even as she thrashed. The blanket she'd been using to hide from him, from the men of the asylum, from the world got caught up around her legs, making it hard to kick him, even harder to get herself free. And he was so much stronger than her. So much bigger. Weighed so much more. How could she ever hope to fight him off? How could she ever—

"Mabbers! Mab! Look at me! Open your fucking eyes! LOOK!" Ander. But Mab didn't want to look. She didn't want to see Bartlett above her, that victorious smile on his face like he'd finally conquered some kind of beast no man ever had. Lain siege to a kingdom he knew he had no right to. Even as that thought struck her, her heart started to slow, her breathing coming a little easier as the next words cut through the panic. "Mab, if you don't open your eyes this instant!"

Ander dropped beside her, wrapped his arms tight around her, and pulled her into his chest. He'd let go of her wrists, or maybe ... maybe he'd never been holding them at all. And slowly, slowly, she came back to herself.

"That's it, Mab. You're okay. I'm here," he said, his tone soft, but not saccharine and lecherous like Bartlett's was that night. "Can you open your eyes now?"

"It's too bright," Mab said, her voice ruined from her screaming. But she peeked through her lashes, and relief washed through her at the sight of Ander's face pressed so close to her own, they were practically nose to nose. He had a red mark on his cheek, likely from her landing a punch, that would no doubt bruise. "I'm sorry. They ... They turned off the lights, and I ... "

"It's all right," Ander soothed, brushing her hair back from her face. It was damp and sticking to the skin of her forehead. And she hadn't bathed in what felt like weeks at this point. Gods, she probably stank. "The alley?"

She nodded, pressing her face in close to his shoulder but not closing her eyes. "The alley."

"He's dead, Mabbers. You know he is. It's been centuries." He pressed a kiss to her forehead, his lips soft and warm.

"I know." Logically, Mab did know that. Even if Ander hadn't cursed Bartlett into oblivion, he would have been long dead by now. He was only human. She also knew, logically, that if she met Bartlett in an alley now, he'd never be able to overpower her like he did back then, even without her wail. Because she and Ander had spent the last several decades learning to defend themselves by any means necessary. Mab Duchan wasn't helpless, she wasn't weak, and she wasn't a maiden anymore. But none of that seemed to matter when her own mind turned against her.

"I could snap you out of here, you know. It wouldn't even be hard." Ander pulled back so he could look her in the eyes, as if he was searching for some confirmation that that's what he should do. "I'll take you to Helicon—"

"I'd just look more guilty for running away," Mab sighed, pushing herself up to sitting and brushing her fingers through her hair, then wincing when they got caught in the knots. "We've been over this."

"And I'm still unconvinced that this is the best option."

"Well, we don't have any *good* ones, do we, Ander?" Mab snapped, exhaustion making her temper flare more than it usually would. She just needed to sleep. But sleep wouldn't come with the screams, and when it did, there were the dreams to contend with. Bartlett and his greasy, sneering face. The pyre. Maybe Ander was right, maybe she should just run away. But Ander and the Schields family would be blamed if she did, and she didn't want that on her conscience. The Schields had been nothing but kind to her—even Quin, albeit in his own, stiff, uptight way—she wasn't going to spit in their faces by getting them into even more trouble. No. She could hang on for a bit longer.

"How's our bar?"

Ander raised his brows at the change of subject but let it slide as he sat up beside her, and they both turned to brace their backs against the wall. "Inferno is fine, Mab. The bar staff misses you. They say no one slings a dirty Shirley like you do."

Mab huffed a laugh and rolled her eyes. "It's just a Shirley Temple with vodka. No need to be all dramatic about it."

"Yes, but most of them are baby bartenders. You've been mixing drinks for how long? Hm?" He leaned in closer to her, his shoulder bumping hers. "You're their hero."

"Shut up." She snorted but didn't move away from him. Instead, she slipped farther down into a slouch so she could put her head on his shoulder. This was the most relaxed she'd felt in what seemed like days. Ander let the silence wash over them because he seemed to know she needed it. Having someone who knew her like that had scared Mab at first. She wasn't used to people seeing down into the depths of her. But it was nice now. A comfort to know she never had to explain herself to him.

He knew, and soon, she'd have less of him. Because Max would marry him, no doubt, and Ander would be a husband first, her brother second. She tried not to let that make her bitter. He deserved to be happy. Max was a good, kind male. Ander was worthy of all the softness and light Max could provide, and Mab wasn't going to take that from him just because she was jealous. Just because it would leave her alone again.

"It's the dark that does it," she said finally, although that was only half true. It was the dark and the quiet. But at least when there was light, she could distract herself with something else. She could read a book—if she could focus on one long enough to really get into it. "It feels too much like the asylum in the dark."

"Then we'll get you a lamp," Ander promised, his fingers moving softly and gently through her hair, his magic working through the snarls before his fingers could ever touch them.

"I don't think there's a socket in here."

"Then we'll get you a magic lamp."

"With a genie inside?"

"Mabbers!" Ander gasped. "I thought I was your genie. Don't I make all of your wishes come true?"

Mab choked on a snort and headbutted his jaw to tell him to keep stroking her hair. "Most of them. But still, a genie would be really cool."

"I'm offended."

"Easily and often." Then she was laughing, soft and a little wretched, and he was chuckling along with her. It was nice. Having him there helped. She knew he couldn't stay; she wouldn't ask him to. He had other places to be, and he should be out there, enjoying his newfound happiness. Not holed up in a cell with her just because someone dumped a body on her beach. Besides, it wasn't like the Schields were going to leave her there to rot. She could last a couple more days. So long as Ander popped in every once in a while to keep her sane.

"I'll still get you that lamp," Ander said when their laughter died away. "Genie not included."

"Thanks."

"No problem, doll."

"Have you heard anything about Enrique while I've been here?" she asked.

Ander stiffened, his hand ceasing its motion in her hair. At first, Mab didn't think he was going to say anything, then his hand waved, and a small black velvet box appeared in his palm. He held it out to her.

"This was in front of my condo door when I got home from visiting you yesterday."

Mab's stomach roiled even before she took the box from him and slowly opened it, the hinges and case making a slight creak. Inside, nestled on black satin, were two golden bands that thrummed lightly with power. Mab had seen a set like these only once before: one on Ander's hand and one on Enrique's.

Aeternus rings.

They bound the couple together so that they could never be parted—literally. Ander had tried to escape, and his ring had prevented him from leaving because Enrique did not wish for him to go. The rings could not be taken off nor destroyed, except by one of the original gods. It had taken Indra to separate them and free Ander at last.

"There was a note," he rasped lowly. "'You promised eternity.'"

Mab's stomach rolled, and she could see the anxious terror building up in Ander that he had been hiding from her. This was clearly a threat. Enrique would be coming for him. "Gods, Andy, are you okay?"

Slowly, her brother turned his head to look at her, fear swirling in his eyes. "He knows where I live, Mab."

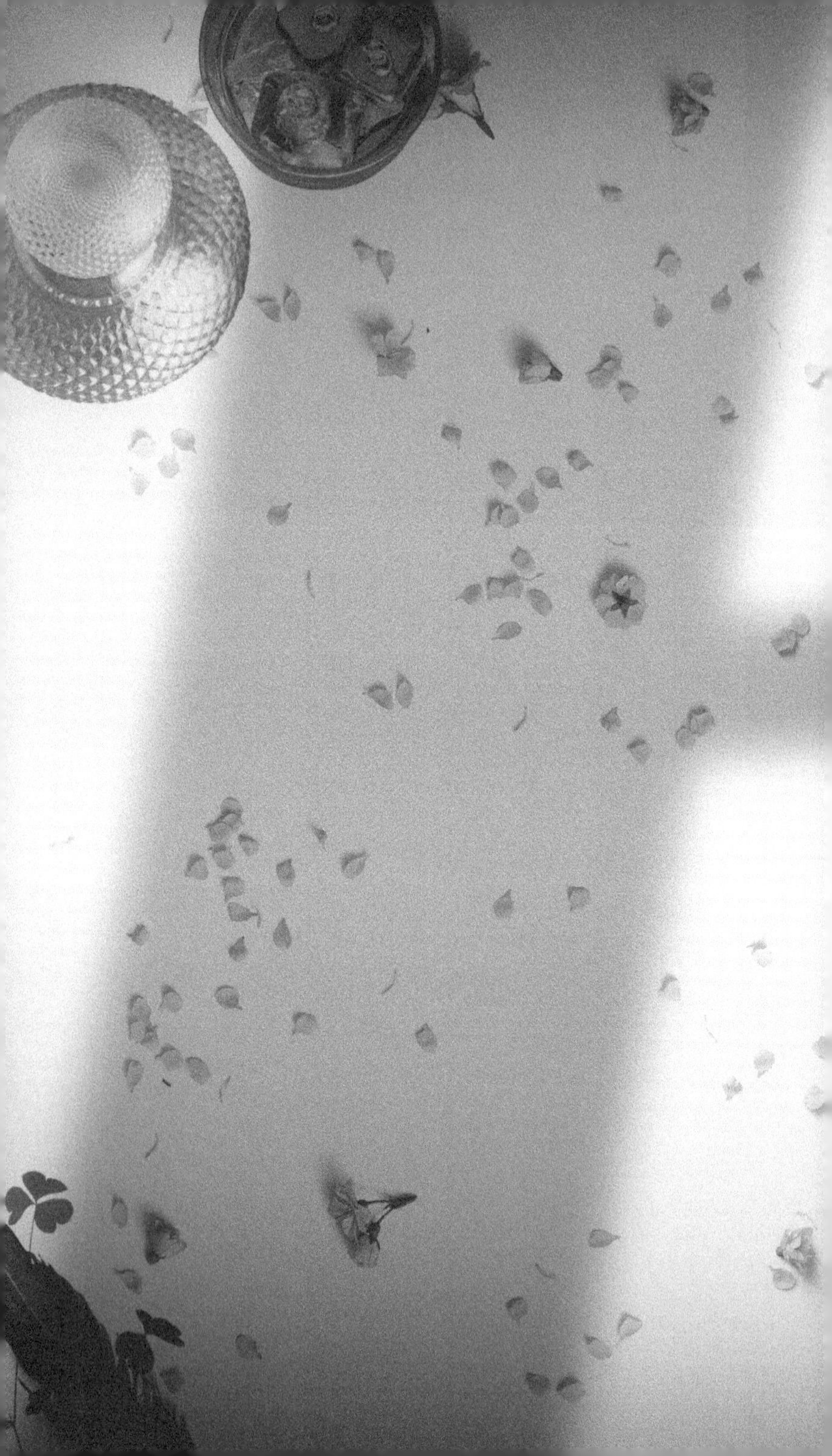

Chapter 17
Max

"You know, I think I hate farmer's markets more than grocery stores," Max said, rubbing at his temples. Farmer's markets in Miami were somehow worse than the grocery store on the Friday before the Super Bowl, and he never really understood why. "It's not even five yet."

Quin made a noise of equal discomfort at his side. If any of the Schields siblings could understand Max's deep abiding hatred for grocery shopping, it was Quin. Which was just kind of funny when he thought about how their parents had met. If it weren't for crowded grocery stores and Ezekiel's inability to throw together a meal on his own, they wouldn't be a family now.

"The fruit stand should be easy to spot," Quin said after a moment of them standing on the edge of the crowd. They were at the end of a long aisle of tents in a parking lot far enough away from the beach that the tourists weren't hogging every available space. "Nox said in all their social posts they had a yellow tent."

"I see at least ten yellow tents from here." Max groaned. "Someone should really tell them that picking a brightly colored tent doesn't make you stand out if everyone else does the same thing."

"I'm sure they'll make a note," Quin grunted, somehow sounding gruffer than normal.

Max snorted and rolled his eyes. Quin was on edge; they all were.

This thing with Mab, and Enrique escaping, was pushing all of them to their last nerve, and Max didn't really know what to do about that. Technically, they were off both cases, but they couldn't exactly disentangle themselves from either. And working on them while dealing with this frankly *pedestrian* fruit stand case was spreading them all a little thinner than he liked.

Max never would have asked that of his siblings. He would have taken it all on by himself. But they'd volunteered, and he wasn't going to turn them down. Not when it came to Ander's safety. Not when it came to Mab being locked up.

"Let's just get this shit taken care of so we can get back." Max shook his head and pushed into the crowd with Quin close at his back. It was a struggle to dodge and weave through the normies, making sure none of them ran into his wings accidentally, but he had plenty of practice in doing it. The first three yellow stands weren't fruit at all. One was for a bakery, the next was for some place called Sunshine Coffee, and the third was artisan bath bombs. "This would have been easier if the twins could have gotten us a map of the market layout."

"It changes regularly." But Quin sounded just as annoyed as Max felt about the fact that they were probably going to have to walk the length of this entire market just to find one little fruit vendor out of the thirty or so there.

He wondered if the normies who'd bought from

Donovan's had done the same. Had they stumbled upon the place, or had someone recommended it? At least one of them had been there before. Maybe it was all a misunderstanding. The normies, for their part, probably thought they were getting some kind of exotic delicacy. Or maybe Donovan hadn't meant to sell to—

"You've got to be fucking kidding me," Max said, letting out a long sigh as he finally got a good view of Donovan's Fruit Stand. It was under a yellow canopy all right, but what stopped Max was the big pop-up banner with a picture of a diaboli fruit on it. Right beside the picture, in big bold print, were the words "Try the New Everfae Diet." Max pinched the bridge of his nose. There went any hope that this was some kind of mistake. "Just once, I'd like one of these things to be an honest mistake. Just once."

"I'll go around the back and head him off."

"Maybe he won't run?" A foolish hope, and he knew it, but Max couldn't seem to help it.

"They always run." Quin slipped away without another word, leaving Max at the front of the stall, watching as more and more normies walked up and bought from the man behind the folding table, who Max could only assume was Donovan.

Max stepped into the line, waiting until he saw Quin in position before he made his move.

"Donovan?" Max asked when he was within speaking distance, only a single normie between himself and the man cheerfully packaging up his customer's order.

"Yeah. Who's ask—" Donovan stopped, his eyes wide, brows high on his face. "Shit."

Then he spun and made a break for it, tripping over the crates lining the back of his stall without so much as trying to grab his cash box.

He didn't make it far because Quin was right there waiting for him with cuffs at the ready. They were drawing a crowd, and Max could see how Quin shifted uncomfortably under the full attention of so many people.

"This vendor was selling without the proper permits. Anyone who has bought food from this stall, please contact us at the station on 2nd Ave for a full refund. Ask for Officer Schields," Max called to all the normies in attendance, already pulling his phone out to call the twins about a clean-up crew and send a text through to Licia that their inside people at the police station would need to be on alert. "And please let anyone else you know who's purchased from this man know as well. Thank you for your cooperation." Then he turned to Quin and nodded toward the way they'd come. "If you'll please excuse us."

By the time they made it back to the sanctuary, Donovan had copped to everything. The only thing he hadn't given them yet was his supplier. That he was tight-lipped about, for the moment.

"Take him to interrogation, then meet me at the command center. I want to go over what we've got so far with the twins before we lean on him too much," Max said, running his fingers through his hair. It was an easy case, open and shut essentially. Apart from this third party who was supplying the diaboli, which might go nowhere or might lead them in circles. Either way, it was a distraction, and Max didn't like it. He had more important things to do than to chase down nefarious fruit vendors. Like chasing down abusive and dangerous ex-boyfriends.

Quin opened his mouth to speak, then stopped, his eyes wide, looking at something over Max's shoulder.

Max frowned and turned to find Ander standing in front of the command center, his arms crossed over his chest.

"Good luck," Quin signed, then disappeared down the hall.

"Traitor," Max muttered, then spun to grin at Ander. "Hi, baby." Max loped up to Ander, hoping desperately that the angry pinch of Ander's brow wasn't directed at him.

"Can we talk?"

"Always." Max winked and reached down to take his hand, then tugged him through the command center—ignoring the twins' catcalls—and into his office. "What's the matter?" he asked when the door shut behind him and he could gather Ander in his arms where no one could see. He pressed a kiss to Ander's forehead and brushed his nose along the ridge of one long, elegant horn, sighing a little as Ander snuggled in. "Did something happen?"

"It's Mab." Ander cleared his throat, but it didn't quite hide the warble in his voice.

"What about Mab? Is she hurt?" If Marius was—

"No. It's not that." Ander sighed, bumping his head against Max's chest, his horns lightly digging in at his collarbones. "But she's . . . She's not doing well down there, Max. She's not eating. I don't think she's slept more than a couple of hours total. We *can't—*" His voice broke again.

Max brushed his fingers lightly through the hair at the base of Ander's skull, gentle and soothing.

"We can't leave her alone in there. I know you guys are trying. But after what happened with the asylum, every day is—"

"Okay. Okay." Max pulled Ander away from his chest and leaned down a little to better meet his eyes. "Okay. We won't leave her alone down there anymore. We'll ... We'll take it in shifts, yeah? All of us. You. Me. The twins. My parents. Georgie. Q. We'll take it in shifts, so she's not alone for very long. Do you think that'll help?"

Ander nodded, sucking in a breath that Max could tell he felt he needed to keep from crying. "Okay. Thank you."

"You don't need to thank me, or any of us." Max shook his head, then pressed his forehead to Ander's. "Mab is family. And I swear to you, she's going to get out of that cell. We're going to clear her name, and she's going to be fine."

"I'm going to hold you to that," Ander threatened, poking him hard in the chest.

"I look forward to it." Max laughed a little and brushed a kiss to Ander's cheek. "Come on, let me walk you out. Then I've got to get back to this case so we can clear it up and hopefully have a little more wiggle room to work on Mab's."

"I thought all of you were kicked off ... " Ander's mouth parted a little as he caught on to what Max was doing. "Oh."

"Mhm." Max took his hand to lead him out.

"You in trouble with your man?" Nash asked when Max returned to the command center.

"Yeah, he looked awful pissed, Maxxy. What'd you do?" Nox leaned forward, her elbows braced on her knees, chin in hand.

"Gossip mongers, the both of you." Max huffed and dropped into one of the extra rolly chairs with a loud exhale. "He's pissed at all of us."

"Us?! What did we do?" Nash gasped, hand lifting to his chest in a truly dramatic display of affront.

"We've left Mab alone down in the holding cells, and she's not doing well." Max scrubbed at his face, weariness settling into his bones. "She's got some ... " He swallowed, pausing a moment to think. He didn't know the whole of it; Ander hadn't given him details. And ultimately, it was Mab's story to tell. But if they were going to protect her—even from herself—they needed more facts. "She's got some unresolved trauma involving being locked up."

"What, like she was in prison?" Nox frowned, turning back to her screen for a moment to pull up Mab's file. "That wasn't in our records."

"Ander said it was an asylum." Which was worse in any time period but especially a few centuries ago. "Either way, we're going to start running shifts to keep her company when we can. Ander was just down with her, so I'll go down for supper. I'm going to call Papa, Dad, and Georgie in on this too. I don't want her left alone for more than a few hours during the day. If visiting hours are happening, someone is going to be there. Am I clear?"

"Yes, boss." Both twins saluted. But Max could see Quin shifting back as if he could disappear into the shadows and not be included in this latest mission.

"That includes you too, Q. I know you're not her biggest fan, but we're not leaving her alone with her demons."

"Who said I wasn't her biggest fan?" Quin signed, his movements slow and almost sulky. But one raised brow from Max had him sighing out a soft, "Fine."

"Good. Nox, work up a schedule. Nash, call Dad and fill him in on the plan. Quin, you and I are going to go chat with our suspect." Max clapped once, and the whole group dispersed to their tasks.

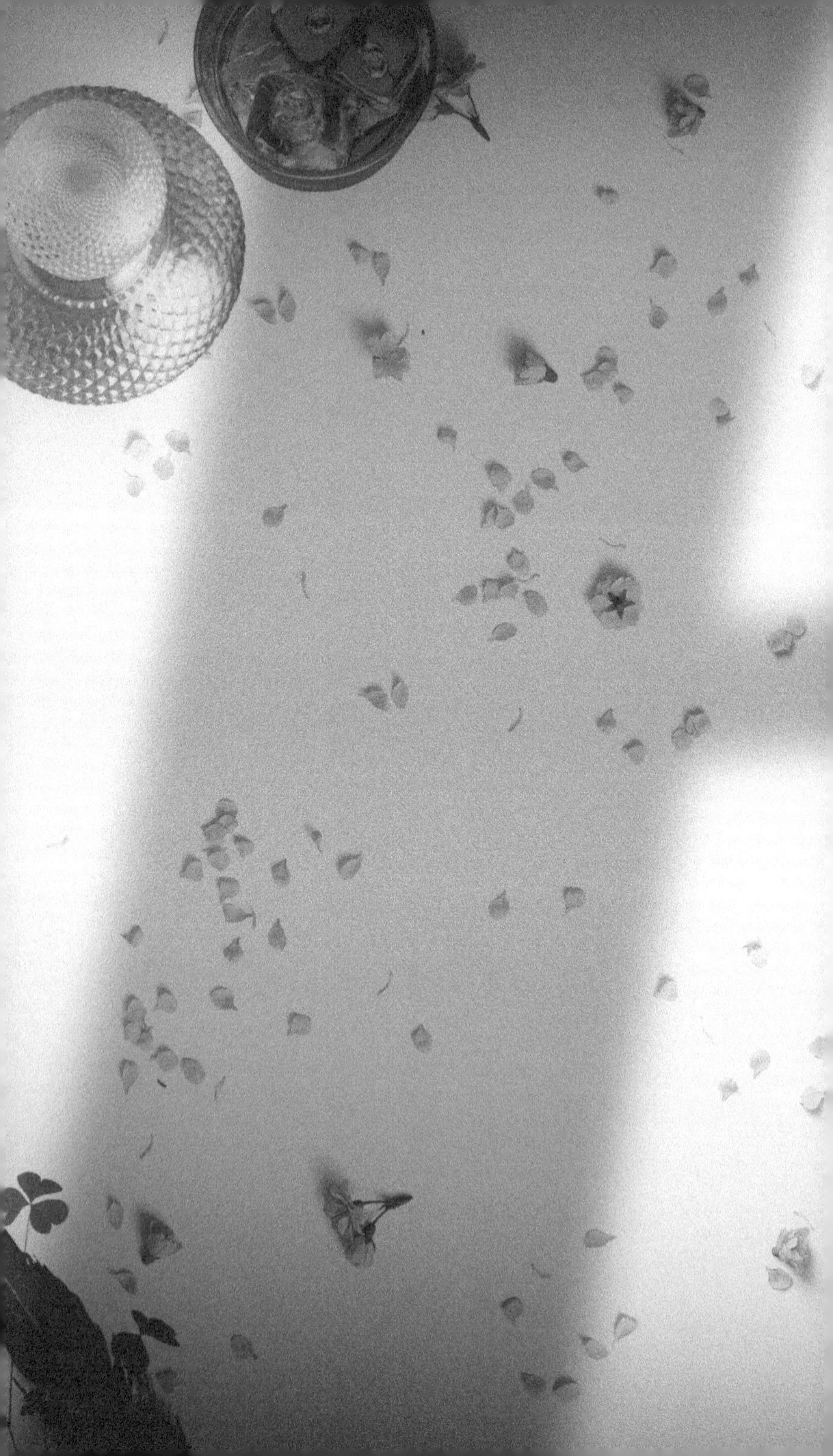

Chapter 18
Quin

"How was your night in the cell, Donovan?" Quin drew out a metal chair, the legs scraping on the floor, and spun it around so he could straddle it backward. He leaned with his arms folded on the back of the chair and rested his chin on them.

The inanimi before him looked sullen, his lips curved down in a pout and his lids half covering his eyes. Despite that, he stared indifferently at the tabletop. His rumpled shirt was untucked from his dirty jeans, and his hair stuck out at all angles from fingers being run through it. There were dark, heavy bags under his eyes, purple and puffy. All of it a sure sign he hadn't slept much in his holding cell.

His only response to Quin was a half-hearted shrug of his shoulders.

Quin snorted. Apparently, a night in holding hadn't made him any chattier. "Any chance you've had a change of heart and decided to tell us who your supplier is?"

Donovan's eyes remained focused on a single spot on the table before him. "No."

"You know, you were targeting humans with an Underworld fruit that is a known poisonous substance. If we ignore the trafficking of foreign substances into the human realm charges . . . you're still on the hook for the death of three normies. Possibly more if we can't track down all your customers. The Princeps don't take too kindly to normie deaths."

Donovan frowned, his lips pursing together. "I told them the amounts to eat and that if they ate any more than that, it could make them really sick. The directions I gave them should have only been enough to give them the shits." He looked up, meeting Quin's gaze for the first time since he had entered the interrogation room. "It's not my fault that idiot humans can't follow instructions."

Quin's jaw ticked as disgust coursed through him. Most inanimi felt no love for the human race inhabiting this realm, but to outright dismiss their deaths . . . It made Quin's internal temperature rise. Anger filled his chest, and he felt the urge to reach across the table and smack the creature before him.

But the one thing that soothed his temper a fraction was the tightening at the corners of Donovan's eyes. He was scared. He knew what kind of charges would be placed on him for his crimes, and he was staring down a very long time in a cell, if not death.

"You know the Princeps won't see it that way. Neither do I. Everyone knows diaboli fruit aren't supposed to cross the portal lines." Quin paused, watching him. "Who's your supplier, Donovan? Give me something to speak on your behalf. You don't want to be executed over a failed diet scheme, do you?"

Donovan's lips pressed more firmly together, like he was

having to physically restrain himself from spitting out the name.

"Let me give you some more time to think about it." Quin stood up and left the interrogation room. He looked at the ignis who was on the other side of the door. "Leave him in there for a bit. I want him to stew on it."

Borialis nodded. "Will do."

Quin strode down the hall, heading back to the command center, where the twins were busy on their computers. He cleared his throat as he came up behind them, and both jumped.

Nash cast him a dirty look for the scare. "Any luck?" he asked.

"No. He's scared, I can tell that. But something is keeping him from revealing who his supplier is. I think we need to dive deep into his family and friend connections. It has to be someone he cares about if he's willing to go to his death to protect them."

"We can do that," Nox said.

"Fishing for personal info is our favorite task." Nash chuckled, biting down on the end of a red vine and letting it dangle from his lips as he chewed on it, slowly inching it into his mouth by way of his teeth.

Quin shook his head at the two. "Just see what you can find."

"While we have you," Nox said, her chair creaking a little under her as she shifted to glance out into the hall, like she was making sure no one was there to overhear, "we found out where the DNA came from in the Duchan case."

"And?" Quin asked, fingers twitching a little at his sides.

"The shirt," Nox said, handing Quin a tablet with a file already pulled up on it. "Mab's hair was on the shirt."

"The trouble is"—Nash wrinkled his nose—"the fury wasn't wearing a shirt when we showed up."

"No. She wasn't." And Quin knew deep in his gut Mab wouldn't have removed it. She'd hardly been able to look at the body, much less go near it to undress it. "Where did they find it?"

"The kitchen trash, it says. But . . . " Nox brushed some of her long, dark hair back from her face.

"*We* went through the kitchen trash ourselves," Nash finished for his sister.

"We have video of it."

Scrolling through the file, Quin drew his brows together. Something wasn't adding up. "Go through the footage again. If it wasn't there when you checked, then it wasn't there. Make sure you didn't miss it. If you didn't, run the footage through our authenticating software. I want to make sure they can't say you doctored it."

The twins nodded as one, then returned to their computers.

"Hello, children of mine," a warm voice said from the doorway.

Quin turned to see his dad standing there. Colt Schields held Tavi on his hip and smiled at them.

"Hey, Dad!" the twins chirped, their eyes staying focused on their screens, fingers clicking wildly over the keys.

Colt chuckled and met Quin's gaze. Tavi seemed to brighten as she caught sight of him, and her arms stretched out toward him.

He crossed the room to take the toddler out of his dad's arms and settle her on his hip. She quickly buried her face in his shoulder, snuggling into him like she was cold. Quin scratched her back gently between her wings, and a happy little murmur left her as she relaxed into him even more.

"What are you doing here?" he asked his dad.

"Tavi and I just came from youngling training. We were going over how to hold a bo staff."

Quin felt his chest tighten at the thought of little Tavi holding one of the child-sized staffs in her chubby little hands. He hated that he'd missed it and made a mental note to work with her on it one-on-one.

"How did that go?"

"Fairly well, though I may be losing my touch. A couple noggins got whacked before I could stop it." Colt's lips twitched with amusement, and his blue eyes sparkled.

Quin smirked. "You handed a group of kids a long stick, of course they're going to hit each other." His gaze dropped down to Tavi, who looked almost like she was going to fall asleep. "Did she like it?"

"She took to it quite well, actually. There was a spark in her eyes."

Quin looked up at his dad and felt a little smile tugging at his lips. "That's good."

Colt nodded. "It is. But that's not why I'm here. Tavi and I visited Mab this morning before class, which means you're up next for the afternoon shift."

Quin frowned. "I'm working."

"You can leave for an hour." He looked over Quin's shoulder to the twins hard at work. "Looks like you're information gathering right now, anyway."

It was true. But . . . small talk. "But what do I say to her?"

"Anything. That's the fun part about someone you don't know well. You have so much to talk about."

Quin shifted on his feet, tension tightening his muscles

as he thought of sitting down across from Mab in the cell and trying to make small talk. They weren't complete strangers, but even still. There had always been something in particular to discuss before. Or something happening that they could focus on.

Colt eyed him, seeming to read the apprehension in his body language. "Take your sketch pad with you." Quin's brow lifted in question. "You always get along with people better when you're able to focus on the paper before you and not the people around you."

Quin sighed. He had promised Max he would do this ...

Colt could see he was folding, because next he said, "Mab may not even want to talk much. Sometimes, just having another person there is enough. Plus, you can take Tavi." He nodded at the youngling in his arms. "She's a good distraction."

"What am I supposed to do with her once I come back up here?" Quin would have to get back to work eventually.

"Text me, I'll come and get her. Now, stop stalling and go." He held out Tavi's small backpack and pointed to the sketchpad that sat abandoned at his little work area off to the side of the room.

"Okay, okay. I'm going." He took the backpack, slinging it over his shoulder, and moved to grab the sketchpad. Tavi peered over her shoulder at Colt and wiggled her fingers.

"Coco will see you later, baby girl. Be good for Quin."

Hating the rigid feeling of anxiety in his bones, Quin carried Tavi down the halls and let them in through the security door with a swipe of the key card attached to his hip.

Inside, an ignis sat perched at the small desk that overlooked the cells. She looked up, nodding at him, then went back to the book in her hands. Security rounds were boring, especially when the inanimi in the cells were behaving themselves.

Quin picked up the pen that sat at the desk and filled his name in on the visitor's log. Dropping the pen, he moved past a number of empty cells and came to Mab's. There was a small wooden stool outside hers that someone had left there. Possibly his dad, maybe even Max.

As he lowered himself down onto the stool, stretching his cramped wings out a little, the wood creaked. Mab looked up, her brows lifting in surprise.

"They're even making *you* do this?" she muttered.

Quin dropped the backpack onto the floor beside him, along with the sketchpad, and shifted Tavi more properly into his lap. "Yeah," was all he said.

Tavi, to his surprise, perked up when she realized where they were. Gone were the droopy, sleep-filled eyes. Instead, a little smile flittered over her face, and she waved at Mab. This action took Mab's attention away from him, and instead, she focused on the youngling.

"Hey there. Didn't think I'd see you again so soon." Mab's voice was soft, the rough quality that was usually there becoming husky.

Tavi pushed against his chest so that she could wiggle back, then slid off his lap to the floor. Quin watched her step up to the cell and press her face between the bars. Her small arm extended, and she pointed at Mab. She pulled back and looked up at Quin. A tiny finger tapped at her forehead, then moved to her chest before she pointed at Mab once more.

Quin tilted his head to the side a little as he tried to understand her. "What?"

Once more, Tavi tapped her forehead and her chest before pointing at Mab.

"What is she saying?" Mab asked.

He looked over at her. "She's saying, me ... " He looked back down at Tavi, then at Mab again, before Tavi's meaning dawned on him. "I think she's saying that you're the same. You look like her."

Tavi's face broke into a grin, and she turned back to Mab, her hand extending again, little fingers opening and closing like she was attempting to reach Mab. Her little green wings with their purple primary feathers began to flutter quickly, which lifted her off the floor a little before she stopped and dropped back down to her feet.

Quin glanced over at Mab and found her smiling in a tender manner. "We do look alike, don't we, kiddo?"

He was surprised as he watched Mab get up off the bench and move to sit on the floor in front of Tavi. With her legs crossed beneath her, she leaned forward to rest her elbows on her knees and held out her hands.

Tavi stooped over, placing her tiny brown hands into Mab's upturned ones, and Quin found himself reaching instinctively for his sketchpad and pulling out the pencil he had stashed in the side of the backpack.

"Your hands are much smaller than mine," Mab murmured.

Tavi, in her quiet manner, only scrunched her fingers over Mab's palms, her wings fluttering again in happiness.

Flipping his sketchpad to an empty page, Quin quickly began to sketch out the sight of the two of them before him. Capturing the gentle light shining in Mab's eyes. The soft, approachable way her body leaned in toward the little girl, hands open in offering. His pencil caught the way Tavi's lips formed the perfect little bow of a smile, her dark brown eyes peering back at Mab in awe and interest.

"What're you doing over there Tall, Dark, and Frowny?" Mab's eyes flitted over to him quickly before she peered back at Tavi, who was reaching out to touch her face.

Quin opened his lips to tell Tavi no but stopped when Mab leaned in and let the little girl trace her fingers over her cheeks, across her brows, and pat lightly at her hair. He forgot for a moment that she had asked him a question, his hand even pausing as he simply watched this interaction between banshee and youngling. His fingers longed for a camera, to capture this moment so that he could pay it proper homage later, on canvas with charcoal and paint. He wondered if his mind would be enough to remember its beauty.

"Well?" Mab prodded, her eyes darting to him quickly, her face scrunching a little as small fingers tugged at a curl.

"Tavi," Quin was quick to say, his tone short. "No pulling hair, that's not nice. Even if you are just exploring."

Tavi's hand drew back, and she looked at him, eyes wide and lip wobbling a little.

Quin's heart clenched at the sight of it. "You're not in trouble," he was quick to soothe. "Just be gentle, okay?" Tavi sucked her bottom lip into her mouth and ran over to him, pressing herself into his side. He rubbed her head lightly and looked at Mab. "I was doing a sketch," he told her at last.

"Of?" she pressed.

Quin shifted, suddenly feeling put on the spot. "Tavi."

It wasn't entirely a lie. Tavi was in the picture. But so was Mab. While he wasn't usually shy about his work, Quin suddenly found himself feeling awkward at the thought of telling her he'd sketched her. He remembered the napkin she'd kept from that night in the bar.

Maybe it was because it was usually his family asking him about his portraits. Or someone he didn't know at all, so it didn't matter.

There was something different about Mab asking him.

Glancing down at the sketchpad, he saw that he had enough done that he could finish at home from memory, so he closed the sketchpad up quickly and set it aside. Lifting Tavi up, he settled her in his lap, cuddling her into his chest to offer her some added comfort.

"Do you sketch often?" she asked.

"It helps me think. And takes me out of what's going on around me."

Mab nodded. "Away from all the noise."

"Yeah." They peered at each other, falling silent for a moment. Quin was the first to break eye contact, looking down at Tavi. "How've they been treating you in here?"

"Oh, like I'm the queen." Mab climbed to her feet, brushing her pants off. She moved back to the bed and drew the blanket around herself.

"I'm sorry you're here."

She shrugged. "Story of my life."

"Do you . . . want to talk about before?" he asked carefully.

"No." It was simple and abrupt.

Quin nodded and fell silent. Maybe his dad was right. Maybe sometimes it was better to just be a presence nearby than to try and talk.

Tavi finally lifted her head from his chest. She sniffled a little but appeared to be okay. Her fingers moved to her hair, tugging on the small fro and then pointing at Mab.

Quin nodded, his own hands lifting to either side of his

head scrunching a little as he made circles to either side of it. "Curly hair," he said along with the sign. "Mab has curly hair like you do." He signed as he spoke, going slow so that she would have a chance to pick up on the motions. "You like that, don't you?"

Tavi's face split into a wide grin, and she managed a slightly mangled version of "curly hair" before pointing at Mab.

"Yeah, Mab has curly hair." He signed it out once more, and Tavi tried her best to sign "curly hair" back, then made an "m" before pointing at Mab. Quin copied her this time, and her grin became even bigger. "Is that her name now?"

"Um . . . what's my name?" Mab asked, a look of confusion on her face.

"In ASL, it's customary to create a specific sign for each person. It represents the person in some way. Essentially . . . yours is now Curly Hair M." He shrugged a little, watching her face closely for her reaction.

Mab chuckled and nodded her head. "Fair enough."

Tavi settled in against his chest now that they had decided that and seemed content to let him wrap his arms around her and draw her close. Quin relaxed a little with Tavi in his arms.

"Is there any word—" Mab paused. "On my case?"

Quin sighed, his shoulders tensing a little. "They found your DNA on the shirt belonging to the victim. According to Marius, it was stuffed in your trash."

"What?!" Mab rose swiftly to her feet. "I didn't take her shirt! Why would I take her shirt? That's just creepy and disturbing and *wrong*. Why would I do that?" Her voice rose more as she spoke.

He extended his hand to shoosh her a little, looking down the hall to see if the ignis on guard was looking their way. "I know you didn't. And Nash and Nox have video proof it wasn't in there. We're working on proving that the evidence was falsified."

"Falsified?" Mab lurched forward, wrapping her hands around the bars to press her face close to it. "You mean framed. Some piece of shit ignis is *framing* me." Her voice lowered to a growl as she spoke.

"Yes," Quin agreed. "Someone is framing you."

The question was, who did Orcus have inside the Miami-Feugo City sanctuary working for him?

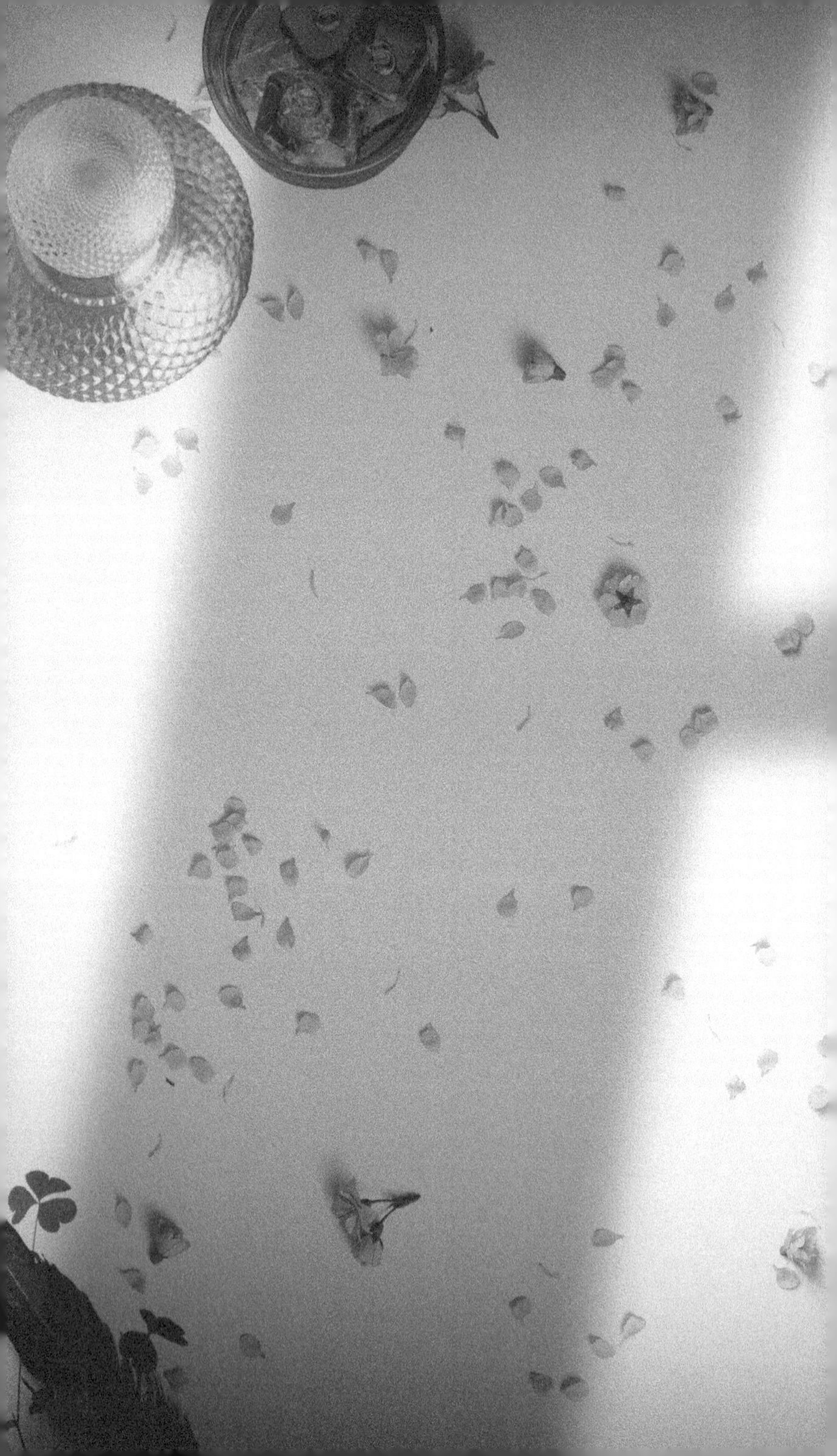

Chapter 19
Mab

The Schields hadn't left her alone for more than a few hours at a time for the last couple of days. It was . . . weird. But also weirdly nice. She wondered who she had to thank for the added attention, Ander or Max. Maybe a combination of the two.

The visits weren't enough to chase away the night terrors—nothing could do that, not when the lights were dimmed and there was no one to distract her from the way the walls seemed to press in too close around her. Maybe she should have taken her own advice and seen someone about it. But she and Ander both would need a therapist who wasn't a normie. Because really, imagine telling a normie that hundreds of years ago she'd been locked in an asylum because some bastard raped her and she reported him. That'd go down *so* well. She'd probably find herself locked up again.

Either way, the days were distinctly better now that she wasn't alone all day. The thought that someone was actively trying to frame her for the murder of the fury haunted her. The why behind it—although as of yet unclear—dredged up even more memories from her time before the asylum. Blamed once more for something that had not been her fault or doing.

Thankfully, there was a parade of Schields family members during visiting hours and meals, swapping out every time so she didn't eat with the same person twice in a row. Colt—who she'd never met before but was hard not to like—and the twins. Quin and Tavi. And even—

"*Ezekiel.*" Mab narrowed her eyes at the man outside her cell door. He was holding Tavi in front of him almost like she was a shield, and there was another girl at his side, her bright pink wings ruffled a little by Mab's tone.

"Duchan," Zeke returned the greeting, his lips curling a little around the syllables of her name. "I'd like to say it's a pleasure to see you again, but that would be a lie, wouldn't it?"

"Papa," the girl at his side chided as Tavi made a small noise of complaint and reached for Mab. "Dad said you have to be nice."

"Yes, well, Georgie, what your father doesn't know won't—"

"Hi there, Tavi," Mab grinned, ignoring Zeke entirely as she made her way over to the bars to offer the little girl her hands again. Tavi's wings fluttered, smacking Zeke in the face, and he grumbled softly before finally putting her on her feet. Mab knelt to be at her level. "You're becoming a regular around here, little miss."

Tavi smiled back at her, not seeming to get the joke, but she reached through the bars to put her hands in Mab's anyway. Both she and Mab ignored Georgie and Zeke as they bickered back and forth. Mab couldn't explain it, didn't want to, but she found Tavi's presence more than any seemed to keep her mind off things. It was easy to forget the cell and the screams when she was trying to figure out what the little girl was thinking based on the movement of her wings and her facial expressions alone.

"Where's your daddy? Hm? He's much better company than *some* people," Mab drawled, her eyes flicking up to Zeke, who was sharing a look with Georgie she didn't think she wanted to understand. The Schields were an interesting lot, but Georgie and Zeke especially confused her. Probably because she hadn't seen enough of them to know how their minds worked yet. "What?"

"Do you need anything?" Zeke asked as if changing the subject, and Mab stilled entirely, her eyes going wide as she turned to look up at him. "Don't look at me like that, Duchan. I'm serious, do you need anything down here? I know Ruin has brought you books and things, but if there is anything I can get you . . . " He shifted on the stool, the wood creaking a little under him. "I'd be happy to help."

Mab raised her brow at the word *happy* but shook her head. "They won't let me keep much down here with me anyway. Ander brought me a lamp a couple of days ago, but they confiscated it because of the glass bulb."

"He got you another one, I see," Georgie said, nodding to the little battery-powered one with the plastic bulb she'd set on top of her stack of books. It wasn't as bright as the first, but it would do. And anything was better than being alone in the dark at night.

"Yeah." Mab shrugged. "I'm Mab, by the way," she said, pulling a hand away from where Tavi was tapping her fingertips against Mab's own to wave. "I don't think we've met, not properly, anyway. You're the baby of the Schields family, right?"

"Georgette. Georgie." She grinned back at Mab. "I've

heard a lot about you. Or rather . . . your bar." Her bright green eyes cut to Zeke, who visibly winced.

"None of it good, I'm sure." Mab smirked a little, then looked back at Tavi when the little girl tapped her wrist to get her attention again. "What's up, buttercup?"

Tavi leaned in closer, reaching for Mab's hair, and Mab tilted her head to put it closer so Tavi could reach.

"Be easy though, right? Remember what Daddy said? No tugging. Right?" Mab kept her tone carefully gentle, hoping not to make Tavi feel like she was in trouble like the other day. There was no harm in the little girl playing with her hair, she just had to learn not to pull on it. "Gentle."

Tavi scrunched up her nose a little, her wings rustling behind her as if she was thinking about it, then she nodded and held her hand out again, reaching for Mab's hair. Mab let her run her fingers through it, tugging lightly at the curls to watch them spring back into place after she'd let go.

"You're good with her," Zeke said.

Mab shrugged. "I've always liked kids. And she's way calmer than some of the muse babies." Not that Mab didn't like the muse babies too, but they tended to be rambunctious and loud. Mab didn't think she was equipped to deal with all that right now. She was just barely holding herself together, she didn't have the energy to calm down a bouncing toddler. "They're always really cute, but they're little hellions."

"That explains so much about Ruin." Zeke chuckled softly.

"Yeah, it does." Mab couldn't help but laugh a little herself. "But I imagine having a bunch of flying babies isn't any easier. This one in particular"—she nodded her head toward Georgie, who made a face like she was affronted—"seems like she'd be trouble."

"Excuse you?" Georgie asked, her eyes impossibly wide. "I'll have you know, I'm the best of all of us. Way better than—"

"Ander told me about you trying to record them when he and Max were a part of the family meeting. Don't play innocent with me, kiddo." Mab snickered softly. "Tell your Auntie Georgie she's not fooling anyone with that act, Tavi." Mab leaned forward again to grin wide at Tavi, her tone going silly as she made a face at her. "Right?"

Tavi's eyes widened for a moment as if she was unsure, then she giggled, the sound so soft, Mab almost didn't hear it. Mab's mouth dropped open a little in awe. She didn't think she'd ever heard anything so sweet.

"You like the funny faces, huh?" Mab asked, still a little starstruck by the fact she'd gotten Tavi to make a sound at all when thus far, she'd been completely silent. She blew out her cheeks, then sucked them in again to make a fish face.

Tavi giggled again, her eyes scrunching in joy, and Mab found herself laughing too. It was hard not to. When she looked back at Zeke and Georgie, they were smiling at her.

"What?" she asked, wrinkling her nose a little.

"Nothing." Zeke shook his head. "So, Quin's been down here to see you?"

"Everyone has." Mab leaned back on her hands so she could look up at Zeke and Georgie without craning her neck so much. "It's been . . . " She bit her lip in thought. "Nice. So, thank you for this."

Zeke frowned a little, shaking his head. "Don't do that."

"Do what? Say thank you?"

"We don't do 'thank you' in this family," Georgie said with a shrug as she bent to help Tavi pull a book from her little backpack.

This family. The words hung heavy in the air between them, hovering over Mab's head like a guillotine. Surely they didn't mean it the way they said it. She shook herself. "Fine. I take it back, then."

"You can buy us all a round when you get out of here," Zeke suggested instead. "Well, all of us except Georgie, she's still a baby."

"Am not," Georgie huffed.

"Sure you are. You're my itsy bitsy wittle—"

Georgie groaned and swatted Zeke lightly with her wing. "Stop it."

"Stop what?" Zeke gasped, holding his chest. "Are you saying you don't love your Papa anymore? But Georgie, you were my favorite!"

"I was definitely not, that's Nox." Georgie scoffed, and Mab couldn't help but laugh a little at the gentle ribbing. "And what're you laughing at? Hmm?"

Mab quirked a brow, her grin ticking farther up her face. "How old are you, anyway, bubblegum? Twelve?"

"Bubblegum?!" Georgie squawked, her wings spreading out behind her and blocking Mab's view of Zeke, who was definitely snickering.

"Oh, I like that one. Can I borrow it?" Zeke asked, poking his head around the edge of Georgie's wing.

"Have at it." Mab shrugged and shot a wink at Tavi, who had been watching the three of them banter back and forth like it was a very rousing game of tennis for the last few minutes.

"You know, I didn't come down here for you two to gang up on me," Georgie grumbled, dropping to the floor, her arms crossed over her chest. Then she scoffed, "Old people."

"Georgette!" Zeke gasped so hard, he fell off his stool.

Then everyone was laughing again as Zeke scrambled back onto it, including Tavi, who may or may not have gotten the joke but seemed to find her grandfather's dramatics funny all the same.

"What in the name of the gods is going on down here?" a voice barked, breaking through the laughter, and the little group all stilled. Tavi's eyes widened in fear, and she ducked herself behind Georgie's wings, hidden from the male coming their way. He was a tall, tan ignis with dirty-blond hair and dusty-blue wings that he had spread behind him as if to make himself look bigger and scarier upon his approach.

Neither Zeke nor Georgie seemed particularly afraid of him, so Mab didn't bother rising from where she'd settled when she was talking to Tavi. The man seemed to clock it as the slight it was because his mouth twitched with distaste when he looked at her. Or maybe he was just an asshole, there was really no way to tell.

"Galeo," Zeke said jovially, pushing up from the stool where he'd been perched a moment ago. "How nice of you—"

"You didn't answer the question, Schields." Galeo narrowed his eyes on Zeke the way someone might look at a particularly annoying little dog, and suddenly, a lot of things clicked into place. This was the guy who Quin and Max reported to. The one she'd gotten the feeling wasn't overly fond of them. So . . . an asshole, then. "What is going on down here? Are you . . . *visiting* with the suspect?"

Mab flinched at the word *suspect*. It was easy to forget that someone was actively trying to frame her when she was surrounded by people who seemed to care for her. Not entirely, because she was still behind bars after all, but it had been pushed to the back of her mind in favor of spending time with the parade of Schields family members that came down to keep her company.

Zeke seemed to sense something about the tone of Galeo's voice that Mab must have missed, because instead of readily acknowledging that that's what he'd been doing, he scoffed. "Visiting a suspect? No, of course not. I was just picking Georgie up from training, and we got a little turned around!" He laughed, the sound forced, even to Mab's ears. "Isn't that right, Georgette?"

Georgie just nodded, her hands moving to brush against Tavi's hair as if to soothe the little girl clearly upset by the confrontational body language of Galeo.

"You wouldn't happen to know how we can get back to the—"

"Bullshit," Galeo hissed.

"Fine." Zeke flicked his eyes back to Mab, and he offered her a little half smile, as if maybe he was trying to comfort her too. It was only then that Mab realized how her hands were fisted in the pair of sweatpants she was wearing, her jaw tense, ready for a fight. "We were visiting. Mab and I go way back. Don't we, Mab? Being club owners in the Miami scene, you know how it is. We're colleagues of a fashion. Right?"

"Right." The word felt heavy in Mab's throat, but she forced it out. She didn't particularly want Galeo looking at her, and already, she was too exposed sitting there in the middle of her cell with nothing to hide behind. But moving would reveal that weakness, and she was not about to be seen as *weak*.

"There? See? Just visiting a friend. Surely you can't—"

"And you brought a *youngling* down here?" Galeo's tone dipped a little lower, something dangerous glinting in his eyes. Then he seemed to make his mind up about something, tilted his head to the side, and his mouth ticked up at the corners in a cold, cruel smile. "Very well. Continue on with your visit with your *friend*, Schields. Don't let me stop you. But bear in mind, I might not be *your* superior, but I am the superior of everyone else in your family. And Colton Schields isn't the only one capable of training younglings."

Zeke flinched at the words but made a show of settling back on his stool and turning away from Galeo as if unbothered, even though Mab could see a tightness around his eyes. Which just seemed to piss Galeo off more, because a moment later, he spun around and left them alone at last. Mab wondered why he'd even come down there. Was it just to berate Zeke and Georgie for visiting her? Or had there been another reason?

"So, that guy, am I right?" Zeke asked a moment later, his lips turning up into a mischievous smile that was so like Ander's, it made Mab smile back out of reflex.

"Mutual nemesis?"

"Oh, definitely." Zeke nodded gravely.

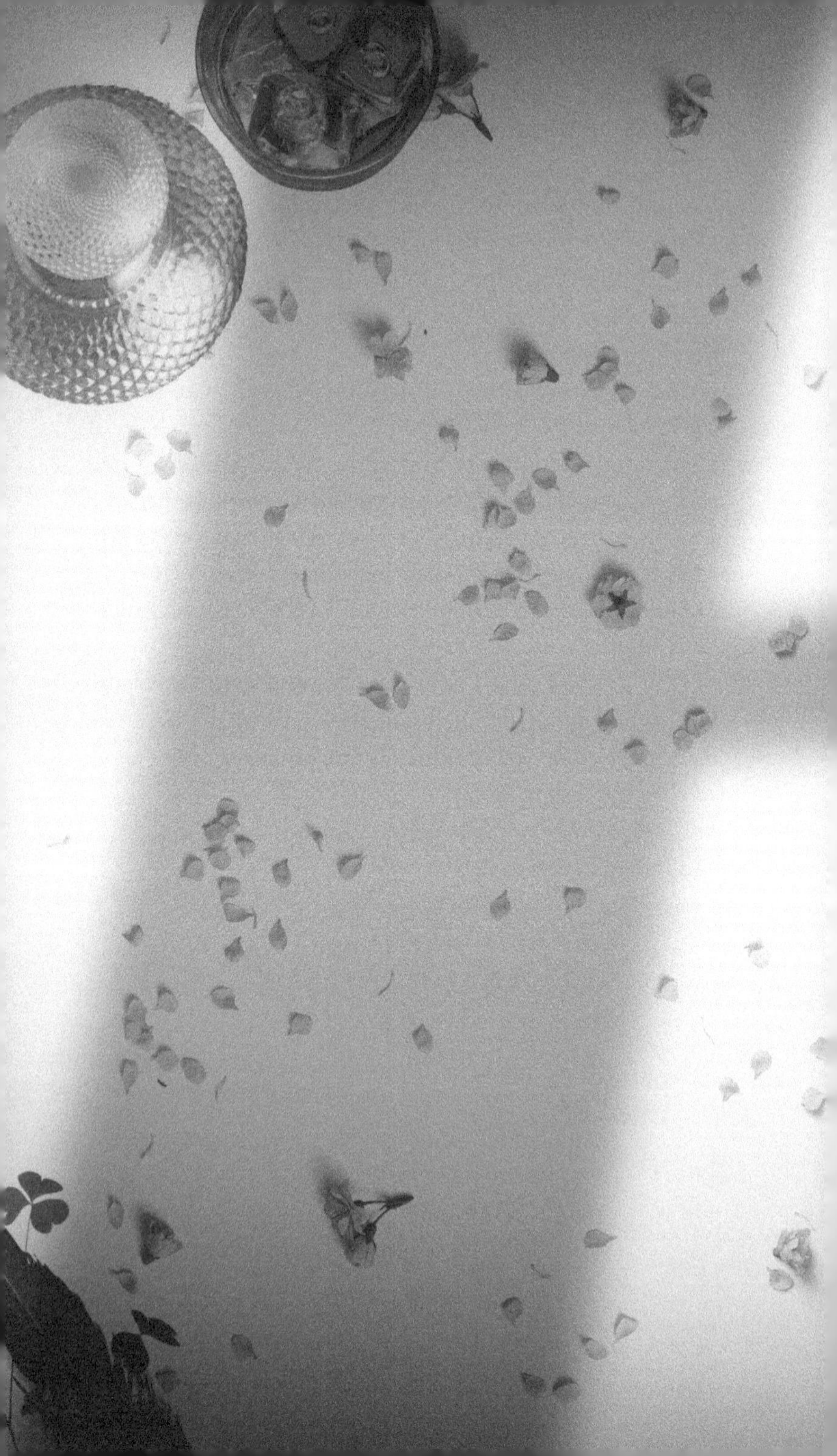

Chapter 20
Quin

"Captain wants to see you. *All* of you," Borialis said from the doorway before disappearing down the hall just as quickly as he'd come.

They had only just arrived for their morning shift. Max was still in the process of pulling on one of his sanctuary sweaters and the twins in the middle of booting up their computers.

"Again?" Quin grumbled. He'd spent far more time in Galeo's office lately than he'd have liked.

"And *all* of us?" Nox looked over at Nash as if to ask him what they had done that she couldn't remember.

"I'm really starting to think that man is in love with us," Nash quipped as he stood up, stretching.

"Let's just get this over with," Max ordered, fixing the collar of his sweater and buttoning the flap that fell between his wings down near his waistline.

Together, the four of them shuffled out of their command center and headed down the hall. It felt ominous, their entire team heading to Galeo's office to meet with him. It was rarely a good thing, and since he'd been pissy with them lately, Quin couldn't imagine this meeting boded well for any of them. Quin prepared himself for another announcement that would only add to the annoyance of their day or prove how much their captain actually despised them.

Galeo sat behind his desk, a stormy look on his face. Dark eyes narrowed, and his lips pinched tight. Quin's back stiffened, already feeling defensive about whatever their captain was about to get on them for.

"So," he began without greeting. "The four of you—and your entire family, might I add—have not stayed away from the Duchan case as ordered. Instead, you've been taking shifts to visit her throughout the day." He said it like he expected them to deny it, his eyes shifting between them all, making a point of making eye contact with each.

"We're not involved with the case, Captain. We haven't touched it, like you ordered. We've just been visiting Duchan to keep her company while she's down there," Max explained. "Seeing as how you haven't released her with a tracking cuff yet."

"Duchan is a flight risk with too many known associates who could help her disappear."

"That's ridiculous," Quin cut in. Something inside him swelled protectively, needing to defend her. To fight for Mab when it didn't seem anyone else could. "Ander Ruin was released with a cuff in the exact same circumstance."

Galeo's eyes narrowed on him, then shifted to Max. "Yes, and he shouldn't have been. That was a decision made by this team."

In other words, another tick against them.

"Tell me, is participating in visitation hours something you do for all murder suspects?" Galeo asked, a brow lifting as he continued to glare at them.

"Well, no—" Max began.

"It seems to me that your entire family is more concerned with what is happening with one inanimi than doing your job protecting the mortals of this city." His face grew stormier, if that was possible, but there was almost a hint of glee behind the rage. As if he was delighted that he was finally able to reprimand the entire Schields family. "And since none of you want to do what you're here to do, I'm suspending the lot of you for a week."

"What?" the twins squawked in unison.

"But, sir—" Max began.

"It's final," Galeo cut him off.

Quin remained silent, doing his best to keep his face neutral while his insides slowly filled up with rage. Their captain didn't care about finding justice. He didn't care about listening to the ones who knew. He didn't even seem to care that this was a special case because it involved an escaped god who was likely out to get all of them, Galeo included.

His hands tightened into fists at his sides, and Quin forced himself to stare at Galeo's forehead instead of into his face. If he actually met his gaze, Quin would be exposing all of his inner feelings through his eyes. He knew he would. Instead, he went into that protective shell that had kept him safe when he was a child. The neutrality in his features that had kept him from showing any of his emotions. It hid his fear when he was facing an enemy much larger than himself back then, and it would hide his fury now.

"I don't want to see nor hear anything of you in this building for seven days."

"What about our current case? We just tracked down Donovan's closest relatives in Feugo that we think might be helping to traffic in the diaboli fruit. Max and Quin were just about to bring them in for questioning!" Nox blurted out.

Galeo's eyes narrowed on her. "Your case has been handed over to Borialis and Kato."

Nox's shoulders sagged a touch, and she nodded. Beside her, Nash huffed. Quin knew that he hated the fact all of their hard work was now being handed off to someone else and none of the credit would be laid where it was due.

"If I catch any of you inside this sanctuary for any reason during your suspension—and that *includes* your inanimi boyfriend, Maximus—you will all be grounded. Understood?"

"Yes, sir," Max said, and the rest of them followed suit.

"Now, get your things and get out." Galeo straightened up and grabbed a file, clearly dismissing them.

As a unit, they turned and left the office. All of them were silent for a moment, the weight of the situation settling over them.

"What is the human version of being grounded?" Nash muttered at last.

"Shut up," Nox hissed.

"No, but seriously. Will he take our toes?"

Quin rolled his eyes, but it was Max who answered. "He'll take your clearances. You'd be stuck doing menial things like filing."

"Oh *gods*," Nash said, horrified.

Being grounded, on the other hand, was an ignis' worst nightmare. When one of them truly screwed up, the punishment had to fit the crime in the Sanctum's opinion. So, the primary feathers at the tip of their wings were clipped. This kept their flight mobility to a minimum. No taking off, no sustained flight, only gliding if they managed to get to a place high enough where they could, effectively grounding them.

They would grow back, but only once the ignis was given permission to pluck the clipped feathers. Even then, there would be no flight for another six months at least while the feathers grew back.

Ignis bodies healed quickly, but their feathers were the one thing that took some time to restore themselves. Prometheus had been sadistic with that little detail.

The remainder of their journey into the command center was quiet. The twins moved to shut down their computers, and Max unbuttoned his sweater to peel it off and return it to his office.

Quin watched them, feeling the weight of this move against their family heavily. Each of them had trained all of their lives to be a part of the Sanctum. They lived and breathed this life, believing fully in protecting those who could not protect themselves. Yet they were looked down on by others because their parents also instilled them with a sense of caring. They raised them as a family rather than just as warriors.

He turned to pack up the few items on his small desk that he didn't want to leave behind for a week and met Max, who was just coming out of his office, a small satchel with a few things over his shoulder.

Max looked crestfallen. "You okay?" Quin asked.

"How am I supposed to tell Ander that we're being forced to abandon Mab in here?"

"This isn't your fault, Max. This is out of your control," Quin tried to console him.

"I know, but all he's going to know is that his sister is being left alone in a place that is filled with trauma for her. And now there's nothing I can do about it." Max scrubbed a hand over his face and ran it back through his wayward dark locks that were always a little bit of a mess.

Apparently, out of the two of them, Quin was the one who had inherited their Papa's penchant for being fully styled at all times.

"We can do something about it." Quin pressed his hand to Max's shoulder. "We'll use this time away from the Sanctum to prove that Mab is innocent."

Max's eyes perked up a little at this.

"Exactly," Nox agreed, stepping up to them. "Now we've got more time to look into Mab's case, and also to hunt down that jackass, Enrique." A *ding* sounded out in the room, and all three of them turned to look at Nash, who made a small noise of excitement. "What?" Nox prompted her twin.

Nash, who had been staring at the screen of his phone, looked up at them and grinned broadly. "Nox is actually right, we *do* finally have the time to work on finding Enrique, and I just got a lead." He flashed them the screen of his phone, showing the notification that had shown up on its surface.

"What is it?" Max asked, some of the stress leaving his face at this news.

Quin looked around them quickly, then held up his hand before any of his siblings could say anything. "Let's get out of here before anyone comes to see what's taking us so long and overhears."

Max nodded. "Right. Come on. We can talk about this once we're home."

There was no need to say any more. The four Schields siblings left the sanctuary quickly, not speaking to anyone on the way out in their hurry to discuss the latest matter at hand. Fortunately, their suspension was seen as reason enough for this, and no one even tried to stop them.

They sat around the dining room table, Zeke out on an errand Colt had sent him on when Zeke's ire at their suspension threatened to be too much of a distraction from their work. Colt, in his typical calm fashion, asked what they needed from him to make it all easier. The twins, as was to be expected of them, asked for hot coffee and snacks.

Quin held his arm out for Tavi, keeping it firmly in place so that she could clutch his hand to steady herself as she worked on keeping herself afloat with her wings. Spending so much time in the cages Orcus and his henchmen had held her in had seriously affected her time to practice and develop wing strength. Quin tried to spend as much time as he could working on it with her each day.

"Okay, now that we're in a safe space, what is this notification about?" Max, to his credit, had held back his impatience as long as he could. But Quin could tell he was chomping at the bit to get moving on this.

Nash plopped down in a dining chair and opened up his laptop. "Back when we were searching for King Dipshit under the name Timoris, we came across a few other names that we thought might be connected to his trafficking ring. The names only ever led to dead ends. Things that were over and facilities obviously long abandoned, even by the ring. But I kept a bug alive out in the dark web for them, just in case." Nash's blue eyes sparkled with pride over his own cleverness. "Orcus knows we're aware of his aliases. So clearly, he can't use Enrique or Timoros, so he either needs a new one or to use an unknown contact to do his dirty work for him. *And—*"

"One of those old contacts has popped up again," Max finished for him.

Nash sent him a withering look—a direct rip-off of their papa's own—as Max stole his thunder. "Yes. It did."

"Which one?" Nox asked, her own laptop sounding as it booted up.

"Lucius Seneca."

Quin frowned. "Why does that name sound familiar?"

The twins snorted at the same time and looked up from their screens to peer at him. Sometimes, their uncanny connection was disturbing.

"He was a famous first century Roman philosopher," Nash began.

"Who was exiled by Claudius but then brought back to tutor Nero," Nox continued.

"And became his advisor, helping to run the government until he was accused of trying to overthrow Nero," Quin finished off, his lessons in Roman philosophy finally coming back to him.

A dawning tingle began at the base of Quin's skull, sweeping up behind his ears and into his face. His eyes met Max's, and together they both said, "It's Enrique."

"Huh?" the twins asked.

"Lucius Seneca—it's not just a contact, it's another alias of Orcus'." The worry in Max's eyes had turned to fire now that they had a definite lead.

"How do you know?" Nash asked.

"Think of the story. Brilliant man, undervalued by most, right hand to a powerful ruler who he then tries to take down?" Quin replied.

Nash scoffed. "Maybe he'll take another page out of Seneca's book and end his life in his disgrace."

"Enrique's too proud to give up yet, he's not the type to learn his lesson and move on." Max had begun to pace back and forth across the dining room.

Quin, noticing that Tavi was getting tired, lowered her to the ground and encouraged her to go over to her play area, where Colt had set up blocks, dolls, trucks and other items for her to have fun with.

"Especially not with an entire ignis army at his disposal, which no one has located yet," Quin muttered.

"Of course." Max stopped pacing. "He's freshly escaped, whoever he has working for him in the Sanctum has proven their loyalty in helping him get out. No one knows where he is . . . It's the perfect time to mobilize his army and prepare an attack."

"Then what was the point of framing Mab?" Quin frowned, not seeing why he would bother to take the time to do that when he clearly had much grander plans.

"Distraction," Nash piped up. They all looked at him in surprise. And he shrugged. "What? It's a perfect battle strategy. Who worked the hardest to find him and put him away last time?" His finger swept the room to indicate all of them. "Who has a boyfriend who's magical and royally connected?" This time he pointed at Max. "Who has the most to lose if he stays free?" Once again, he indicated all of them in the room.

Several curse words slipped out of Max's mouth that had all of their brows shooting up in surprise. A tiny squawk released from Tavi in the corner, and Max's face turned bright red as he remembered, only too late, that there was a youngling in the room.

Quin shot him a glare, and Max mouthed, "Sorry," before he moved on.

"You're right, Nash." Their little brother beamed at this. "Enrique wanted us distracted with Mab so that he could scheme unhindered."

"Then let's use this week to find him," Quin stated.

Max nodded, then looked at Nox and Nash. "We're counting on you."

The twins saluted just before their fingers hit the keys, and their real work began.

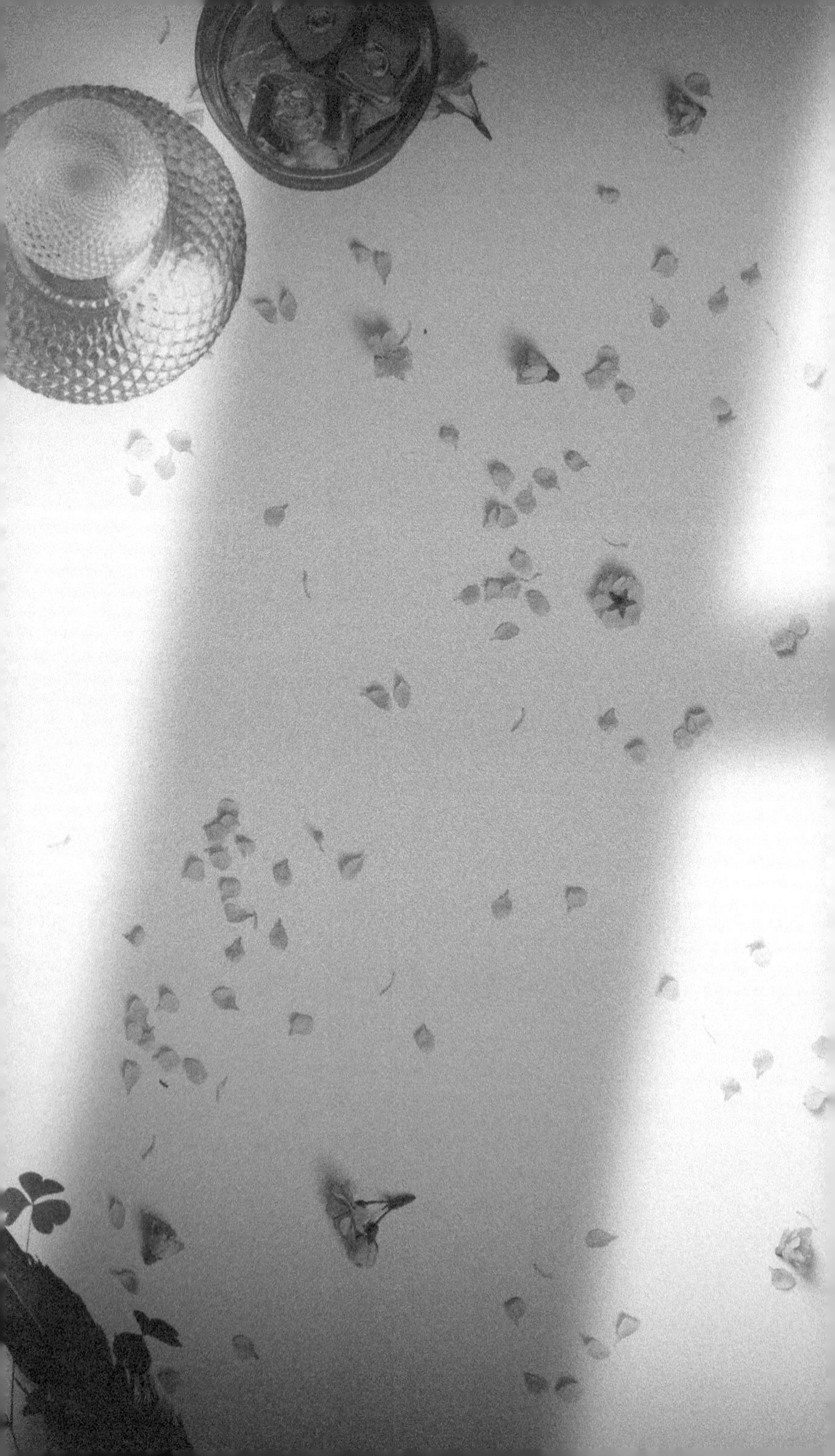

Chapter 21
Mab

Breakfast came and went.

Lunch, too, passed without any sign of the Schields.

And by the time it was supper, Mab knew something was wrong. They wouldn't just leave her like this, surely. Not without a word or a note or anything. Something had happened. They'd gotten into trouble. One of them had gotten hurt while on a mission. Enrique had attacked. *Something* had happened, and she'd been left down there in the cells.

Alone. In the cells.

The walls inched in a little closer, and Mab hunched her shoulders to make herself smaller. The walls had closed in with every passing hour she spent there alone. And although she knew it was her imagination, she couldn't turn it off.

"It's the same size," she told herself as the walls scooted another half a foot closer.

"Stop it," she chided, and she felt them loom taller around her, threatening to crush her under their weight.

"I said, knock it off!" Even with the blanket wrapped

tightly around her and the pillow over her head, Mab couldn't seem to ignore the way the space was becoming tighter and tighter. Gods, she couldn't *breathe*. Something was sitting on her chest, crushing her lungs beneath the weight of it, and she couldn't fucking breathe. She was going to suffocate in here. Curled up on a cot in a cell surrounded by cement on all sides.

The lights went out, signaling that a whole day had passed without anyone to visit her, and Mab steeled herself against the screams that came with the night as the room around her disappeared entirely and she was buried in the dark.

It was like a tomb. A mausoleum. And it would be where Mab Duchan, the banshee, the lady of the manor, met her end. A place for the lost and the abandoned.

"They didn't abandon you. Stop being dramatic."

Didn't they?

If they didn't abandon her, where *were* they? They didn't just forget that she was down here. No. They had left her here. Left her behind. Ander too, it seemed, had given up on her. And why shouldn't they? What did she provide to any of them? She was just a burden. Hadn't she proven that over the last week? She was *weak*.

"That's a lie. They wouldn't do that. I'm part of the family, they said so." She sucked in a breath, tightened her fists, and tried to fight against the thoughts, but they came just the same.

Ander had Max now, he didn't need her companionship. He'd found his soulmate. Something she'd never have because the ignis she'd been tied to was probably Quin. And even if they weren't? What were the chances she'd ever find them? Well. None now that she was probably going to be executed for a murder she didn't commit. But without that? Without the guillotine hanging above her head? Why would they *want* her? She had nothing to offer them. No bright smiles. No charm. She was just . . . Mab. And no one wanted just Mab.

Clearly. As everyone had left her.

"They didn't!"

She sniffled, scrubbing at her face. When had she started crying? *Why* had she started crying? Wasn't this where she'd known she'd always end up? Hadn't Bartlett proven that to her once upon a time? That this was the end she deserved. This was where she belonged. Buried beneath the earth, forgotten.

A chill settled into her bones, and Mab buried her wet face in her pillow, almost thankful once the screams hit a fever pitch. At least then she couldn't hear her own thoughts anymore. At least then she couldn't think about how no one cared for her. No one wanted her. No one loved her. And now she'd die before even knowing what the bond felt like blooming painfully in her chest.

And there she was mourning—stupidly—a thing she'd always said she didn't even *want*.

The lights kicked on, brighter than before, it seemed, burning Mab's eyes. It hadn't been an entire night, had it? Or had she just . . . disassociated the whole time? Well. It wouldn't be the first time. But it might be the last.

"Get up, Duchan," an ignis called through the bars.

When she didn't move, they snarled, muttering curses under their breath that she was thankfully too tired to hear. Oh. Or maybe it was the fact that she still had the pillow shoved so hard against her ears, they were aching. That could be it too. Mab made the mental effort to unclench her fingers one by one until the pillow fell away from her head.

Not that it mattered. A moment later, the ignis grabbed her by the wrist and ripped her from the cot.

"Weren't you *listening*?" they hissed. "Your trial is in a few minutes. Make yourself presentable."

"My—My trial?" Mab's head spun. "But it's only been a week! Tops! The investigation can't be over. It *can't*." Was she begging? She felt like she was begging, but the voice that came out of her mouth didn't really sound like her own anymore. She couldn't remember what her own voice sounded like, actually.

"It is." The ignis brushed her off, moving away from her as if her mere proximity would sully them. "Now get cleaned up. You'll go before the judge in a half hour."

"What about the Schields family? They were looking into—"

"The Schields family is not looking into anything for *you*," the ignis snarled.

Mab's heart stopped beating in her chest before it kicked up again, thundering against her ribcage. They *had* abandoned her. They'd left her alone in here, and now they were leaving her to die. Just like Edward.

"What about a lawyer? Surely I'm supposed to have someone speak on my behalf? I haven't had any counsel." None of this seemed right. All of it too rushed. Forced. Pushed along without following procedure so Mab could be hidden away forever.

Forgotten.

"I said, get ready." They stared at each other, neither moving. "Fine. If you're not going to take the time, let's just get this over with." The ignis' hand tightened around her wrist, grip hot as a brand. Mab was sure there would be blisters left behind, scars, if she lived long enough for them to become that.

"Let me go!" Mab struggled against the hold, but she was weak, so *weak*. She always had been, hadn't she? She'd always needed saving. That's why no one wanted her. That's why they'd abandoned her, left her to rot. Who would want someone as weak as her at their side? No wonder her soulmate had never surfaced.

The ignis didn't answer. They just dragged her along, her feet skidding against the floor. She thrashed. She pulled. She struggled. But nothing would slow their progress to wherever they were going. And soon, the dark wooden door that must have led to the courtroom loomed like a black hole, threatening to suck her in and leave her floating in the dark.

"I said, let me go! I don't want to go in there! Take me back to my cell! Let me rot there! I don't care! Just don't make me—"

But the door opened, and she was shoved through, and it was just like the last time.

All eyes were on her. Their gazes heavy and grating. Mab's shoulders stiffened, then curled in further to make her smaller. Maybe she could make herself small enough that they wouldn't even be able to see her. Maybe she could make herself so small that she'd just disappear entirely. That would be better than facing whatever came next.

The ignis didn't stop. They dragged her up the main aisle and deposited her in a caged-off box at the front of the room. Right where everyone could see her. Could watch as she unraveled.

Mab curled further in on herself, ducking her head into her knees. She couldn't watch this. Not again. Her hands moved to her ears, to block out the noise of the courtroom. Not that she could hear anything very well with how hard her heart was pounding in her chest. Everything was swimming. The room. The voices. Like she was under water. Drowning.

She tried to suck down another breath, but all she wound up doing was choking on it.

Gods. Mab was going to die in this courtroom before they even dragged her away to be executed, wasn't she?

Tears stung her eyes, making it somehow *harder* to breathe around a sob.

And just when Mab thought the weight of all those eyes on her would crush her. Just when it felt like water was filling her lungs. Just when she was sure she'd die on the spot . . .

The doors to the courtroom crashed open, banging loudly against the walls on either side.

Mab flinched, and her ears rang.

"Queen—Queen Aemiliana!" someone sputtered. "To what do we owe the—"

Mab's head jerked up, eyes wide. Aemiliana? What was she doing here? And . . . Ander! Andy was here. And behind him, big dark wings spread wide enough to make him appear larger than life, an angel of vengeance, was Quin. They were . . . were they here to help her?

"Someone had better tell me very quickly why you have my daughter in a cage," Aemiliana said, her voice sharp. Mab didn't think she'd ever heard the queen sound so angry.

"Your daughter?" It was the judge. The judge was the one asking the questions, her face shell-shocked at the appearance of Underworld royalty.

"Yes. My daughter. I demand you release her this *instant.*"

"Andy?" Mab asked, her voice small and choked and rasping. It grated coming up, like she'd swallowed glass. But nothing could hurt her now that Ander and Aemiliana were there. They would get her out of this. They would help her.

"Mab!" Ander rushed across the courtroom, ignoring all attempts to stop him. "Mabbers, are you all right?"

"No." She shook her head. She wasn't going to lie to him. She couldn't. Besides, he had to see that she wasn't. "I'm not okay."

Ander nodded, his hand slipping through the bars to grasp her fingers. "Don't worry. We're going to get you out of here."

"How?" It seemed impossible. If the Schields hadn't been able to find enough evidence to free her, how would Aemiliana, who had probably only just heard about the case the day before? And why would the ignis listen to her anyway? She was a queen, yes, but she was also an inanimi. How far would her word even stretch?

"You can't just come in here and demand we release a murderer," the judge said sternly, leaning forward as if trying to impart some serious wisdom to Aemiliana.

She did not look at all impressed. "What proof do you have that Mab is guilty of this crime?"

"Well, the victim was found on her private prop—"

"The victim could have been led there by anyone. Next." Aemiliana waved her hand, brushing the argument aside.

"It was clearly a banshee—"

"What? And Mab is the only banshee in the United States? And even if she were, she's not the only one who has access to a portal to this area, is she?" Aemiliana crossed her arms over her chest.

"We found DNA from Duchan on the body." The judge lifted her chin as if this were some kind of victory, and Mab's stomach dropped.

Quin stepped forward, his shoulders tight as he slipped a thin folder across the podium to the judge. "The tech first on the scene took their own samples. These are the results." He flipped the folder open to point to a page at the top. "You'll see here there was no DNA at all found on the body at the time. Likewise, the shirt the DNA was found on was not at the scene. The report from the primary ignis said it was in the kitchen trash, but the techs in charge of the kitchen have video footage of them going through the trash, and there was no shirt found during their search. If you need the techs' credentials, those would be on the last page. They're highly competent and have an extensive record of closing cases." He picked up the paper and moved it aside to reveal another page beneath. "These are witness statements from all neighbors within a mile radius—the radius estimated that a banshee wail would have been heard. No one heard anything that night. Not even Duchan's closest neighbors. Even with silencing magic, those closest would have heard something, but there was nothing."

"So, from what I'm hearing"—Aemiliana tilted her head, one dark brow raised high on her face—"all of the evidence you have is either purely circumstantial or proof that Mab was framed for this."

"Your Majesty, I can assure you, the Sanctum is an honorable body which would not stoop to falsifying evidence. And we are speaking of a defendant with plenty of history—"

"History?" Aemiliana's eyes darkened, and a hardness settled over her features that chilled Mab a little, making her very happy it wasn't directed at her. The queen of Helicon took a step forward, her armed guards that flanked her taking one unified step behind her as Quin slipped out of the way to allow her to face down the judge head-on.

"My daughter has *no* history of violence toward another being, let alone murder. What I see here is a case of prejudice and a Sanctum which feels no need to prove guilt before sentencing, at the very least. And if not that, then one corrupt and intent on framing an innocent inanimi simply so they can keep their record clear."

"Your Majesty, we have done—"

"Do I need to bring the King of Olympia into this?" Aemiliana asked, her tone suddenly low and dangerous. "Because not only can I, but Indra will *also* personally vouch for Mab Duchan's innocence, as she is a close, personal friend of his."

"I—Well, I—" The judge sputtered, leaning back in her chair, and Mab's fingers flexed around Ander's. Was it a good or bad sign that Aemiliana had struck the judge dumb? Mab wasn't sure . . .

"That being the case, I'm sure you'll be more than willing to release Mab into my custody while you continue investigating. I mean . . . we'd hate for you to rush the process and execute someone who was innocent, wouldn't we? How would that look to the king of the gods?"

"Yes. Yes, of course." The judge cleared her throat. "Release Miss Duchan into Her Majesty's custody. Immediately."

Mab couldn't get out of the cage fast enough, and Ander was waiting for her when she did. He scooped her into his arms, pressing her in so tight to his chest that she could feel every rib in his torso. It hurt like hell, but it also felt wonderful. Relief flooded her so quickly, she nearly sagged with it. "You came and got me," she whispered, half in disbelief.

"Of course we did, darling," Ander whispered back. "You're our family."

A choked noise came out of Mab's throat, but there were no words. None at all.

"He's right," Aemiliana added, wrapping her arms tight around them both. "You're my daughter, whether you like it or not."

Behind them, Quin stood a distance off, his back straight, face serious. Aloof but respectful, his eyes averted as if he did not wish to intrude on their family moment.

"I do like it," Mab muttered, but she ducked her head into Ander's chest where she could hide the heat on her face.

"Hmm. Good. Now, let's get you back to Ander's so you can eat, shower, and get some real rest, yes?"

"Yes," Ander agreed on Mab's behalf, and they both started ushering her to the door, Quin bringing up the rear of their little entourage. She noticed the way they kept themselves between her and the eyes that had come to the courtroom to watch the spectacle. It was . . . nice to be protected by them. To let her family look after her. Maybe . . . Maybe she didn't have to be the one that had something to offer constantly.

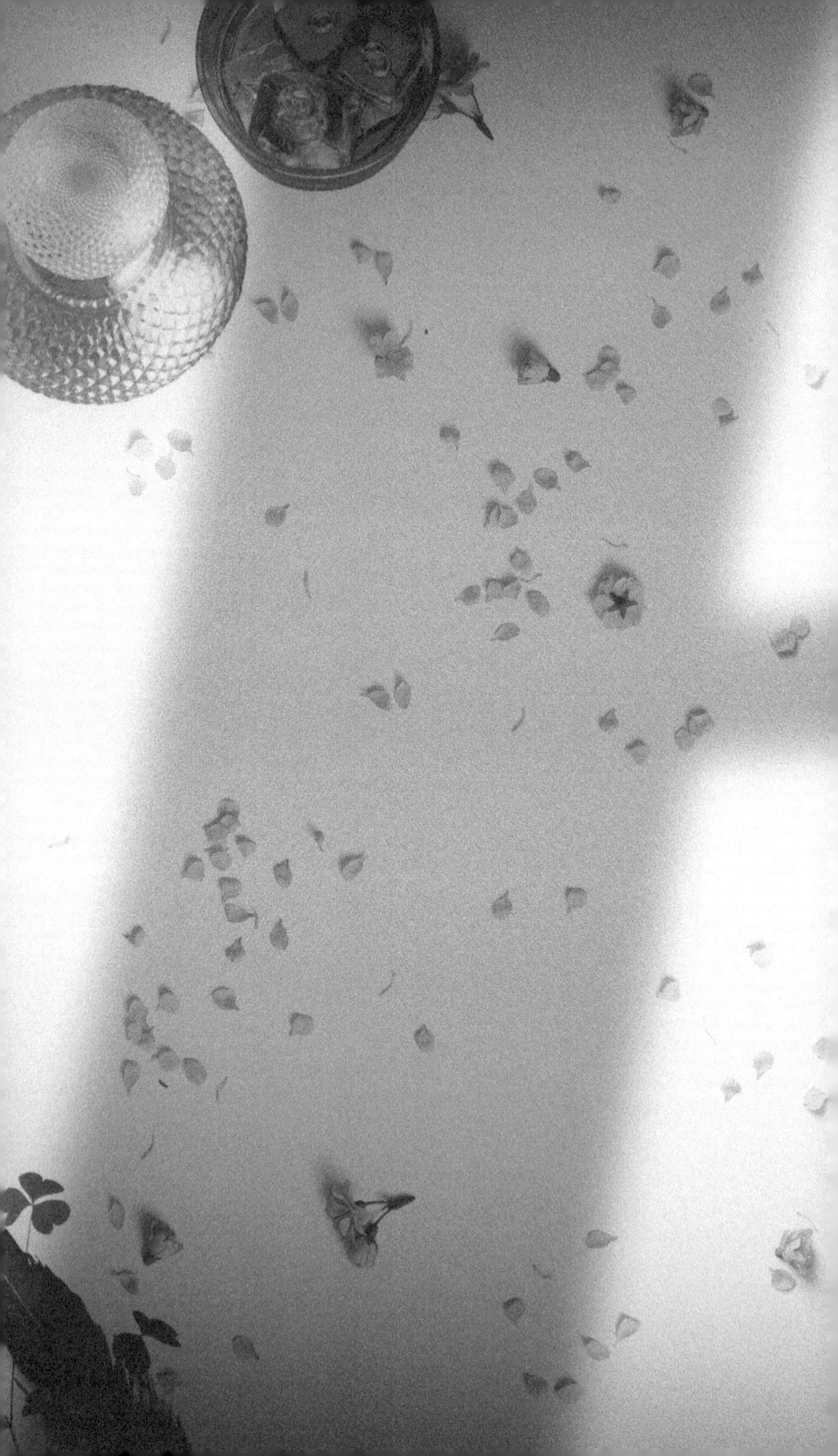

Chapter 22
Ander

He was going to kill whoever had put Mab in that cell and placed her on trial for something she hadn't done. Just like he had cursed that prick of a mortal who'd attacked and placed her in a cell so long ago to die with his dick shriveled and diseased.

Ander had only killed twice in his life, and once had been for Mab. He would do it again.

In a heartbeat.

Without pause or care of consequence.

No law or force in this universe was going to stop him from exacting punishment on every inch of their flesh.

As they stepped outside of the sanctuary and into the mid-morning Miami sunlight, Ander pulled Mab closer to him, curling her protectively against his chest. He had come so close to losing her; the thought chilled him to the bone.

There were shadows beneath her eyes and a haunted look in their depths. She'd been reliving those night terrors they'd worked so hard to chase away. Ander thought they had been successful in mostly eradicating them. But they were back, their presence a dark stain on Mab's spirit. He hated seeing it. Hated thinking of the pain and torment that raged in her mind. Hated that he'd had to be apart from her during all of this.

"Let's get you home," he murmured, then looked over at his mother. "Mum, will you do the honors?"

Aemiliana nodded and stepped up to encircle both of them protectively in her arms.

Ander glanced back at Quin, who seemed to be hovering just out of reach, as if he had been a nuisance rather than a great help. Ander knew he'd risked his career coming today when he had been banned from the sanctuary all together.

"Come on, Quin, the least we can do is transport you back quickly."

He looked uncomfortable at this. "I can fly."

Aemiliana tutted. "Nonsense. Join us."

Unable to refuse a queen, he stepped up to their little huddle. Ander took ahold of his elbow and pulled him into his and Mab's side. Instinctively, it seemed, Quin's wings spread out to engulf them slightly.

Aemiliana pressed a kiss to Ander's cheek and one to the top of Mab's head. "Hold tight, my babies," she murmured to them lovingly.

Ander's heart swelled with love for his mother just as she nodded her head, and the four of them were transported from outside the sanctuary into the middle of Ander's condo.

The loud, active buzzing of three busy people came to a halt as the Queen of Helicon, her son, Quintus, and Mab suddenly appeared.

Four sets of eyes turned to look at them from where they were scattered around the condo: the twins on the floor at either end of the coffee table, busy clicking away at their laptops, Gizmo in Nox's lap, Max pouring over a map on the kitchen island, and Tavi and Monnie playing under the dining room table.

"Mab!" the twins trumpeted together, both moving to stand up.

Max also took a step forward.

Ander held his hand up. "Mabbers needs a chance to bathe and attend to herself. If one of you would please order us green coconut curry with coconut rice from Shandi, the large mixed sushi platter from Nami House, a large Greek pizza with a house salad from Tony's, and honey garlic wings and teriyaki strips from Cluckers, that would be fantastic."

"I'll handle that," Quin offered and quickly stepped away from their group, moving over to the other side of the room, pulling out his phone as he did.

Mab looked up at Ander, eyes wide. "All my faves."

Ander kissed her forehead. "I know. Come on, time to get you into a bath." He looked over at his mother. "Why don't you come with us?"

"Of course, darling."

For a brief moment, Ander's eyes caught Max's gaze. He smiled softly, though there was a nervous quality to him which Ander suspected had to do with his mother being present.

In the bathroom, Ander began filling the tub, tossing in an orange-scented bath bomb as well as some Epsom salts.

"You guys don't have to do this," Mab said as she began to undress.

Ander cast her a quick glance. "Yes. We do."

He remembered the day Mab and his mother had brought him back from Enrique's clutches in Acheron. How Mab had been there every step of the way. He wouldn't abandon her now, not when her healing from this hadn't even begun.

Once Mab was in the bath, Aemiliana sat behind her and began to tenderly wash her hair, working soap and fingers through it in a manner that Ander remembered. His mother had always been fabulous in her ministrations. Her hair washes came along with a head massage that made a person want to fall asleep where they sat.

While his mother worked on Mab's hair, Ander picked up a sponge, file, and pick and took Mab's hand to work on cleaning and fixing her nails.

Her eyes were droopy, and she looked at him with both thanks and resistance.

"Stop trying to fight it, Mabeline, we're going to take care of you."

"But—"

"It's what family does, sweetheart," Aemiliana stated simply, fingers carefully unknotting a tangle of curls.

Mab's eyes filled with tears, and she bit at her lip to contain them. Seeing this, Ander reached out to tap her nose. "We've got you, snookums, just leave it all to us."

Just as he hoped, Mab snickered a little at the action and endearment. "You're such a dork sometimes."

Ander winked at her, adding some extra sauce to it. "Don't tell Max."

"Oh, I'm sure he knows."

Ander huffed, and another soft chuckle came out of Mab, which made his heart swell.

"So . . . " Mab closed her eyes as Aemiliana tipped her head back and gently poured water over her hair to rinse out the soap. "What's with the command center in your living room?"

"They decided it was safer to work out of the condo." Ander carefully picked dirt out from under her nails.

"But . . . why? Where have they *been*? What happened?" There was pain and worry in her voice that was unmistakable. And Ander realized she didn't know about the suspension.

"They've all been suspended," he started, setting the pick aside and picking up the file to start shaping her nails. "Quin actually risked quite a bit coming with us today. None of them are supposed to go near the sanctuary." Ander fought against a growl. "Now I'm starting to see *why*."

"What?" Mab's head came back up, and she looked at him. "Suspended? Does this have something to do with me?" Her brow furrowed.

Ander sighed and nodded. "That asshat Captain Galeo saw their family visiting you as a sign they weren't focusing on their work. So he's suspended them all for a week, and they're not allowed to step foot inside the sanctuary under threat of grounding. He even said if I went in, they would still be grounded." The mere thought of the threat Galeo had issued made Ander want to rip the ignis' own feathers out and see how he liked it.

To think anyone would even *mention* the possibility of doing that to his Max made him livid.

Too many people were coming for those he loved most. Ander felt a deep need to start righting some wrongs, and soon.

"Grounded? What does that mean?"

"It means," Ander growled, concentrating on filing the edges of Mab's nails, "they'll clip the first four primary feathers on each wing, effectively grounding them. Just like any bird, they can't take off, they can't fly, all they can do is hold on tight and glide downward if they get a good enough updraft."

"Shit," Mab hissed, then her brows shot up, and the water splashed as she straightened quickly. "Is that going to happen to Quin now? Why did he come today?" Her eyes pinched at the corners.

"He had proof you were innocent, and he felt you deserved to have an ignis in your corner. Protectiveness is a Schields trait, I think." Ander had wanted to kiss the ignis when he came to Ander, letting him know that the trial was going to take place and insisting that he come along. Quin was grumbly, but he was honorable.

"I think my presence there today will act as some protection," Aemiliana offered soothingly.

It seemed to help, and Mab settled back into the end of the tub, though there was still a slight furrow between her brows. "Okay." Mab fell silent for a moment. "Thanks . . . for coming for me." Her voice was soft, husky.

Ander glanced over at her, his own expression softening. "Mabbers, I would go to the ends of the earth for you. I owe you my life, and I will never let anyone hurt you." He squeezed her hand, and Mab squeezed right back.

"Honestly, I don't know why you waited so long to come and get me, Ander," his mother spoke up, rinsing out the last of the suds.

Ander winced and looked at Mab, making an "I'm in trouble" face.

"Don't blame Andy. He wanted to snap me out of the cell and whisk me away to Helicon as soon as he found out. I told him not to," Mab announced.

"Well, I'm glad he eventually ignored that. Next time, I want to know the *minute* anything like that happens to either of you. Am I understood?" Her tone was stern, and though she couldn't see Mab's face, her dark eyes moved from the top of Mab's head to Ander and back again.

The both of them shrank a little, like young children scolded. And together, they said, "Yes, mum."

Aemiliana smiled. "Good. Now Ander, let's leave Mab to finish washing up and relax. In the meantime, you've got a young ignis lad to introduce me to."

Ander's eyes widened, and he stared at Mab. "Help," he mouthed to her.

Mab smirked and shook her head. "That's a great idea, I'd love to just soak in here for a bit." Her eyes narrowed in delight. "Have fun, Andy," she called as Ander got to his feet and followed his mother out of the bathroom.

He paused in the doorway. "After everything I've done for you today . . . "

Mab blew him a kiss then sank deeper into the bubbles, a loud sigh releasing from her that sounded like a great deal of stress and torment leaving her body.

Ander watched for a moment, making sure that she was okay, and finally released a weighted breath of his own. She was home. She was safe. He had his Mab out of that hellhole and back with them where she belonged.

Finally assured that Mab was going to be okay alone, Ander closed the bathroom door and turned to his mother.

She held out her hand, smiling at him gently, and he took it without hesitation. "This isn't exactly how I planned on you meeting Max . . . " he muttered.

"Mmm . . . I'm sure it was *much* later than this." She eyed him pointedly, and Ander had the decency to blush.

He took a deep breath. "Maybe." There was a loose, wild sort of energy shifting through him that made Ander move his weight from one foot to the other. Was he nervous?

Aemiliana noticed and pressed her free hand to his cheek. "Sweetheart, just let me meet him."

"He's really sweet, Mum. I swear. He's the kindest, gentlest soul you will ever meet, and he loves me so, so much."

She smiled more. "Then I am sure I will love him as well." Her head tipped in the direction of the living room, and Ander nodded.

Still holding her hand, Ander led his mother back out to the ignis-filled room. Max, who had been seated, instantly stood up. As did the rest when they saw that the queen had reentered the room.

Aemiliana reached out her hand, motioning downward. "Sit, sit. Please. No need to stand on ceremony in my son's home." She smiled at them.

Ander noticed that the twins both gave a semi-awkward half-bow/curtsy before returning to their spot on the floor. Quin, stoney-faced as ever, seemed to only straighten more, standing with his arms folded behind his back.

It was Max though that stole Ander's attention. His white wings, which always gave him an angelic appearance, shifted lightly behind his back, almost seeming to tremble. He clutched his hands together before him as he moved across the floor, hesitant but hopeful.

Once he was close enough, Ander reached out to take his hand instead, cupping it between both of his. "Mum, this is my Max. Max, this is my mother, Queen Aemiliana."

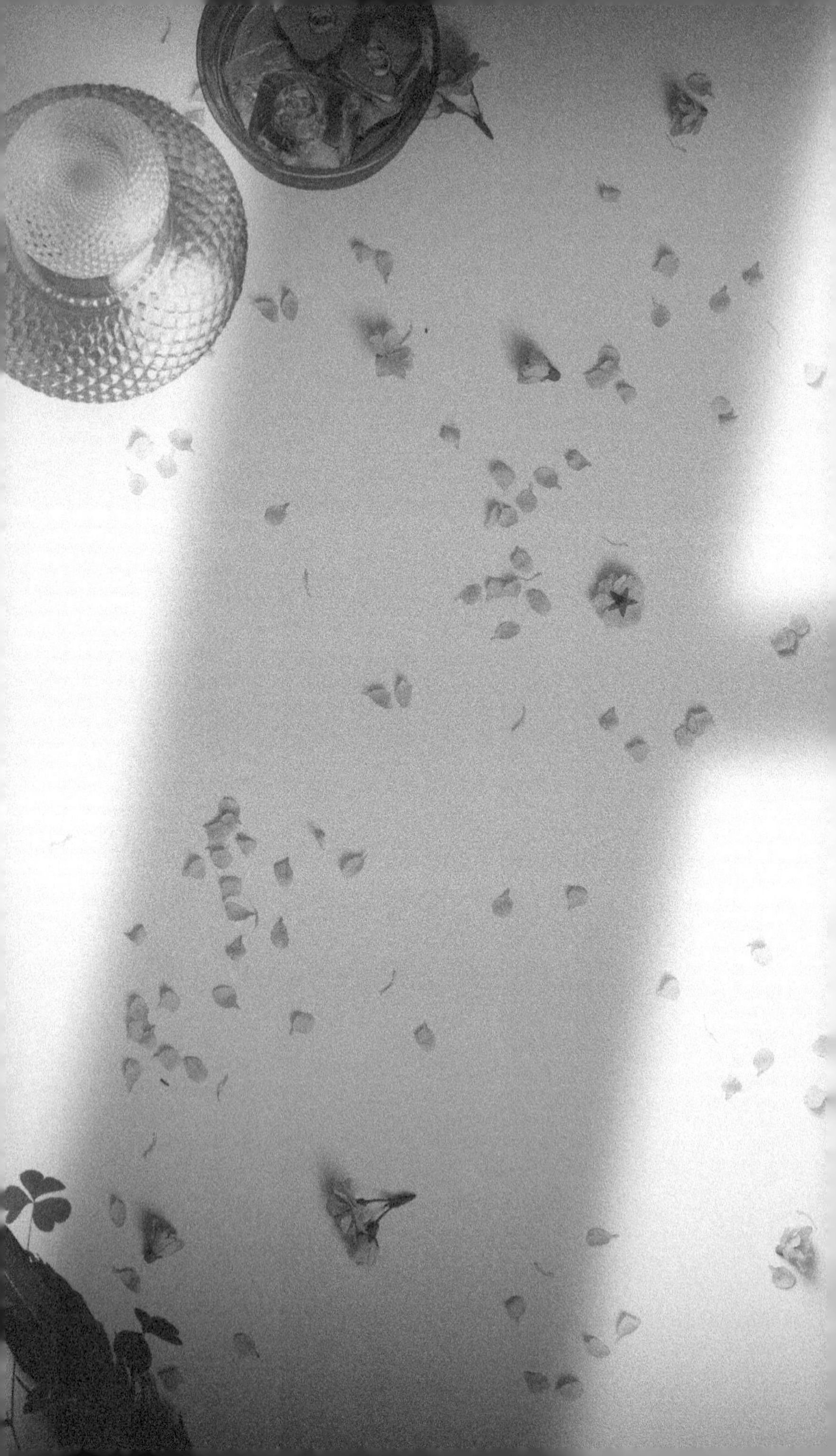

Chapter 23
Max

Max had faced down monsters ten times his size. He'd fought alongside his brother for *years*. He'd been in situations that would make a grown man cry. And yet ...

And yet, as Aemiliana came back into the living room, Ander at her side, an expectant look in her eyes, it was *this* that made Max trip over himself. At least his hands weren't sweating; he didn't want Ander to know just how nervous he was to meet his mother when they held hands.

"Uh ... Hi," Max said, offering a too-big smile and a little wave. Shit. That was weird, wasn't it? Like Stitch meeting Lilo for the first time. Who *did* that? What was wrong with him? "I'm Max."

And ... didn't Ander just say that?

"I've heard a bit about you," Aemiliana offered, one finely shaped brow lifting in judgment.

Max shifted more under her gaze.

"All good, I hope?" Gods, his throat was dry. He always kind of forgot that Ander was a *prince* of Underworld. That his boyfriend wasn't just some really good-looking guy he'd met at a bar one night but actual, legit royalty. Max's Disney

Prince come to life. And here was his mother, the *queen*. Damn it.

"Some of it."

"Mother," Ander chided. "I've never had a bad word to say about Max."

"Well, you aren't the only one giving me information, are you? In fact." Aemiliana seemed to lift her chin higher, her eyes narrowing on Ander. "You didn't tell me you even had a soulmate until about a month ago. Did you?"

"What's that?" Ander tilted his head as if listening to something, his brows pinched in concentration. "If you'll excuse me, I think Mab is calling."

"I didn't hear—" But Ander had already snapped himself into the bathroom, leaving Max to face his mother alone. "Anything … "

"He does that," Aemiliana said, a little smile ticking up the corners of her lips. "You'll get used to it."

"I suppose I will." Max nodded. "Look, I'm sorry that we're meeting on such … weird terms. This isn't at all how I wanted to do this. But here we are." He shrugged helplessly.

"Yes. Here we are." Gods, did she have to say things like that? All … regal? Max was definitely botching this whole "meet the parents" thing. And of course Ander left him to flounder. "You know he's been through heartache."

"Yes. We've talked about his past." Max nodded again, standing taller, suddenly serious. "I know about Enrique and Estelle."

"Then you know I will not see my children hurt again by the people they choose to care about." Her gaze flicked to the rest of the Schields family, and Max wasn't really sure what she was implying there, but he knew he couldn't let it go unanswered.

"We take care of our own, ma'am, and Ander and Mab are as much a part of the family as anyone else in this room," Max vowed, trying to pour every ounce of feeling he had into the words. He loved Ander. Desperately. He'd do anything to make him happy, to see him thrive when so many others had tried to stifle him.

Aemiliana hummed. Max wished he knew her better so he could understand what that meant. Was she impressed? Was she skeptical? His wings shifted behind him, betraying his uncertainty.

"Is everything okay over here?" Quin asked, stepping up beside Max and offering Aemiliana a curt nod of respect.

"Everything's fine, Q." Max turned to shoot his brother a grateful smile. "I was just telling Aemiliana how I'd die protecting her children if I had to."

"I'm not asking for you to die for them." She tilted her head, but there was a little frown at the corners of her lips as she shifted her gaze to Quin. Like she was seeing something no one else could. "Dying for them is easy. Living for them, and fighting every day to ensure they're happy, is harder. Any ignis can die in a fight, but only his soulmate can keep him smiling. Which are you, Maximus Schields?"

"I, uh . . . I . . . " His tongue felt suddenly too big for his mouth. Why was he stumbling over this? Maybe because, after years of living as a tin soldier among the ignis, he wasn't sure that he *could* live for someone. Even though his father had taught him he was more than just a warrior, more than just a weapon, everyone else in Max's life had hammered into his head that the greatest thing he could ever do for someone was to die protecting them—that's what he was good for, in the end. And now, Aemiliana was asking him specifically *not* to do that, to consider a future that was infinite with the man he loved, and Max was

. . . he was stumped. "I'll do my best," he finally choked out.

"See that you do." Aemiliana nodded, and her gaze flicked to Quin as if including him in this warning. "I'd hate to see what becomes of those who break the heart of the Prince of Helicon."

"Daaaaamn." Mab whistled from behind them. Max didn't know when Ander and Mab had returned from getting Mab dressed. All he could hope was that they hadn't witnessed all of that. But the look on Ander's face told him that was far too much to hope for. "That was some shovel talk, mum."

Aemiliana hummed, and this time, Max was pretty sure it was out of amusement.

"*So* much scarier than mine." Mab came over to stand on the queen's left, leaning into her space a little, as if perhaps Mab needed the added comfort of her mother in that moment. "He laughed when I gave him mine!"

"That's only because I was so excited to get one." Max huffed but couldn't help the smile that ticked at the corners of his lips at seeing Mab like this again after so many days of her being silent and withdrawn. They didn't know each other well, but she was family, as he'd said. And he'd hated seeing her down in that cell. "Baby, they're making fun of me."

"You'll get over it." Ander grinned, moving to lean heavily against Max's side and watch Aemiliana and Mab interact with a pleased little smile on his face.

"Well, I am much older than you, Mab," Aemiliana said, a little laugh in her voice. "I've had more practice."

"No, you haven't," Mab snorted. Much of the life had returned to her eyes, but Max could see the way her shoulders still curled in a little on themselves as if preparing for a blow. The words were light, playful, but they were a mask. One that Max would let her keep. "But if that was your first try, I pity whoever has to sit through the next one."

"Fine, not more practice. More time to think about it. Now, come around here and let me see you." She tugged Mab so she was standing between all of them and tilted her head to look her over. "Much better. Don't you think, boys?"

"She'll be even better once we get some food in her," Ander grumbled. "You've lost so much weight."

"You sound like one of those aunties from the dramas I like," Mab grumbled back, swatting his hands away as Ander went to pinch her cheeks and pull at them a little. "Stop it. Max, make him stop."

"You know I literally *can't* make him do that," Max laughed softly.

"The food should be here shortly," Quin supplied, although Max wasn't sure who he was trying to help. Maybe he was just supplying information.

"Mum . . . " Mab whined when Ander grabbed her and pulled her into what looked like a bone-crushing hug. Then he grabbed Max's wrist to pull him in too, squashing her in between them.

"Sorry, Mab, you're on your own." Aemiliana laughed softly. She'd taken a step back from their little group, watching them, a gentle smile on her face.

"So," Mab said, leaning her head against Ander's shoulder and bumping Max lightly with her hip. "Food?"

"Didn't you hear Q? It'll be here soon." Max laughed, giving her and Ander one final squeeze before he pulled away again.

"I hate to break up this cute little family moment," Nox called from where she was still sitting in front of the couch, her nails loud against her keyboard. "But I think we've got something."

The little group broke apart and moved to the living room area. Mab, Ander, and Aemiliana went to the bar in the corner, while Max leaned over the back of the couch. "What is it?"

"Someone on one of those cryptid boards is saying they saw angels in Port Arthur, Texas." Nox chewed on her lip.

"Are there pictures?" Quin asked, he and Max both making their way around the couch to stand behind the twins and look at their screens.

"Not very good ones," Nash volunteered, turning his laptop so they could see.

"Those could be shopped." Nox wrinkled her nose.

"But why angels? Why not something else? Like Bigfoot?" Max asked. "Nash, download the pictures, run them through our software. See if you can determine if they've been doctored. Nox, look for more sightings."

The twins nodded and got back to work.

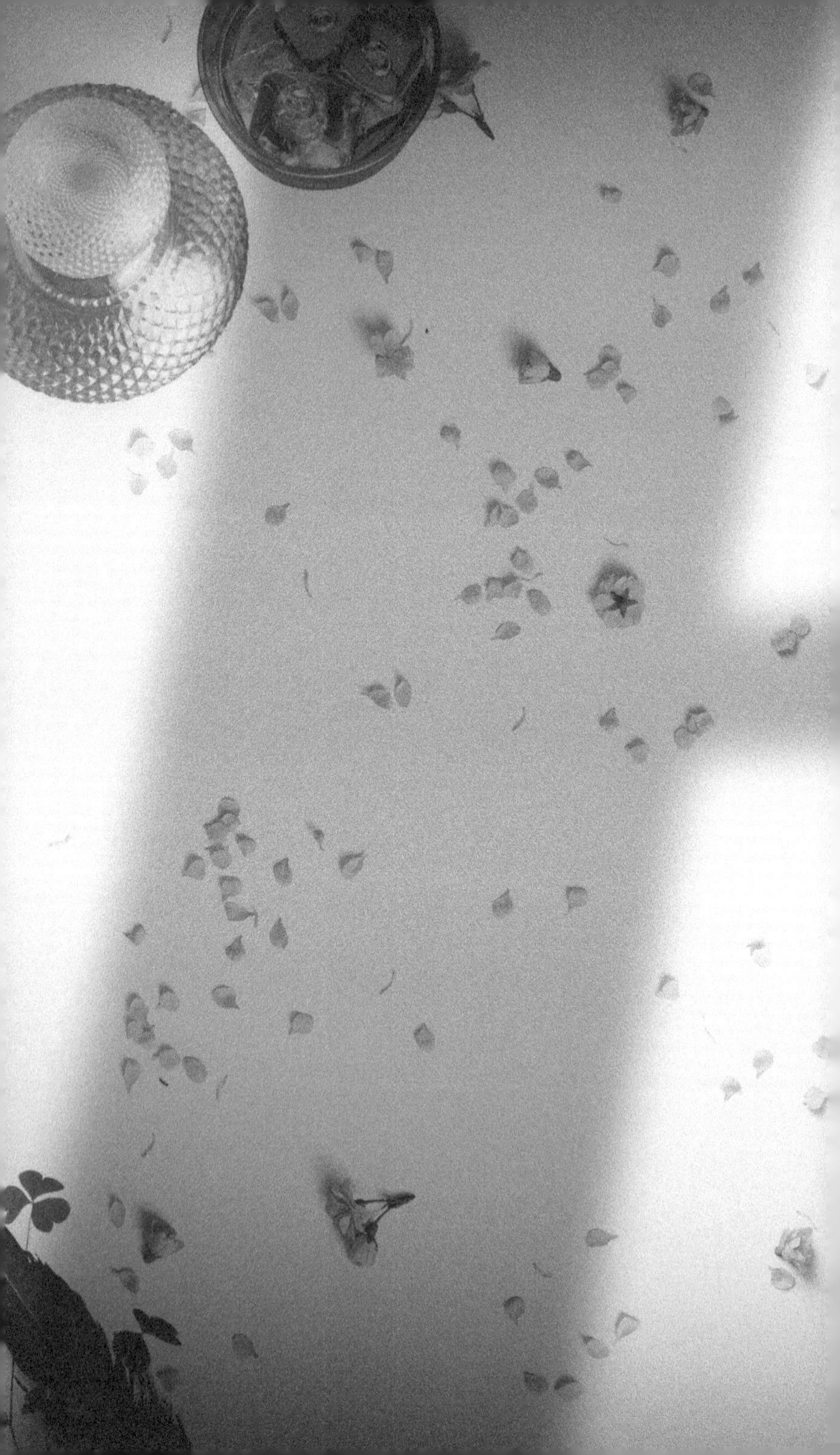

Chapter 24
Quin

"Well, my darlings, while I hate to leave you, I think it best that I return home," Queen Aemiliana announced.

Quin looked at Max, then back to Ruin and his mother, wondering what the proper etiquette was for saying goodbye to a queen as she departed the condo you just so happened to be in. Max, to his credit, held up reasonably well beneath the queen's scrutiny, but Quin could tell he was relieved to hear she was leaving.

"Goodbye, Your Majesty!" Nash and Nox called out together, looking up just briefly from their laptops before they ducked back to work.

Quin, sensing Max could use a little support, followed him back to where Queen Aemiliana stood with Ruin and Mab.

Queen Aemiliana drew Mab in for a tight hug, holding her closely and whispering something in her ear that even Quin's great hearing wasn't able to make out, but he could only assume they were words of love and encouragement. She pressed a kiss to Mab's forehead before pulling away.

When she turned to Quin and Max, he felt the need to stand straighter and did so.

"Max, it was a pleasure to meet you and your family. Until next time." She bowed her head a little. Though it was said in a refined manner, Quin heard the subtle undertones. If Max didn't treat her son well, there would be a lot of pain the next time he met her.

In unison, Quin and Max dipped a little into a bow.

"The honor was completely mine, Your Majesty," Max was quick to say.

When Queen Aemiliana turned to Ruin, the love she felt for her son was evident on her face. Quin noticed for the first time that Ruin was the spitting image of his mother. The same dark hair, tanned skin, and brown-lidded eyes. Whoever Ruin's father was, the only mark he'd left on him were the long, elegant horns protruding from Ruin's forehead, proclaiming for all to behold that he was not entirely muse.

"Should I walk you back to the portal, Mum?" Ruin asked.

"No need, Theandros is waiting downstairs for me," she assured him.

"What? He could have come up!"

Queen Aemiliana chuckled and pulled Ruin in for a hug. "He didn't wish to intrude. I love you, my darling. Please don't wait until there is another tragedy to come visit me." She cast a purposeful glance between him and Mab, then she pulled back, and with a light hum and a flick of her wrist, she disappeared.

Her sudden absence made Quin's ears pop, and he had to drive his knuckles into them to release the pressure.

"There ... that wasn't so bad, was it?" Ruin was saying to Max, who'd moved over to him to pull him into his arms.

Quin turned away, giving his brother and his boyfriend some space, and found that Mab had done the same and was now staring at the twins in the living room.

"Why did you all decide this was the safer place to be?" she asked. "And not at your home?"

"Max thought it would be better if we worked from the condo where Ander could put up charms rather than our parents' place where we could potentially be watched. We're . . . not supposed to be working on finding Orcus," Quin explained.

"But you are."

Quin nodded. "We're trying to find him before he strikes again."

Mab looked at him. "Again?"

"It's no longer just my assumption. We're pretty sure at this point he's the one who set you up."

Mab swore a blue streak at this, and just like before, there was a small squeak from under the table. Tavi reminding everyone that she was there.

"Oh, shit. Sorry!" Mab's eyes were round, and she darted a quick glance to the table.

"Max did it yesterday . . . so it's not the first time," Quin grumbled. At this rate, Tavi's first words when she decided to finally speak were bound to be a curse of some kind.

"He left Ander a threat," Mab announced suddenly.

Quin's eyes shot to her. "Who? Orcus?"

She nodded. "A small box of aeternus rings at the front door of this condo. I'm assuming since you all thought this was the best place, he didn't tell Max that."

This time, it was Quin who was fighting back curse words. He pressed his lips tightly together and stared across the room at Ruin. "No. Max hasn't mentioned anything about it. When did the rings show up?"

"The day after I was arrested."

Quin huffed and shook his head, crossing his arms over his chest. "Then your arrest was absolutely his doing, and he's been up to something big while we've been focused on you."

The issue was, what? A dawning sense of dread swept over Quin, landing on his shoulders to try and bear his body down with the weight of it. He knew the twins would locate Orcus one way or the other, but Quin's fear was that, at this point, it would all be too late.

Suddenly, the door buzzer announced that the first of their food had arrived. After that, it was a steady stream of delivery people bringing all of the different dishes Ander had asked them to order.

In the end, they decided to spread the food out on the coffee table, everyone taking up a position somewhere in the living room. The twins pulled their laptops away to sit them on the couch near their heads, their programs still up and running and visible if they needed to do something but out of reach of any sauces or spills.

"Time to eat, Tavi. Come out." Quin bent over to peer under the table, where the youngling was still playing with the tiny white fluff of fur Ruin called a dog.

Tavi stared back at him, eyes round and body hesitant. She pointed at Monnie, seeming reluctant to come out.

"She can come too. Come," he encouraged.

Still, the little girl didn't move. Not until Ruin whistled and opened a can of dog food in the kitchen, and the little white fluffball scurried out from under the table and ran for the kitchen, yipping all the way.

Once Tavi was out from under the table as well, Quin took her tiny hand in his and walked her over to the living room. Max had grabbed her plate and fork from out of her backpack, along with her non-spill cup, which was now filled with milk.

"Thanks," Quin said. Max only smiled and set the items down in front of Tavi.

With Tavi settled, he began pointing to different things, asking her what she wanted to try until he had a bit of almost everything on the little pink plate, then he set it in front of her. Tavi peered slowly at each item, then, picking up her yellow fork in a clumsy, untried manner, began to stab at the salmon nigiri.

Quin waited until everyone loaded up their plates and he was sure Tavi was content to make his own plate. Settling down with some rice and curry, a slice of pizza, some tuna sashimi, salmon nigiri, and a piece of California roll, he sat on the floor, plate in hand, and began to eat.

"So, is the plan that we all go to Texas?" Nox asked.

Quin looked at Max, who was looking back at him.

"I think we have to," Max said.

"We need to plan it well," Quin added. "We don't have any clearance to be in Texas."

A small hand reached over to pluck a piece of olive from his pizza, and Quin watched Tavi place it on her tongue. Her tiny face scrunched up a little as she thought about it for a moment. Then her fingers went back into her mouth to fetch it out, and she dropped it back on top of his pizza.

"Thank you . . . " he muttered.

The youngling smiled up at him brightly, letting out a cheesy little chuckle, as if she were deeply proud of herself.

"I have a factory!" Nox suddenly announced, a piece of pizza in one hand and her other flying over her keyboard. "Seems this is where the 'angels' were mostly seen flying in and out of."

"Where is it?" Max hopped up from his spot beside

Ander and moved over to the whiteboard Ander had snapped them to use.

Nox listed off the address of the warehouse, then hit a couple more keys on her computer, and the printer they'd set in the corner of the room began to whirr to life. "Picture of it being printed now."

"Thanks." Max went to grab it and tape it to the whiteboard.

"Are there any other factories or warehouses around it?" Quin asked, clearing the sushi from his plate in quick bites.

"No, everything around it appears to be empty."

"Typical Enrique fashion," Nash piped up.

"He may have bought the properties around him to purposefully keep them empty," Max suggested.

"Print us off a map of the surrounding buildings, Nox. We need to figure out where we can sneak in so they don't see us." Quin finished off his pizza and stood up. The curry could be eaten later now that plans were happening.

"How safe is it going to be for you two to go in there on your own?" Ruin asked, his brow furrowing in concern.

"We won't be going in on the offensive," Max assured him, coming forward to squeeze his shoulder and bending down to pluck up a piece of dragon roll. "It'll be for recon, to see if we can figure out where Enrique's main base of operations is." He popped the piece of sushi into his mouth.

"I still don't like it," Ruin muttered.

Quin walked over to the printer, pulling off the several sheets of paper that made up the map of the buildings and streets around the old factory. He walked to the whiteboard, and grabbing the tape, began to tear off strips and piece the map together. As he got to the last page, the tape dispenser ran out.

"We're out of tape," he called out and tossed the

dispenser over his shoulder into the little waste bin beside the printer.

"Four points!" Nox yelled.

"Oh, come on," Nash argued. "That was at least six. It was over his shoulder and not looking."

Max seemed to also have an opinion. "Yeah, but it was plastic, so weightier than if it had been paper. I agree with Nox, four points."

Quin snorted. "You only agree with Nox because I'm beating you."

Max gasped. "I would never!"

They eyed each other until Max laughed and held his hand out to Ruin. "Hey babe, can you snap us more tape?"

Ruin obliged, and soon Max was bringing Quin another dispenser to finish putting the map together.

Once it was complete, he and Max stood looking at it.

"Lots of coastline," Quin muttered.

"And they'll see us coming from a mile away." Max tapped his fingers against his lips.

"I don't think there's an area where we can fly in without normies seeing us." Quin glanced over at him.

"I can portal you." It was Ruin; he had come up to stand beside Max to peer at the board along with them.

Max looked down at him, slipping his arm around his waist. "You sure?"

"It'll bring me some peace of mind to get you there directly. I need to help out some way."

Max kissed the top of his head. "Thank you."

"We still need to decide where the best landing spot is. Since we'll be able to portal in directly wherever we choose, let's make the most of it." Quin scanned the board over.

"Before you decide anything, let us map out the entire area and find any pitfalls," Nox called to them.

All three turned to look back at the others still seated around the coffee table.

"We should talk about us coming too," Nash added. "If this is recon, you need a recon team, and who better than Nox and me to help you capture everything as well as monitor the situation with thermal gear?"

"Well . . . It would help." Max chewed on his lip.

In tandem, the three of them returned to the coffee table. Quin settled back down beside Tavi, who had green curry spread across her face and seemed very happy to shovel it into her mouth with both the fork—which she dropped a lot off of—and her fingers.

He picked up his own plate to eat the curry he had abandoned before, agreeing with Tavi that it was quite delicious.

"We're going to need to know if there are any security cameras, where the closest normie building is, and if there's any schedule Enrique's men stick to," Max said, reaching for another piece of pizza.

Nox eyed him. "Yeah. We know. We do this for a living."

Max rolled his eyes at his sister. "That's enough sass out of you."

Nox silently mocked him as she grabbed a piece of sushi with her chopsticks.

"Brat!" Max threw a piece of salmon sashimi at her, which stuck to her cheek.

Nox gasped. "Max!" Peeling it off her cheek, she threw it back at him, hitting him square in the face.

Across the table, Tavi giggled and picked up a handful of rice, tossing it in Nash's general direction. It spattered over his shirt, hit a portion of the laptop behind him, and pinged off the couch.

"My shirt!" Nash wailed, and looking behind him, paled even more. "My computer!"

"My *couch*!" Ruin was aghast.

Quin glared at his siblings as he reached down to take ahold of Tavi's hand, stopping her from throwing another round. "Could we *not* teach her to throw food?" he growled lowly.

Nox pointed at Max. "He started it."

And Max looked apologetic. "Sorry, Q."

"Sorry, Q?!" Ruin sputtered and pointed at the green spots of curry-soaked rice on his couch. "My couch!"

"Oh, stop fussing, Andy," Mab cut in. "You know you can clean that away with magic."

Ruin huffed but didn't say anything more. He did, however, wave his hand, and the curried rice disappeared not only from his couch but from Nash's shirt and computer screen too.

"Oh, bless you!" Nash smoothed his hand over his now pristine white V-neck shirt.

Choosing to ignore all of them, Quin looked down at Tavi. "We don't throw food." He signed it as well as spoke it, just to make sure his words hit home and were seen as serious.

Tavi looked confused and pointed over at Max, shaking a tiny fisted "M" his way, as if to say, *Why him but not me?*

"Max isn't supposed to do it either. He was being bad," Quin explained softly but firmly.

Tavi looked over at Max, who gazed back at her in a contrite manner, and nodded. Huffing, the youngling flapped her wings in irritation then returned to her food.

"Brothers, am I right?" Mab leaned in toward him a little to say.

Quin snorted. "And I've got two," he drawled.

"Well, Andy isn't safe around anyone, let alone kids." Mab smirked a little.

Quin lifted his eyes from Tavi to look at Mab. Her sudden nearness made him pause. It felt like a lot, to have her so close, but not necessarily in a bad way as it usually did with most people. Simply, he was very aware of her shoulder being so close to his.

"I've noticed," he muttered back.

"It's what makes him fun but also a huge pain in the assss-phalt." She managed to correct herself just in time, brown eyes darting to Tavi, then back to him. They seemed to sparkle with an unspoken apology, and he noticed for the first time that there were light golden specks of color in the brown, reminding him of warm honey nestled in chocolate. She mouthed a quick, "Sorry," her full lips wincing at the end.

"It's okay." Quin glanced at Tavi, who was busy in her own world. "I don't think she noticed."

Mab nodded. "I think I'm as bad as them. I'm not used to having kids around either."

Quin nodded. "It's been a while for me too. It seems like a very long time since Georgie was a baby."

"Yeah, but you're a natural at this whole thing." She nodded at Tavi, and her head tipped a little as she watched the youngling poking experimentally at her salmon nigiri.

The angle of her head highlighted the sleek line of her chin to her jaw, fading into the soft rounded curl of her white hair. There was something about how the light from the fading sunshine outside made Quin's fingers itch for a piece of charcoal. He suddenly had the strongest urge to sketch Mab and capture her beauty.

Beauty.

Typically, the sight of something beautiful made him

want to sketch, but it didn't usually cause this strange tightening in his abdomen. Shifting a little in place, Quin jumped up quickly to shake off the foreign feeling and walked over to the board as if he had something he needed to look at.

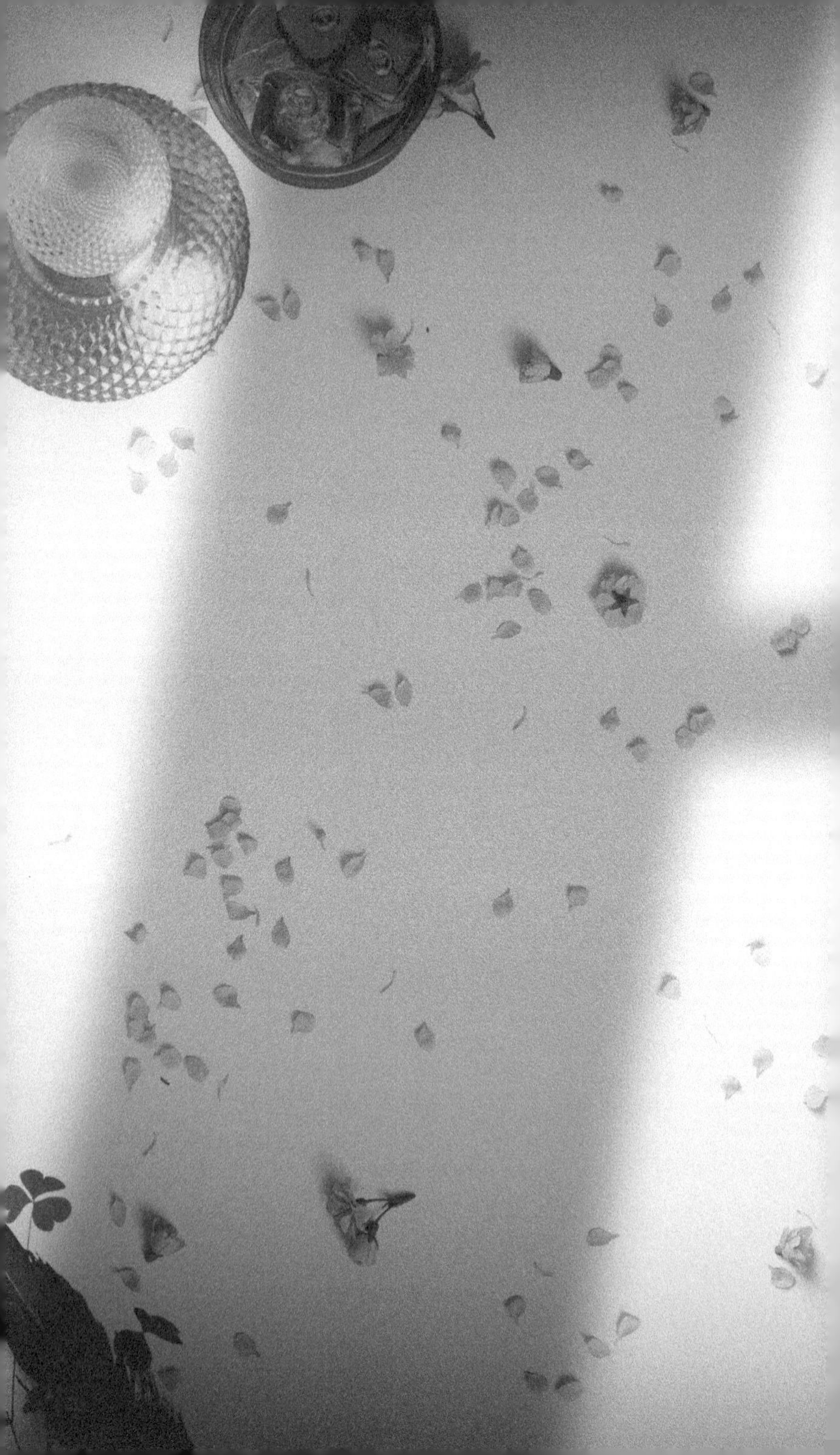

Chapter 25
Mab

Tavi was out. The twins were slogging through the hell that was online message boards. Max and Ander were cuddling on the couch, talking quietly. That just left Mab and Quin.

And sure, yeah, she could avoid him if she wanted to. She could go hide in her room and pretend the rest of them weren't there at all. But Tavi was in her bed, and she'd been alone so much over the last week or so . . . She was loath to leave these people who had done their best to help her when no one else would and adopted her in their own weird way.

So, she stayed.

She curled up in one of the chairs near the doors to the balcony, Gizmo in her lap, just watching all of them as they went about their tasks. Quin was beside her in another, his back to the goings-on as he looked out over the city.

"So. I never did thank you," Mab said into the quiet that had settled between them. She didn't know what it was about Quin, but she kind of liked just sitting with him. There was no pressure to talk like there was with so many other people. But even without the pressure, she *wanted* to. Which was just ... *wild*.

"Thank me for what?" Quin glanced over at her from the corner of his eye, and Mab felt Gizmo shuffle a little in her lap.

"For coming to visit me and coming to the trial to help get me out. It was nice of you. You didn't have to, and I know you risked a lot doing it." Mab shrugged.

"You're welcome." Quin shifted his gaze back to the sliding glass door. "What's its name?" he asked, tilting his head toward the large calico-colored, lop-eared rabbit in her lap. "Tavi was asking."

"His name is Gizmo." Mab gave Gizmo's ears a little scritch, smiling when the rabbit went somehow more lax across her legs. "You know ... she seems to be getting on well with Gizmo and Monnie. Maybe you should think about getting her a pet. It might help her open up a bit more."

"Ignis don't keep pets." Quin turned his attention back to the window, and Mab half thought he was dismissing her out of hand, but his jaw ticked a little in irritation, like maybe he didn't quite agree with that rule.

"Ignis don't go to Disney World and collect souvenir popcorn buckets either." Mab grinned a little. "Nor do they rent out whole abandoned warehouses to act as an art studio where they make frankly beautiful portraits of normies."

Quin shrugged, almost shy. "Papa always encouraged us to embrace human things."

Mab murmured, understanding. "This doesn't have to be any different. And I could help you pick a critter right for her. I've had a lot of different kinds of pets through the years." And the more she said, the more she was sure this was a good idea. Every little girl needed a pet, especially little girls who had been through what Tavi had. A pet would make an excellent companion. "Dogs, cats, a lizard or two, although after the last tantrum Andy threw about how things with scales were not meant for cuddling, I kind of gave up on that. Just . . . no birds."

"Why not?"

"I could never really get behind the whole wing clipping thing. Just didn't seem right to me to keep them from doing what came naturally to them just so I could have a friend." Mab curled her knees up close to her chest, lifting the rabbit to her face so she could bury her nose in his fur. Gizmo didn't exactly smell pleasant, all wood chips and musty down, but he smelled like home. A home she couldn't go back to right now because she was still in danger and her home was still a crime scene. "I had an admirer buy me a pair of love birds once, early on. You know, back when people did things like that."

"What happened to them?"

"The birds or the admirer?" Mab chewed on the inside of her cheek as she spun her chair to face his reflection in the glass overlooking Miami. She'd spent a lot of years alive, centuries, and not all of them had been good. Some of it got hazy, especially those early years when she and Ander were partying almost non-stop and she was still recovering from the trauma of the asylum.

Quin made a soft questioning sound.

"The admirer got the boot. I mean, they were going to anyway. I wasn't looking, and they were . . . " Mab winced a little at the memory of Avidan. They had been objectively gorgeous, but Mab had always needed a little more than that. "Well, let's just say, I've never been very keen on the whole 'gifts to express affection' thing. And I get why they did it, that was all the rage back then. But then, so were whale-boned corsets, and honestly . . . fuck corsets."

Quin huffed, a sound that might almost have been a laugh.

"The birds I kept until they'd healed up, then Andy and I took them back to where they came from and set them free." They lapsed back into silence as Mab watched Quin think it over. His eyes were still fixed on the Miami skyline, the lights reflecting in them, making them sparkle. He really was unfairly attractive. Like, who gave him the right to look like *that*? She cleared her throat and forced herself to look away. "All I'm saying is, after I escaped the asylum, I needed a little something extra to get through everything, and Ander got me a kitten."

"The asylum?" Quin tilted his head, his eyes meeting hers in the reflection on the glass.

"We're not talking about that," Mab said, a little more bite to her words than was strictly necessary. She couldn't talk about that with anyone who didn't already know about it. Not with the memories so fresh. "We're talking about pets."

Quin raised his brows but nodded his understanding.

Mab let out a long breath and forced herself to relax. He hadn't meant anything by it; he was just asking. Anyone in his shoes would. It was normal to be curious. Rude. But normal. "Sorry."

"No. It's fine. I shouldn't have asked." He didn't say it, but she could imagine him tacking on *you're not ready*. And honestly . . . how did he know? Was it because he was actually starting to get her? Gods, wasn't that a weird notion?

"Right. So. Like I was saying, a pet for Tavi." She

nodded to herself. "What sort of little critter do you think she'd like best?"

Quin murmured in thought before saying, "Nothing too big or rambunctious. She still gets nervous around loud noises. And anything too hyperactive might scare her."

"So dogs are out," Mab said thoughtfully. "Unless you go for a senior dog. You'd have to find one that's already been exposed to kids, though, not always the easiest. I had a dog a couple decades back named Buster, he would have been great. Cats?"

"Well, we already have cats at home. Dad and Papa have cats. She could just . . . "

"Nope. Nuh-uh. That's not the same and you know it." Mab laughed a little, shaking her head. "So if your house is already cat friendly, why not get her a kitten?"

"I'll, uh . . . I'll give it some thought." Quin nodded, then he turned his head to look her in the eyes. "Thank you for your suggestion. I really appreciate the care you're showing Tavi. It means a lot to me."

Mab sucked in a breath, her heart clenching hard enough in her chest that she nearly doubled over from the pain. What the fuck *was* that? "Uh, yeah, you're, uh, you're welcome," she sputtered out, trying to breathe through the tightness.

"Are you okay?"

"Yup. Fine. Just . . . just indigestion, I think. Too many different kinds of food all at once after, you know . . . not eating much the last few days." Mab rubbed at her chest. It eased off a little, and she was able to sit back in her chair, her breathing evening out. She cleared her throat and pressed on. "How're Tavi's flying lessons going? It seems like she's gotten better since last I saw her."

Quin tilted his head a little, a smile ticking up the corners of his lips. She didn't think she'd ever actually seen him smile before. Not really. "She's doing great." The little grin widened, making wrinkles appear around his eyes, and holy shit, he was—

Mab's chest clenched again, and she doubled over, wheezing through the pain as her heart pounded in her chest. Shit. Fuck. Damn. What *was* that? She fisted her hand in her shirt, pressing it against her chest to relieve the ache, but nothing helped. And her head was starting to swim with it. Her vision and hearing went fuzzy.

"Mab? Mab, are you all right?" Quin asked, worry in his tone, and when she looked up at him again, his blue eyes were *so* wide. Why did he have to look so damn pretty, even worried and upset?

"Yeah," she choked, the word coming out rough. "I'm good. I just . . . I'll be back." Then she grabbed Gizmo, dropped him in Quin's lap without a word, and raced across Ander's condo till she could lock herself in her bathroom.

Her knees hit the cold tiles with a *thud*, the sting of it only just recognizable through the continued clenching in her chest. Was she having a heart attack? Could banshees *have* heart attacks? Gods, she was going to be sick.

"Mabbers." Ander's voice came through the door, soft concern lining his tone. "Mabbers, are you okay?"

"I'm fine. Just . . . just some bad sushi." Maybe he'd just—

"Bullshit." Ander's voice was clearer now, as if he'd snapped himself into the room with her, and he came to sit on the tub beside her. "What's going on?"

Nope. He wasn't going to just go away. She supposed she should have expected as much from him. He knew her better than that.

"I think I'm sick." Mab leaned her head on his lap. "Or

maybe I'm having a heart attack. Can—" She winced at another sharp wrench in her chest. "Can banshees do that?"

"No. They can't." He frowned, his fingers brushing her clammy forehead. "You don't have a fever. And nothing you ate tonight is any different than you normally eat. You aren't even drunk, Mab." His lips twisted into a worried little scowl as he brushed her hair away from her sweaty temples. "It feels like a heart attack?"

"Sure. Yeah. What I imagine a heart attack would feel like. I've obviously never had one before, so . . . " She hissed, rubbing at the spot on her chest that was starting to feel like a bruise, an ache, that would never fade.

Ander made a quiet, delighted sound that almost might have been a squeal, and Mab turned her head in his lap so she could glare up at him.

"What the fuck are you so happy about? Your best friend might be dying."

"Not dying, Maberella. Gods, you're so dramatic." He swatted her on the shoulder lightly. "And it's not as bad as a heart attack, honestly. Calm down."

"You're one to talk." She snorted.

He swatted her again for good measure. "It's the *bond*."

"It's the *what*?" She sat up abruptly, her head spinning, and she really was going to throw up if she kept doing that. "It *can't* be the bond, I've only been around the Schields all day today. And I was just talking to Q-ball . . . When . . . "

"When whaaaat?" Ander asked, his smile growing wider by the second. It was terrifying, and Mab wanted to shove him until he fell backward into the tub, but she didn't. Because, of the two of them, he was the only one who had survived this shit.

"When it felt like someone reached into my chest and squeezed all my organs in a vice. Gods, it hurts, Ander.

Can't you do anything?" she whined, leaning forward to peer at him imploringly, then what she'd said caught up to her. She'd been talking to Quin when it started. He'd *looked* at her when it started. Met her eyes. And she'd thought ... "No ... No-no. Nope. Nuh-uh. Not doing that."

"Not doing what, Mabelina?" Ander bent down so he could press his face in close to hers. "It's Quin, isn't it?"

"The fuck it is!" she hissed, and this time, she did shove him, but not nearly hard enough for him to topple back into the tub, nor hard enough to stop his sudden laughter. Bastard. "It can't be Quin!" she huffed plaintively. "It just can't."

"And why can't it?" Ander asked through his laughter.

"Because he *hates* me, Andy. He has from the beginning." Maybe hate was too strong a word. But he sure as shit didn't *like* her, not in the way a soulmate should, anyway. Her eyes were *not* burning with tears. She was not going to cry over some *guy*. She wasn't. That was just stupid. And she wasn't stupid. She was Mab Duchan, for gods' sake.

"He doesn't hate you, Mab," Ander sighed. "Come on, get cleaned up, and let's go back out there. I'll get you a nice drinky drink, that'll help."

"You could give me a nice drinky drink in here." Mab huffed, pulling her head off his lap so she could curl her legs into her still aching chest. Bonded. Arrow-bound. To Quin Schields. To the one ignis in the entire world, probably, who would want nothing to do with her. And wasn't that exactly right? Hadn't she known it would end that way all along? Maybe it would have been better if she hadn't met him at all. She could have gone the rest of eternity never knowing that he didn't want her.

"Yeah, because that wouldn't be weird at all. Come on.

Put on your big girl pants." Ander stood up and held out his hands to her. "You can do this. It should have faded a little by now. The initial bonding is the worst bit."

"It still hurts."

"Yes, but not like it did, right?"

"No, not like it did." She groaned, leaning her head back to glare up at him. "Come on, Andy, haven't I been through enough?"

"Normally, I'd say yes. But you ran out of the room like a bat out of hell and freaked everyone out. You kind of have to come out and at least make an appearance to let them all know you're not dying in here."

"Maybe I *am* dying in here." That'd probably be preferable to what would come next. To a life with this hollow feeling living in her chest.

Ander tsked and flapped his hands a little to make her take them. "Big girl pants, you've got this, Mab."

"I hate you."

"I know." He ushered her back into the living room, not once pausing to let her dig her heels in. And when they came back out, the Schields family was suiting up.

"Everything all good?" Max asked as he came over to Ander, a worried crease between his brows.

"Yeah, we're fine," Ander assured him.

Max nodded. "We're about to head out."

Mab peaked around him to see Quin twirling a bo staff lightly between his hands, and her chest gave another kick. "Balls."

"What was that?" Max frowned at her.

"Nothing. Just ignore her. Come along, darling, let's get you ready for your mission."

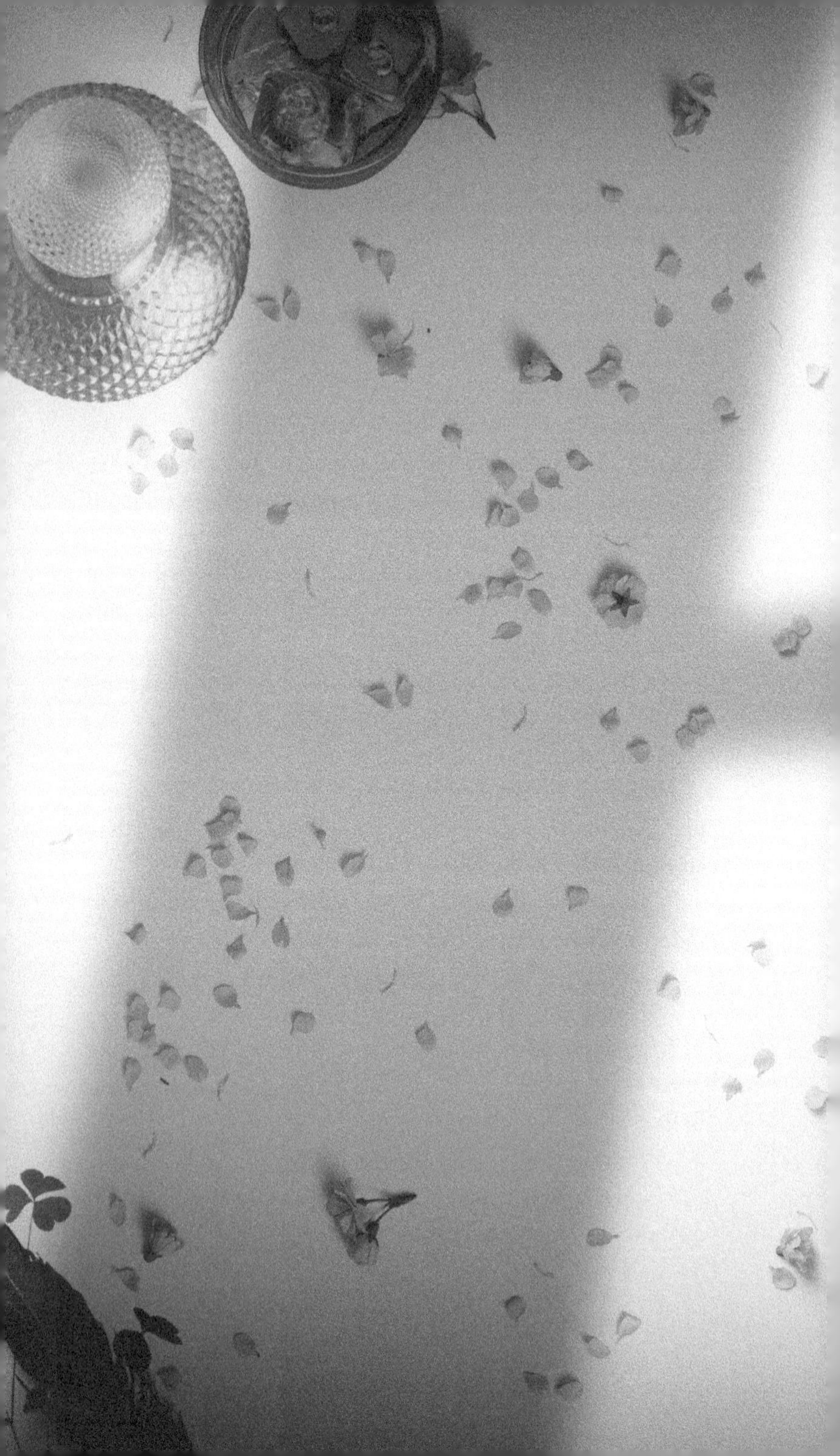

Chapter 26
Quin

Quin wasn't sure what had happened. One minute, he and Mab were discussing what kind of pet he should get for Tavi, and the next instant, he had a rabbit thrown at him and Mab was gone.

He'd tentatively sat the rabbit down on the floor, letting it hop away to wherever it had hidden for most of the evening, and looked at his siblings. They had all looked just as confused as he felt.

"Ander's got her, let's get ready." Max had climbed to his feet, a serious look on his face.

Now, they all stood in the middle of Ruin's condo, dressed in pieced-together assault gear—items that they'd had at home that would work or were at least black—and strapping on their weapons.

"How am I going to know when to bring you back?" Ruin's hands clutched onto the front of Max, and Quin was sure he didn't want to let him go. "Do I just wait for a phone call? What if you get hurt or captured and can't phone?"

"Actually, we've got you all hooked up." Nash appeared, seemingly out of nowhere. He held his hand out to Ruin, who eyed it suspiciously, glancing to Max, then placed his hand tentatively in Nash's.

Nash, holding his hand like he was leading a queen to her throne, drew Ruin to the couch where one of the laptops was set up. "Take a seat," he instructed. Once Ruin was on the couch, Nash clicked a button, and four different camera views appeared. "Each of us has a camera on us." He showed the little black pin attached to each of their collars. "When you click this button right here"—he pointed to a key on the laptop—"you'll get audio. Don't do it until we're over there or you'll get a lot of feedback. I also don't know what a portal will do to mics. So just wait."

Ruin watched the screen for a moment, his eyes flicking to each of them to see which screen was who, then he grinned up at Nash. "Thank you!"

As Nox stepped up to the two of them to begin going over some other things, Quin turned to Max. "Are you ready?"

Max nodded. "Let's get this done and destroy this asshole's plans."

Quin's lips twitched a little, but he nodded. "Agreed."

"Okay, babe, I think we're ready," Max called out to Ruin, who was instantly at his side, hugging and kissing him.

Quin turned away from the PDA and found that Mab was suddenly there right before him.

"You okay?" he asked her.

She nodded. "Yeah. Perfectly fine." Although she didn't seem able to meet his gaze. "Spy good, or whatever . . . " She huffed a sigh and patted his shoulder, all the while looking anywhere but up at his face. "Just, uh, don't get hurt."

"Uh . . . thanks." Quin eyed her for a moment,

wondering what exactly had happened in the living room to change her entire demeanor. He was usually really good at reading people, but he found everything about Mab right now to be confusing.

"All right, let's go," Max called, and the rest of them assembled around him.

"I've done my best to figure out where you need to end up, bless *Google Maps*, but because I've never been there myself or seen it . . . you could come out somewhere wonky. Just be aware of that," Ruin warned as his hands began whirling in front of him.

As a large portal took shape in the middle of the kitchen, Quin frowned. Was this going to work? Or were they going to end up stuck in the middle of a wall, or right in the center of the enemy encampment? Quin looked at Max, about to ask him if he was sure about this, but Max was staring at Ruin with his standard blind faith in those he loved.

Quin grumbled to himself, staring at the portal with disfavor. If he lost a wing or a foot to this . . .

"See you when we get back." Max kissed Ruin quickly, then darted through the portal, his sword in hand.

Quin's fingers tightened on his bo staff, twisting around it a little. He nodded to Nox and Nash, who both carried heavy bags slung over their shoulders. They looked grim but passed through the portal next. With his siblings through, Quin threw one last look to Ruin and Mab, then stepped through the portal himself.

The sensation was like flying and drowning all at once. It felt as if there was nothing and yet everything in his lungs. As he came through the other side, he had to look himself over to make sure he wasn't dripping wet or coated in some sort of film.

But he was fine. He was normal. And he was inside a dark, empty warehouse.

"I think he brought us to the right place," Max murmured quietly to keep his voice from echoing in the space.

Nash flicked on a flashlight and shined it along the floor, checking to make sure there were no hazards in their vicinity.

"Looks it," Quin responded. Stretching out his wings, he gave them a little shake, making sure they hadn't been harmed in the portaling. Feeling that they were fine, he flapped hard twice and jumped into the air.

Since it was hard to see what was on the floor, he chose to fly over to the large set of windows on what he could only assume was the east end, closest to the water. Once there, he landed gingerly and peered through the glass.

Next door, there was a large warehouse that looked rather decrepit but glowed warmly with lights from inside. Out on the wharf in front of the factory, a large cargo ship sat docked, lights glowing all over the top of it as shipping containers were offloaded onto the dock itself.

"What do you think is in them?" Max asked, landing softly beside him. He tucked his wings in against his back, as if worried the bright whiteness of them would shine like a beacon through the windows.

"Nothing good."

His earpiece crackled suddenly, and Nox's voice came through. "We've found a mezzanine with a good view of the factory and the harbor. We're going to get situated up here. Over."

"Perfect. Let us know once you've got thermal imaging. Then Q and I will head out. Over," Max replied.

Quin retrieved the camera out of his pocket and began

snapping shots of the ship and the unloading of containers that was taking place. He zoomed in on a few men that he could see. "I think we've got inanimi," he muttered.

Max pulled out a small set of binoculars and held them to his face. "Yeah, I'm seeing satyrs for sure, possibly a couple of minotaurs, and what looks like a demogorgon."

"We've got the right place, then." Zooming in on the inanimi, Quin snapped several more pictures, capturing their faces as well as their activities.

"Okay, we have thermal imaging up and running. Over," Nash announced into Quin's earpiece.

"What kind of numbers are we looking at?" Quin asked his brother. "Over."

"About ten out on the docks, and another ten, maybe twelve, inside. Place is crawling with them. Guys, be careful," Nox said. "Over."

"Stealthy and quiet, just like a mouse," Max muttered, then looked at Quin. "Ready?"

Quin nodded. "Let's come in from the west side. The street that runs perpendicular to these buildings should give us access without blowing our cover."

"I agree," Max said softly, then pointed to a door on the opposite side of the building. Together, they ran over to it and slipped out into the night.

"Looks like you're coming up on a single lookout on that side. Upper southern corner of the building. Over," Nox's voice cut into their earpiece.

"Roger that," Max whispered into his mic. He signaled to Quin to take the man, and he would continue along the outside of the building.

Quin motioned his understanding and took to the air. With his black wings, he would be more camouflaged with the night. This was definitely one of those times when

Max's angel-like wings were more of a hindrance than a help.

Soaring above the factory, Quin spotted the sentry looking down over the street. He saw him take notice of Max and reach for his radio to call it in just before Quin landed behind him on the roof. He withdrew his bo staff from the holster on his back and snapped it into full extension.

The minotaur spun, shocked at the sound of feet on gravel, and crumpled to the ground as Quin's bo collided with the creature's head. As his form fell, Quin yanked several cable ties from his pocket and tied the minotaur's ankles together and his hands behind his back.

"Sentry is taken care of. Over," he said into the mic on his chest.

"I've got the building," Max began. "You head down to the dockside and see what photos you can get. Over."

"Roger that." Quin ran quickly across the top of the building to peer down at the docks. Several inanimi were steadily offloading sea cans from the container ship. Some of the cans went into the building beneath him, while others were being loaded onto large trucks.

He waited until everyone's attention was on loading a current sea can, then he leaped off the roof. His black wings stretched out, capturing the air beneath him, and he glided silently down to the ground.

Furling his wings tight against his back, Quin ducked behind one of the trucks, pulling out a tracker to stick to the bottom of the transport. He ran along the side of it and peered around the corner carefully, then ran to the next, doing the same to the bottom of it.

Whatever was coming off that ship was going somewhere, and they needed to know where.

At the end of the second truck, Quin waited until two inanimi walked past him, then he hurried over to one of the shipping containers they hadn't moved yet. Pressing his ear to it, he attempted to hear inside. With his knuckle, he tapped lightly on the cool metal and waited until a *bang* came from inside.

"There is something alive inside the sea cans, at least some of them. Over," he whispered into his mic.

"There's only drugs inside the warehouse," Max responded. "But I see empty cages. I think they've held ignis here before. Over."

Quin cursed silently. This was definitely Orcus' operation, but it wasn't the final destination. They'd only found another rest stop on the god's way to his true base of operations.

"Quin, you've got two figures on your six," Nash warned.

Quin spun just in time to block a fist with his bo but not in time to stop a second punch to his abdomen. Grunting at the pain blossoming through his stomach, Quin kicked out at the knees of the demogorgon before him, then blocked its next punch, spun himself, and used his wings to send the beast flying backward into the side of the sea can.

It caused a loud crash to echo into the night, and several shouts rang out after.

"Q, what was that?" Max shouted over their comms.

"I've got a situation," he grunted back, fighting with the second inanimi, who this time wielded a long knife.

Quin struck out with his bo, trying to swipe the knife out of the creature's hand. However, he was too fast and spun out of his way, grabbing onto the end of the bo staff. Quin glared at him as the inanimi snarled.

"Not a good idea," Quin warned and yanked on the bo.

It was enough to send the creature stumbling, and when he did, Quin shoved forward with the bo, and it connected with his forehead.

The inanimi didn't go down, but he staggered. Quin took that as his opportunity to drive the pad of his hand up into the beast's nose. This time, his eyes rolled back into his head, and he crumpled to the ground.

However, the demogorgon had found its bearings. Coming up on Quin from behind, it wrapped large, stone-like arms around Quin, pinning his wings and arms to his body and lifting him off his feet.

Quin growled and kicked back with his heel, connecting with the demogorgon's knee. It dropped Quin, giving him the opportunity to go all the way to the ground, roll, and pop back up onto his feet several yards away.

But the demogorgon was not alone, and Quin found himself surrounded.

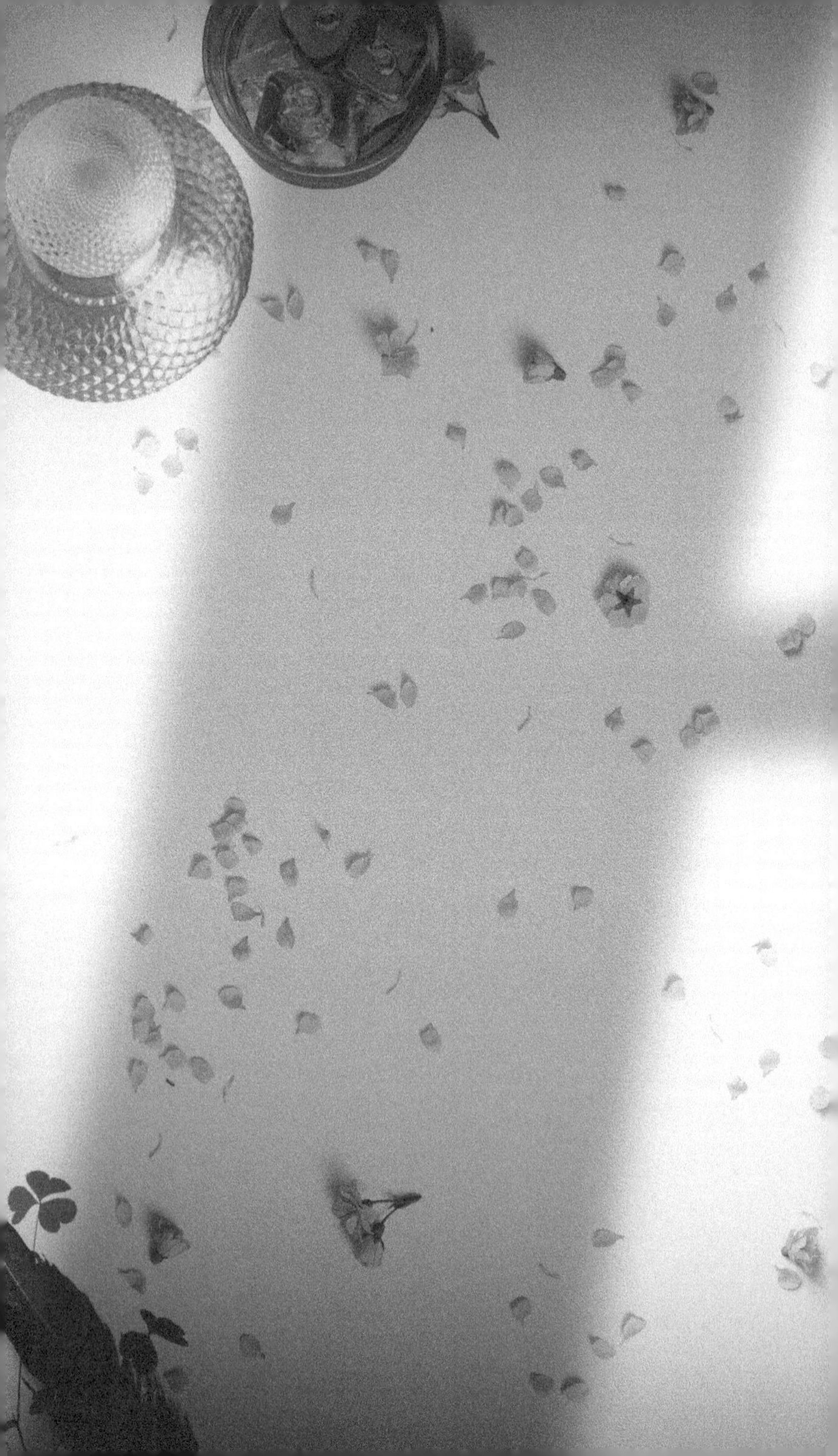

Chapter 27
Mab

"Spy good, huh?" Ander teased, bumping his shoulder into Mab's where they sat on the couch, watching the laptop screen.

"Don't start." Gods, could she get any more pathetic?

"Seriously, Mab, what *was* that?" Ander nudged her again, and she swatted at him, but he didn't back off. Not that she'd thought he would. She knew him better than that, and he wasn't going to drop this amare bond thing. Especially after she'd been *so* understanding of him when his bond had snapped into place. Karma was a bitch and a half as far as Mab was concerned.

"That was me trying to be nice." Which was really her first mistake, wasn't it? Mab wasn't nice, not by nature. Maybe she had been, once upon a time. Before Edward and Bartlett. Before the asylum. "Cynical" was an understatement. And there she was trying to be *nice* to her soulmate. "I promise I'll never do it again if you stop."

"You are aware that's really not an incentive for me to stop, right?" His grin was way too large for how much she was suffering. She really did hate him sometimes.

"Well, damn it." She curled more firmly around Gizmo where she'd dropped him in her lap again. Mab needed something to keep her mind off the utter shit show that was her life right now. Especially as she watched her literal soulmate put his neck on the line and throw himself right into Enrique's warpath. They hadn't even gotten to . . . well, anything, really. And already, Quin was off putting himself in harm's way. It just didn't seem fair.

And Mab was *worried* about him, which was just *so* stupid. She didn't even like him. Hardly even knew him. And he for damn sure didn't like her or know her. So what was with the gnawing in her belly?

Movement flickered on the screen, but it wasn't anything serious. Not yet, anyway. But it would be just Mab's luck that she'd find her soulmate and the utter bastard would up and die, wouldn't it?

"You should tell him," Ander said, breaking the tense silence that had settled between them.

"Like hell I should," Mab snorted. She shook her head, pressing her face in close enough to Gizmo's fur that she was practically inhaling it with every breath. "You saw how awful I was at wishing him good luck. Can you imagine how that would go?"

Ander didn't say anything, but his gaze was heavy on her, and she knew him just well enough to know without looking that he'd raised an eyebrow, his expression lined in judgment.

"Oh, hey stranger, I know you don't know me at all, and hell, might even hate me—"

"He doesn't hate you, Mabbers," Ander murmured, and his tone was so gentle, so small, that she lifted her face from Gizmo's back to eye him.

"Fine. He doesn't hate me." She nodded in

acknowledgement, then pressed on anyway. "But he doesn't like me either. So it'd go something like this: Hey, stranger, I know you don't know me and don't even really like me, but surprise! We're arrow-bound. So I guess you're stuck with me for eternity. Or until one of us dies. Which, hey, with how things are going, might be sooner rather than later."

"Mab."

"No." She glared at him, her mouth twisting into a vicious scowl. "Let me finish." Because she knew how this was going to end. Because it was the same way it always ended. "And he'll say," Mab continued, unable to stop herself, even though she really wanted to. Because it hurt too much to say these things out loud. It ached in her chest, a hollow feeling right alongside the bruise left behind by the bond snapping into place. "'Well, that just sucks. See you never.' And I'll be—" She choked, burying her face in Gizmo's fur again, and cleared her throat to regain control over herself. "It won't be like you and Max, Andy. I know you think it will be, but it won't. I'm not you. And Q isn't Max."

"Oh Mabbers," Ander sighed and pulled her into a tight hug, forcing her to lean her head on his shoulder. "I think maybe he'll surprise you."

"Maybe. But it's doubtful," Mab mumbled into the fabric of her shirt, hiding her face until she'd sucked back her tears, then she turned back to the screen, and what she saw made her heart skitter in her chest.

Quin was surrounded. She couldn't see everything, but she could see what he was seeing. There were at least six inanimi around him. All wielding blades. All advancing on him as one. He couldn't . . . he couldn't fight them all off at once.

"Andy . . . Andy, what do we do?"

Ander had already grabbed his phone and was making a call to the twins to get an answer to that question. But Mab could only watch as the camera jerked around. Quin dodged as best he could, but some of those movements were blows. There was blood glittering on the pavement in the dark—it might have been his, it might have been his attackers'. She couldn't tell from this angle.

Before she could think better of it, she clicked the button to turn on the audio to Quin's camera, and her heart gave another terrified lurch in her chest. He was panting hard, his breathing labored. Likely by a broken rib, if she were to guess.

She couldn't hear anyone else, but she could hear Quin's hiss as one of his attackers landed a blow with their blade, then Quin talking to someone through the coms. Max, probably. "I'm going to need an extraction. I can't get out of here on my own."

He didn't sound scared. Which was frankly baffling. But he didn't sound like *himself* either.

"Yeah, I can wait another couple of minutes," he agreed like an idiot.

He'd only managed to take down one of the six, and there was movement in the shadows beyond the circle of inanimi around him. More were coming.

She didn't know when Ander had risen from the couch, but he was up and across the room, working to reopen the portal and give them a quick exit. Her gaze flicked back to the screen. The angle had changed. It took her a minute to figure out why. Quin was on the ground.

"You need to get him out of there. *Now*, Ander." She shoved Gizmo off her lap onto the couch and got to her own feet.

"I'm working on it, Mab. Max will be there in—"

"He doesn't have time for that, Ander. Get him back here *now*. Whatever it takes." She should have gone with them. She should have been there. She wasn't an ignis, she wasn't trained for intel-gathering missions. But she could fight. She could have had Quin's back. She could have been one more pair of hands, one more set of eyes, and she could have prevented this. "I'm going to get the first aid kit. Get him home!"

She didn't wait to hear Ander's response. She ran through the condo to her bathroom and ripped open the cabinet, pulling towels and medical supplies from beneath the sink. They hadn't needed any of this in a long time, but Mab was loath to stop stocking it on the off chance that they got into a bar brawl. This *wasn't* a fucking bar brawl, though, and she probably didn't have everything she'd need to stitch Quin up once he was back. She'd . . . she'd just have to make do. She'd done more with less, in worse situations. Stretched supplies thinner when she'd been a nurse on the front lines. She could do this.

Not that she'd have much choice in the matter, really. It was that or watch her soulmate bleed out in front of her. Fuck!

By the time she made it back to the living room, the twins were coming through the portal. Mab's heart lodged in her throat, her hands shaking where they held the supplies as she waited one beat, two, before Max came through, practically dragging Quin with him.

"Get him on the couch," she ordered, not even waiting for anyone else to say anything. Her hands no longer shook as she set her kit on the coffee table and started pulling out everything she'd need. This she could do. The logical, methodical patching up of someone else she knew how to handle. Could practically do it in her sleep.

Feelings were messy. But this she understood. "Andy, I need—"

"Sorry, love." Ander shook his head. "It'll have to wait till after I've patched up Max. You've got this covered, though."

When she lifted her head to glare at him, there was a not-so-subtle twinkle in his eyes that made Mab want to throttle him. That would have to wait. She could shake the shit out of her brother after she was sure Quin wasn't going to bleed out on his fucking couch. Gods, she hoped he left stains behind for Ander to deal with.

Quin groaned as Max helped him sit, the sound drawing Mab's attention away from Ander and back to the injured ignis in front of her.

"We need to get you out of this shirt, at the very least. But—" She winced, glancing down at his legs. His pants were torn, blood oozing from them. The cuts didn't look as deep as the wounds on his torso, but that didn't mean they didn't need to be treated. For all she knew, the inanimi who'd attacked him could have laced their blades with something. She wouldn't be able to tell until the fabric was out of her way. "Eventually, I'll have to look at your legs too. But let's start with the worst injuries first."

Quin grunted a reply and shifted to unzip the flaps connecting the front of his shirt to the back, but he stopped midway there with a sharp hiss. His hand flew down to the wound on his stomach, which gushed a little more with the movement.

"All right. All right. Let me do it." Mab swatted his hands away gently and reached for the zipper herself. "Just sit still and try not to make my job any harder than it has to be."

"Is there anything we can do?" Nox asked. "I have some medical training, but it's mostly . . ."

"Mostly what?" Mab asked without even looking up from where she was peeling the fabric out of the wound. She tossed the soiled shirt over onto one of the chairs, thankful that Ander was preoccupied and didn't see the mess she was making of his furniture. "Fuck, did they *have* to jam it into the stab wound like that? I need tweezers."

"I mostly work with corpses," Nox finished and held out the tweezers to Mab.

"Well, that's better than nothing. Thanks." She crouched down onto her knees to get a better look. "Nash, if you're not doing anything, could you get me a bowl of hot water?"

"Roger." Nash gave a quick salute and disappeared into the kitchen.

"If you're going to help, Nox, you need to clean up. We can't risk infection."

"Right." Nox disappeared behind her twin.

"All right, this is going to hurt," she warned, glancing up at Quin.

"Yeah, probably," he agreed. His skin had gone pale from the pain and the blood loss, and his expression was decidedly pinched. But he looked . . . Gods, he didn't look any less beautiful than a few hours ago when they'd been talking about getting Tavi a pet.

"If you need pain meds, I might be able to find some. But I don't have anything that'll numb the area."

"It's nothing I haven't dealt with before. Just get it over with."

Mab nodded and ducked her head back to her work. While she carefully picked the chunks of fabric out, she patted his knee soothingly. "Almost done. And then I think we can stitch this up. It's deep, so I'll have to do an inner and outer stitch."

"Okay."

"Got the water," Nash crowed proudly, setting it on the coffee table next to Mab's little med kit.

"Where do you want me?" Nox asked.

"How is your stitch work?" Mab moved to start getting the needle ready.

"I've never had any complaints."

Mab turned to look up at where Nox was standing with her hands clasped in front of her, a nervous little grin on her face, and had to remind herself that Nox was just a baby. That she didn't know all the shit going on in Mab's life right now. That maybe humor was how she diffused tension. With a shake of her head, she turned back to the wound in question. "I'll handle this one, but once I'm done, we're going to ditch his pants, and you can check the cuts on his legs while I deal with wrapping the broken rib and checking his wings."

"My ribs are fine," Quin protested, but Mab shot him a little glare as he shifted and winced at the movement.

"Yup, totally fine, big guy. And I've got some oceanfront property in Minnesota I can sell you."

Quin huffed, but his lips twitched upward and, shit . . . that might have been a laugh. Mab had made him laugh! She'd celebrate that little victory later.

"Before we let Mary Shelley back here dig in—"

"Hey!" Nox protested, but she sounded like she might be laughing too.

"I know you don't drink, but it'll numb you at least a little."

"I could use a drink," Nash volunteered.

"No one asked you, Thing 2," Mab answered, shaking

her head. The joking around was helping to steady her out. While her hands had been steady, her insides trembled more than Jell-o in a stampede. But this helped.

"How come she gets to be Mary Shelley and I'm Thing 2?" Nash griped.

"Because she knows how to work a scalpel." Mab tilted her head back to look at Quin again. "You sure you don't want that drink?"

"No alcohol." He shook his head.

Mab returned to the suture kit and the wound. It took an agonizingly long time to stitch it up the way she knew it needed to be. And her work was a little crooked. She was out of practice. Now that she was bonded to an ignis, maybe she should see about reupping her certs and practicing again. Who knew how many times she'd be—

No. No, she wouldn't let herself think like that. Chances were, once Quin found out about the idiotic bond, he wouldn't want anything to do with her. And that was fine. Just fine. Because she didn't need some stoic, handsome, artistic, soulful, kind, caring—She didn't need him, either. He'd just gum up the works. The thought sobered her, and the rest of the wound tending went by quickly enough with Nox's help and only slight grumbling from Nash until she sent him away to check in with Max and Ander.

By the time she was finished, the twins had wandered off to find their laptops, and she was left with cleanup.

"You can use my bed," Mab said, wiping the blood from her hands on one of the warm rags that was left marginally clean. "Tavi is already in there, and there's plenty of room for the both of you."

"Where are you going to sleep?"

"Couch, probably." Mab pushed to her feet. Truth was,

she probably wouldn't sleep. Not after everything. It was better to push off the night of terrors that awaited her until there weren't so many ears in the house. "Don't worry about me. You need to lie flat, you're practically being held together by thread."

Quin frowned at her and looked like he might want to argue, but she pulled him to his feet and ushered him gently down the hall, only stopping when they were in front of her bedroom door and he dug his heels in so he could turn around and look at her.

"Thanks for this, Mab," he murmured softly.

Mab shrugged, unable to think of anything of use to say to that. She didn't need another *spy good* debacle.

Don't say something stupid. Don't say something stupid. Don't say something stupid.

"Good night, handsome." *Fuck!* She spun around so quickly, she saw stars, then raced back to the living room, where she threw herself face down on the couch and screamed into the pillow.

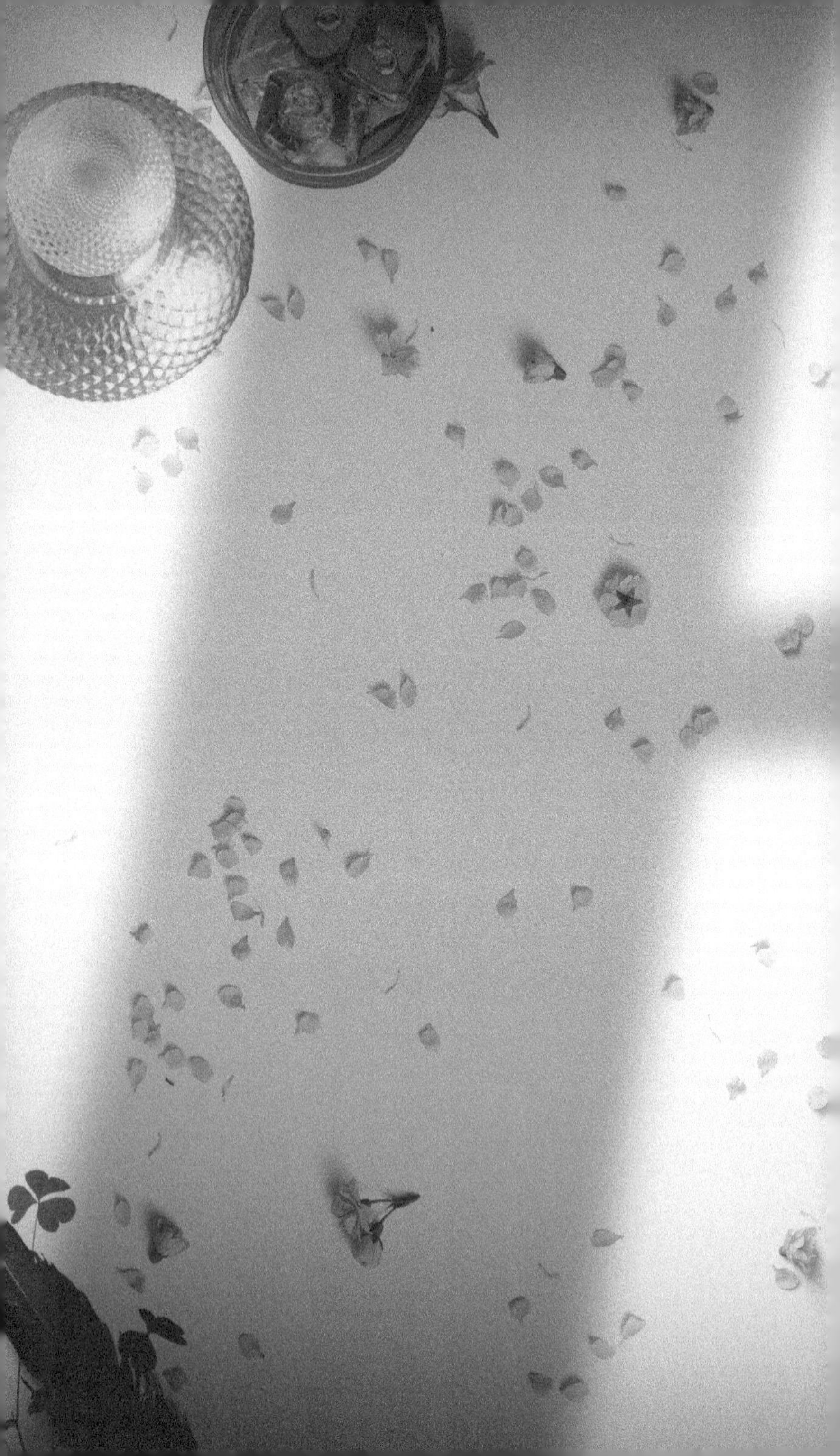

Chapter 28
Quin

Quin awoke to pain and aches all over his body and a toddler's hand splayed over his face.

He would heal, and while he hurt now, only a few hours after their mission finished, in a couple of days, his body would be as good as new, and this would all be a memory. Possibly with a fresh scar where he'd been stabbed, but a memory nonetheless.

The condo was quiet, and from the looks of the sky outside his window, it was still early. The sun was just rising, staining the darkness all shades of light pinks and oranges. But he was awake, and he needed food as well as coffee.

Quin reached up to carefully extract Tavi's hand from his face, placing her arm down by her side. She shifted a little but stayed asleep. Her tiny brown cheek, which was becoming a little chubby from actually being fed properly, was smooshed into her pillow, and her long black lashes splayed out in all their glory.

Looking at the youngling, he knew that he would do

whatever it took to keep her happy. She deserved a good life. People around her that she could count on no matter what came along.

Tavi deserved to know she was safe.

He brushed a thumb along her cheek, which didn't even make her stir, and carefully sat up. His ribs screamed. His wound protested. Even his wings were displeased. His main problem, however, was that all of his clothes from the night before were destroyed. He hadn't intended to stay the night and so he had nothing to wear except for the cotton pajama pants Max brought in to him just as he was going to bed.

Just after Mab walked him to his door. Just after she called him handsome.

She meant nothing by it, he was sure. She'd been in the middle of calling everyone a name of some sort while she'd worked on stitching him up. Quin was used to her calling him anything but his name. He simply wasn't used to the names being nice or complimentary.

Quin held in a groan as he stood, pressing a hand to his abdomen over the gauze that covered his wound. Maybe he'd actually suck it up and ask Max if Ruin would give him a little of that healing magic he could do, just to take the edge off.

When he slipped out into the hall, the condo was pitch black except for a light shining from the direction of the kitchen. His nostrils also picked up on the scent of coffee in the air. Someone was awake.

The hardwood floors were cold on his feet, and Quin found himself missing his parents' house. While they were humans and suffered from the heat, they'd always found a way to evenly balance out keeping the house cool enough for themselves but not freezing for their three ignis children.

Ruin, however, hadn't seemed to figure out yet that he was likely freezing Max out with all the AC.

As Quin came into the open-concept living room-dining room-kitchen area, he spotted Mab seated alone at the kitchen island, sipping coffee, and the twins asleep at the dining table. Their laptops were still open before them, but at some point, they had leaned forward onto the table and fallen asleep with their heads pillowed on their arms.

They hadn't intended to sleep here either, but he had a feeling they went right to work following their trackers to see where they'd ended up.

Quin walked over to them, resting a hand on each of their shoulders and giving them a gentle shake. When they peered up at him with blurry eyes and a slight scowl on Nash's face, he spoke. "Go take my bed. Tavi's in there, but you should fit."

Nox rubbed her eye. "You sure?"

"Don't argue, just go."

Nash stood, rolling his neck and shoulders. He leaned in and kissed Quin on the cheek. "Thanks, bro." Then he took Nox's hand and tugged her down the hall.

When Quin looked toward the kitchen, Mab was standing at the island with a coffee pot in one hand and a new mug in the other. She wasn't meeting his eyes but looking somewhere around his upper chest until finally, she looked up at him and nodded at the pot.

Quin nodded back to Mab's silent question as he moved over to the island and took a seat on one of the plush velvet stools Ruin had placed there. The condo was still very much him, but there were small touches of Max around. A Mickey cushion on the couch, a cardigan slung over one of the dining room chairs, and a display of popcorn buckets all across the top of the kitchen cabinets. Quin squinted and realized they even appeared to be purposefully backlit.

"You're up really early," Mab said, pushing the coffee mug toward him. "What do you need in it?"

"Just a little sugar. And I rise early."

Mab's brow lifted. "I didn't take you for a sugar man." She spun to reach for a little marble dish beside the coffee maker and came back to set it and a teaspoon in front of him. "I thought you'd be more, *I take my coffee strong and bitter like the regimented soldier I am.*" Her voice grew a little gruff as she imitated a stiff, unyielding person.

Quin's brow lifted. He couldn't tell if she was teasing him or mocking him. But as he looked at her, her air became almost demure-like as she ducked her head and sipped at her own coffee.

He took up the teaspoon, scooped just enough sugar to cover half of it, and stirred that into his coffee. "I drink it like my Papa. He's the one who got me drinking coffee, and he just made it for me how he takes it." He shrugged and instantly regretted it as his ribs protested.

"Ah," was all Mab said in response.

"Why are you up?" He looked over at the couch. "Was it that uncomfortable? You really should have taken the bed. I can sleep anywhere." And he meant it. After spending the first ten years of his life in a cage, sleeping on a couch was practically a luxury.

"No, it was all right. Sleep's just . . . " She shrugged and sipped more coffee as her words trailed off.

Quin studied her, seeing the way her eyes seemed a little narrowed with anxiety. There were dark patches beneath to show she hadn't slept. And if Quin wasn't mistaken, her lips looked a little raw, as if she had been worrying them with her teeth a lot.

"Are you okay?" he asked gently. Quin wasn't the best at consoling—the twins always said he was too straightforward and pragmatic. They didn't want honesty when they vented, they wanted an ear. So he thought of his dad and how he would handle this situation.

"I'm fine." The smile she offered him was entirely false. Quin could see right through it. "It's nothing you need to concern yourself with."

Quin took a slow sip of his coffee as he studied her. She wasn't all right. She'd just gotten out of a holding cell she'd spent almost a week in, and he'd seen firsthand her reaction to being put in that cell. It was the response of someone who had serious trauma.

He knew because he also hated small spaces.

"Did you know that when Prometheus sends down a new batch of ignis infants, he doesn't send them directly to the Sanctum?" Which would have made more sense. The whole process was just asking for them to be lost, stolen, or killed. "We have an oracle who gives us fair warning that more are on their way and a general idea of where to look, but we have retrieval teams who go out to find them."

Mab was watching him as he spoke, a little furrow to her brow, likely wondering what he was going on about.

"Sometimes, when the teams aren't fast enough, infants go missing."

Mab nodded. "Like with the asshole."

"Yes." He didn't need her to explain that she meant Orcus. "When I arrived, I was sent to Syria, and my retrieval team wasn't fast enough." He saw Mab's brows shoot up as she sipped her coffee, eyes focused intently on him as she listened. "Inanimi got to me first. There's this camp Jasko kept the infants in, not just ignis but also anything else he could get his hands on. We stayed there, watched over by nasty women he paid to rear us until we were old enough to hold a weapon."

Quin paused, sipping his coffee and thinking about the horrors of those first days. Knowing nothing but pain, hatred, and fear. Often, he wondered if he was broken. Maybe that was why Max had managed to fall in love when he hadn't. Why he'd never felt attached to anyone romantically before.

Or maybe he was simply the way that an ignis was supposed to be, and it was Max who was broken. Changed by the arrow Erotes shot into him. Bonded to another being so it overwrote his true ignis nature.

"What would they do with you then?" Mab asked, eyes wide.

"They had fighting rings. Other inanimi would come to watch and bet on us. When we were little, it was to first blood, but when I turned eight and I started getting taller than all the other kids and my ignis strength started coming in, they pitted me against adults."

Mab gasped. "What the *hell*? *Eight*?"

Quin nodded. "When we weren't in the ring fighting, they kept us locked up in cages. Spaces so small, we could barely move. It kept us more restrained. Meant we couldn't fight back as well when they opened the doors to pull us out."

At some point, his eyes had dropped to the island as he found himself being drawn back into the cramped cage, the feel of stone and sand beneath him, the chill of the cave surrounding him. His mouth dry and his belly empty.

"How long?" she rasped. "How long were you there?"

Quin took another sip of coffee and pulled himself out

of his memories so he could meet her gaze once more. Her dark brown eyes were filled with concern and a mirror of her own pain. He could see that on some level, she understood.

"Until I was ten. That's when the ignis discovered the fighting ring, and Dad brought me back here to Miami."

"Fuuuuuck," Mab whispered, hitting the "k" hard at the end. "I'm sorry."

He shrugged. "It was a long time ago."

"Not *that* long." She pressed her fingertips to the scratch marks on her cheeks. "Not even hundreds of years can wash away the horror of imprisonment."

He waited, quiet and patient, to see if she would continue.

"I was attacked by a piece of shit nobleman," she began. "And when I told the police, he said I was making it up. That I was crazy. Just out to ruin him."

Quin's hand tightened around the handle of his mug, threatening to crush the ceramic beneath it.

"They came for me, in the night. I was still wearing my nightgown when they hauled me out of my townhouse and into a locked wagon. I was in the asylum for a decade at least, maybe more. I don't know, I kind of lost track. Just . . . listening to the madness and screams all around me. With nothing but stone walls to stare at." Her face had gone blank, and Quin wondered if she were attempting to disassociate from the pain of that time.

"How did you get out?" he asked, barely above a whisper.

"A guard tried to attack me in my cell." As she spoke, Quin had to set his mug down before he shattered it. The rage that was overtaking him at something that happened so long ago was nearly blinding. "And when I screamed, my banshee wail appeared for the first time." As she continued, Quin had a dawning sense that things were only going to get worse. "He left with his ears bleeding, but more of them appeared later and hauled me out to a pyre. They tried to burn me at the stake for being a witch."

Quin wasn't one to swear, but he found a curse slipping from his lips as he stared at her, horror and revulsion filling him. He was aware that it had happened in those days. Normies so disbelieving in the magical that they burned whatever they couldn't explain. But he'd never spoken to anyone who had experienced it firsthand. "How are you alive?" *And functional?* Her care and concern for others was honestly admirable after everything she had suffered through at the hands of humans.

"Ander. He appeared like a demon in the night. Scared them away and managed to put the fire out just as it reached my feet. Left me with some scars, but . . . " She took a deep, slightly shaky breath but straightened her back and tipped her head up proudly. "I'm here," she said, making a motion like *ta-da* with her free hand.

"And that's why you love him," Quin said simply.

A small smile broke through the stoney look on her face. "Among other reasons. But yeah. That's why I love him."

Quin nodded. "That's Dad for me. The first kind face I remember seeing over me, the one who pulled me out of hell."

"Zeke must *love* that," Mab said, a smirk forming on her face.

"I think sometimes he wishes he and I were closer." Quin shrugged. "But the twins are his mini-mes, so I think he's okay."

Mab snorted and sipped more of her coffee.

"I'm sorry," he started, then continued when he saw the

questioning look on her face. "That we triggered all of that pain for you by locking you up. I wanted to keep you out of there until there was proper evidence, but my hands were tied."

"It's okay, Stink Eye." This time, as she said the nickname, Quin could almost swear there was a touch of fondness behind it. "I know you did everything you could."

He still didn't feel like he had done enough. Even though he'd risked a grounding by showing up in court. In all honesty, that was the least he could have done. He should have gone to Galeo with the evidence earlier. Fought against Marius and Cedaloin taking over. But he'd let himself be steamrolled. Accepted what Galeo forced on them simply because he was their captain.

It chafed at him a little, to blindly follow. To not be allowed to question or protest. It reminded him a little too much of the fight camp, where the handlers' word was law and no one was able to fight back.

The shrill ringing of a cell phone interrupted their quiet moment together. Recognizing it as his own, Quin moved into the living room, fishing through the pile of equipment that was his. Galeo's name was lit up on the front.

Pressing the green *Accept*, he held the phone to his ear. "Quintus."

"Where is Maximus?" Galeo growled. "He's not answering his phone."

"I can only assume he's still in bed, sir." Quin's voice was dry and emotionless. "We're suspended, so there's no need for him to be up."

"Well, drag his ass out of bed, and the twins, and get yourselves to my office, *now!*" Galeo didn't wait to hear a response from Quin. Instead, he hung up and left Quin staring at his phone.

"Is everything okay? I could hear the yelling from over here."

Quin looked at Mab. "It's our Captain ... He wants the four of us to come in."

"I thought you were suspended?"

"We are."

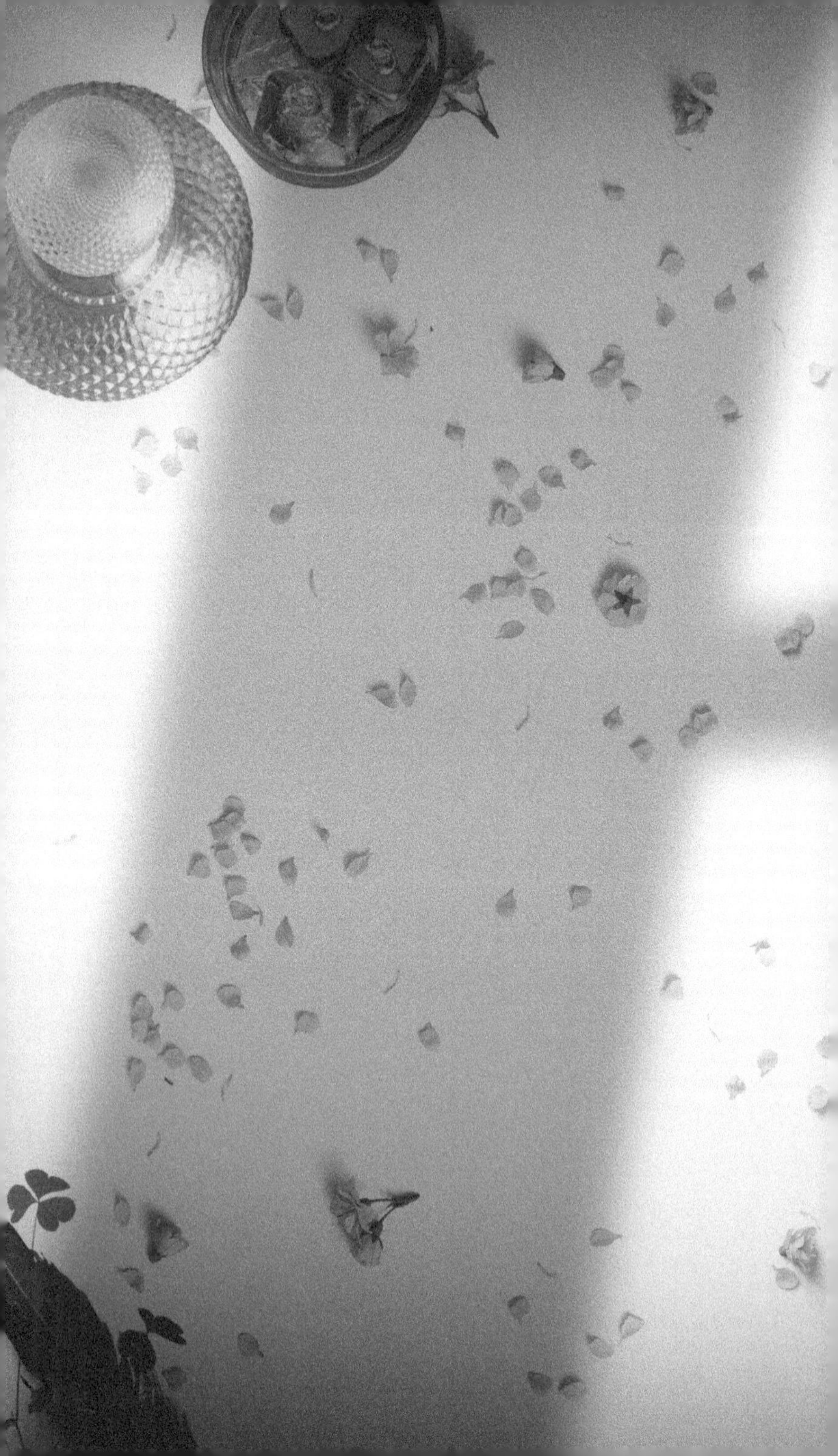

Chapter 29
Max

Max didn't like going into any given situation without some knowledge of what was going on. Call it the soldier in him. Call it the leader in him. Call it an ignis trait. Whatever it was, walking into the sanctuary without any knowledge of why Galeo was calling them in while they were all supposed to be suspended unsettled him.

He couldn't shake the feeling that something terrible was about to happen. Something he couldn't stop. Something he couldn't protect his siblings from. And what kind of leader—what kind of *brother*—was he if he couldn't protect them from everything?

Those suspicions were only confirmed when they rounded the corner and caught sight of their command center. There were two human techs inside, dismantling the twins' workstation. Throwing cords into a box and carefully setting aside computer screens. The chairs had been wheeled into the hall, out of the way, while they worked. All five of them, one for each Schields sibling—Georgie included, once she was old enough.

That wasn't what stopped Max cold, though. What

stopped him cold, his muscles locking up where he stood in the hall, was the trash bag sitting outside of the door, an olive-green sleeve hanging from it haphazardly.

His sweaters.

The bag was full of them. And they hadn't even bothered to fold any, by the looks of it. Just balled them up like they were nothing more than empty fast food wrappers and stuffed them into a bag.

He wanted to storm in there and ask them what the hell they were doing. Demand an answer for why all of his belongings had been thrown into a black trash bag. But he already knew the answer, didn't he? And it was his own fault. He'd been the one to bring this down on their heads. All because he couldn't leave well enough alone. All because he hadn't followed orders.

They should hate him for this. Maybe they would by the time it was all over. But for now, when Max turned to look at his siblings, all he found were three faces pressed into grave determination.

"We've got your back," Nox said, and their brothers nodded firmly.

Max lifted his chin. Right. His siblings knew what they were doing was the right thing. And above all, they were loyal to their family, to justice, not to the Princeps who sat high on their thrones in Rome, far enough away from the action that they couldn't understand what was really going on. And it would stay that way, no matter what punishment was handed down to them by Galeo.

With a deep breath, Max led them the rest of the way to Galeo's office.

"Close the door behind you," Galeo said without looking up from whatever was on his tablet.

None of them spoke, but the door shut with a finality that made a trickle of sweat crawl down Max's spine.

Galeo made them stand there waiting while he finished looking over whatever was in front of him. Max recognized it as an intimidation tactic. One that Galeo had used on them a few too many times to really be effective anymore. But still, he stood straighter, ready to take whatever was coming their way on the chin.

If he could protect his siblings, he would. But he knew them well enough to know they were ready for this. They had known the potential consequences when they decided to help Mab and Ander. He wasn't going to disrespect them by thinking they hadn't. By thinking he'd tricked them into this somehow. They were all adults. Not just adults; capable, trained professionals. They had gone into this with their eyes open, and even if he couldn't protect them from the fallout, they had been willing to help anyway.

"Effective immediately, I am reassigning Nox and Nash to other teams," Galeo said, his words calm, measured.

"Team*s*?" Nox hissed and took a step forward until she was on Max's right. Her hands clenched into fists at her sides, clearly ready for a fight.

"Yes. Teams, plural. I'm separating you." Galeo's tone was detached, impersonal, and cold. As if he didn't realize or perhaps didn't care what effect that would have on the twins and their productivity. Max knew from experience that they couldn't *be* separated, not if one wanted them to continue to perform. They were at their best when they were a unit.

"We won't work with anyone else," Nash said, coming up on Max's left. His posture mirrored his twin's, anger rolling his shoulders back and making his chin tremble. "You can't separate us."

"We won't work with any other techs," Nox agreed.

Max held back a growl. He wanted to tell them both to shut up and just take it for what it was. Promise them that he'd figure a way around this. But he didn't . . . He wasn't sure that he *would* figure out how to solve this for them. This might be . . . This might be the end of Team Schields. His breath caught in his lungs, lodging there. Gods, he was going to throw up.

"Now, no need to throw a tantrum, you'll still be—"

"I'll *show* you a tantrum!" Nash snarled. "If you think this is a tantrum, you haven't seen *anything*." And he took another step forward, but Max put his arms out and stopped both twins from advancing farther. He didn't need them to get themselves locked up and possibly executed for attacking an official. That would be worse than his team being disbanded. He couldn't lose them.

"Enough." Max's tone was firm. "Nash, Nox, stand down."

"We won't—" Nox started, but Max cut her off with a firm shake of his head.

"Those are your orders; you will follow them." The *until I figure out another way* went left unsaid, but he knew they heard it all the same. They were too damn smart not to. "Am I understood?"

"Yes, boss," the twins said in unison, the reply so practiced, it came easily to their tongues, even now.

"Good." Max nodded and returned his attention to Galeo. "Will that be all, sir?" He knew it wasn't. His gut churned with the knowledge that there was more—*worse*—coming. Galeo wouldn't have called them all in if he was just going to punish the twins. He had something for Max and Quin as well. Although Max thought maybe it was a good sign that he wasn't dolling out their punishments publicly. Maybe that meant they weren't too bad?

Foolish. Naive. Hopeful.

"No. That will not be *all*, Maximus," Galeo spat, his wings shifting behind him in clear anger, spreading out as if to puff himself up to be bigger than he was. Another intimidation tactic that had stopped working on Max shortly after he came of age to run his own team and grew taller than Galeo. A fact that infuriated Galeo further as Max watched the movements with a blank look. "You and Quintus will be grounded."

Max's heart lurched into his throat, and it was only by sheer force of will that he didn't vomit on the floor. "What?"

Grounded. Their primary feathers would be clipped. They would be unable to lift off from the ground. Unable to fly as they were accustomed.

"Please, sir," Max gasped through a throat gone raw with acid. "That's a little extreme, isn't it?"

Instead of answering, Galeo turned his tablet around to show them footage of the fight in Texas. How he'd gotten it, Max didn't know. But it didn't matter. The fact was that he had, and now he knew they'd ignored a direct order. "Tell me, Maximus, does insubordination not warrant such a punishment?"

He couldn't save himself. He couldn't keep the twins together. Maybe he could still save Quin. "Quin had no choice in that mission. I ordered him to go with us. I'm his superior. If anyone should be punished for that, it's me. You don't need to—"

"I warned you *both* what would happen, didn't I?" Galeo asked, his head tilted to the side, questioning, curious. Like a psychopath watching a fucking trainwreck. "I told you if you continued to investigate Orcus, this would be the cost."

"Yes, but—"

"Quintus has his own infractions, bursting into the courtroom unrequested in direct violation of his suspension. And as far as this stunt in Texas goes, he could have said no. He could have come to me and told me what you were doing. He did neither of those things. Instead, he went along with it." Galeo tapped on the screen, and the image shifted to clear footage of Quin sneaking through the trucks on the dock. "Thus, he will be punished the same. Superior officer or not, he could have said no."

"But, sir—"

"Take them away." Galeo spoke into the intercom on his desk, and the door was flung open as four ignis came in, iron shackles already in their hands that would block the flow of Max and Quin's fire, keep them from lashing out at their captors. Not that it would really stop them from fighting. They were both trained soldiers.

"You can't do this!" Nox shouted and stepped in between the approaching ignis and her brothers, Nash at her side, both ready to fight to protect their brothers.

"They didn't do anything wrong!" Nash agreed, raising his fists.

They would be no match for ignis, no matter how they'd been trained by their fathers to protect themselves. Not in this setting, where they were surrounded. They were just humans. Unarmed humans. And they'd be hurt in the process.

Max took their shoulders and gave them both a firm squeeze. "It'll be all right, you two," he lied softly.

It wouldn't be. Nothing about this situation was all right. And already, Max could feel Quin at his side, tensing up, his entire body going rigid. Max's heart sank in his chest, his hands starting to shake. He couldn't protect them, any of them. He couldn't save them. And Quin was going to— Gods, this shouldn't be happening to Quin. Not after everything he'd gone through. Max had promised him once, when they were children, that he'd look after Quin. That he'd make sure no one ever put him in a cage again. In many ways, this was just another cage.

"Max," Nox whispered, the word a choked, broken mimicry of how she usually spoke.

"It'll be all right," he repeated. Because what else could he say? He couldn't let the twins get hurt trying to protect him and Quin. Not when he'd brought this down on all their heads. "Go and . . . " He cleared his throat. "Call Dad and Papa." He glanced back at Quin, then ducked his head to whisper to her. "He's going to need them after this."

Nox nodded and let him brush the tears from her face. Her expression was resolute but still furious.

Max could understand that. He was just as angry. Because how *dare* Galeo, after all they had done for this sanctuary, after all Quin had suffered through, after their many years of service, how *dare* he clip their wings.

The four ignis who Galeo called in to get them had hung back until that point, looking nervous about what was going on, uncomfortable with what they were going to have to do. Max could understand that too. No one wanted to watch as an ignis was grounded. No one wanted to even think about that as a possibility.

Still, he could go into this with as much dignity as possible. He turned to look at Quin one more time and murmured gently, "You aren't alone. I'm right here with you. And I'm going to stay right here with you."

Although he didn't know how much good the words

would do. But he needed to say them, needed to try to reassure Quin one more time before this happened.

"I'm fine," Quin said roughly.

Max turned and nodded to the ignis.

"You won't need the iron for me. I won't fight you." It wasn't himself he was worried about. It wasn't himself he'd fight for. It was Quin.

"Sorry," one of them murmured softly, her tone almost regretful, apologetic. "Orders."

He nodded his understanding. Because wasn't that all an ignis was? They were orders, packed together and given flesh. Nothing more. It was only them, only the Schields family, that thought they could be more than that. How wrong they'd been. How arrogant.

Then she clapped the cuff around Max's wrist, and he went cold.

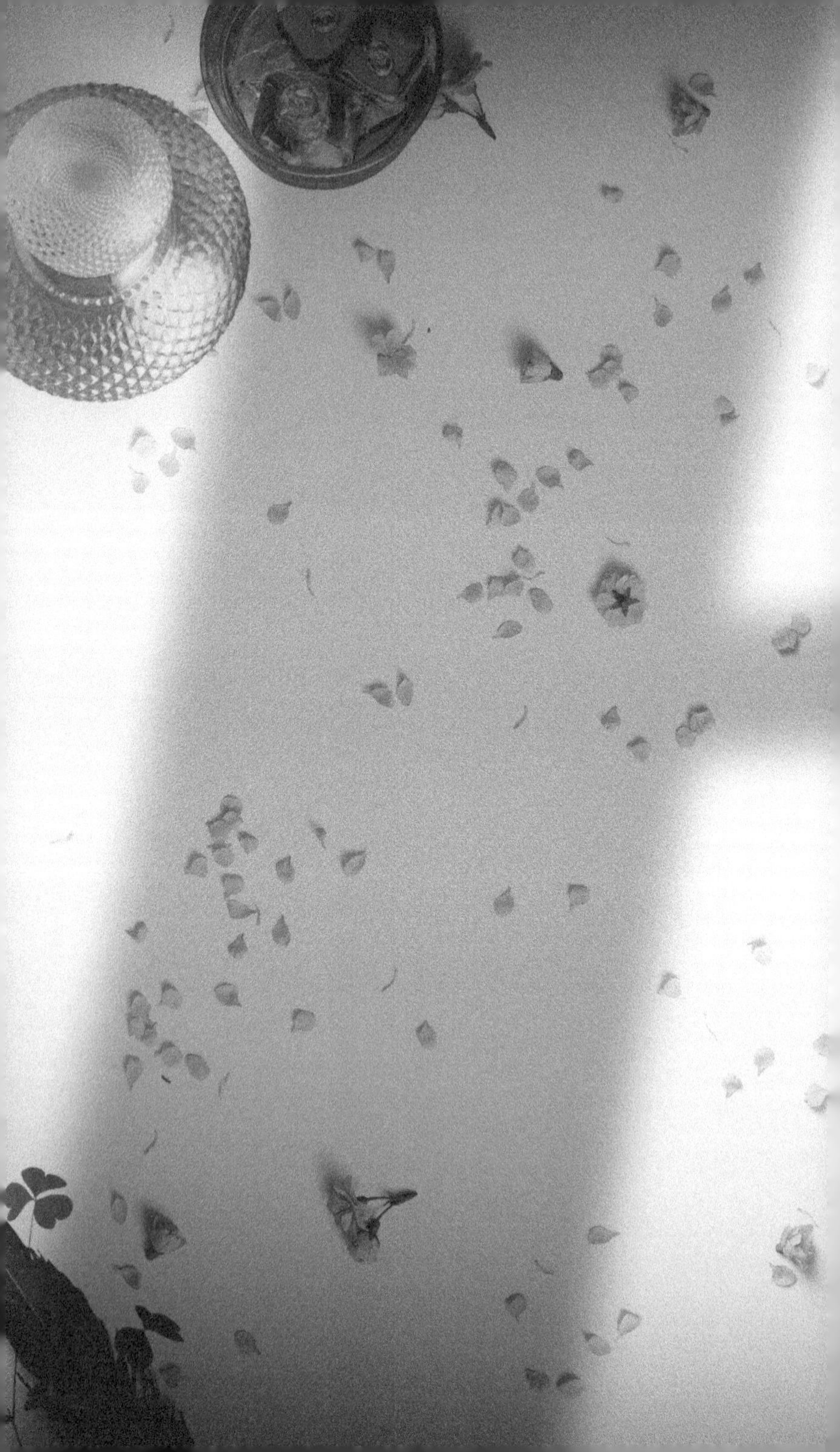

Chapter 30
Quin

Quin had been grounded before.

He had been about seven or thereabouts—it was hard to tell time, let alone age, when one had no guidance in the matter—when he tried to fight back. After winning his match, he turned his weapon on his handler, taking him in the side of the head with the sword he had been given. He'd struck him with the broad side of it, not the edge, and so his head remained intact, but it dropped his handler to his knees. When the camp leader appeared out of the shadows to stop him, Quin had turned his sword on him, and one good swipe scoured down his face, slicing through his eyes and cheek.

He could remember the scream of pain and fury to this day. As a child, he'd been filled with fear as well as anger and had sought to behead the handler still on his knees, childish naivete making him think he could fight his way out to freedom.

Quin never got that far. Another handler shot him with a tranq gun, and Quin's knees had fallen out beneath him.

When he came to, they dragged him out of his cage,

having purposefully waited until he was aware. Then two of them held him down with his face in the dirt while a third clipped his primary feathers.

It had severely hampered his ability to fight in the rings, nearly ending with him killed. But worse, it destroyed any hope he'd had of one day escaping into the skies. Quin realized then that he would never be able to get himself out of the rings, and he would be there until the day someone finally killed him. Defeat had set in.

Quin wanted to fight again. He wanted to lash out at the two ignis surrounding him, one holding a set of wrist cuffs, the other a taser in case he fought back. He wanted to blast a hole through the sanctuary wall and fly away. Free.

This place was only one more fighting ring, was it not? Another place that had locked him up. Forced him to submit to a specified mold and threatened punishment if he stepped out of line. Their cages were gilded and formed in the shape of protecting society, but they were cages all the same.

He resisted the instinct within to protect himself and instead held his hands out so that they could clamp the thick irons on him. As the cold metal encircled his wrists, Quin did his best to empty his mind.

He didn't do well with tight spaces or being confined. When he was younger, he would nearly black out if someone pinned him down. Training had been a process until he dealt with the worst of it.

As the two ignis fell to either side of him and began to walk him out of the office, Quin kept his eyes straight ahead. He didn't dare look at either Nox or Nash to see the fear on their faces. Nor did he let himself look over at Max. Max, who he knew was trying so bravely to hold himself together for Quin. Feeling like he needed to be stronger just so Quin could fall apart.

He hated that about himself. Hated the weakness that could be triggered by the silliest things. Hated the trauma that had broken him in so many ways.

Quin wanted to be strong now. Wanted to hold it together so that, for once, Max could fall apart. But as they walked the white halls of the sanctuary and approached the door that led into the clipping room, beads of sweat began to form at his temples, and his wings twitched, threatening to take flight.

His hands were bound, but he'd fought with worse odds. His ribs were broken, and there was a wound still healing in his abdomen, but he'd fought with worse injuries.

Could he forgive himself for the fallout of fighting back? Could he forgive himself if he *didn't* fight back?

The door to the clipping room whooshed open, and a draft of cold air met them. The chill settled into Quin's bones, and the tension in his body mounted.

This couldn't happen again. He was no longer a child. He was no longer weak and unable to protect himself. He could fight this, and he could escape.

Inside, there were two separate clipping stations. Quin had never been in this room before, but he knew them for what they were the moment he saw them. His feet halted, his breath catching as the chill of the room settled further into his body. One of the ignis beside him muttered for him to move, and when he didn't, they grabbed him roughly by the shoulders and forced him forward.

"No!" It was ripped out of him like one would yank a tooth. Forceful and tearing. Clawing up his throat to burst out unbidden and unwanted.

Quin had tried to remain stoic and silent. But this

couldn't happen again. He was no longer a captive. He was meant to be in control of his own life.

He and his siblings had only done the right thing. They were ignis. They were meant to find terrible beings and bring them to justice. They had simply been hunting the worst out there.

He had begun struggling even before he realized it. His wings spread out wide, and he twisted to bat one of his guards with his left wing. It caught the ignis by surprise and made him stumble sideways. His other guard jabbed the taser into his torso, forcing the breath out of his lungs as she struck his broken ribs.

He wheezed as the shocks of electricity coursed through his body. Every muscle tensed in agony, and his injuries screamed even more from the force of it. When the volts stopped entering him, his knees threatened to cave below him.

His guards were quick; they grabbed his arms and rushed him forward, shoving him down onto the clipping station. Braces shot out to clamp around his ankles, pinning them down, then his knees as well, holding him in a kneeling position. As if he were a lowly slave, bowing to his master. They lifted his cuffed wrists up and slid them into the stand in front of him, through the hole in the middle of it. As his hands went through, it closed around his wrists, effectively holding him captive.

The last, most degrading part was the hooks that descended from the ceiling. Knowing what was coming, Quin yanked at the stand, pulling with all his might, despite the way his hands screamed at him to stop. Trying to break them free.

"Stop making it worse for yourself," the ignis above him whispered. Timoteo, if Quin remembered correctly.

"We were just trying to hunt down a criminal," Quin rasped.

"We know." But he still reached for the hook, still stretched it down to slip it through Quin's feathers and around the upper arm of his wing. Blindly following orders, as they all did.

Never questioning. Never stopping to wonder whose best interests they were listening to.

The same treatment was given to his other wing, and the hooks pulled upward, stretching him out so that his body was held taut between the three points.

Quin couldn't move. No matter how he struggled, he could only inch himself slightly one direction or the other.

They could do anything they wanted to him, and there was nothing he could do to stop it. His heart pounded in his ears, threatening to burst from his chest and take flight on its own. No matter how much air he breathed in, he could not seem to get enough oxygen.

In the back of his mind, he heard deep, sadistic laughter. Almost like a dry, hacking cough that went through to his bones.

"You thought you could get away from us, did you, little birdie?" Hidalgo rasped, his voice a tumble of gravel falling over the stone walls of the cave. Blood streaked down his cheek and the side of his neck, a red, angry wound garishly splitting the side of his face. "Hold him down, boys."

456 was shoved violently forward so he fell face-first in the red dirt. Larger, stronger bodies pinned him to the ground, making it so no matter how badly he struggled, he could not get free.

His cheek was forced into the ground, dust and dirt breathed in and out of his nose as he frantically tried to break out of the hold. But nothing worked.

Hidalgo laughed darkly, the bark of it scratching at 456's ears and insides. Scraping its way down into his being. "Struggle all you want, little birdie, this is happening. You're lucky Jasko makes the money off you that he does, or you'd be strung up and left to die instead."

456 couldn't see what they were doing, but he could feel them stretching his wings out. A newfound terror filled him. Were they going to take his wings?! Would they strip him of the only thing that gave him any kind of peace at all? The brief flights he could take in the ring. When he felt the air beneath him, a gentle, loving caress that lifted him up. Bore him away from this hell.

Tears pooled on the sand and stone beneath him. Starting as perfect drops of water, resting on top of the dry, parched earth, before seeping down into the abyss.

456 hated showing weakness. Hated anyone seeing how this place affected him. But he sobbed uncontrollably. And screamed. Angry, hate-filled screams of fury. He struggled and fought, cried and screamed, until the darkness threatened to take him under.

When at last they let him up, his wings were still attached, but he saw how the first four primary feathers on both wings were shorn in half. Scrubbing the back of his hand across his eyes, he climbed defiantly to his feet. Stretching out his wings, he leaped into the air, flapping forcefully to launch himself upward.

He faltered and landed heavily on his behind in the sand.

All around him, his captors laughed. Except for Hidalgo. He simply stared back at 456 with a dark, pleased look. His black eyes almost seemed to glow red as his lips twisted into a vile smirk of pleasure.

"Put the birdie back in its cage."

"Quin!" Snapping out of the tailspin his mind had gone

down, Quin looked over at Max, locked in the same way. "It's going to be okay."

It wasn't. And Quin knew that as he watched them bring out the silver shears that glistened in the bright LEDs from above. As the sound of metal blades slicing through the cartilage of feathers echoed out in the room, Quin forced himself to keep his eyes on Max.

He wouldn't fail his brother. Not in this. He would make himself strong enough to be in this moment with Max. He couldn't hold his hands like they would when they were little, but he would hold his gaze.

Max, for his part, only flinched a little as they cut through the feathers. His eyes stayed on Quin's. The look in their depths tried to convey that everything would be all right, but behind that was the dawning understanding that it wasn't going to be. That something truly awful was being done to him right now. To his body.

One of the greatest violations you could inflict upon a bird of prey.

When they clipped the last feather, Max's eyes snapped shut. Quin didn't know if it was because he didn't want Quin to see his desolation or if he was hiding tears. Either way, Quin's heart broke.

They had done this to Max. They had grounded him. Stripped him of his flight. Taken from him part of what made him who he was.

Quin let out a howl of fury. A rage from so deep inside him that his hands sparked with fire. "You all have no honor!"

He struggled, fighting the bindings. Fighting the hands pinning him down in the sand and stone once more. Struggling to block out the manic laughter echoing through his mind.

He barely felt the clipping. Hardly heard the snip of the metal blades as they cut through him. But he saw the tips of the black feathers as they fluttered to the ground. A stark contrast against the light gray tile beneath him.

He stared at them, a haunting, garish sight, and his body went slack. The fight drained out of him. He was seven years old again. Weak and defenseless. There was nothing he could do to protect himself or anyone else around him.

A short half-sob, half-laugh left him, and Quin hung his head.

As they unhooked his wings, released his hands from the hold and the cuffs, and unstrapped the bindings on his legs, he didn't even move. Why bother? It was over now. He and Max had lost.

Because in this world, goodness was seen as weakness. And the world would try to take from you every chance it got.

"Quin." Max was at his side, his hand on his shoulder, his gaze soft and concerned.

Gods . . . Max. How did he manage to stay so good and pure in this life? How did he remain this light of love no matter what was going on around him?

He shook his head and, unable to find the words, he signed with limp, lackluster movements, "No. Just 456."

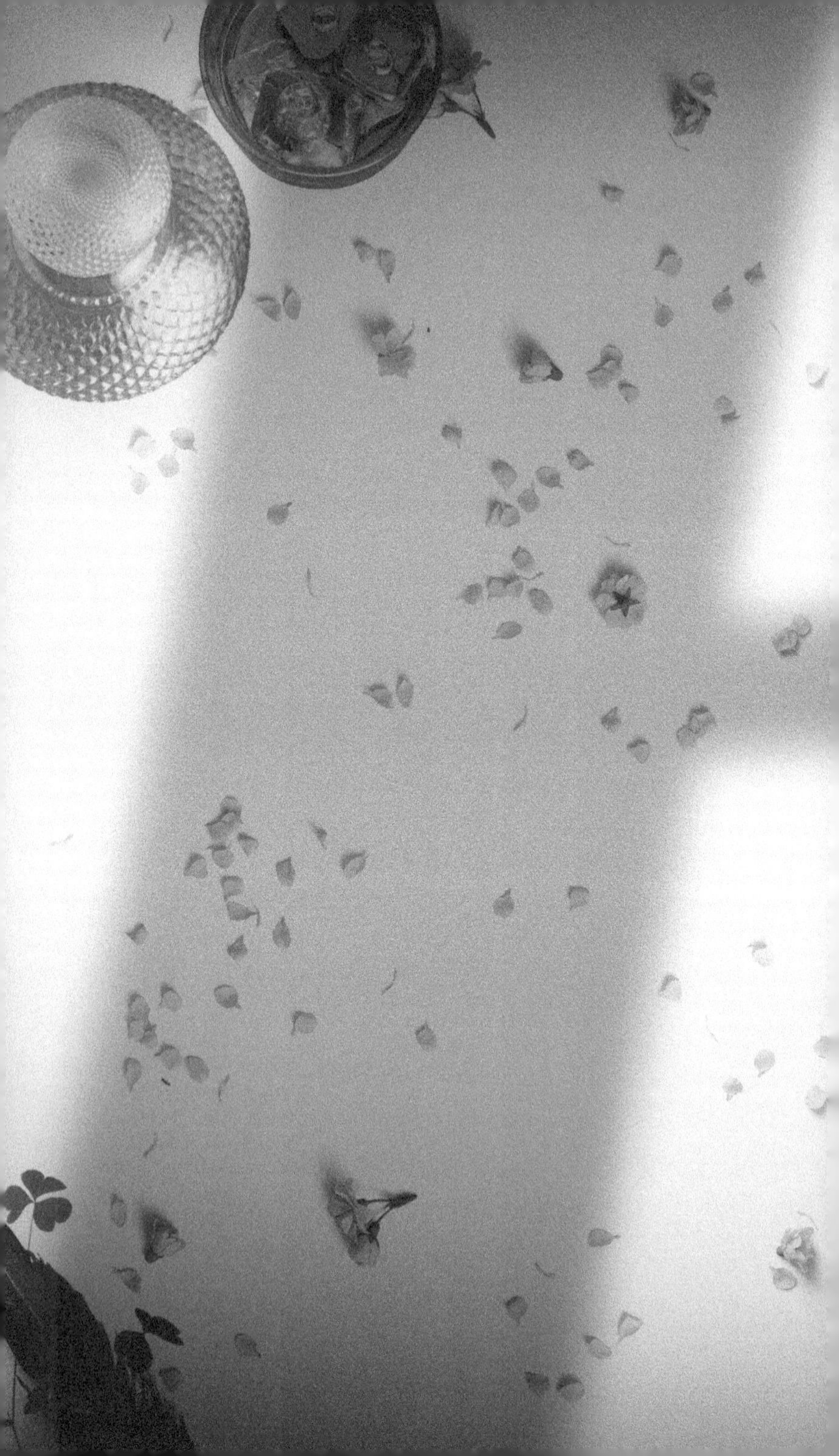

Chapter 31
Ander

Once the Schields cleared out, Ander and Mab sat at the kitchen island, their respective pets in their laps and a cup of coffee before each of them.

The air was heavy with trepidation that neither of them wanted to voice, so Ander poured a little whiskey into both their mugs to take the edge off. Although Mab didn't say it, he knew she needed the added warmth settling in her belly to soothe her nerves just as badly as he did.

When his phone finally rang, he was surprised to see Nox's name come up instead of Max's. He reached for it so quickly, the phone slid across the marble counter and he had to use his magic to keep it from falling to the floor.

"Hello?" he asked, breathless and harried even though he hadn't done anything but sit here.

"They know about last night's mission," Nox began, not even bothering to say hello.

"Fuck." Ander rubbed at his forehead.

Mab's brows shot up, and she mouthed, "What?"

"They're splitting me and Nash up," she continued. "And putting us on different teams." In the background,

Ander could hear Nash complaining how it was complete and utter bullshit.

"And Max and Quin?" Ander looked over at Mab as he asked it.

"What's going on?" Mab asked, her face twisting with worry.

Ander waved her away so he could hear Nox. Except Mab had other things in mind and stole the phone out of his hand, hitting the Speaker Phone option. "Say that again, Nox, I just put you on speaker," she announced to the room.

Ander glared at her, but he supposed he couldn't blame her. She was waiting on news of her soulmate as well.

"They've sentenced Max and Quin to be grounded." Nox's voice was hollow and pain-filled.

"What the *hell*?!" Ander shouted. "I'm on my way! I'll get them out of there before they can do anything!"

"It's already happening as we speak."

Mab cursed heavily.

"What do you mean?" Ander's head was light, dread tingling up his spine to tickle at his skull. A heavy, itchy kind of panic settled over him that made him antsy with the need to be doing *something*.

"They've got them in the grounding room already."

Ander covered his face. His Max. His sweet, dear-hearted Max, who wanted only the best for everyone. They were going to clip his feathers and keep him from flying. They were damaging a part of his body against his will.

"I am going to fucking burn that place to the ground," Mab growled.

Ander seconded the notion. "And I am going to help you. This is *barbaric*." How could they still adhere to such practices?

Of Hope & Blight

"No, you can't do anything. Ander, Max is going to need you. Please ... you just need to be here for him. He's going to try to be strong for Quin and everyone else. He needs someone to be strong for him. To help him through this. *Please.*" It was the "please," the desperate sound of begging, that Ander wasn't used to in Nox's voice that made him settle.

Max needed him. Not to go on a crazed, revenge-filled frenzy but to be the one person who had himself together so that Max was allowed to break down.

Ander took a deep breath and nodded, more for himself than anyone else.

"Okay. Okay. Do your parents know?" he asked.

"Not yet. He wanted us to call them, but we thought you should know first so you could get here," Nox informed him.

"All right. You two stay where you are in case they come out. Mab and I will snap to your parents' home and grab them. We'll be at the sanctuary as soon as we can." Ander met Mab's eyes, and he knew that she was ready to bring the whiskey bottle and the cloth so long as he brought the matches.

But the Molotovs would have to wait until they at least got their boys home and settled.

"Thanks, Ander." There was relief in Nox's voice.

"We'll see you soon, kiddo." Ander hung up and was instantly on his feet, setting Monnie down on the floor.

He didn't even have to pull Mab to him; she was already at his side, slipping her arm around his waist. Ander met her eyes and saw in them her consent. With a snap of his fingers, they left the condo and popped up in the middle of the Schields family home.

The house was quieter than Ander expected. Even

though almost all of the Schields were gone, for some reason, he'd thought they would be coming into chaos.

As they popped into the kitchen, Colt turned from the counter to look, and Zeke walked in from the hallway with Tavi on his hip.

"What—" they both started to say.

"Max and Quin are being grounded. You need to come with me to the sanctuary right now!" He didn't let either of them finish. There was no time.

To Colt and Zeke's credit, neither of them protested. Both hurried forward.

"Georgie!" Colt shouted out. "We have to go to the sanctuary, we'll be right back!"

Ander wove his hand before him, opening up a wide portal. "Okay, everyone through!"

"What?" Georgie shouted from somewhere in the house. "Dad?"

But the Schields were already through, and Ander was pushing Mab after them when he shouted back, "Sanctuary! Emergency! They'll be back!" Then he followed them into the portal.

On the other side, they came out into the crappy little alley where the portal into the Feugo City sanctuary was located. The twins were waiting for them, with no sign of Max and Quin yet.

Nox and Nash ran up to their parents, beginning to spill out the entire story. Off to the side, Ander stuck out his hand to Mab, and she responded in kind. Holding onto her tightly, he stared at the area where Max would appear. Waiting for him to exit. Trying to be prepared for whatever version of Max would come out.

Ander was holding his breath, anticipating the worst, lungs screaming for oxygen but his body too tense with anxiety to let it happen. So when Max eventually did emerge, his precious white wings folded in against his back, Ander released a big woosh of air. Gasped another breath in.

Max looked the same as he had this morning. Almost as if nothing had taken place. Unless one looked closer and knew his face as intimately as Ander did. Then one would see the haunted look behind his eyes.

It made Ander's stomach roil with sickness.

Ander knew Colt and Zeke would want to check on their son, but Ander didn't care. He released Mab's hand and ran forward, meeting Max, who looked surprised to see him and yet all at once not.

Max's arms slipped around Ander's waist, and he pulled him in tight against his chest, burying his face in Ander's shoulder. Ander accepted the weight of Max's lean, his own arms circling around him.

"I'm so sorry, baby," he whispered into his ear. "I'm so sorry they've done this to you." Ander wanted vengeance. He wanted to make whoever had done this bleed. "Who made the decision?"

Max shook his head. "Galeo warned us he'd do it," he rasped.

When he lifted his head at last, the gold in his hazel eyes seemed to gleam behind the unshed tears.

"What can I do?" Ander rasped.

"I'm fine," Max insisted. "It's Quin . . . I'm so worried for him, Ander. I don't know . . . " Max broke off, looking back at his brother, who was currently surrounded by their family.

Ander noticed there was a bleakness to Quin's features that wasn't typically there. While he was a quiet being, and fairly reserved, he seemed shut off entirely now.

Completely closed to the outpouring of love coming his way.

He even ignored Tavi, who held her hands out to him.

Ander swallowed. "Let's get you all back to the condo. Away from these assholes and back where you're safe. Once he sees he's still got all of you to support him, he'll come back."

Ander knew what it was like to have trauma thrown on you. To have so much awful piling up, you could barely breathe. Sometimes, it was hard to accept the love people were offering when you didn't even know quite *how* to take your next breath.

Quin just needed a moment to sit. Center himself and learn how to bear it all again.

"I hope so."

Ander glanced back to find Mab, who was staring after Quin with a look of deep longing. He knew she wanted to be over there. Wanted to help comfort him in some way. Now that the bond had snapped into place for her, it was hard to keep herself separate.

His heart broke for her in this moment. At least he could hold Max.

It made him want to murder Galeo. To make him pay for what he had done to Max and Quin. To bring him agony over the way he was tearing up Mab's insides all over again.

Ander's eyes narrowed as he stared back at where the sanctuary stood hidden behind glamours. Under his breath, he began to hum, his mind weaving the spell as he pictured Galeo, concentrating on the head of the Feugo City Sanctum.

When he finished, he bowed his head so no one would see his smirk. Galeo had taken Max and Quin's flight; now they would all see how Galeo handled a severe, unstoppable case of molting.

"Come on, let's get you all home." Ander wove his hand in front of him, opening up another large portal. "Everyone through the portal!" he shouted, calling the family forward.

He waited for them to go through into the condo, holding Max's hand as he did. Then, when Mab was beside them, he encouraged Max through and took Mab's hand. He stopped her from going in, leaning in to press a kiss to her cheek.

"I cursed his ass," he whispered.

"What?" Mab blinked.

"Galeo." Tugging her hand, he pulled her through the portal.

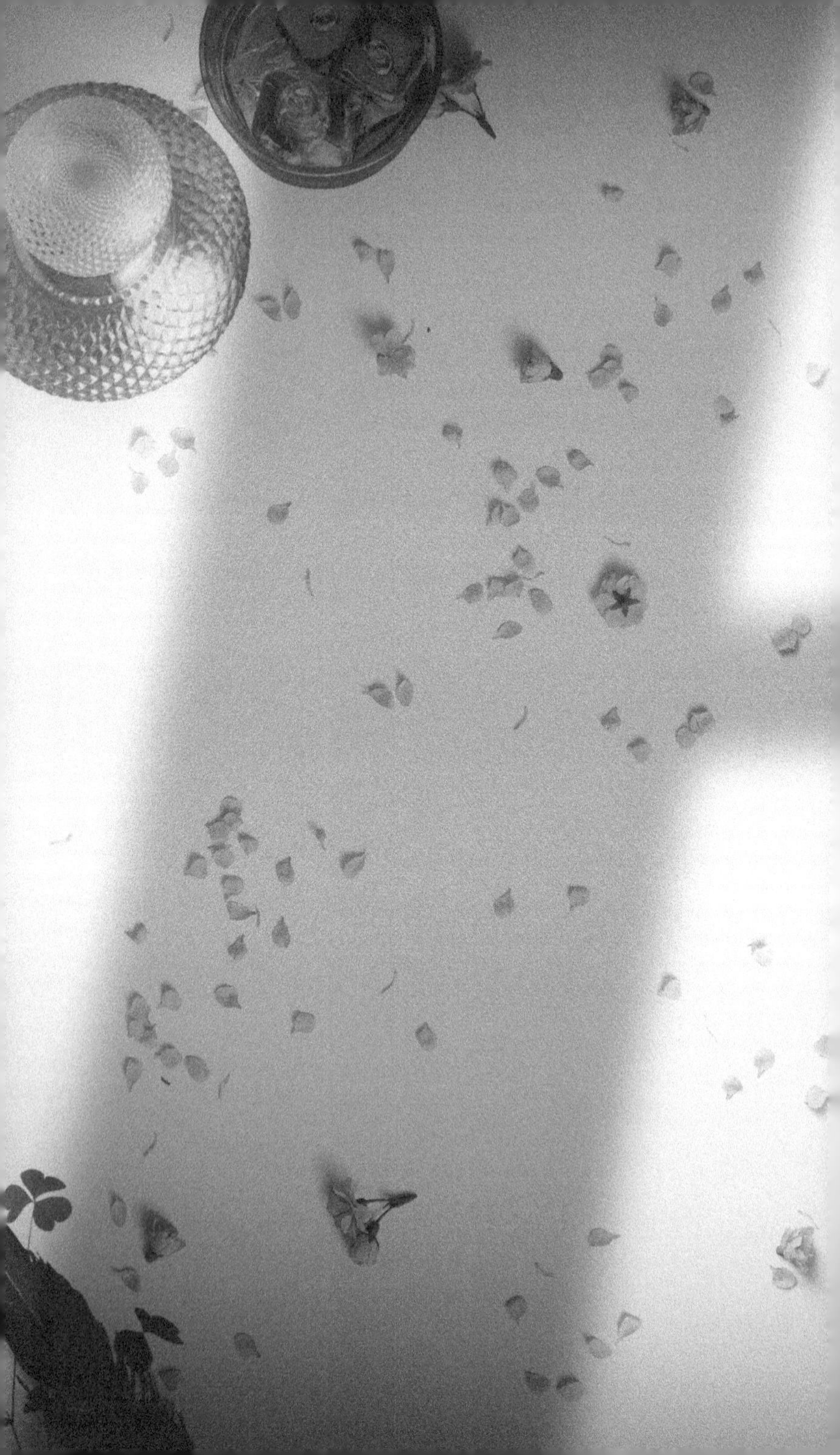

Chapter 32
Mab

Birds were meant to fly.

It was a law of nature.

Bunnies were meant to hop. Dogs were meant to chase. And birds were meant to fly.

Mab meant what she'd said the night before when she told Quin why she never kept birds as pets. She didn't like the idea of essentially injuring someone or something just so she could keep them close. She didn't like the idea of putting whatever she loved in a cage and forcing them to love her back.

So yeah, birds were meant to fly.

And now . . . and now Quin *couldn't*.

And maybe . . . gods . . . maybe that was *her* fault.

He couldn't, and she'd never seen him look so small before. His big oil-slick wings, which usually caught the light, reflecting back rainbows with their every movement, were curled in so tightly against his back that they didn't even move when he did. Like he thought if he could just keep them still long enough, hold them close enough, that it would protect him. But the damage was already done.

"You all are free to stay here for the time being," Ander declared once the portal snapped shut behind them. "It might be best if Max and Quin do, at the very least. In the last couple of days, I've put wards out the wazoo on this place."

Mab's place would have been better, but she hadn't been back since the investigation started and didn't know when they were going to clear it for her to return, despite what had happened at the trial. So she couldn't take anyone there, not right now. Not until she'd at least gone home and made sure it was all clear. Ander's place would be fine.

She lost track of what else he said, her eyes focused on Quin, who was still surrounded by his family. They had pressed in so close to him, she couldn't see how he was even fucking breathing. But they were his family. He loved them. So they'd know what was best for him, right? His family would do what he needed, right? And what right did she have to try to insert herself into that? None. She wasn't anything to him. Just the snarky bartender who called him in the middle of the night because she found a dead body on her beach. Were they even friends?

Gods, she needed a drink.

Her chest ached. Her eyes burned. And every muscle in her body spasmed with the need to reach out to him. To pull him close. To let him hide away from the world like he so clearly needed.

Wait.

Mab stepped forward, her eyes narrowed on Quin's hands. They were moving in tiny, jerky motions. Almost too quick for her to catch. But she didn't have to know the words to understand the panicked tone and the overwhelmed look on his face.

"Hey." Everyone ignored her. And yeah, maybe they

should, because who was she? But Quin was curling tighter in on himself. Making himself smaller and smaller. "Hey!" She pushed forward, nudging the twins out of the way as gently as she could. "How about we give him some room to breathe, yeah?"

Then she put herself bodily between Zeke and Quin. *Bold move, Duchan.*

Colt's brows lifted, and Zeke opened his mouth as if to argue.

What was she even *doing*? "Just . . . just give him a minute. Okay?"

Someone tugged at the hem of Mab's T-shirt, and she looked down to find Tavi at her side, her eyes wide with worry as she pointed behind Mab to Quin. Mab whipped around, and what she saw made a whimper crawl up her throat, though she swallowed it down. Quin's chest was rising in quick, desperate breaths, on the verge of hyperventilating.

"Shit." Gods, she was a fucking idiot. "Shit, you're having a panic attack." She should have seen the signs. She'd been so wrapped up in her own heartache, she'd missed it. But this, this she knew how to handle. This was something she could deal with. And like that, everything else fell away. Her sole focus was getting Quin to feel safe again.

"All right. Okay. Blankets. We need blankets. And someplace quiet. With a door," she murmured softly to the group around them. It would be easier if they were busy, then they wouldn't be hovering so much. With a deep breath, Mab took a slow step toward him. "Q, luv, I need you to look at me," she implored, careful to keep her voice low and soothing. "Can you do that for me, handsome? Just for a minute."

Quin's eyes jerked up, finally. They were darker than she'd ever seen them, the pupils dilated so much, she almost couldn't see the blue for all the black.

"There you are," she murmured the praise gently. "I'm going to hold out my hands. When you're ready, I want you to take them, okay?"

Quin shook his head, curling in on himself a little more.

"All right. You don't have to do that. If you don't want to be touched, that's fine." She nodded. "But I need to get you somewhere safe, so I need you to follow me."

Quin shook his head again, unsure, his rapid breaths only increasing, and Mab had to bite down hard on her cheek to hide the flash of hurt that washed through her. It wasn't fair of her to be hurt over his instinctive response when he was in fight-or-flight mode. Then his gaze flicked down to Tavi.

"Tavi is coming too. And we aren't going far, just down the hall," Mab promised. She hadn't moved her hands from where she held them out in between them, hadn't moved any part of her body except her mouth to speak. No sudden movements. Nothing he couldn't see coming. For his safety as well as her own. "And I promise, once you're there, I'll leave you be. Okay? You can lock me and everyone else out for a little while if that's what you need. But just ... " Her voice broke a little, and she cleared her throat against the tightness that settled there. "Just let me get you somewhere safe and warm first, all right?"

Quin was still staring at her, his brows drawn together in the middle, rooted to the spot.

"C'mon, handsome," she murmured, and his brows lifted just a fraction, his expression easing just a little. Which was enough of a sign that she was getting through to him for Mab to take a step back, trusting everyone else to get out of her way as she backed toward the hall. He took a step to follow her, his hands twitching at his sides like maybe he wanted to reach for her hands finally but wasn't sure he should. "There we go, that's great." She smiled a little and started humming, rough and quiet, an old sea shanty she'd heard a couple times in the pub. More to keep herself from freaking out than to help him.

But he seemed to like it, following after the sound like a sailor of legend would a mermaid's call.

"Just a little farther, handsome. We're almost there." She didn't turn around to see how close they were; thank the gods she'd walked Ander's condo when she was three sheets to the wind, exhausted, and everything in between. Otherwise, she might not have been able to make it to her room without looking over her shoulder to check. From the corner of her eye, she could see the painting hung just outside her room, and she turned, leading Quin through the door, Tavi following close behind him. Once they were inside, she guided him to the bed.

He settled down onto it, a little unsure, and another shiver went through him. He was still panting and looking a little paler than before, like maybe he was nauseous, but she'd have to deal with that later.

"Your parents will be here with the blankets in just a moment, all right?" She didn't move. She stood across the room, giving him space to feel safe and not encroached upon. "But in the meantime, I need you to start working on your breathing. You know the drill: slow breath in through your nose for a count of four, then a slow exhale for a count of four."

Quin didn't meet her eyes, but he nodded quickly, then he drew a slow, shaky breath in.

"What can we do?" Zeke asked, holding out blankets,

and when Mab turned around, she found all of the Schields had piled into the room, and Quin was starting to curl in on himself again. He had Tavi in his lap now, at least, but his wings were wrapped around them both like he could shield them from everyone and everything.

"Can you give us some room? I'll let you guys know when he's come down. But right now, he just needs a minute. Trust me," Mab murmured as she took the blankets from Zeke.

"But—"

"Come on, hun," Colt said, giving Zeke's arm a little tug. He looked over to meet Mab's gaze, and Mab thought maybe there was some kind of understanding in his eyes. Like he saw more of her than she'd like. Too late now, she supposed. "He's in good hands." He cut a look to the twins and jerked his head toward the door. "Let's go check in with Max and Ander. And call Georgie." His voice faded as he tugged Zeke down the hall, and Nox cast one more worried glance toward Quin before shutting the door most of the way.

With the room quiet again, Mab turned slowly back to Quin, the blankets balanced across her arms. "I'm going to sit these here," she said, pointing to the chair. "You take what you need. Okay?"

Quin nodded, still working on his breathing, but didn't unfurl his wings, and even once she'd set the blankets down, she had the sinking feeling that he wasn't going to reach for them. He'd stay there, shivering, until he eventually passed out. She couldn't have that.

"All right, I fibbed," she sighed and pulled one of the softest from the middle of the pile. "Can you maybe . . . uncurl your wings a bit so I can get a blanket on Tavi? I think she's cold."

Quin narrowed his eyes on her, like he didn't quite trust her. And really, hadn't she just told him that she'd lied once already?

"I know. I'm terrible. But, Q, honey, we need to get you warmed up. I can hear your teeth chattering from all the way over here. And look? This is the best one of the lot, promise. Super soft and snuggly." She held it out so Tavi could reach for it, and when Tavi let out a happy little murmur, Quin took it to drape across his and Tavi's legs. Which was a start. "That's good."

Tavi wiggled a little, clearly unhappy at not being able to see what was going on around them, and Quin let his wings drop a fraction so he could scope out their surroundings. Whatever he saw must have eased his mind because his wings settled back behind him, a little more relaxed than they'd been out in the main room.

"Hi there, handsome." Mab smiled at him, happy she could see him now. "All right, you've got blankets. I'm going to just ... " She cleared her throat. She didn't want to leave him like this. Already she could feel the bond pulling her in, their connection drawn so taut, it might snap her in fucking two. But she'd told him he'd have privacy once she got him someplace safe, and she wasn't going back on that, not now. He needed to feel like he was in control of something, and if that something was her bedroom, that was fine. "I'm going to go back out into the main room. I'll come back in a bit to check on you and bring you and Tavi some water. Okay? Grab as many of these as you need"—she patted the stack of blankets—"and if there's anything else ... just ask."

Quin nodded. He was taking slower, deeper breaths, the panic beginning to ease, if even only just a little.

And Mab turned to go. It would suck to go sit out in the living room and just wait, but she'd promised. And she—

A little hand wrapped around her pinky and gave it a careful tug. When Mab looked down, she saw that Tavi had scrambled over Quin's lap to grab her before she could get to the door, her dark eyes wide and pleading.

"You want me to stay?"

Tavi nodded.

"Only if your Daddy says it's okay." Mab's gaze flicked back to Quin, brows raised in question.

He nodded once, short and sharp, but he wouldn't look at her.

"All right. But if you change your mind, just let me know, and I'll leave." She moved to grab the blankets and heft them onto the bed beside Quin, then settled into the chair. Tavi crawled back into Quin's lap, and they settled in.

It was quiet. Too quiet for Mab, who was still jittering with the anxiety of needing something to do. She was used to being the caretaker in these situations, and sitting still waiting for something to happen always set her on edge. Fiddling with a loose thread on her T-shirt, she did everything she could to not stare at Quin as he came back to himself. It was awkward, wasn't it? To just sit there next to someone while they stared off into the middle distance, reliving their trauma?

She should probably look at his wings. Some of the feathers didn't look so good, probably from him struggling against whatever they'd done to hold him down while they—

She shook herself, breathing through her mouth to curb the swell of nausea. Point being, they needed to be tended to. At least straightened out so they were all laying right. But he didn't want anyone touching him, and she could respect that.

But, gods, she needed something to do with her hands.

"Do you want me to do your hair, Tavi?" she asked suddenly, her gaze sweeping to the little girl playing with the edges of the blanket.

Tavi looked up, eyes wide, then she nodded so quickly, she nearly sent herself toppling. Her wings fluttered behind her, moving so fast, it was a miracle she didn't vibrate right off the bed.

"All right, come here." Mab pulled a brush from the nightstand and scooted the chair a bit closer until her knees were almost pressed into the bed. Then she set to work on Tavi's hair, brushing it out slowly and sectioning it off so she could work it into six big twists. Not too tight, otherwise she'd wind up with a headache, but tight enough that they'd hold through most of her wiggling. Mab hummed softly to herself as she worked, the motions well practiced and calming.

She didn't know how long it took. She took her time, if only to delay the moment when she wouldn't have something to do with her hands anymore. But once she was done, Mab tilted her head and smiled to herself.

"There we go. What do you think?" She pulled a hand mirror from the drawer and let Tavi look at herself.

Tavi gasped, delighted, her eyes bright.

"I needed to find someone to help with that," Quin said, his voice rough from disuse, or panic, or some combination of the two.

"Yeah?" Mab asked, tilting her head so she could look at him again. Most of the color had returned to his face, and his pupils were almost the right size again. He was coming out of it. That didn't mean he should move, but at least it meant he was out of danger. "Well, all you had to do was ask."

Quin grumbled a soft acknowledgement but didn't say anything else.

"I didn't want to ask before because you were really upset, but can I look at your wings? They're a little ruffled. I won't touch—" She swallowed against the rage that threatened to take over. "But some of the upper ones could use some attention."

Without a word, he spread his wings wide and turned so she could better reach them. His back was stiffer than before, but she could understand that. Mab rose slowly from her seat. She could feel his attention on her out of the corner of his eyes.

Tavi watched them, her wings flapping a little behind her.

Mab hummed while she worked, slow and steady, her fingers brushing lightly over his black feathers to find the ones that needed straightening, careful to avoid the clipped primaries.

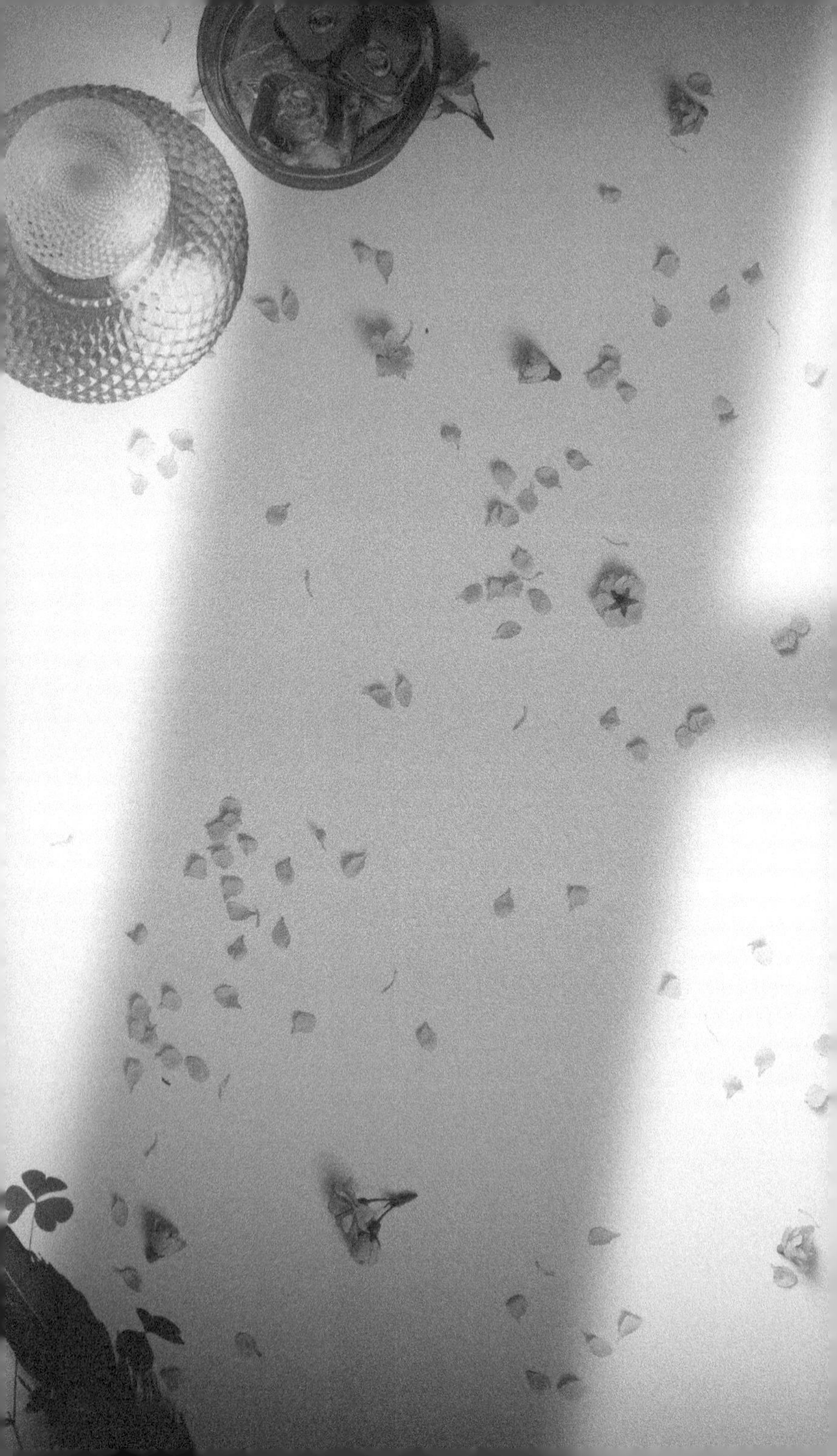

Chapter 33
Quin

Her fingers were soft through his feathers. Her actions tender and careful. Each brush sent a little fissure of pleasure through him, like slowly being lulled to sleep. He'd expected to hate every minute of it. But there was a soothing nature to the movement of her fingers that calmed the frayed nerves inside him still firing with adrenaline and warning.

Quin wasn't usually big on touch. Perhaps that's what happened when you went without it for the first ten years of your life. The sensation of having it caused too much stimulation. And too much was overwhelming.

Especially right now, when the ghost of his past haunted every recess of his mind and lurched into the forefront whenever it could.

"There, you're all fixed up," Mab murmured, and he felt her shift on the bed, her weight sliding back and giving him more space.

Tavi, for her part, had settled down now that Quin himself was doing much better. And she was using the opposite side of the bed as a jumping-off point to flutter into the air for a moment then fall onto her bottom, bouncing.

Watching her, Quin couldn't help but think that this was about all he was good for now. A brief, desperate flutter into the air, then falling.

Falling.

How many times did he need to fall before he was allowed to stay aloft?

How many times would life bring him these blows and expect him to keep going on?

His breathing picked up, his heart hammering wildly in his chest as the hand of anxiety curled around him. Gods, he was weak. He was broken. Max wasn't out there currently falling apart because he'd had his primaries stripped. No, he was handling it like a soldier. Like an ignis should.

Quin was always the liability.

Quin twisted on the bed so he was facing out toward the door once more and took a deep breath. He focused on the feel of his feet firmly planted on the floor and the softness of the mattress beneath him, how the blankets strewn about him tickled lightly at his wings. Tried to count the number of things that he could hear: the murmur of voices in the condo, Tavi bouncing on the bed, Mab's steady breath beside him. Listed off the things he could see in the room: lamp, chair, portrait of a lady, nightstand, curtains, door. Gradually, his breathing slowed, and he was in control of his thoughts once more.

He glanced over at Mab. "Thank you."

She shrugged. "It was nothing. Just some feather rearranging."

"No, I mean for earlier. Out there. I was getting overwhelmed, and you sensed it."

If he wasn't mistaken, Quin could almost have assumed a faint blush stained her cheeks. But Mab spoke without any hesitation. "No thanks needed. I recognized the signs is all. Between me and Ander, we've sort of run the gamut of emotional responses to bad things."

Quin nodded. She understood. There was something nice about being around someone who understood.

His family cared. They were considerate and more patient than anyone should ever have to be. But none of them understood what his life had been like before he came to Miami. They could sympathize, but they couldn't understand.

Mab did. She got what it was like to be locked away from the rest of the world. To have no autonomy over your own body, let alone your life.

"Why are you doing all this for me?" he asked. It was the only thing that didn't make sense. Why she seemed to care so much.

Mab shrugged and looked down at the floor. "I know I can be a hard-ass . . . but I don't like seeing people hurting."

She cared more than she let on. She was also a lot sweeter than her gruff exterior would lead anyone to believe. And Quin was finding that being around her felt safe. Quiet. Easy. He didn't feel the need to pretend to be happier or lighter than he actually was. He could simply be.

Quin wasn't sure he'd actually ever felt that way before.

He drew in a deep, steadying breath, then slowly let it back out. This attack had been a bad one, lasting much longer than his others. The clipping had awoken trauma responses in Quin that he hadn't had to relive in a long time. Because of it, there was an ache deep inside him that had nothing to do with physical injury. But his mind, at least, was his own again. There was calmness around the ache.

Thanks to Mab.

Max had always been a safe space for him, but Quin also felt like he needed to present a happier front to Max so that he wouldn't worry or be upset he couldn't fix something that wasn't fixable.

Here, right now, however, Quin felt that it was okay to simply exist. Mab didn't need him to show that he was okay with everything that had happened or pull out a smile. She was just glad he was able to sit calmly and talk.

Quin unfurled his wings a little and wrapped them around himself so that he was able to actually take a look at the clipped feathers for the first time. The sight of their shorn lengths made his stomach clench, and in his mind, the echoes of little 456's screams replayed over and over again.

As Quin brushed a thumb over one blunt end, he once again felt the dirt and stone beneath his cheek and the press of hands holding him down. His stomach rolled in protest as hopelessness and loss emptied out his insides and left him aching and alone.

But he wasn't alone. If he concentrated, he could feel the shifting of the mattress as Tavi bounced. Could feel the comforting presence of Mab in the room with him, even though she didn't speak. 456 was still there, a small voice of sorrow and agony that would never leave him, but Quin didn't need to be swallowed up by him.

Quin let out a slow, shaky breath and shut his eyes for a moment, tucking his wings in against his back once more. He had fallen, and the Sanctum had taken something from him he didn't think he'd ever have to lose again. But all around him were people who cared, and there was a freedom in that that little 456 never had in the cages. And there was hope.

"You're nicer than you let people think," he said at last.

Mab snorted, but it turned into a little chortle. When she looked at him, her brown eyes sparkled with a dark humor. "If people don't know you're nice, then they don't try to get things out of you."

"So it's to stay lazy?" Had he just tried to tease her?

Mab smirked. "Exactly. I don't like doing things. If they think I'm mean, I don't have to."

"It's why sometimes I don't speak."

Mab laughed honestly this time, and Quin found that the sound of it settled happily in his chest. It was different than when one of his siblings chuckled at him. Harder to earn.

Tavi suddenly crashed down between them, landing with her head off the end of the bed and her legs flailing out to connect with Quin's chest and Mab's chin. He reached out quickly and grabbed onto her, keeping her from flipping off the bed entirely.

Quin picked her up and sat her on her bottom between them on the bed. "Tavi, you have to be careful. You hit Mab in the face."

Tavi's eyes turned big and round, and she looked over at Mab with a distraught look as she began to sign "sorry" over and over again.

"She says she's sorry," Quin translated for Mab.

"It's okay." Mab looked from Tavi up to him, then back down again. "Accidents happen. Just be careful not to hurt yourself." She reached out and tapped Tavi on the nose.

The youngling wiggled at the action, then turned to Quin, signing again.

"What? What is she saying?" Mab asked.

"She wants something to eat." Quin held his hands up so Mab could see and mimicked Tavi's movements. "This means food."

Mab watched his hands closely and moved through the motions herself. He watched as she mouthed the word "food," making the sign several times. As she did so, Tavi nodded her head and repeated the sign herself.

"Well . . . I guess this means we'll have to go back out there." Quin sighed and eyed the door. He loved his family, but he wasn't sure he was ready for all that.

"Nah, let me call Ander. I'll make him snap us some food." She picked up her cell and held her phone up to her ear. "It's fine. We're fine. No, I don't have an emergency, but I do have a hungry youngling in here." She paused, then nodded even though Ander couldn't see her. "Yeah, I think pizza would be fine." She glanced at Quin quickly, who nodded in agreement. "Just make it a large cheese to be safe. And we need some drinks."

There was more chatter on the other end, then Mab ended the call.

"Thanks." Quin felt like he was doing nothing *but* thanking her. But he really did appreciate the help.

"Honestly, no trouble at all. Andy's the one having to snap it all here." She flashed a grin. "Benefits of having a magical brother."

"The only thing the twins can do is reroute shipping processes to make our packages arrive faster."

Mab opened her lips to respond, but then a knock sounded on the door just before Colt and Zeke entered. One with the pizza, the other with a tray of drink options.

"We're not going to stay," Colt was quick to say.

"We just wanted to check and make sure you were okay, then we're going to head home," Zeke finished off.

Quin nodded and forced a little smile for his parents. "I'm okay. I just can't deal with crowds right now."

They both nodded.

"It's okay, Quin, whatever you need right now is fine. We just wanted to check in on you real quick." Colt stepped forward and kissed his forehead. "Is Tavi okay to stay here, or do you want us to take her?"

"She can stay," he said softly.

While technically it was more work, there was also something right about having her here with him. Having her where he could see her meant he wasn't going to be sitting here worrying about her. Right now, he just needed the assurance that she was okay, and the best way to have that was to keep her close.

Colt nodded and smoothed Quin's hair down. "Okay, love, we'll see you tomorrow." He moved over to Tavi and held out his arms. "Can Coco have a hug?"

She leaped into his arms, and he squeezed her tight, then passed her on to Zeke for another cuddle. When he set her back on the bed, he also stepped up to press a kiss to Quin's forehead.

"Behave yourselves, you three." Zeke smiled down at Quin, and Quin could tell his Papa desperately wanted to bundle him up and take him home where he could watch over him. But he was respecting his need for space. Quin appreciated that more than he would ever know and also recognized how much of himself Zeke was holding back and fighting to do so.

With a wave of their fingers, the two of them left, and the door to the outside world was closed once more.

While it had just been his family, Quin still breathed a little easier.

"Okay, let's eat!" Mab said.

They all shifted to sit better on the bed. Mab moved so she could lean against the headboard, and Quin sat back on his own side of the bed with several pillows stuffed behind him so there was room for his wings. Tavi, for her part, chose to sit in the center of the bed with a piece of pizza on a paper plate that had been left on top of the box.

Quin watched her as she clumsily lifted the large slice and took a big bite, tearing at it with a little growl that made both him and Mab chuckle. When her cheek was rounded with food, sauce smeared all over her lips, cheeks, and chin, she looked up at them and smiled broadly.

"Do you want me to cut that up?" he asked her, only to grin a little as Tavi just glared back at him, face serious and eyes squinted as if he had insulted her. He held his hands up in surrender. "Okay, I'm sorry."

Mab snickered and bit into her own piece of pizza. "You're going to have your hands full with this one. She's going to be dynamite."

"I hope so." Quin watched her take another bite, shoving far too much into her mouth, but could only shake his head. "I hope we got to her in enough time that she's able to take on the whole world fearlessly."

He didn't want her to have the lingering issues that he did. To feel like the world had far too many people in it and hiding away was better. Or to only experience it as an observer, there to take pictures and paint it from the safety of his studio.

"She's going to do just fine. She's got great support." Mab looked over at him, and Quin found his gaze meeting hers. "Someone who understands what she's gone through."

"Thanks."

They fell into silence then, both eating their pizza, Mab with a beer, Quin with a bottle of Powerade, and Tavi with her sippy cup of water.

It felt easy to fall into silence, but not an awkward silence. It was comfortable. Safe. And for the first time in hours, Quin was able to let the tension out of his muscles and just relax.

When the pizza was done, they tossed the empty box onto the floor and watched Tavi jump, flutter in the air, and bounce onto her bottom until she dropped to the mattress and let out a deep yawn.

Quin held out his arms. "Come here."

Without hesitation Tavi crawled over to him, and he pulled her into his arms, tucking her against his chest.

He wasn't sure how it happened, but eventually, the three of them were laying on the bed, Quin and Mab facing each other so that Quin's wings could hang out over the edge and not be in the way, and there was room for Tavi in the middle.

The minute they laid down, she passed out, her thumb going into her mouth to be sucked on. Quin supposed he'd have to break her of that habit eventually, she really was too old for it, but for now, he would let her have the comfort. Whatever helped her sleep at night.

"You're so good with her," Mab whispered.

Quin shrugged, tucking his arm beneath his head. "I just treat her the way I wish someone had been there to treat me when I was her age."

A sadness spread into Mab's eyes. "It's an honorable thing, to raise a child that's not your blood."

He didn't say anything, but he felt like there was more behind her words. The quiet hung in the air between them for a moment, then Mab spoke.

"My mother died giving birth to me, and my father was dead long before that. Shipwreck somewhere in the Indies."

"Who raised you?" he asked softly, not wanting to wake Tavi and also not wanting to press too hard.

"The housekeeper. The butler. Sometimes it was the

cook, and other times the gardener. I had a lot of parents and yet none at all."

As Quin looked at her, he saw the lonely child that she kept buried deep inside. Perhaps not even admitting to herself she still existed. "No one ever fully took you as their own?"

Mab shook her head. "I was the lady of the house. They loved me, but there was still distance. I didn't really have a family. Not until Ander." Which meant not until after the asylum. Quin frowned. "Hey, don't look like that. I didn't mean to bum you out. I was supposed to be in here cheering you up."

Quin forced his expression to become neutral. "It's okay. I'd much rather have a real conversation than something just meant to force happiness at me."

"Yeah," Mab whispered. "Me too."

"I was grounded before." Quin didn't know when he'd decided to tell her, or even if he had. The words simply seemed to slip out of him.

Mab's eyes widened a little at this admission. "You were? Noone out there said anything about that."

Quin shook his head. "None of them know."

"Why?" She bit her lip, as if needing to hold herself back, like she was asking too many questions.

Quin didn't mind the questions. Not from Mab. There wasn't pity in her eyes when she looked at him. Rather, there was a deeper well of understanding forming in them that he was finding more and more comforting.

"They saw firsthand how broken I was and had to deal with piecing me back together. I know it wasn't easy on them. I suppose I never wanted to add to the pain they already felt over all of it."

Mab's face softened. "You're not a burden to them,

Quin." Her words were soft, whispered so they didn't wake the slumbering Tavi.

"I am." He spoke simply, without complaint. He loved his family and appreciated everything they had done for him, which was why he didn't want to continue to add more to what they had already gone through because of him.

"They love you."

"They do." He knew it. There was never any doubt about it.

"How old were you?" she asked at last.

"I never really knew how old I was in there; no one celebrated birthdays with us or even spoke about the day we were born. But there were ways to tell the seasons were changing and gather that we had aged another year. So I think I was around seven when it happened."

Mab's features pinched in disbelief. "Seven?" Her voice trembled a little, and she reached out to take his hand.

He looked away from the concern in her eyes; otherwise, it might stop him from speaking. From unburdening himself upon her. "I fought back against my handlers, and in return, they pinned me to the ground and clipped my wings. The next day, they threw me in with a much larger opponent, and I barely made it out alive. It was the day I realized I was going to die in the cages. That I wasn't ever going to be able to break free."

Her sharp intake of breath was what brought his eyes back to her face, and while he didn't find pity in her gaze, he did find tears. "At seven, you were contemplating your own death?"

Quin could only nod, this moment with her holding him firmly in her grasp, and his fingers tightened a little around Mab's.

"Oh gods, Quin. That's awful."

"It's why this afternoon hit me so hard. It took me back there, and I felt it all again. The pain. The grief. The loneliness and hopelessness. It just reminded me of how broken I am. Possibly beyond repair."

Mab's hand held his more firmly, and she sat up, her eyes hardening—but not in anger, more in resolution and conviction. "We are not broken, Quin."

The way her voice shook on the word "we" made his breath halt, and every part of him zeroed in on her voice. Her words. Her lips forming each syllable.

"We were damaged, yes. Horribly, terribly damaged. But we are not beyond repair. Because we are not alone. We have family who loves us and who will never abandon us. And we'll have setbacks. Times when the past rears its ugly head and makes the pain all come back. But that doesn't mean we're broken. Those are just the days we need a little more love than the rest."

As Quin stared into her teary eyes that met his unblinkingly, he realized he'd never felt so seen or understood. That perhaps there were times when Mab herself had wondered if she was broken beyond repair. Yet, he didn't think she was. Instead, he thought she might be the bravest, strongest person he'd ever met.

He didn't have words to speak; his tongue felt glued tight against the roof of his mouth, pinned there by the emotions wreaking havoc inside him. Pain. Grief. Hope. Comfort. Fear. Connection.

It was overwhelming, and yet he did not want to pull away. There was something here, in this moment with Mab, that simply felt right.

So Quin nodded, never breaking eye contact with her, and Mab's frame slowly relaxed, and the ferocity faded from her eyes.

When she settled back down on the bed, their hands fell to the mattress between them, fingers still lightly entwined. Silence overtook them, but it was a silence of understanding and comfort.

At some point, Quin wasn't sure when, his eyes fell closed, and sleep claimed him.

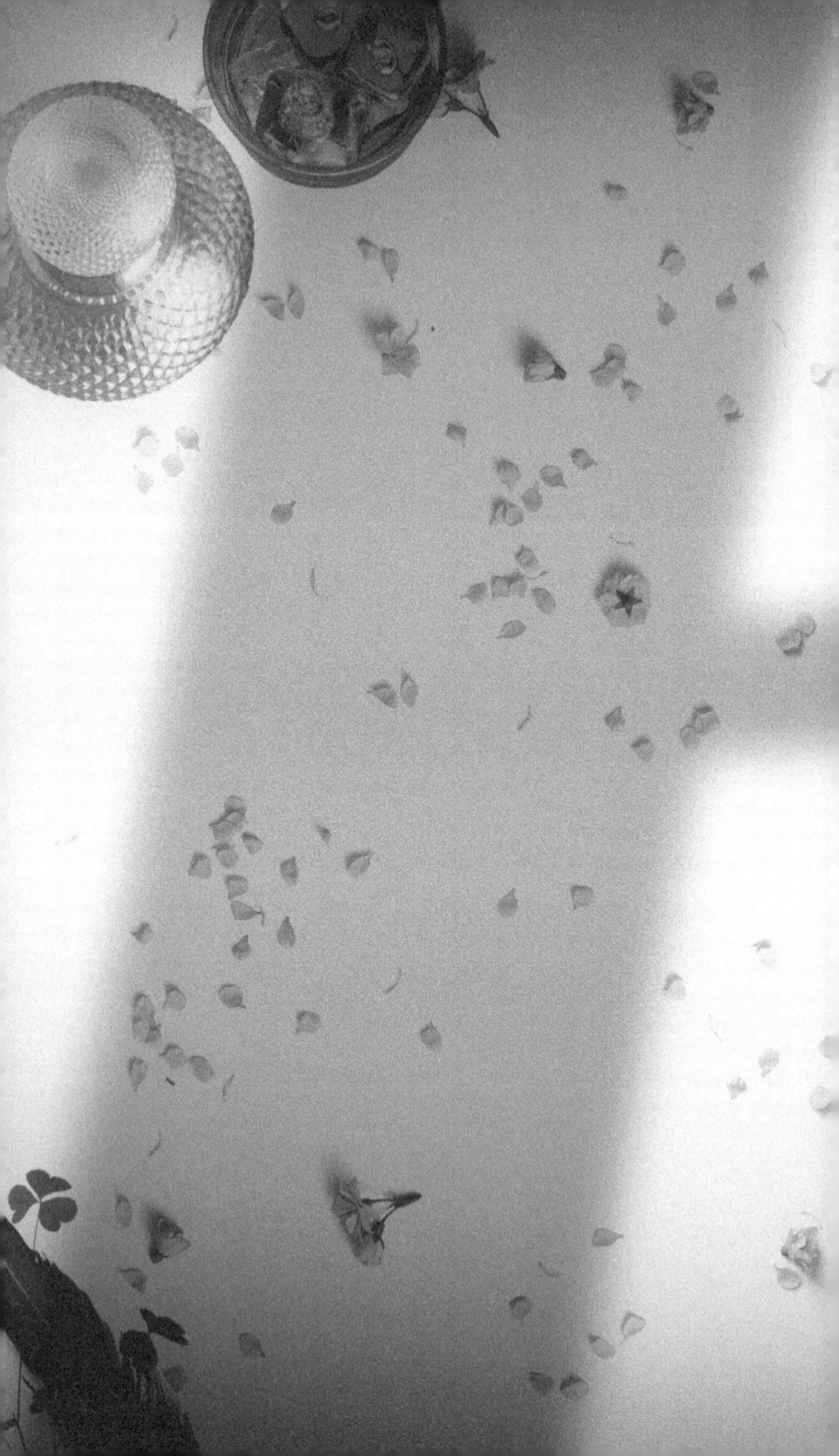

Chapter 34
Mab

Mab didn't know when she had drifted off. She'd meant to leave after Tavi was out and Quin was asleep. Meant to give them space again. Because as right as all of this felt, as at home as she was there with them, she knew the truth of it. They weren't hers. Not to keep. No one ever was. These few scant moments were stolen. Borrowed. And they couldn't last.

But somehow, one minute had dragged on into two. Had dragged on into an hour. And every time she told herself to leave, she didn't, until she just fell asleep.

What finally woke her in the morning was a tiny foot pressed into her bladder. She groaned, dragging her eyes open, and looked down at where Tavi was drooling into the pillow between herself and Quin.

Neither of them are awake yet. Good. I can get out of here before anyone notices.

She shifted carefully, trying to scoot back off the bed little by little, but the movement was enough, apparently, to wake Quin. His eyes shot open, alert in a moment.

"I was just ... " Mab felt heat crawl up her neck. Gods,

was she blushing? Like a girl with her first crush! How ridiculous. She hadn't been a girl in *centuries*. "Bathroom," she finished awkwardly, hooking her thumb over her shoulder.

Quin nodded. "We should get up and get home too."

"Yeah, I'm sure your dads are worried. I think Andy said he left the portal to your parents' place open in the dining room." She didn't want him to go. The urge to ask him to stay crawled along her tongue, threatening to make a fool out of her, but she swallowed it down. Then she forced herself to spin around and head to the bathroom without another word, because she knew if she stayed, she would definitely say something stupid.

Instead of returning to her room when she was done, she went through the door into the hall and slunk toward the kitchen to hopefully hide from any prying eyes. And it worked too. By the time she had the coffee pot going, Quin was at the portal, Tavi in his arms, both giving her an awkward little half wave that she returned with a salute. Because she was a weirdo.

Letting out a loud groan, she leaned forward, smacking her head on the counter. What was *wrong* with her?

"Your phone is lit up," Ander said. He appeared suddenly at her side without her noticing, drawing a yelp from her.

"Don't sneak up on people," she hissed and grabbed her phone to check the notification. It was a text from the ignis on her case, letting her know that they were releasing the seizure of her house.

"Can't sneak up on someone in my own home." Ander shrugged, grabbing her coffee mug and gagging. "It's gone cold."

"Yeah, I was a little busy having an existential crisis over here." The ceramic was cool under her fingers when she grabbed it and moved to pour it out in the sink. Not like she needed coffee anyway; she was jittery enough.

"Why are we having existential crises before breakfast?" Max asked, moving around Ander to get to the coffee pot and pour some for himself. His hands brushed Ander's waist in a move that was so natural, so innate, it made Mab want to sob. "I mean . . . aside from the obvious."

"I got my house back." Mab jiggled her phone so they could see the text thread.

"And that's cause for a crisis . . . why?" Max tilted his head. He looked sleep-rumpled and content.

Mab wondered if she'd soothed Quin the way Ander seemed to have Max. He'd appeared better last night after she helped him fix his wings. But . . . what did she really know about him? Could she really tell if he was better or not? It wasn't like they were . . . *anything*.

"This is about Quin, isn't it?" Ander sidled up beside her, bumping his shoulder against hers. It was a careful, companionable gesture, one they'd shared time and time again, one that usually made Mab feel all warm inside. All it did now was make her want to shy away. "You should just tell him he's your arrow-bound. Everything will click into place and—"

"I'm sorry. He's what?" Max stopped with his mug halfway to his lips, his hazel eyes wide.

"Q is Mabberella's arrow-bound. Her soulmate." He drew the last word out dramatically, wiggling his eyebrows.

"For crying out loud, Ander! Can't you keep a secret for more than seventy-two hours?!" Mab snarled.

"Not from *my* soulmate." He pressed his face in close to hers, a delighted, mischievous smile on his lips. Brat. "Which you'd know if you'd tell yours—"

"Stop it." Mab shoved him by the cheek to get his face away from her own.

"Never." Ander snickered.

"Wait," Max said. His coffee cup clicked against the counter where he set it down so he could come around the island and stand in front of Mab, his brows high on his face. "Quin is your arrow-bound? My Quin? My brother? About yea high"—he held up his hand to indicate how tall Quin was—"black wings, doesn't talk much, likes to glare at people. That Quin?"

"Don't strain yourself, Wonderboy," Mab muttered. Ander hip checked her and shot her a glare before turning his smile back to Max.

"Yes, baby, keep up." Ander laughed. "And now that I think about it . . . he's perfect for you, isn't he? You can both be growly and glarey and scare everyone in your vicinity together! Perfect bonding!"

"Shut up," Mab hissed, her cheeks heating further.

"Isn't that a little coincidental?" Max tilted his head in thought. "I mean . . . weird how you two wound up bound to brothers, right? And Quin was all the way in Syria. Anything could have happened. But he wound up here."

"That's fate, babe." Ander patted his cheek lightly. "Don't overthink it, you'll only upset yourself."

"Coincidence. Fate. It doesn't make a difference." Mab flopped forward again, her forehead pressed to the cold granite countertop.

"Why not?" Mab heard one of the stools scrape lightly against the floor as Max sat across from her.

"Because Quin has been through *enough*. He doesn't need to add all of this"—she gestured to herself all over without lifting her head—"mess in his life too."

Ander scoffed, and she could just imagine him rolling his eyes.

"I don't really think you should be making that decision for him." Max sounded like he'd gotten closer. He'd probably leaned forward on his elbow on the counter. "Do you?"

"I'm older and wiser. And even if I wasn't." Mab lifted her head to narrow her eyes at him. "Do you really think if I told him, he'd be okay being bound to someone? Isn't it just one more cage? Hasn't he been trapped enough?"

"I don't feel trapped."

"Yeah, well you're special, Max." With a huff, Mab turned away from them to make herself another cup of coffee. She couldn't keep looking at them while they talked about this. It was embarrassing. It left her feeling raw. "Besides, I don't even know how to talk to him. Not really."

"You were talking to him fine last night," Max insisted. "In fact, I don't think I've seen anyone be able to talk him down like that. He's a tough nut to crack. Warms up slowly to people. Doesn't really like to let people in."

"You know, Max, you're not helping me feel any better about this." Her shoulders hunched in closer. Maybe if she made herself small enough, she could disappear entirely, and they wouldn't have to have this conversation.

"My point is," Max huffed, then waited until she turned around to look at him before continuing. "Maybe you shouldn't tell him you're bound yet. But maybe you should ask him out. Get to know him as a friend first. See how things progress from there. Who knows, maybe you won't even have to tell him. Maybe he'll just feel it, like I did."

"And if all else fails, you could try flirting again!" Ander snickered, then ducked when Mab grabbed an orange from the bowl on the counter to chuck at his head.

"I am never. Ever. Trying flirting again," she hissed, doing her best not to think about what happened last time. Why did things have to change so much over the years? Why couldn't social conventions stay the same to some degree? She'd been able to adapt to everything else life threw at her, but flirting? She'd never had to *do* that, not even to get out of a parking ticket. One of the many benefits of having a very alluring, very magical brother. And even before, when she'd been looking for someone, when she'd wanted the attention, she'd never flirted. She'd just kind of . . . shown up and smiled at people, and Edward fell right into her lap. It had been easy. Which, now that she was thinking about it, might have been part of the problem. Maybe he'd never loved her at all. Maybe he'd just wanted a rich patroness to fund his—

"Mabbers." Ander snapped his fingers in front of her face, ripping her out of her downward spiral. "Wherever your head is at, get it out of there. Now."

"Edward." The name came out on a rasp, and Ander scowled, reaching up to take her cheeks in his hands and fix her with a hard expression.

"Edward didn't deserve you."

Mab let out a soft noise of discontent but didn't try to shake him loose.

"None of that," Ander chided. "He didn't. Quin, on the other hand, is great. Maybe a little grumpy for my taste, but hey, you've always been into the brooding type."

"What do I do?" Her tone was plaintive. She wanted this. She wanted this so badly that she ached with it. But there was no way it could work, was there? It was pretty clear that Quin had no romantic interest in anyone, least of all the bitchy banshee who'd fallen headfirst into his life.

Of Hope & Blight

"You go home. You get your shit straight. And you call him."

"*Call* him?" That sounded like a disaster waiting to happen.

"Yes. Call him. Invite him over for lunch. You can make those ribs I really like."

"So just . . . lunch?"

"Among other things." Ander wriggled his eyebrows again, signifying that he was done being serious, and she groaned even louder. But he was right, wasn't he? The worst thing Quin could say was no. And already, a plan was beginning to form.

"Just be yourself," Max advised.

"Great advice. Super. You guys are *real* helpful." But they were right. She could do this. She'd already spent a few hours with him just talking and being present for him. What was one afternoon? She chugged her coffee, grabbed her keys and her rabbit, and headed home to get to work.

The house was a complete and utter shit show. The ignis that searched her place had just thrown everything onto the floor once they were done, leaving nothing untouched apart from her purse and the few jackets hanging near the door.

Seeing it like this left her aching. This was her *home*. Her safe space. And it had been violated. But . . . But still, she was going to get this mess handled, and then she'd—

The beach. She grinned a little to herself. The beach was perfect. Sea-salt air and sand always brought her peace. She was sure it would do the same for Quin and Tavi.

Yeah. That'd work great.

With a nod, she pulled out her phone and dialed Quin's number.

"Is everything okay?" was the first thing he asked, his voice taut with worry.

"Yeah, everything's fine." It wasn't really, not yet. But it would be. Soon. "I was just thinking . . . My house was cleared last night. Maybe you and Tavi would like to come by for a beach day? I'm making some ribs, and the sea air would probably be really good for the both of you."

Quin was silent for what felt like too long, and anxiety reared its ugly head again.

"You can say no, Q. I just thought maybe it'd help to have a day away from *everything*, you know? Just unwind a little." She chewed on the inside of her cheek. "I promise I won't be offended if you're not up for it, though, I get it."

"No." Quin let out a long, slow breath. "No, I think a beach day might be just what we need. What time do you want us there?"

"I've still got some cleaning to do, and the ribs to put on. So let's say around one?"

"One is great."

"Great." She tugged on a loose curl, straightening it to its full length before she released it to let it spring back into place. "Great."

"Yeah. Great."

"Right. So I'll just . . . I'm going to go get to work. Bye!" Then she hung up without leaving him time to say goodbye as well.

When she was done, she fired a quick text off to Ander.

> Doing lunch. Need ribs. Who's the best brother around?

> Already in the fridge

You owe me

Max says good luck [thumbs up emoji]

Right. Luck. She was going to need quite a bit of that if she was going to spend an entire afternoon with Quin without making a complete ass of herself.

She looked down at Gizmo, who hadn't moved from her side after she settled him on the floor, as if he didn't know where he was allowed to go with all of her shit just thrown around.

"I know, buddy, we've got a lot to do, don't we?"

Gizmo's ear twitched.

"Helpful," she huffed. First things first: she needed to put his pen back together so he at least had somewhere to hang out while she cleaned.

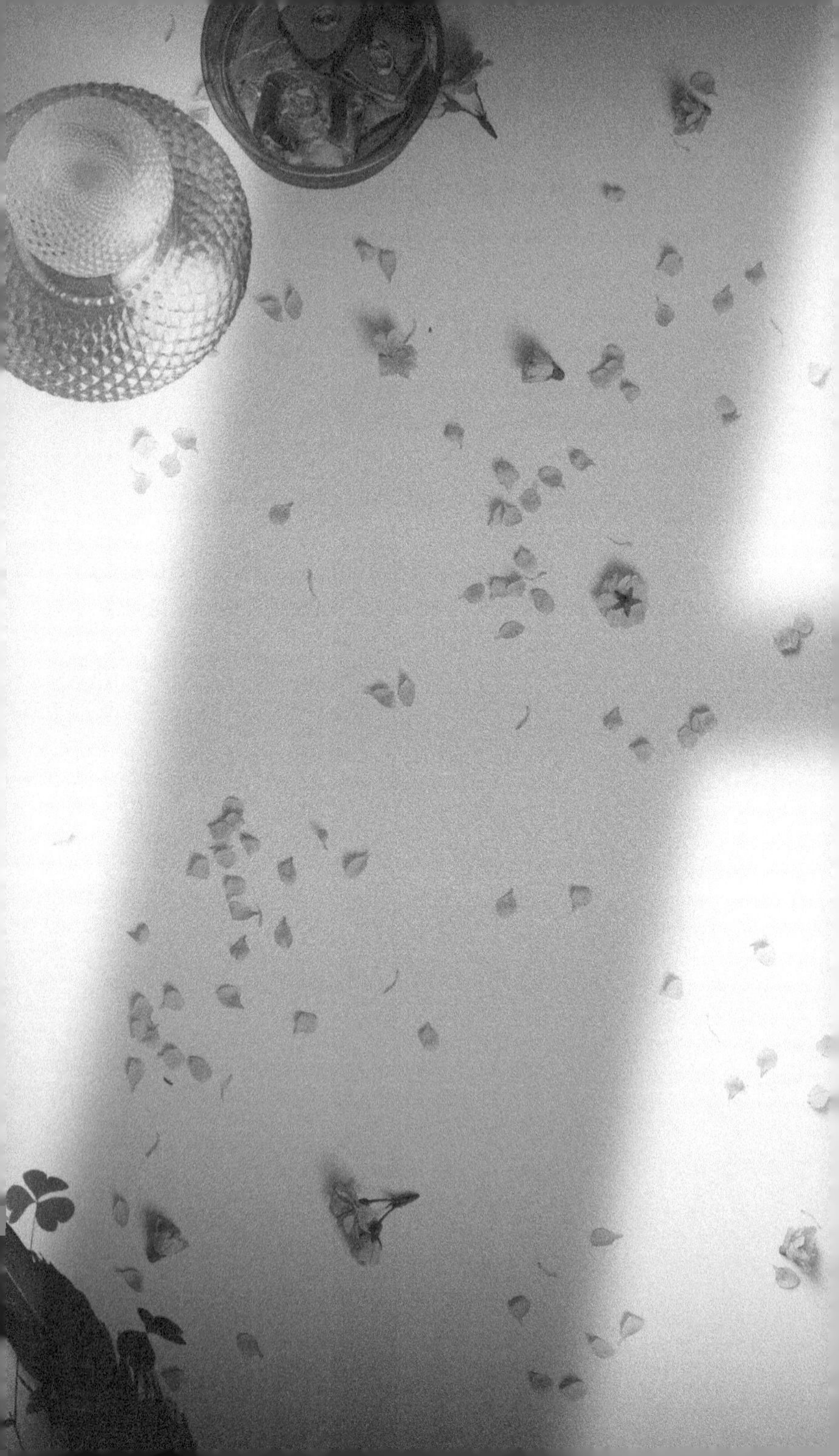

Chapter 35
Quin

Quin sat at the counter in the kitchen watching his dad wash dishes. Meanwhile, Papa moved around the room, picking up mail to sort through, going to the fridge to see if there was anything in there, moving to the pantry to see what was inside.

"Do you want anything? Need anything? Hungry? I'm peckish. Is anyone else peckish?" Zeke rattled off.

He was hovering. They were *both* hovering. Attempting to seem nonchalant as they found reasons to stay as close to him as they could. They were doing it because they loved him, he knew that. It didn't make it any less cloying.

"I'm fine," Quin insisted.

"I could use a snack," Nash called from just behind Quin, where he and Nox were at the dining table.

They were attempting to follow up on their trackers. The trucks had gone farther inland in Texas, stopped for the night, then continued on. But not back toward the coast. Currently, they were trying to figure out where the trucks had stopped and what they had been doing while they were there.

It required hacking into one of the normie's military satellites, which apparently was giving them some issues.

"What do you feel like?" Zeke asked. He looked relieved, obviously happy to have been given a reason to stick around the kitchen for longer.

"Quesadillas pleeeease," Nox called out, her eyes not lifting from her screen.

"Perfect, three quesadillas coming right up!"

"I don't need a ques—" Quin began.

"Nonsense. You can always use a snack. Plus, if you don't eat it, Nash will," Zeke cut him off.

"Yep!" Nash agreed.

As his phone went off, Quin sighed in relief, until he saw whose name was on the screen. Picking it up, he slid off the stool and accepted the call. "Is everything okay?" he asked as he left the kitchen.

Mab's call had been a blessing he wasn't expecting. Quin loved his family, but they seemed to think they needed to be around him at all times to make sure he knew he wasn't alone. Problem was, he wanted to be alone. Or at least . . . have a little more space.

Though they meant well, all their hovering was doing was making him think about *why* they were hovering. Right now, the last thing he wanted to be reminded of was the clipping room. He needed a distraction. Desperately.

The beach was a perfect idea. Especially Mab's private beach. Away from everyone, outside, and doing something that Tavi would enjoy. Quin couldn't remember the last time he had done something for leisure like swimming.

He almost felt normal while he changed Tavi into her bathing suit and packed them both a change of clothes. Like he was just going out for a nice afternoon in the sun on one of his days off. That was until he reached for his jeep keys because he wouldn't be able to fly them to Mab's house. His jeep was fine. He liked his jeep. But the reminder that he *had* to take it changed everything.

The Sanctum had never felt like home, but it had felt right. Given purpose to his life. Made it so he could help protect other people. Stop the monsters out there who tortured, killed, stole, and destroyed. Be for others what he had needed for so long.

But now, he questioned it all. Galeo had always hated them, everything about them. And it was an opinion that only seemed to strengthen over the past two months. This didn't just feel like a punishment. This felt like someone who had it out for them finally getting to dig in and hurt them.

Quin's hand tightened around the bag he carried. He took a deep, steadying breath. He didn't want Tavi to see how upset he was. Didn't want to worry her again like last night. Dropping their bag in the back, behind his seat, he picked Tavi up and plunked her down in her toddler car seat, especially adapted to make room for her wings. Strapping her in, he brushed his fingers along the twists in her hair. Mab had done a good job, and they'd held up well while she slept. Tavi also adored them, beaming at herself in the mirror this morning as she checked them out.

Once Tavi was secured, Quin hurried around the front and climbed in. With the open top and the modified front seats to accommodate his wings, the jeep was the perfect vehicle for him to get around the city. Max preferred his bike, but Quin had always needed the trunk space to haul his canvas and paint around.

"Ready to go?" he asked Tavi, glancing at her in the rearview mirror.

She looked up at him, a bright smile on her face, and nodded, pointing out toward the road.

Quin smiled. "Good."

The trip through Miami wasn't the same as flying; nothing could ever make him feel as light or as free. But the wind whipping through his hair brought him a little of the feeling. He hated enclosed vehicles.

Tavi seemed to agree. She lifted her arms up into the air, fingers wiggling as the wind tickled through them.

When they arrived at Mab's, the delicious scent of barbecue pork greeted them. Settling Tavi on his hip and grabbing their bag, he smiled at the girl. "Smells good, doesn't it?"

Tavi tapped her nose, agreeing.

There was music coming from the back yard, so Quin walked around the side of the house toward where the patio and pool were. There, Mab stood at a grill, slathering more sauce on a couple racks of ribs.

She was dressed in a white one-piece bathing suit, an orange sarong tied around her waist and a floppy sun hat on her head. As they walked up, she looked over and smiled.

"Hey! The ribs still need some time, so do we want to go down to the beach for a bit?" She set down her sauce brush and wiped her hands off, then came over to them.

"Yeah, I think Tavi would enjoy playing in the water and the sand."

As they headed down, Quin saw that the mess was all cleaned up, which was a relief. Looking at the sandy beach, there was no way to tell that a dead fury had lain there just a week ago.

When they hit the sand, Tavi squealed and took off running. She only got so far before her feet slipped, and she face-planted. Sighing, he dropped his bag to head over to her, except she was already pushing up to her knees and grinning, sand covering her cheeks.

Laughing a little, Quin reached down to pick her up and set her on her feet. He brushed the sand off her face. "Careful there." Tavi giggled, then hurried toward the water. "Only up to your knees in the water!" he called out after her.

Mab came up beside him, a smile on her face. "She seems very excited."

"Yeah, I don't think she's ever been to the beach before." As Tavi hit the water, she stopped, stomping her little feet in it. Then she rushed in, up to her thighs, and began patting the surface.

Quin couldn't resist pulling his phone out of the pocket of his swim shorts and snapping photos of her and a quick video. He added them to the family chat, knowing everyone would love to see it.

"Well then, you should go in there and share this moment with her," Mab said.

Quin looked at her. "You coming too?"

She smiled and nodded. "Wouldn't miss it."

While she slipped off her sarong to set it on the beach lounger, Quin retrieved his bag and placed it and his phone on the spare sun chair. He unbuttoned his T-shirt at the back behind his wings, pulled it off, and laid it on top of his phone to protect it from the direct sunlight. Then he kicked off his sandals and headed down to the water's edge. Tavi was busy splashing and looked up at him happily. She signed the word for water, and Quin laughed.

"Yeah, it's lots of water."

"Hey, do you think she'd like to play with this?" Mab called out.

When he looked back up at her, Mab was pulling a pink flamingo floaty out from under her beach lounger.

"Is that yours?" A grin slid over his lips as he pictured Mab floating on the water in that.

She stared at him for a moment, and Quin wondered if he had said something to offend her. Then she blinked and shook her head. "No. It's Ander's."

That made more sense.

Before Quin could respond, Tavi answered for them. She let out a squawk of excitement and pointed at the pink floaty. She then started signing her sign name for Georgie. Quin laughed and nodded.

"It does look like Georgie, doesn't it? You want to float on it?" Quin asked.

Mab waded into the water, setting the floaty on the surface. "I'll hold it, you set her in it."

Quin nodded and picked Tavi up. Carefully, he set her in it so that her wings were hooked over the edge and in the water and her bottom nestled safely in the open middle.

The minute she was floating, Tavi began to kick her feet happily, her hands splashing in the water, which made her spin. All of it seemed to bring the youngling pure delight, and her giggles drifted into the air.

It was wonderful, and Quin was able to take another deep breath and release it just as easily. A little more of the tension slipped out of him. Was it possible someone else's joy could heal the wounds inside you?

Mab was also laughing as she watched Tavi. She

grabbed onto the neck of the flamingo and began to pull it through the water. Tavi's hands lifted into the air, and she smiled even more as her floaty zoomed around.

Quin watched her happy face, just glad to be out here experiencing her, experiencing this. But gradually, his eyes drifted up the slender length of Mab's arms, over the curve of her shoulders to the elegant slope of her neck. Her lips bowed in a happy smile, and her eyes crinkled warmly at the corners with pleasure. Even her white curls seemed to shine more beneath the cover of her sunhat.

A nervous feeling settled into his belly, and his blood almost seemed to buzz in his ears.

It was hard to take his eyes off her. To not watch every movement as she ran around the water, pulling Tavi behind her and wringing laughter out of the toddler.

She was beautiful and—

"Is everything okay?" Mab had stopped and was looking over at him in question.

As their eyes met, Quin gasped, a sharp pain shooting through his chest and making his heart clench. Wheezing, he lifted his hand to his breastbone and rubbed. "I'm, uh . . . okay."

At least, he thought he was okay. An ignis couldn't have a heart attack. Or . . . he didn't think so, anyway. That, however, didn't explain what was going on. The fierceness of the ache faded a little, but it remained there, a pang of annoyance he couldn't quite forget.

There was a puzzled look on Mab's face, but she bit her lip and nodded. "Okay."

With her attention back on Tavi, Quin decided to dive into the water. Distract his mind from whatever was going on and hopefully make it all go away. Whatever this was, he'd never felt anything like it before.

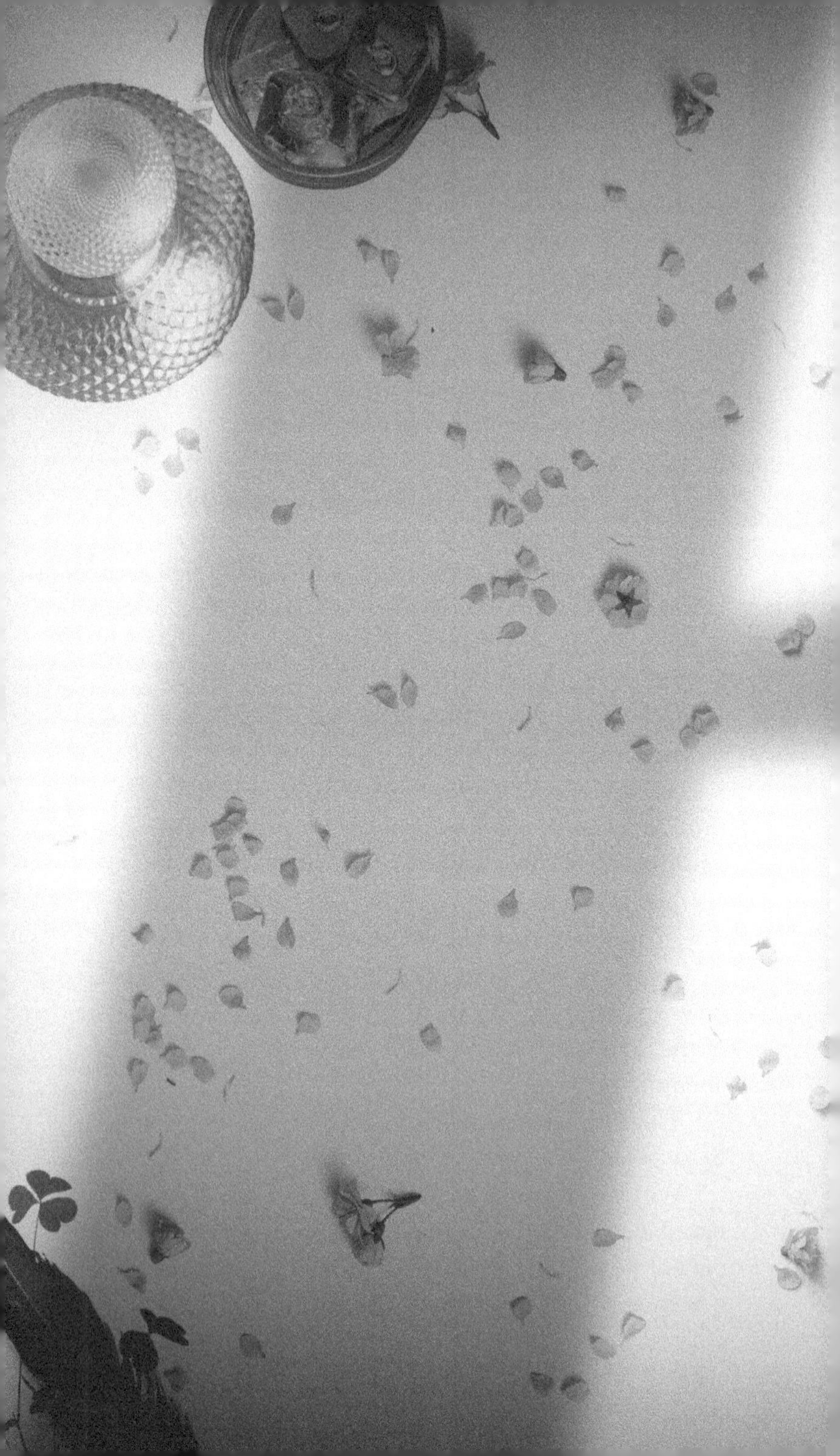

Chapter 36
Mab

It was hard to explain, even harder to put a name to, but there was something . . . *light*, about Quin like this. Surrounded by the sun shining off the water and the salty air of the sea, he looked like an entirely different person. Like someone had reached into his past and erased every bad thing that had happened to him. He looked . . . at peace, she decided. Settled in a way she hadn't seen him up till now.

It looked good on him.

And sure, the lack of a shirt and the swim trunks that clung to his thighs when he rose up out of the water like some deity of the sea coming to land to grace all the mere mortals with just a glimpse at him helped. Poseidon would throw a tantrum if she could see the way Quin put even her beauty to shame when surrounded by the clear blue waters. It helped a lot.

But mostly—*mostly*—it was the lack of a furrow between his brows. He wasn't smiling, but she didn't think she'd ever seen his face so relaxed before.

This had been a good idea. A spectacular idea. Brilliant.

Even if every single time he came out of the water Mab nearly had an aneurysm. She was totally fine. It was a small price to pay for the sheer joy burbling out of Tavi's mouth and the little grin that had begun to creep up the corners of Quin's lips.

They couldn't be hers, but she could give them this. It would just have to be enough.

A few more spins through the water, twirling Tavi until her eyes were sparkling so much, they outshone the sun reflecting around them, and Mab's phone alarm went off.

"That'll be the ribs," she called out to Quin, who was swimming a little farther out. "Let's go have lunch, then we can build a sandcastle, all right Tavi?"

Tavi nodded, and signed, "Food."

"Yup. Lunchtime." Mab lifted Tavi carefully from the floaty, perching her on one hip, while the other arm grabbed the floaty as they made their way to the beach. Once there, she grabbed Tavi's little towel and started to help her dry off. "Your twists still look pretty good. Did your Coco help you bonnet them?"

Tavi frowned a little like she didn't understand. So that was probably a no.

"Ah, well, I'll talk to your daddy about it later. It'll keep them from getting frizzy." She smoothed her hand over one of the twists. It had begun to frizz a little with the humidity and the salt water. "I'll give him some product he can use too."

"What was that?" Quin asked, drawing her attention back to where he was walking out of the surf, droplets shimmering off his muscled chest and stomach. He stretched his wings out to their full, glorious length and shook the water out of them. Gods, how did someone get that good looking? Oh, right. They were literally crafted by a god.

She shook herself. "I've got some spare product and a bonnet in my bathroom I can send you home with for Tavi. It'll help with the frizzies from all the Miami humidity."

"Oh." Quin blinked, his eyes flicking from Mab's face down to where Tavi had taken her hand and given it a little tug back toward the house. "Thanks."

"Sure thing, handsome." Mab spun on her heel and let Tavi tug her toward the patio, where the pool and a little table sat under an umbrella. Scooping Tavi up, she deposited her into one of the chairs, tapping her nose playfully. "Sit tight, princess. I'll get us some grub."

Then she spun to head back to the grill and almost face-planted into Quin's chest where he'd been right behind her. She wobbled a little on her feet in her haste to put space between them again, and Quin grabbed her by the waist to keep her from falling.

"Careful," he murmured softly.

"Mhm," she agreed, the sound a little too high even for her own ears. He was so close. Too close. *Too* close. *Too close*. She took a step back, putting an arm's length between them again. A careful distance. "I've gotta . . . check the ribs." Then she sidestepped him and headed back to the grill like the fucking coward that she was.

"*Be yourself*, he said," she grumbled as she gave the ribs one more helping of sauce before plating them. "*It'll be fine*, he—"

"You okay, Mab?"

"Peachy keen, jelly bean." What the *fuck*?!

"Okay. I'm just going to head inside and grab some drinks, if you don't mind."

"There's fresh-made lemonade in the fridge."

"Fresh-made like you bought it from the store? Or like you made it from . . . " He trailed off, and when Mab turned around to look at him, his expression was absolutely priceless. There was a mixture of horror, curiosity, and disgust all mingled into one there. It eased some of the panic that had been building up in her chest.

"Ander told me not to think about it. So I'm not thinking about it, and you shouldn't either." She pointed her barbeque tongs at him. "Just bring out the pitcher and the cups sitting on the counter."

"Okay. Okay." He held up his hands in surrender, and backed toward the door, a little grin on his face.

"And the potato salad!" she called just before the door slid shut behind him, shaking her head. "What're we going to do with your daddy, huh, mo stoirín?"

Tavi tilted her head and shrugged her shoulders, then held out her hands for the plate of ribs Mab was setting in the middle of the table.

"All right, all right." Mab laughed. "Let me put one on your plate. And be careful, they're hot. Blow on them like this." She took a rib and blew lightly on it to cool it down, then set it on Tavi's plate. "Maybe this wasn't such a good idea. You're going to be a mess, honeybun."

"We can always hose her off in the ocean, right Tavi?" Quin grinned at her from the door.

Tavi wrinkled her nose as if she didn't find the joke very funny and promptly took a big bite of rib, smearing her face in sauce as if to prove them both wrong.

Mab laughed softly. "Come sit down and eat, Woodstock, or the little one will finish them off before you even get any." Then she dropped down into her seat without ceremony and started to fill her own plate. Quin joined them a moment later, pouring lemonade for everyone and settling in across from her. Their focus turned toward the food. Which was a relief; it gave Mab a minute to breathe before she had to play hostess again.

After lunch came more swimming and sandcastles that were a little lopsided but managed to stand the test of the tide as it rose farther up toward her lounger. Then Mab went out for a swim of her own, and by the time she got back, Tavi and Quin were sprawled across the other lounger, Tavi's eyes growing heavier by the minute.

"I think we wore her out," she said, grabbing her towel to dry off.

"Yeah. I should probably get her home. It's getting close to nap time."

"You could—" Mab stopped herself as Quin's eyes snapped up to her, and she felt every inch a mouse caught in a trap. She swallowed hard. "She could take a nap in my guest bedroom. Then you don't have to move her far and risk waking her up too much."

"You sure you don't mind? She's going to get all sorts of sand in the sheets."

"It's fine." Mab shrugged. "Come on, grab sleeping beauty, and I'll show you where you can put her to bed." Then she bent and gathered up what was left of their towels and toys and trekked up to the house with Quin behind her.

She clearly hadn't thought this through, Mab realized a few minutes later, once Tavi was tucked in and there was no longer a child-sized barrier between them to keep shit from getting too awkward. She hadn't thought this through at all. The last few times they'd sat and chatted, it hadn't been too bad. But there had been panic attacks and wound tending and all manner of other things she needed to split her attention between. Meaning she didn't have time to think about the stupid shit that could come out of her mouth sometimes because she lacked a filter thanks to living with Ander for the last couple of centuries.

"You want to go hang by the pool? We can leave the door cracked; we'll be able to hear her when she wakes up." Mab hooked her thumb over her shoulder. At least outside they'd have the sound of the waves to drown out the silence that was no doubt about to ensue between them.

"Yeah. Sure."

She flopped herself onto one of the chairs on the pool deck and let out a long sigh. It had been a long time since she'd done a beach day like that, and honestly, Tavi wasn't the only one who could use a nap. She heard the chair beside her creak a little under Quin's weight as he settled in too.

"So, thanks fo—"

"I'm going to stop you there, Tweety." Mab held up her hand but didn't turn to look at him. "You've said enough thank yous to last us a lifetime. You don't need to thank me for anything I do for you guys. I like hanging out with you both. Tavi's sweet, and you're . . . " She bit the inside of her cheek to keep herself from saying something stupid and instead muttered "bearable" in a voice she hoped he recognized as teasing.

"Bearable?"

"Mhm."

"Is that the best you've got?" Okay. He sounded like he was laughing now. She lifted her hat to cut him a glare, and he held up his hands in surrender. "I'll take bearable."

"Good. It's better than most people get." A grin tugged at the corners of her lips, and she didn't try to swallow it down.

"And what do most people get?"

"Barely tolerable." If Ander heard her quoting *Pride and*

Prejudice at the guy she liked, he'd probably burst a blood vessel from laughing, but thankfully, he wasn't here.

"I'll definitely take bearable, then." A soft chuckle shook his voice, and Mab decided she liked that sound. He should do more of that. It made him sound so much younger. Unburdened in a way she knew neither of them were.

Mab huffed in response and turned her head back, flopping her hat over her eyes. "You thought any more about getting buttercup a pet?"

"Buttercup?"

"Octavia."

"Do you make it your mission to come up with a new nickname for people whenever you talk to them?"

"Only the people I like," Mab murmured, her neck heating a little from embarrassment, but she couldn't quite tuck the smile away now that it had taken up residence on her face. "Answer the question."

"Haven't had time."

"Ah. Well, let me know when you do. I'd love to be there to help." And to see the delight on Tavi's face when she realized that the little critter in front of her was her new friend. It'd be adorable.

"I'd like that," Quin mumbled back, and he sounded so damn sincere that Mab could hardly be held responsible for what came out of her mouth next.

"You two should stay for dinner."

"What?"

"For dinner. Give you a bit more peace and quiet. Let Tavi play a little more in the water before you have to head home."

"I don't want to overstay—"

"You won't."

"Okay."

Dinner wasn't anything special, just a quick chicken stir fry, but there was plenty to go around, and Mab didn't think she wanted to go back to being alone, not yet, anyway.

So she and Quin settled into the kitchen to work. Tavi was perched on one of the stools at the island, picking uncooked veggies out of the bowl where Quin was dropping the freshly chopped ones, and Mab was busy with the chicken.

She headed to the fridge just as Quin did, and they bumped each other, Mab's head smacking against his chest. Gods, he was so fucking tall, wasn't he?

"Sorry," Mab laughed at the same time that Quin muttered a quiet, "Sorry."

And then they were both laughing softly, standing in the middle of her kitchen, and Mab's chest gave a traitorous lurch. This house had been hers for years now, but it had never really felt like home before. Not like it did now. Funny the things a person realized when something changed. How the status quo could stop being enough so suddenly.

The song on the radio changed, and Mab shook her head a little, tilting it back to grin at him. "Excuse me, good sir, but may I have this dance?"

He blinked at her for a moment, confused, and all at once Mab realized how stupid that sounded. See this? This right here. This is why she didn't flirt. Gods, she was such an idiot.

"I'll just . . . " She tilted her chin back to the chicken sizzling on the stove.

"Oh. Yeah. Sorry," Quin muttered again, stepping out of her way.

She was grateful for the heat off the pan. Hopefully, it would hide the shamefaced flush settling into her cheeks.

With dinner complete, they settled on the back patio again, enjoying the warm breeze off the water and the slowly setting sun. It was quiet, but not too quiet. Companionable.

"I meant to ask," Mab said softly into the silence, and Quin lifted his head. "How are you?"

Quin shrugged, and yeah, Mab got that. Sometimes, there wasn't really a good answer to that question. She probably understood better than most people that sometimes, you just weren't okay, and nothing anyone could say or do would make you okay.

"All right." She nodded. "Would you, um . . . Do you think you'd mind if I texted? And checked in with you? I'm just. I'm a little worried, and I want to make sure you're all right. You know, in case you need another escape from your helicopter parents," she joked, hoping to ease some of the vulnerability that had crept into her words.

"I think that'd be nice."

"Okay." Mab let out a long breath.

They were gone an hour later, leaving Mab with a kitchen full of dishes that she refused to let Quin help clean up and a ringing silence in her ears. Alone. She was alone. And her house had never been so quiet before. Had never felt so empty. Her chest ached.

She grabbed her phone and dialed Ander. Thank the gods he picked up on the second ring.

"How'd it go?" he asked before anything else.

Her only response was a long drawn out "fuuuuuuuck" before she recounted every weird little thing she'd done all night, over-thought every reaction it had garnered, and generally told him what an idiot she'd made of herself.

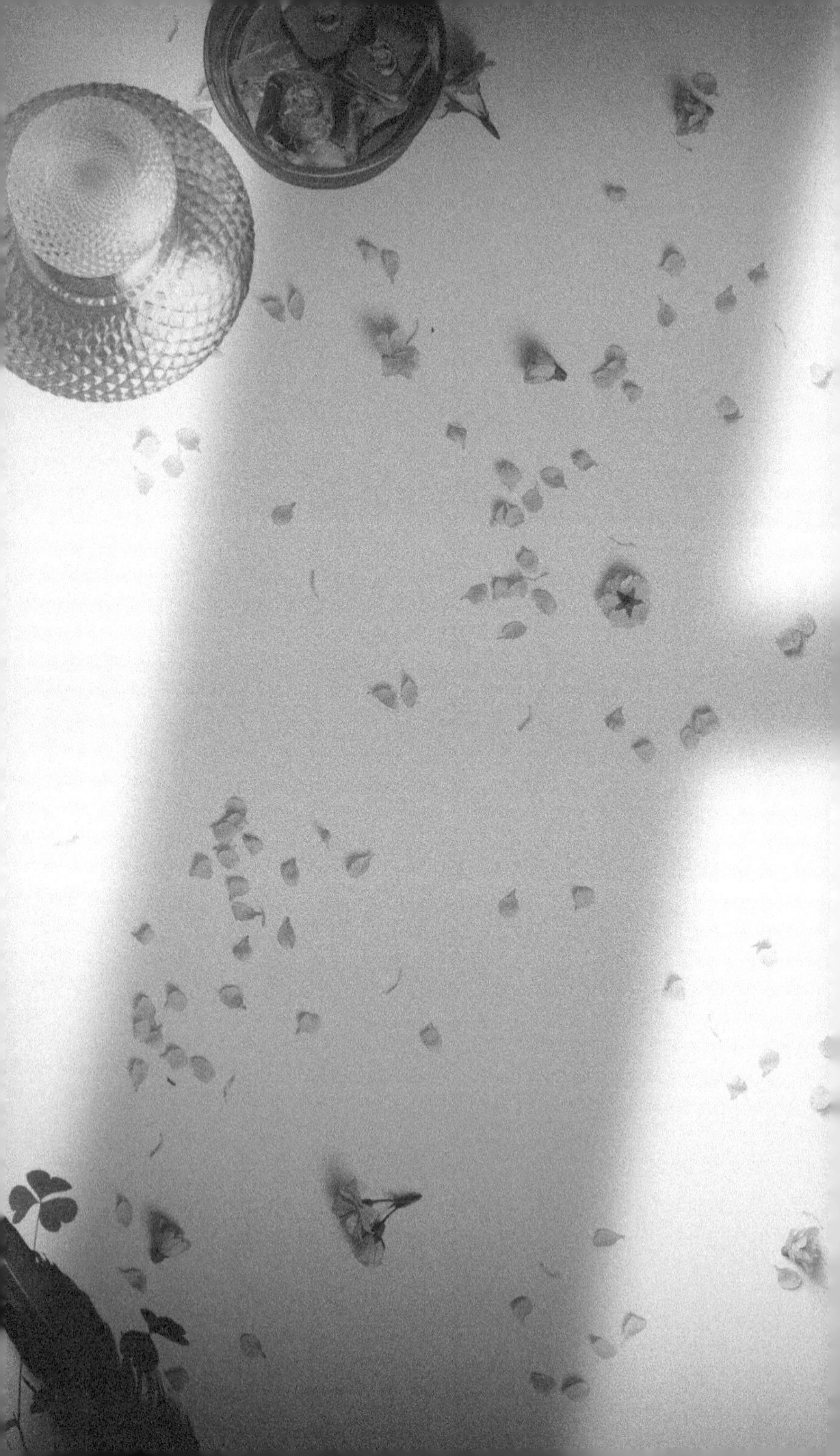

Chapter 37
Quin

Mab walked toward him, a flowing skirt fluttering around her slender ankles. It was hard to breathe while watching her. His heart beat wildly, and as she stopped before him, he couldn't find the words to speak.

She lifted her hand and pressed it against his cheek, a move he'd seen his papa do to his dad many times just before a kiss. Quin's eyes widened. Was Mab about to kiss him?

Her hand was warm on his cheek, and soft. Slowly, she pulled his head down closer to hers, and his heart picked up so hard, he was sure it was going to explode out of his chest. Their faces drew closer, and Quin could swear he felt her breath on his lips—

Quin's eyes opened, and he was staring up at the ceiling of his bedroom, not looking down at Mab. He pressed his fingers to his chest. His heart still hammered wildly, as if he'd run ten miles.

What was that? He'd never had a dream like that before. Suddenly, the image of Mab in the water with Tavi sparked to mind, her happy smile, Tavi's laughter, the peace of that moment. His heart lurched, and his chest tightened.

Quin pushed himself up into a seated position. His mind whirled. Nothing made sense. What was wrong with him?

Maybe it had something to do with his reaction at the beach, and maybe it didn't.

Quin threw off his covers and climbed from the bed. He stretched carefully, checking his ribs, and was happy to find they were feeling much better. His fingers pressed lightly at the space where his wound had been, and while the flesh was healed, there was a little tenderness beneath. Tenderness Quin could handle.

He bent to grab his sweats from off the floor, slipping them on overtop his white boxer briefs, and stepped out into the hall. It was still early, so Quin wasn't really expecting to see anyone up, but his papa was in the kitchen.

Zeke stood dressed in a silken robe that was tied around his waist, and he hummed softly to the radio as he made a fresh pot of coffee.

"You're up early," Quin said, stepping farther into the kitchen.

His papa gasped, not having heard him approach, and turned to look at him. "Quintus! You almost made me mess myself."

"Sorry. I'll take a cup of that when it's done." He nodded at the coffeemaker before taking a seat at the counter.

"Of course, love." His father turned back to finish making the coffee, hitting Power, then moved to lean against the counter and gaze over at Quin. "What's wrong?"

Quin shifted and looked down at the counter. He wasn't used to his papa being the one who read him so well.

Typically, it was his dad who saw through him. And yet . . . Zeke Schields may have been the best person to talk about this with.

"How do you know if you're attracted to someone?" he asked softly, keeping his eyes on the counter until he was done, then he darted his gaze up to look at his father.

Zeke gasped, his eyes widening and his mouth falling open a little. "Oh. My. Gods. Are we finally going to have this conversation!?" He practically went dog-whistle high as he spoke, his body vibrating with what Quin could only assume was excitement.

Quin winced at the pitch and made a face. "Shh . . . don't wake everyone." He looked back over his shoulder to make sure no one was coming down the hall. The last thing he needed was for one of the twins or Georgie to overhear this conversation. "If it's going to be a big deal, I can wait and talk to Dad."

"No, no! I can do this!" He took a deep breath, brushed his hands down over his body as if he could wipe away the excitement, and spoke more calmly the second time. "I can do this." Zeke cleared his throat. "What's bringing on the question?"

Quin blushed. How was he supposed to admit what just happened?

"Love, you can tell me. No judgment."

Quin stared back at his papa, and his shoulders relaxed. He knew he was being honest. It was why Quin had known Zeke would be the right one to talk to about this. Not just because of all his experience dating but because he always preached to them that, whatever their preferences, so long as their partners were consenting and of legal age, it was okay.

"I had a dream." Quin paused as he saw his papa's eyes

begin to gleam, but Zeke just nodded for him to continue. Behind him, the coffee pot began to gurgle as coffee streamed into it. "About Mab." He swallowed. "She put her hand on my cheek, like you do with Dad, and she was just about to kiss me. But I woke up."

Zeke just nodded and waited.

"I've never dreamed of kissing someone before, and when I woke up, my heart was pounding." He rubbed at the spot on his sternum once more, remembering.

"What else happened in the dream? Did she touch you in any other way? Did you touch her?"

"No, but I was staring at her as she walked toward me, and I couldn't stop noticing how beautiful her ankles were."

An uncontrollable snicker tore itself out of his papa's lips. It was high-pitched, and he had clearly tried to keep it down, but it came out of him anyway. Quin frowned at him.

"I'm sorry!" Zeke held his hands up. "That's just ... possibly the most adorable sex dream I've ever heard."

Quin frowned more. "Is that what ... But I've never ... It's—"

His father came forward to lean on the counter and took his hands, brushing his thumbs over the backs of them in a soothing manner. "Tell me about yesterday. What happened that changed everything?"

Quin looked at him in surprise. How did he know? "I don't know. We were in the water, and she'd brought this floaty out for Tavi to get in. Mab was pulling her around on the water and Tavi was squealing and Mab was laughing and they both looked so beautiful and happy and—" This was ridiculous. He should stop. What did any of this even matter?

"And what?" Zeke pressed.

"And my heart clenched and sped up, and I felt breathless looking at her."

Zeke smiled softly and nodded. "How were things between you the other night? When you stayed over at Max's after the terrible-thing-that-shall-not-be-named?"

"Safe," Quin whispered without thinking. Because that was how Mab had felt. Safe. Peaceful. Someone familiar to him even though they were only getting to know each other. "I think she understands me. She suffered through something terrible too. She knows what it's like to be held against your will."

Zeke was still gently stroking the tops of his hands. "You like her as a person, don't you?"

Quin thought about it for a moment, then nodded. "I do. She's a lot sweeter than she lets on. She's great with Tavi and really brings out a lighter side to her. And I don't know . . . She doesn't expect more from me than I'm able to give."

Zeke smiled more. He drew back, knowing that soon, the soothing touches were going to become overstimulating for Quin, and turned around to pour them coffee, a teaspoon of sugar in both, no milk or cream.

When the coffees were ready, he turned back to Quin, bringing them over to the island and sliding one across to him.

"You're romantically interested in her," he said at last.

"Huh?"

"Oh, baby." Zeke smiled at him as if he were simple and reached out to pat his cheek. "I think you're demisexual. The reason you've never felt attracted to someone before is that you've never really had the chance to get to know someone on a personal level. Now you have, and you're connecting with Mab. You're forming a romantic attachment to her." He smiled more and sipped his coffee.

"And now, because of that, you're finding yourself sexually attracted to her."

Quin's hands wrapped around his mug, and he stared back at his father. "But how do I make it *stop*?"

Zeke laughed. "Well, you don't have to act on anything you're feeling. You can ignore it and stop hanging out with her so much until it passes by. *Or—*" He paused, eyeing him. "You could try to get to know her even more. Spend more time with her. Do something with Mab where it's just you and her, no Tavi."

Quin swallowed. The thought of being alone with Mab made him incredibly nervous. He could face off with monsters in the dark, battle six inanimi at a time without blinking. But the thought of it being just him and Mab alone was terrifying.

"You mean like a date? But I don't know how to do that!"

Zeke reached out to pat his hand once more. "It doesn't have to be complicated or fancy, Quinny. Just find out what she likes to do and do it with her. If it's something you've never done before, get her to explain it to you. If it's something you have, you can compare notes. Find out what draws her to it. See what you have in common." He sipped his coffee once more. "Dating is just hanging out with another person."

Quin inhaled a deep breath. Could he actually do this? Did he, Quin Schields, actually want to *date* someone? His father was eying him expectantly, as if he wanted to sit and plan out every detail of a date for Quin and Mab. Quin could barely conceive of the *idea* of a date right now, let alone spitball ideas with him. Quin's eyes searched the kitchen for a distraction and landed on the coffee canister.

"Dad is going to kill you if he finds out you've been getting up early to sneak caffeine."

Zeke scowled. "That decaf is awful. Who wants the placebo when they can have the real thing?" He narrowed his eyes on him. "If you tell your dad . . ."

Quin held up a hand. "I won't say a word."

By the time the twins came out of their bedrooms, laptops tucked beneath their arms, he'd had some time to think and had almost convinced himself it was something he could do. That letting another person into his life, into his inner circle, was a good idea.

"You two look terrible," he said, scanning them over.

Nash scowled and plopped down beside him at the island. "That's because we barely slept. We've been following the trackers you placed on the trucks all night."

"Until they *stopped*," Nox cut in.

"Stopped?" That piqued Quin's interest.

"Yes, and then we had to figure out where they had stopped *at*. Last place was just a bunker of sorts. A place for them to sleep during the day so they could drive at night," Nash continued. His fingers moved over the keys so that he could bring up satellite imaging for Quin to look at.

Nox moved around the kitchen, then approached them, a mug of coffee in each hand. One she handed to Nash, the other she curled both hands around and lifted to her lips for a drink. Her bright green eyes lacked their typical sparkle, and her lids were puffy.

Quin realized that sometimes he and Max forgot how much extra work the twins put into their missions and how much sleep they lost regularly because of it.

"We think it's a compound," she explained as Nash turned the computer for Quin to look at. "Large enough to have barracks, mess hall, weapons rooms, and massive fields for training."

"But it looks empty." Quin leaned in more so he could see better.

"We think they keep inside during the day. Less likely to be spotted by normies that way." Nash stifled a big yawn and gulped down some coffee, wincing at the scalding heat.

"We're doing our best to keep an eye on it so we know as soon as there's movement, but we have to keep hacking the normie government satellite to get a look. It's time consuming."

Quin nodded. "I'm gonna call Max and let him know."

He slid off his stool and went to his room to collect his phone. Dialing Max's number, he waited.

It didn't take long for Max to pick up. "Yeah?"

"The twins have found something. Looks like a large compound that could be Orcus' main base."

There was silence on the other end, then Max spoke. "I'm glad to hear it. Can I leave you to take point on this for right now and monitor it with the twins? Gather what information you can?"

"Is something wrong?" Quin asked, frowning.

"No, I've just got something important I need to do."

"Do you want my help?"

"I've got this," Max assured him. "And I'm going to make Mab assist me on this one. The best thing you can do is keep an eye on this Enrique matter."

At the mention of Mab, Quin felt that weird fluttering sensation in his stomach again.

"Okay. I'll keep you posted."

"Thanks, Quin." Max hung up.

Quin stared down at the black screen of his phone.

What was so important that Max wasn't going to rush right over?

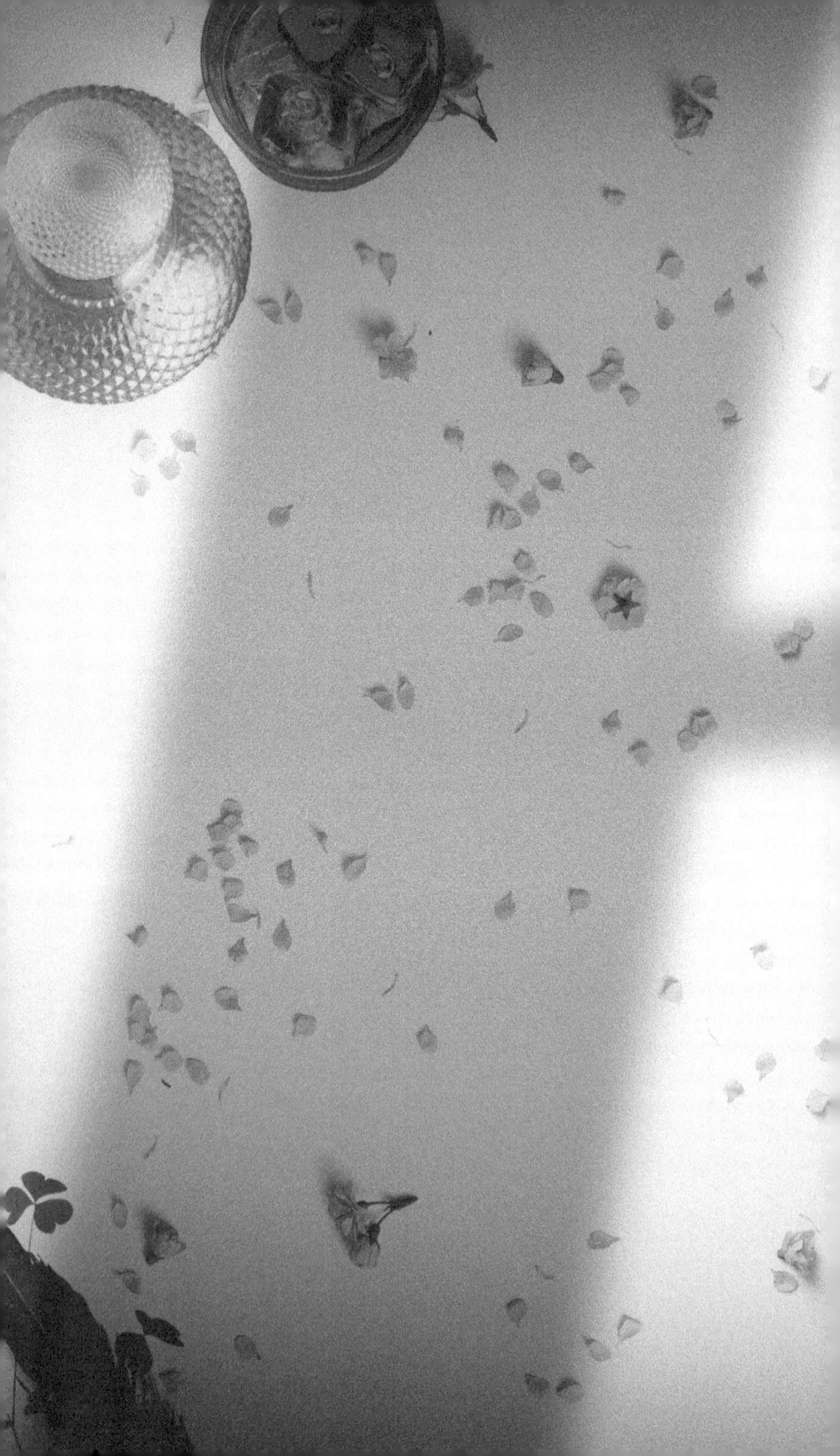

Chapter 38
Max

I'm going to marry him, Max thought as Ander checked over his wings, making sure there was no damage aside from the obvious. It was a passing thought then.

I'm going to marry him soon, Max thought the following morning, after Mab and Quin left and Ander worried himself practically sick about what would happen to his sister now that she was bonded. He'd done his best then to ease Ander's worries. To assure him that Quin would be good for Mab once he realized their connection. It helped, but the depth of Ander's care for his family—for *their* family—over the last few days struck Max right in the chest.

I'm going to propose to him tonight, Max thought again while Ander puttered about the kitchen, putting together a breakfast tray and brewing coffee, and the thought nearly bowled him over. It had always been a foregone conclusion. Something Max had always known but had only just voiced to himself. Ander was his soulmate; of course they'd get married one day. But to propose? That was a different matter.

Although he shouldn't have been surprised, with

everything that had happened in the last couple of days. The way Ander fit so neatly into Max's little family and how he took charge when Max needed him most. How Ander had become Max's port in the storm ... Why wait?

I need to get a ring. I need to make this perfect.

"Babe," Max called, swallowing down the smile that threatened to take over his face. He didn't want to give it away, not yet. If he was going to do this, it had to be a surprise. It had to be special. It had to be a night Ander would remember for the rest of their long lives. "Why don't we go on a date tonight?"

"Tonight?" Ander whipped around so quickly, it was like he was wearing roller skates, but he was smiling, and that was all the answer Max needed. "I can get us a reservation at—"

"No. No. I want to plan it. I just want you to show up looking pretty. Okay?" He was going to have to call in some help on this if he was going to get it all done. Good thing he had just the woman for the job, and she shouldn't be otherwise occupied today ... "But that means you'll have to keep yourself busy today. Is that all right?"

"Yeah. I've got some stuff I need to do at the club. I've kind of let all the paperwork pile up. What time do you want me back?" Ander came over to lean into Max's space, his chin resting on his shoulder, the warm line of his torso pressed against Max's back. It was comforting. Soft. Max loved every minute of it. Wanted to lean back into the touch like a cat begging for pets.

"How about I pick you up from the club around ... " Max thought for a minute. "Eight?" That should give him enough time to get everything ready.

"Eight is perfect," Ander purred into his ear, the sound tickling. "Should I wear anything special?"

Max wrinkled his nose in thought. He hadn't figured out where he was going to take him yet. He just knew it needed to be a night to remember. But . . . well, what better place than the scene of their first date? "No heels. Only requirement. And something that makes you feel pretty."

"Color me intrigued, sweetheart." Ander pulled back to grin at him. "But that's the only hint I'm getting, isn't it?"

"It is." Pushing himself from the stool, Max moved after Ander, reeling him in close again so he could tilt his chin up carefully and press a chaste kiss to his lips. "I want it to be a surprise."

"Fine. Fine." Ander's smile went soft and languid. "Keep your secrets."

"I will. Now, go and get ready for work." He grabbed Ander's hand and spun him away before swatting his butt lightly. "I've got things to do."

Ander laughed brightly, his hips swaying all the way to the bedroom, but that gave Max enough privacy to send a quick text to Mab and answer a call from Quin before he was on his way.

Getting to Helicon without the use of a Sanctum-sanctioned portal was a pain in the ass. He had never really thought about how easy it was to get from place to place with the sanctuary at his back. But thankfully, Ander wasn't at the club yet, and Mab was able to smuggle him through the portal in Inferno's storeroom that led directly to Helicon.

"I'm not coming with you," she said, her arms crossed

over her chest. "And if Andy is going to be working here, you'll have to find your own way back."

"Sure, if Aemiliana doesn't eat me alive first." Max grinned at her, brushing his hair back from his face. It likely only made it look messier, but he was beyond caring at this point. He was too nervous about meeting with his future mother-in-law and asking her permission to marry her son.

"That is a very real possibility." Mab's expression turned sharp and predatory as she opened the door for him, then shoved him through without preamble. "Break a leg, Wonderboy!"

Max stumbled, only just caught himself from falling face-first into a hedge, and spun around to cut Mab a glare, but she was already gone. The door closed behind him, the portal disappearing with it, and like that, there was no way back unless Aemiliana decided to send him back. Well. He took a deep breath and stood up a little taller. He supposed the only way out was forward.

"Maximus," a soft, warm voice said from behind him.

Max jumped, spinning around, hand reaching for a weapon that wasn't there, and came face-to-face with the queen herself. "Your Majesty," he yelped, his voice too high, too panicked. "Uh ... hello?"

"Greetings." Aemiliana raised an eyebrow, her head tilting to the side as if she was looking for someone behind him. "You're alone."

"Oh. Uh. Yeah." Max shifted awkwardly, clearing his throat to try to make himself sound more like himself. It likely wouldn't work. He was freaking out. He really should have brought backup. Quin wouldn't have said anything, but having him there would have made Max feel less like he was drowning in his own insecurities. "I actually came to, uh ... to talk with you."

"I assumed." She didn't look at all amused nor entirely surprised by his arrival. Had she known he was coming? Well, clearly she'd known someone was coming because she'd appeared in the gardens a moment after he stepped through the portal. She must have a ward set up to alert her when anyone came from Inferno into Helicon. That was . . . oddly sweet. Her wanting to know when her children were home, first thing. "Come. I've had tea prepared."

Then she turned and swept through the gardens, leaving Max no choice but to follow her. He wiped his hands on his jeans, hoping no one noticed how they shook as he followed Aemiliana through hedges and down paths, then into the palace and down gilded halls. A little smile ticked up his lips as he imagined little Ander running along the marbled floors, laughing and bright. He had probably been adorable. Even when he got older, drunkenly swaying with Mab at his side. Max imagined these halls held a lot of good memories for him. A lot of bad too, based on what Ander had said about his grandfather.

Max shook those sad thoughts aside and focused on settling into the cushions placed around a low table on the floor in what appeared to be Aemiliana's private sitting room. The carpet beneath him was lush and colorful. He couldn't see any of the walls for the draperies. But the space had a light airiness to it, even with all the rich, gem-toned textiles.

"Now," Aemiliana said, neatly pouring them each a cup of tea, "tell me why I should allow you to marry my son."

"How did you know I was—"

Aemiliana raised one dark brow, the expression so oddly like Ander's when he was annoyed, it stopped Max dead. "There is only one thing that could have brought you to Helicon without my son." She paused for a moment. "Well.

One thing that would bring you here without you looking frantic and panicked. But let's not speak of *him* right now. If this is what you mean to do, then you don't have much time to put together a proposal that will be good enough for Ander, so you'd best get on with it. Why should I let you marry my son, and so soon into your relationship?"

"Because I love him." No. That wasn't enough. There was so much more than just love. That didn't cover even half of the reasons Max wanted to marry Ander. It was at the heart of all of them, sure, but it wasn't the whole of it. Those words seemed so trite, so shallow compared to the depth of what Max felt for Ander. "He's . . . " Max's throat clogged with emotion, and his eyes burned with tears. "He's *everything* to me, ma'am. I don't know how else to explain it. I can't imagine my life without him in it."

Aemiliana stared back at him unblinking, and Max shifted a little under the searching gaze. "That's what he does for you. But what do you do for him? What reason does his mother have in offering his hand to someone who may only love him because of some ridiculous spell he cast when he was drunk?"

"This has nothing to do with the amare bond!" Max snarled, anger making his face hot. "I'd love him even if we weren't bound. I'd take care of him even if he had nothing to offer me in return. If he didn't want me, I'd still try to make his life as bright as possible. Even if he chose someone else. His happiness is all that matters to me. Yes, he brings me light, and he's the first person I've allowed myself to lean on since I was a child, but there's so much more than that. And I'd do the same for him tenfold. I'm devoted to him. I'm willing to give him everything, anything. If tomorrow he asked me to clip my wings and leave the Sanctum, I would. But he'd never ask that of me, just as I'd never ask him to give up his club. We understand each other. We make each other better. We're *good* together."

Aemiliana lifted her cup to her lips for a careful sip, and Max wondered if she was doing it just to make him sweat. He didn't know her well enough to recognize her ticks the way he did other people's. But if he were in her shoes, that's what he'd do.

"Please." He gasped the word like a drowning man. "Please, Your Majesty."

Her cup settled against the saucer with a soft click. Her lips formed a soft, subtle smile. "Very well. I give my consent for you to marry my son. All I ask is that you love him the way he deserves. The way he will love you. All-consuming and absolute. But be aware, Maximus Schields, if you hurt him, there will be nothing left of you to return to the fires of Prometheus."

"Yes, Your Majesty." He dipped his head in respect, in understanding. "If I hurt him, I wouldn't want to return to them anyway. I wouldn't be worthy of it."

"No. You wouldn't," she agreed readily. "Now, you've much to do. So I suggest you get moving." With a soft song to call forth her magic, she raised her hand and opened a portal in the far wall. "That will take you to Mab's home. She should be waiting for you to go ring shopping, I believe."

"Thank you, Your Majesty." Max scrambled to his feet, nearly knocking the table over in his rush. But he didn't slow down. Because she was right, he didn't have a lot of time to do everything he needed to do. "You won't be sorry!"

"I had better not be," she murmured just as the portal spat him out on the patio around the pool at Mab's.

"Took you long enough," Mab said from where she sat on one of the pool loungers, sunglasses covering her eyes.

He felt her gaze rake over the way he was bouncing on his heels, hands trembling just the same. She lifted a brow. "She said yes, I'm guessing."

"We've got to go ring shopping, Mab! Come on. Come on. Let's go. Get up." He moved to her to grab her hands and pull her to her feet.

Mab groaned, pulling her hands from his, but she headed into the house anyway to grab her purse and a ring of keys. "Fine, but we're taking my car."

"Okay!" Max inhaled deeply and tried to settle himself, but it didn't work. He was a riot of emotions, most of them good, some of them nervous. Every muscle in his body twitched with anxiety. Every nerve ending hummed with excitement. He was going to burst apart at the seams if they didn't get moving right away.

Mab led him into the attached garage, where two old cars were parked side by side. Their bright colors gleamed under the light. He didn't know anything about cars, but he could tell that Mab had taken care of these. "Woah, nice wheels."

Mab scoffed. "Just don't scratch the paint, Schields, or you'll never make it to '*I do.*'"

Max saluted and slid carefully into the teal convertible closest to them. "So. Cars, huh?"

There was no answer, just the roar of an engine as Mab pulled out of the garage and onto the street, heading for the heart of Miami.

"I would like to go on record as saying that Ander owes me *big* for this," Mab grumbled from where she was pressed into his side behind a glass case full of engagement rings.

It was the third place they'd been to, and Max still hadn't found exactly what he was looking for. Not that he *knew* exactly what he was looking for, but he'd know it when he saw it. It would scream "Ander." Still, Mab was growing increasingly grumpy.

"And if one more normie assumes we're a couple, I'm going to scream so loud, I shatter every piece of glass in this godsforsaken—"

"What can I help the happy couple with?" the salesperson said, and Max heard Mab take a deep inhale. He nudged her with his hip, and she coughed on it.

"We're not a couple. This is my soon-to-be sister-in-law. I'm looking for a ring for my boyfriend." Max had gotten that down after the first time because he didn't want any extra questions that might imply Mab was anything but what she was. Gods, he was so done with the heteronormative nonsense from normies. "I'd like to see this one up close please," he said pointing to a ring through the glass.

It was a little more understated than the pieces Ander usually wore, but Max didn't think he wanted something too terribly flashy. Nothing that was so big it would feel clunky for everyday or get caught on things. But it still had to look like something Ander would wear ...

"That's too small," Mab grunted at his side.

"It's the biggest one in this case." Max sighed, rubbing at his face. "Why did I bring you again?"

"This case sucks. What do you want from me?" Mab shrugged. "Show us your statement pieces. Stuff that almost looks like costume jewelry but isn't."

"That collection is prohibitively expensive, ma'am."

The sales associate looked Max over in his jeans, loafers, and sweater with patches sewn into the elbows. Max knew what he looked like. Was more than aware of the fact that the man was probably sizing him up as some kind of professor type who maybe wasn't even tenured yet, considering his age. "I don't think—"

"Did we *ask* what you thought?" Mab spat, leaning over the glass to get closer to the man's face. Max was suddenly very glad he'd brought her along.

The man cleared his throat and pushed off from the glass to stand up straight again. "Right this way."

"I didn't know you could do that," Max whispered to Mab as they both followed the man to the back corner of the store.

"You pick up a thing or two when you spend a couple hundred years with Ander." Mab shrugged again, stuffing her hands into the pockets of her cut-off shorts. "Like how to talk to snobby salespeople." Her smile turned a little feral when they came up to the next case. "Now *this* is more like it. All right, Maxxy, see anything you like?"

Max leaned over the glass, his eyes wide and searching. There were lots of pretty pieces in there but nothing—

"That one." He pointed to what looked like maybe it was a stacker set. The main ring was a large set of wings with diamonds set in where the feathers should be. At the center, between where the two wings almost touched, there was a tear-shaped ruby. The second smaller ring was a rounded row of diamonds that nestled perfectly along the curve of the ruby, like a crown. "We'll take that one."

"Yes, sir," the man said, and Max hardly heard the price over the drumbeat of his heart in his ears.

He was going to propose to Ander.
Tonight.

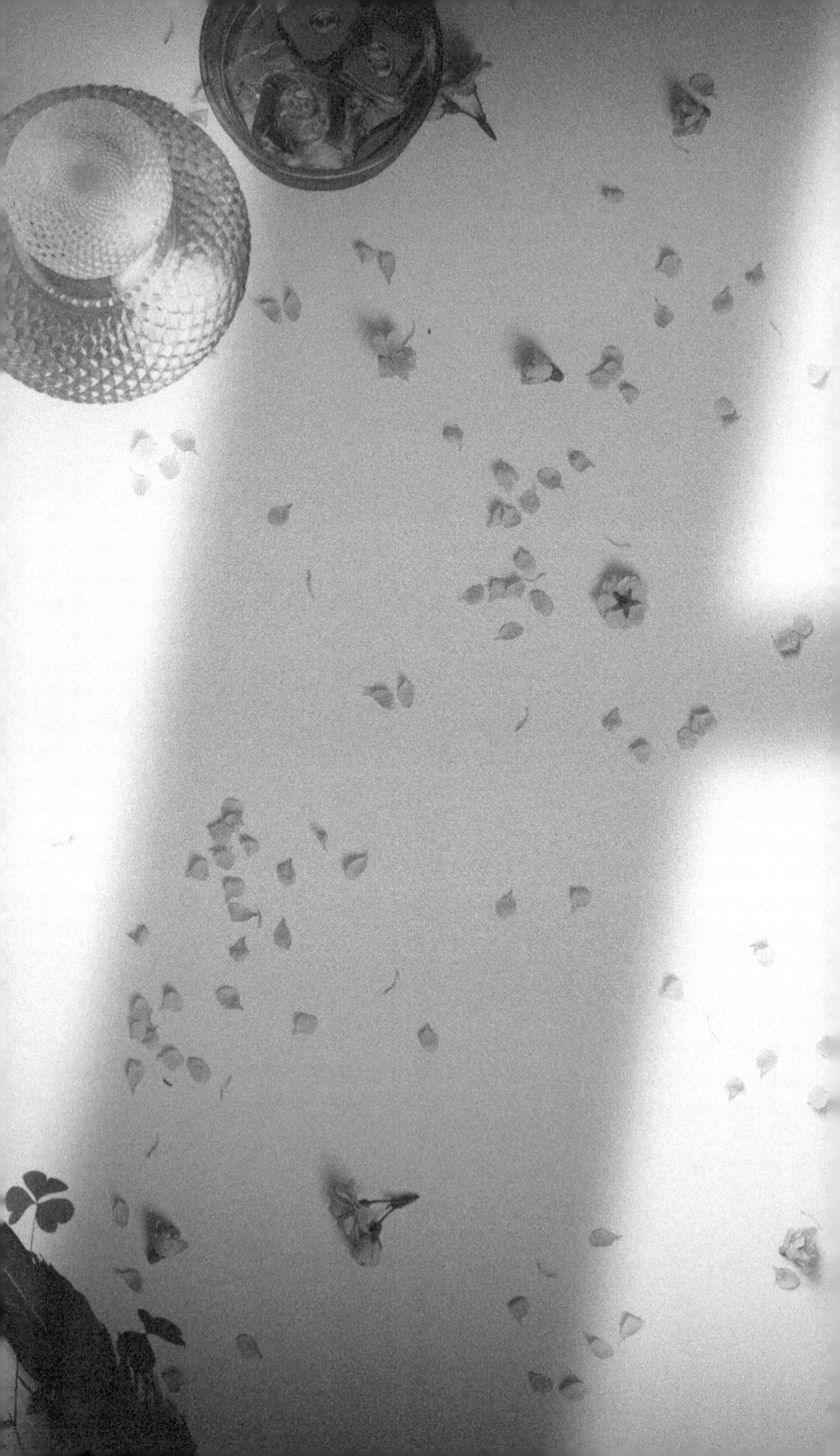

Chapter 39
Ander

Max told him to dress pretty. And so he had. He wore a loose-fitting black Balmain shirt with a silver embroidered damask pattern up the sides. He styled it with a white collared dress shirt beneath and tucked only the front of the black blouse into his tight black skinny jeans. On his feet, he wore pointed black shoes.

He coiffed his hair back off his forehead but teased it high into a wide mohawk. There was a gold cuff on his right ear and a chain with a small heart pendant dangling from the lobe of his left. His nails were painted black and his fingers covered in gold rings with red and black gems.

He lined his eyes with black and a smudge of black over his lids. Ander felt pretty. And when Max arrived to pick him up, the pleasure that bloomed over his face at the sight of him made Ander's insides buzz.

"Wow," Max breathed out, and Ander was sure that he would never grow tired of the way Max looked at him. Like he was the most beautiful thing in the world.

Ander slid his arms around Max's neck, pressing a warm kiss to his lips. "Hi, sweetheart."

Max grinned, his arms sliding around his waist. "Hey."

Ander laughed, unable to stop himself. "Ready to go?"

"Absolutely." Max pulled back, threaded their fingers, and tugged him from the office and down the stairs into the club.

It was early, but the club was already filling up. It pleased Ander every time he saw it. "Should we snap wherever it is we're going?"

Max shook his head, pulling him through the crowd and outside, where his motorbike sat. "Nope! We're taking this."

Ander chuckled. "I do like sitting with you between my thighs." He winked at Max and smirked at the faint blush on his boyfriend's cheeks.

Soon, they were cruising down the street, Ander's arms around Max's waist and Max's wings fluttering around him. Ander still didn't know where they were going, but he didn't care. He was with Max, and that was all that mattered.

He wasn't exactly surprised when they pulled up to the taco truck. Max did love this spot. Though when he'd told him to dress pretty, he'd thought he would be taking them to a place a little fancier than this. His comment about no heels should have been warning enough.

"Eating here?" Ander asked as he slid off the bike.

"Nope!" was all Max said, and it made Ander chuckle.

"Okay, mister mysterious."

Max winked and grabbed his hand to tug him up to the truck. While they waited for their food, they stood in each other's arms, and the simplicity of it made Ander happy. He rested his head against Max's shoulder, making sure his horns didn't poke him in the head, and hummed softly to himself.

Max turned his head to look at him and smiled, pressing a kiss to his forehead. "I love you," he murmured.

"And I *adore* you," Ander said back.

They were busy staring at each other when their order was served up. They almost didn't hear it until the shout of their number being called finally broke through.

Max hurried over to grab the bag, then they were back on the bike and headed off once more.

Ander realized what Max was doing when they pulled up to the botanical garden.

"Ahh, I see what you're up to."

Max's face almost seemed to blanch. "You do?" he rasped.

"Well, yes, our first date was only about two months ago." Ander snickered and poked Max's side. "It's cute."

Max's shoulders relaxed, and he breathed out. "I thought it might be nice . . . to come here again."

"It is."

They held hands once more as they entered the gardens, walking through, gazing at the beautiful flowers and enjoying the sweet scent in the air. Eventually, they found a nice spot beneath a tree, and Max suggested they take a seat.

Ander snapped his fingers, and a blanket appeared, along with a bottle of wine and some glasses.

Sitting down, they unpacked their food. Max took his pile of tacos, and Ander accepted his burrito. It was huge, and he wanted only about half of it.

"We should have gotten you less tacos . . ."

"What?" Max asked, eyes going wide as he pulled his pile toward him protectively.

Ander chuckled. "No, I meant because I'll only eat half of this. You can have the rest."

"You should eat it all," Max said.

"This will be enough." He held up the half he'd picked up.

Max shrugged. "I'll still finish it for you." His face split with a grin.

"Of course you will." Ander smirked, then took a bite of his burrito.

They ate, occasionally reaching out to touch the other's arm or leg. It felt so good to be with him. To look over and see Max's smiling face beaming back at him. When Erotes first shot his arrow into the descending ignis, Ander had been positive he'd cursed him.

Now . . . now, he would thank Erotes if he saw him again. Quickly and possibly under his breath so Erotes didn't hear it, but thank him, nonetheless.

Ander sighed contentedly and looked around them. "This was a good idea, baby."

He watched a butterfly flutter above them in the air, smiling, then turned back to Max when he saw him moving out of the corner of his eye. At the sight of Max propped up on one knee, holding a small velvet box in his hands, Ander gasped.

"Max?" He whispered. "What are you . . ."

Max smiled gently and opened the box to show off a gorgeous ring. A sparkling teardrop ruby with a splay of diamond-encrusted wings. It was the most beautiful thing Ander had ever seen.

"You . . . are everything and more than I could have ever dreamed of," Max began. "I know it's only been a few months, but I can't imagine living life without you. I know I want to spend every day of my eternity with you."

Ander's heart was beating so wildly in his chest, he

could barely hear Max, but he strained, focused on his lips. On the beautiful words coming out of his mouth.

"Ander Ruin, Prince of Helicon and my heart, will you marry me?" Max's hazel eyes were wide and lovely, filled with so much love, Ander couldn't believe all of this was his.

"Are you sure?" he gasped. "Are you absolutely sure? I mean . . . it's me! I've—"

Max took his hand and pulled him closer. "I love you just exactly as you are. Be my husband?"

A rush of pure joy threatened to make Ander pass out, he threw his arms around Max's neck and began kissing him through his laughter and the tears that were pouring down his cheeks.

"Yes! Yes-yes-yes-YES!"

Their lips were together once more. The kiss was deep and happy and filled with so much love, Ander knew that all the dark, long-buried wounds inside of him were beginning to heal. Max loved him. Max loved him in a way no one else ever had. He knew the bad and saw past it. He saw to the good that lay within Ander and did his best to bring it out of him.

Ander pulled back. "Oh my gods, put it on me!" He held out his hand, beaming as Max took the ring from the box and slid it on his ring finger.

Ander pulled his hand close, gazing at the ring in awe.

"Do you like it?" Max asked hopefully.

"Sweetheart, it's perfect! Absolutely perfect!" Ander leaned in and pressed another kiss to his lips. "Gods, I love you," he breathed against him.

"I love you too," Max murmured back. He kissed the corner of Ander's lips, then along his jaw, and finally pressed a kiss to his throat.

Ander groaned. "Can I snap us and your bike home," he

whispered. "I wanna show my new fiancé just how much I do love his ring by pleasing every inch of him." He purred the words, leaning into Max even more.

Max shivered and nodded his head. "Yes, please."

Smirking, Ander pulled Max into his arms, kissing him firmly as he snapped them home and straight into their bed.

Then he made slow, thorough love to his fiancé until he was a happy, panting, sated mess.

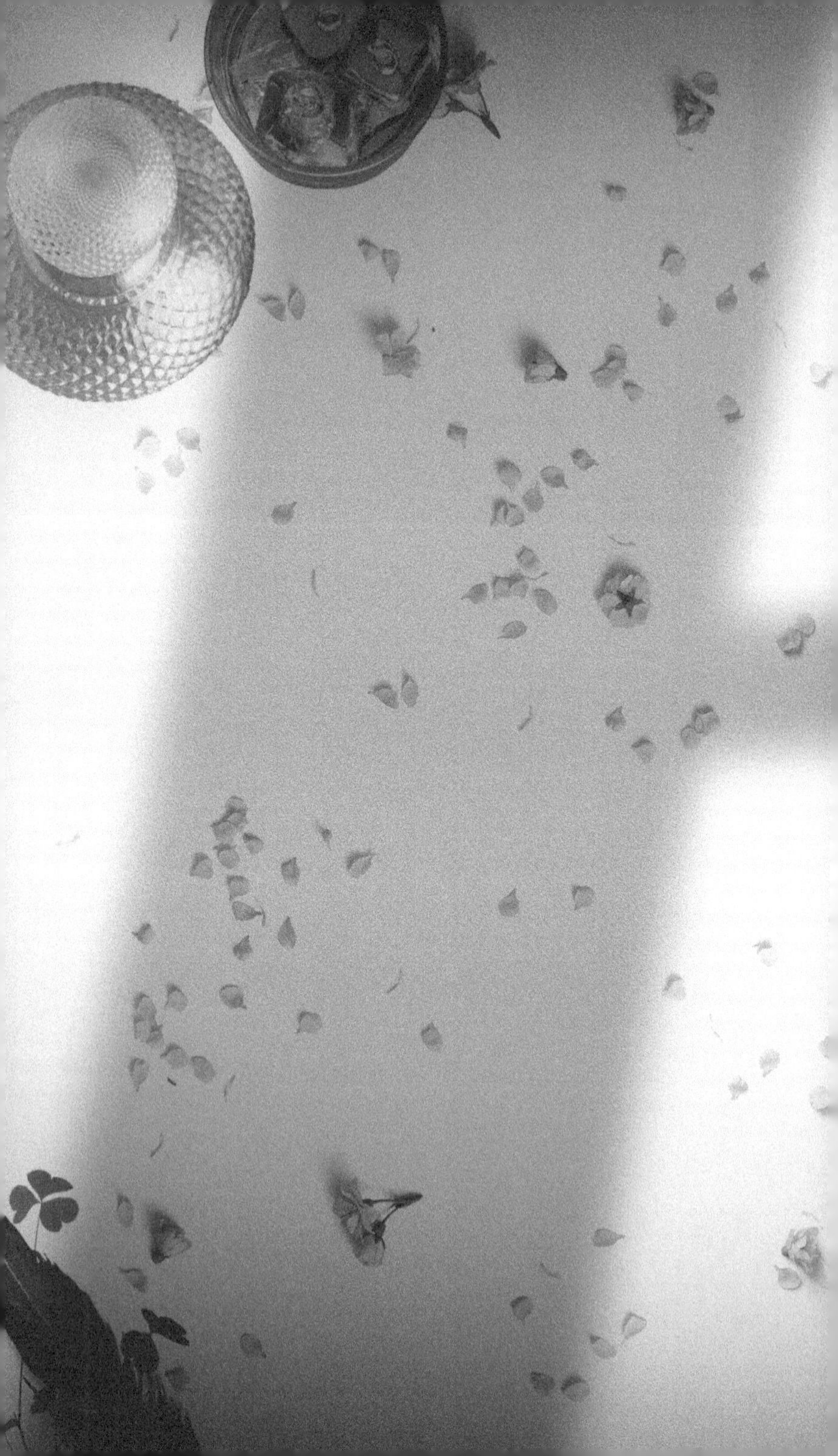

Chapter 40
Mab

All Mab could say about this whole fiasco was that it was a good thing she hadn't planned to have a surprise party for the two numbskulls that had just gotten engaged. Because when she showed up to their door, it was very clear that they'd spent the last couple of hours in bed.

"Mabbers! What a surprise!" There was a dark hickey forming on Ander's neck, and Mab resisted the urge to roll her eyes and groan. "What can we do for—?"

She didn't wait for him to finish the question, just pushed past carrying the box of booze. "Twins and Q will be here any minute. Food is on the way. Get dressed."

"Get dressed for what?" Max asked, coming down the hall in only his boxers. His hair was an absolute disaster, and there were red marks all over his chest. Peachy. Just peachy.

"Your engagement party, dipshit. Now go make yourselves presentable, I've got work to do." She pulled out a banner to prove her point and moved into the pantry to grab the step stool, turning her back on them both without another word. There was some shuffling behind her, so she assumed they'd left, but a second later, the banner flew from her hands and attached itself above the cabinets. "I had that handled!"

"You *always* hang them crooked," Ander called back.

"You always hang them crooked," she mocked and went back to pulling the rest of the decorations from the box.

The twins arrived promptly twenty minutes later with Quin dogging their steps, and then the drinks started flowing.

"Can you show me how to make that drink again? The one with the raspberry syrup?" Nox asked, tilting back a little to look at Mab better.

"Sure thing, kiddo." Mab tapped her nose and grinned when Nox only giggled.

"So, I heard about the last time you guys partied . . . How did you wind up in a tree?" Nox tilted her head in curiosity, and Mab couldn't help but smile back at her. She'd never been the big sister type, but she could see being that to Nox and Georgie. Now that she was kind of-sort of part of the family.

"*Ander* is the one who got us stuck in a tree." Mab snickered and started mixing ingredients together in the shaker.

"Mama always says never to drink and teleport." Ander tapped his nose sagely.

"Too bad you never listen." Mab snickered when he squawked and threw a pillow at her, which she ducked all without spilling a single drop of the drink she was making. She was old hat at Ander tantrums. "She also told you to never drink and spell, and look how that turned out."

"I don't know what you're talking about, Mabbers," Ander said, dropping down onto a stool next to Nox in the kitchen and sliding his empty glass her way. "That worked out famously for the *both* of us."

"What did?" Nox tilted her head in curiosity.

"Nothing. He's talking out of his—"

"The love spell I cast!"

"You what now?" Nox shifted on her stool, clearly getting comfortable.

"Ander," Mab warned, her hands tight around the shaker. She did not want anyone hearing about that, especially anyone who was likely to tell Quin. He didn't need to know that she was bound to him. It would only complicate what had the potential to be a decent friendship. And she wasn't ready to say goodbye to that, not yet, not if she had a choice. Even if it hurt like a heart attack every time they were close to each other and not touching.

"Oh, come on, Mabbers. Noxxy-kins wants to hear the story."

"The story is, he cast a love spell and got us both into a lot more trouble than he should have, that's the story. Not very interesting, but have you ever asked him about why we weren't able to return to France for a half a century?" Mab shoved a drink into his hand and hoped he got the hint.

"It wasn't *that* long," Ander huffed, taking a sip.

"Definitely was. And we almost got shot in the process."

"Oooh I want to hear this story even more." Nox rested her chin on her hands and looked delighted at the prospect. Mab and Ander delved in deep, playing off each other as they relayed the events of France, and the love spell was quickly forgotten, thank the gods.

"And that's why we couldn't go back to France for fifty years." Mab shrugged.

"How do you know you couldn't—"

"He tried," Mab snickered. "But someone had stolen one of his portraits from the townhouse and was still passing it around twenty years later. He caused a riot when he showed up. Not to mention, they thought he was a witch."

"Normies," Ander sighed. "They think *everyone's* a witch." Then he and Mab snickered, a private joke between them. She wondered for a moment when there had been enough distance between her and that pyre that they could laugh about it and decided it didn't matter. It was just nice that it wasn't haunting her anymore. The cell was. But not the pyre.

Mab was in bartender mode for a hot minute, until the shaker started slipping through her fingers, then Nox pulled her out onto the makeshift dance floor of the cleared-out living room.

"C'mon, Mab!" Nox crowed above the music, her green eyes bright in the lowered lights.

Happiness buzzed through Mab's system right along with the alcohol. Her brother was in love and engaged. Max was going to take such good care of him. And the Schields family? Well, they'd pretty much welcomed her as one of their own. Sure, her soulmate was avoiding her, but that was all right. And so what if she was drinking a little extra to try to push him from her mind and the ache of his absence from her chest? No one had to know that but her ... and probably Ander.

"How did they dance back in the day?" Nash asked, a laugh on his lips.

"*Which* day?" Mab snickered. "I've seen a lot of days, kiddo. You're gonna have to be more specific."

"Show them a proper waltz, Mabbers! You always were the best at waltzes!" Ander was clapping along to the music. He hadn't moved much at all from Max's lap the entire night, and Mab didn't have the heart to try and tear him away. They were happy. Let them be happy. Gods only knew what tomorrow would bring.

"A waltz?" Mab laughed, her head falling backward. "To *house* music?"

"Oooh can't do it?" Ander's grin had gone sly. "Is the Lady Duchan finally backing down from a challenge? I never thought I'd see the day!"

"Oooooo!" the twins hollered, their hands over their mouths. It was ridiculous. Everything about this entire day had been ridiculous from start to finish. But Mab didn't think she'd have it any other way. It felt like those early days with Ander. The ones before Enrique, when he wasn't as damaged, and they spent their time hopping from party to party causing mischief. Only they weren't likely to get chased out of this one by gun-toting Frenchmen or an angry, cuckolded love god.

"Put your money where your mouth is, Ruin." Mab held out her hand, dipping into a formal bow in front of him, a wicked smile crawling up her face. She knew this was going to be absolutely the stupidest shit they'd ever done, and that included getting stuck in a tree and having to have Max and Quin come get them out. But it was fun. And she felt so light. And she wasn't going to overthink it as she swept Ander into her arms and they started through the steps, albeit much quicker than they ever had before because the music warranted it.

The dance was almost too fast, but thankfully, Mab had done these steps a million times over when she was far drunker than she was now. The spinning, however, was likely going to make her so dizzy, she wouldn't be able to walk for a while. But that was fine too. Then she could just lay on the couch with her head in Ander's lap and let him pet her hair.

"I'm not doing the lifts," Ander said, a little breathless.

"Coward," Mab shot back, a laugh on her lips. It was hard not to laugh. Hard not to be happy. When she was dancing with her best friend. However ridiculous they might look. The first lift was fine, even if they both wobbled a little from drunkenness. The second nearly sent them both to the floor, but Mab somehow managed to put her arms out to the sides and only just hold her balance. "God, I'm so out of practice. I look like a drunk chicken!"

"But a pretty drunk chicken," Ander cooed to her, his head bent low where only she could hear.

"Shut up." She laughed, giving him a little shove, and he spun her out away from him, keeping ahold of her hand so he could reel her back in when she was done. Her head spun with it, but it didn't make her feel nauseous, it made her feel light. Lighter than air. Gods, it was good to be happy like this again.

"I'm just telling you what he's thinking," Ander murmured, and when he pulled back, she saw his eyes glittering with mischief, the absolute brat.

"He who?" Mab frowned, her nose curling up a little.

"Your admirer." Ander nodded his head behind her.

"I don't have a—" They twirled, and she caught sight of Quin, standing beside the couch where Max and the twins had taken up residence, his gaze fixed on the pair of them dancing in the middle of the living room. "Don't be silly, Ander. He's just watching us make asses of ourselves, just like the rest of them."

"Maybe," Ander conceded. "Maybe not." His grin turned wicked.

"Ander, what're you doing?" But it was too late. He'd grabbed her by the wrist and spun her out, letting go of her at the last possible moment so she went spinning across the floor and straight into Quin.

A yelp tore its way from her throat as she stumbled into him, and he caught her around the waist to keep her from falling to the floor.

"Are you all right?" he asked in that soft, careful way of his that made her heart slam into her ribcage.

"Yup. Fine. Perfect. Phenomenal." She giggled nervously.

"Are you keeping my partner, Quin? Or are you going to send her back to me?" Ander called, delight making his words wobble. Bastard.

"Oh . . . I . . . " Quin's hands flexed around her waist.

"Just grab my hand and push me out toward the dancefloor. I'll do the rest, handsome." Mab winked and held up her hand for him. He took it, unsure, but did as she asked, and Mab spun back out to Ander, feeling more lightheaded than ever before. "I'm going to kill you for that."

"Oh, shush." Ander laughed, pulling her into a tight spiral that was sure to send them both reeling. "He liked it."

"You don't know that," she hissed. But they were spinning so fast now that she couldn't stop the burble of laughter that crawled up her throat, spilling out of her in wild abandon as they twirled and twirled, then wobbled, and both of them stumbled onto the floor, laid out flat on their backs on the plush carpeting.

"You know," Ander said, giving her hand a playful squeeze, "I forgot how much cardio that is."

"Well I didn't! I think we're getting too old for this," Mab snickered.

"Speak for yourself, wench!"

"Shut up, you geezer, you've got at least a couple centuries on me!"

Then they were both cackling so hard, Mab felt a stitch forming in her side but couldn't seem to stop. It had been so long, it seemed. Since they'd been well and truly drunk and silly. And never before in such comfortable company. Usually when they got like this, they were alone.

"You two okay over there?" Nox called.

"Peachy keen, jelly bean!" Mab held up a thumbs-up, but the words just sent them into another delirious round of laughter.

"I think it's time we got you into bed, baby," Max said, standing over them, his hair messy and his eyes fond. "You too, Mab."

Ander blew a raspberry, and they were laughing again.

"Are they always like this?" Nash asked, peeking at them from the couch. "Should we be worried?"

"They're fine." Max shook his head. "Come give me a hand, Q."

Quin murmured his agreement, then he was standing over them too. The lights just behind him shined like a halo and reflected rainbows off his wings. Gods, he was beautiful, with that soft press of his lips that Mab had once thought was disapproval but now wasn't sure *what* it was.

"I wish I could stick my fingers into your brain and pull out all the words you don't say." She wiggled her fingers at

Quin, and he frowned at her, but Ander was cackling from where Max had scooped him up into his arms. "Shit. Did I say that out loud?"

"Totally did. It was kinda weird, not gonna lie," Nash commented from where the twins were laying on their sides, each in the opposite direction on the couch, his feet in Nox's face.

"Bite me," she fired back without any heat because her neck was getting unbearably hot.

"Quin," Max called over his shoulder. "Just pick her up and put her in bed. I'll make them both some toast."

"No toast!" Ander squealed.

"Yes, toast."

"I'd like some toast!" Nox raised her hand. "With cranberry jam."

Quin sighed a little, his shoulders hunching. Then he bent and scooped her carefully into his arms.

"This is why we shouldn't drink tequila," Mab whispered to Quin like it was a secret.

"You didn't drink tequila, you twat!" Ander called from what sounded like the other room. How was he even still listening?

"Oh, shut up, Andy!" she shouted back, careful to curl her body so she wasn't shouting right into Quin's ears.

"Hey, how come she gets to be carried to bed?" Nash whined.

"Cause I'm a-fucking-dorable." Mab blew a raspberry at him over Quin's shoulder. "Right, handsome?"

Quin blinked at her a moment, his cheeks looking a little ruddy. Maybe it was hotter in the condo than she realized? It was hard to tell, what with the fact that she couldn't feel her fingers anymore. "Be quiet and go to sleep,

Nash," he said instead, then carried her carefully down the hall.

She kind of lost track of time then, her head on his chest, the soft *thump-thump-thump* of his heartbeat in her ears. It was lulling her to sleep, making her mind stop spinning, spinning, spinning like it always did.

The bed was soft beneath her, and he tugged the covers up to her chin with gentle movements. But just as he went to move away, Mab grabbed him by the wrist and pulled him toward her again. He bent closer, confusion creasing his brows, and Mab reached up to touch his cheek, her thumb brushing over the high cheek bone.

"You're really nice," she told him, a little hypnotized by the brush of her thumb against his stubble. It was a lot softer than she would have expected. She wondered what it would feel like rubbing against her neck. "I like you *sooooo* much."

"You're really nice too, Mab," he murmured, then blinked, his lips pursing like he hadn't meant to say it.

"No, I'm not. But it's nice that you think so." She shrugged. "Good night, luv."

"Good night, Mab."

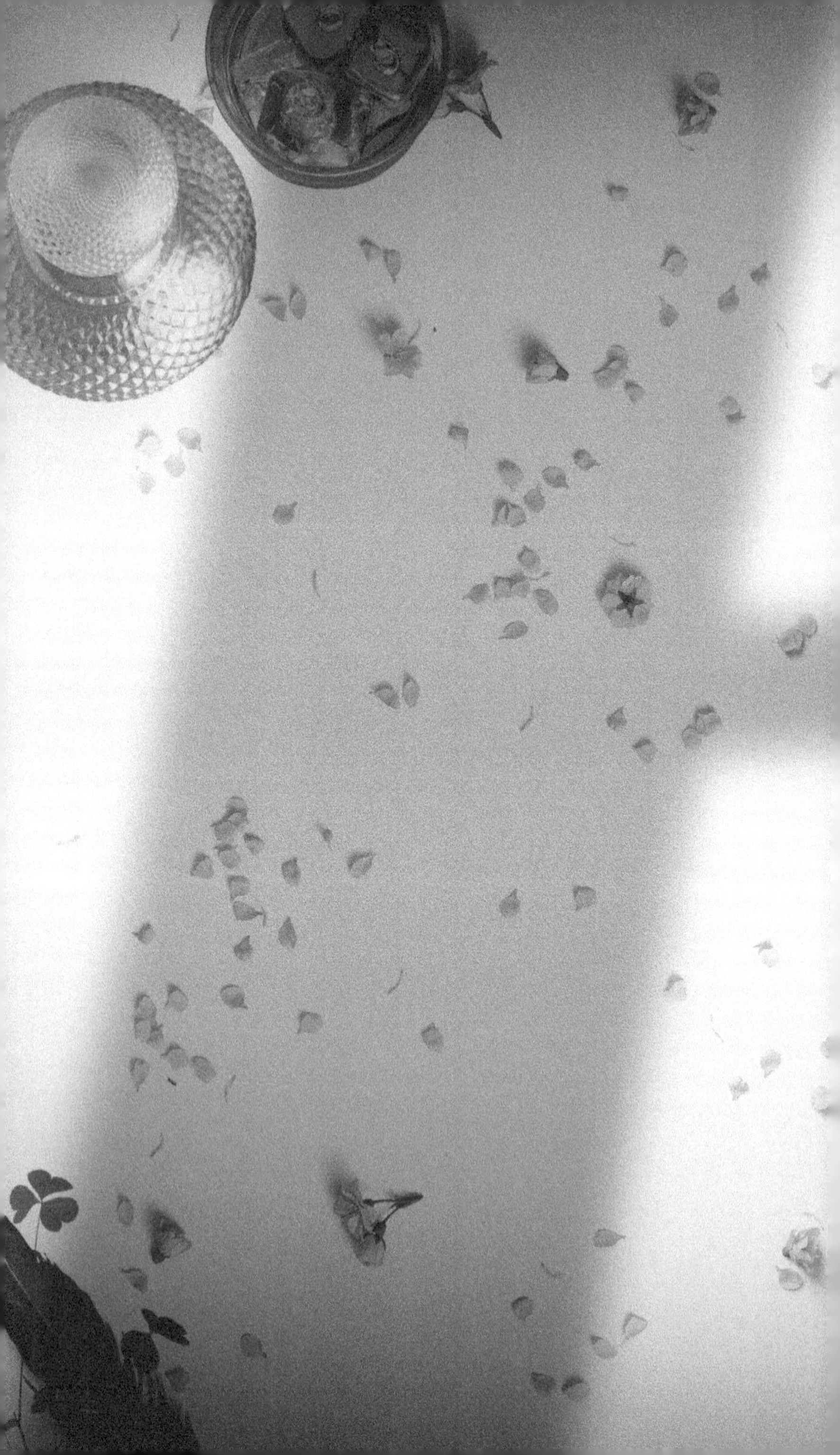

Chapter 41
Quin

Bacon snapped in the pan while potatoes roasted in a cast iron skillet. An electric griddle sat on the counter beside him, where he had several pancakes frying.

No one had woken up yet, which he wasn't surprised by. But he planned to pull them from their beds, get grease and carbs into them, and sober them up. If he was nice, he'd have let them sleep, but they had things to talk about. To plan.

There was a shuffle of noise behind him, and Quin turned around to check, wondering if it would be Mab. His heart beat faster. Last night, as he watched her dance with Ruin, a part of him had wanted to dance along with her. To see what she looked like when she was smiling at him with that much joy.

To hear her say that she liked him while her fingers gently caressed his cheek.

It wasn't Mab, it was Max. His skin looked a little gray, and his hair was a mess, standing up all over the place. He looked awful, and yet he also looked deeply and completely content and happy.

"Morning," Max croaked.

"Morning." Quin eyed him. "You look terrible."

Max sat down on one of the plush stools and leaned forward with his elbow on the counter and his chin in his hand. He gave a goofy smile. "Thanks."

"I'm happy for you." Quin hadn't gotten a chance to say it last night, not amidst all the drinking and dancing. Or the fact that Max hadn't been able to let go of his fiancé. "Have you told Dad and Papa about you and Ru —Ander?"

Max's eyes narrowed on Quin. "Ru-Ander?" He sat up, hands slapping on the counter. "You still think of him in suspect mode, don't you!" he taunted, the light in his eyes saying he was going to make Quin pay for this later.

"What?" Quin frowned and shook his head. "No."

"But you still think of him as Ruin! Not by his first name."

Quin's lips opened, but no sound came out. Max wasn't wrong; he *did* think of him as Ruin. But that's how he'd first referred to him! "Stop dodging the question about our parents," Quin deflected the moment back onto him. He held up his hand to stop Max from speaking when his lips opened. "And I promise I'll start thinking of my new brother as Ander."

Max sagged back in his chair, content once more. "Thank you." He began searching the counter for something.

Quin grabbed a mug out of the cupboard, pouring coffee into it and fixing it how Max liked it. He then slid it across to him.

Max grinned brightly, took a big drink, and sighed. "We didn't have a chance last night. I want to tell them in person. But Ander wants to do it over the phone. He thinks that's the only way for him to avoid Papa throwing something at him."

Quin went back to the stove to flip the bacon over and stir the hashbrowns. "He might be right."

"Baaaabe . . . " a groggy whine called from the hall. "Why are we up?"

It was Ruin . . . *Ander*, dragging a squinty-eyed Mab by the hand.

"No," she rasped, voice rough and unused. "The question is, why do *I* have to be up just because you are?"

Was "adorable" a word you were supposed to use to describe a grown woman? Quin wasn't sure. But there was something about Mab looking sour at being woken up, most certainly hungover, but still trudging after her best friend that made Quin want to pull her into his arms and hold her.

Which was a strange thought for him in general. Cuddling was not his preferred method of affection.

"Why are you all so *loud*?!" Nash half-yelled, half-groaned from the living room, only to have Nox smack him in the face with a throw pillow.

"Shuddup," she moaned.

"Both of you get up. Breakfast is just about ready, and I'm making a fresh batch of coffee," Quin called to them.

He took the current pancakes off the griddle, adding them to the stack in the oven, and poured on four more.

"Do you need any help?" It was Mab, eyes still droopy from sleep, with just one curl escaping from her silk bonnet that he wanted to carefully tuck away and looking so endearing, it made his heart thump several times. Hard.

"You can do up the coffee?"

She nodded, and as she passed him in the kitchen to move to the coffeemaker, her hand rested just for the briefest moment on his elbow.

It shouldn't have mattered. It was just a touch to let him know she was passing by and to make sure that he didn't step back. But it sent shivers up his arm and into his neck, making the skin behind his ears and along his skull tingle.

Was that normal?

While the last of the pancakes cooked, Quin whisked up a large batch of scrambled eggs. He didn't bother asking anyone what they wanted. If they were craving something specific, they could cook it themselves. Once the eggs were done, he plated everything, passing a plate out to everyone, even the twins, who had trudged their way over to the counter still wrapped in their blankets.

He pulled the plate of pancakes out of the oven, added the last four, and set that in the middle of the island while Mab set mugs of coffee down in front of everyone. Quin watched her from the corner of his eye, that fuzzy, tingling, humming feeling coursing over his skin once more. There was something nice about doing this together.

Nox and Nash took a couple of pancakes each, then carried their plates and mugs over to the table, sitting down in their bundled little cocoons. That left the last two stools for Quin and Mab to take.

Sitting down at the opposite end of the island from each other, Quin found that Mab's eyes met his, and they sat like that for a moment before Max broke the silence. Quin looked down at his food quickly, grabbing his coffee mug to take a sip and give himself something to do.

"These pancakes are really good, Q. Thanks for making breakfast," Max said around a mouthful of said pancakes.

"Mhm," was all Quin said in reply. He suddenly didn't feel like talking. Every nerve seemed to be firing, and that dull ache in his chest had sharpened. It lanced through him with each beat of his heart, igniting a yearning inside him that he didn't understand. But there was a want, a *need* that called out for something, or some*one*.

"So, is Max aware of everything we found out yesterday?" Nox asked, then crunched down on some bacon.

Quin watched her for a moment. "I didn't really have time to tell him with everything he was doing." She knew that. Quin had been *with* the twins until Mab called them all here.

"What did you find out?" Max stared at him, interest all over his face.

Quin pointed over at Nox, indicating she should take point on the information. She and Nash had been the ones to gather it all, after all. Quin took the time to dig into his breakfast.

"Well," she said around a mouthful of eggs, "Nash finally managed to hack into the government satellite and keep a connection long enough for us to do some proper snooping. We got heat signatures on the compound. It's chock full."

"Stuffed," Nash seconded.

"Of?" Max pressed.

"Looks like ignis. And we've got video of more trucks coming in at a constant stream. And not just from the port like the ones we traced. We think they're coming in from somewhere else." Nox sipped some coffee.

"Enrique's amassing his army of ignis." Max frowned.

"Why is he using trucks?" Ander asked. "Why not portal everyone there so you can't watch?"

"That much portal activity would give off too large of a magical footprint. Sanctum radars would pick up on it right away. He's actually being incredibly clever going the normie route," Nox piped in, sounding a little annoyed at having to give praise to Orcus.

Ander snorted. "Clever. You mean backstabbing and conniving. I wish I had the ability to kill the bastard."

Quin watched the emotions play themselves out over Ander's face and knew that he was being honest. He wasn't sure if that made him feel better or worse about the half-muse who was planning to marry his brother.

"Get in line," Mab muttered, and Quin's gaze flew to hers.

Most would likely have been less surprised Mab would say something like that, but not Quin. He recognized her hard exterior as a way to keep people at arm's length. Life had taught her not to trust them. It was all to protect her gooey center. And yet, recognizing the same traits that resided within both him and Max, she would protect her brother over herself any day. Protective and loyal, Mab would protect her family even if it meant hurting herself. He saw that in her, just as he knew it within himself.

"So, this raises the question, what do we want to do with this information?" Nox asked.

Without missing a beat, Max responded, "We plan our attack."

"*What?*" It was Mab and Ander together, both of them staring at Max, horrified.

"Now that we know where Enrique's base is, we plan our attack to go in and get him." Max's words were simple, confident, and serious.

Ander shook his head. "No. Babe . . . darling. Sweetheart." He reached out to take Max's hand, the ruby and diamonds on his finger sparkling in the kitchen lights. "You took him down once. You've sacrificed yourself, your flight, and your position to track him down. But I think now it's best you let Indra and his ignis do the rest."

Quin snorted, scowling at the thought. All eyes turned to focus on him. "Indra's ignis have supposedly been looking for him all along and found nothing yet. Some of the top ignis in both realms have gotten nowhere? Don't you find that odd?"

Ander blinked. "Are you saying—"

"We don't know if we can trust them? Yes. Someone in Olympia is helping Orcus," Quin said firmly. His fingers tightened around his fork.

"Galeo *did* have all that footage of us at the Texas port," Nox supplied.

"Exactly, and where did that come from? I mean . . . maybe it was from the local sanctuary, but if they weren't aware of Enrique's operation there at all, would one portal they don't have tabs on be enough to alert them?" Nash finished for his sister.

"It was weird," Nox added.

"Super weird." Nash took another bite of eggs.

"So you think the whole Sanctum is corrupt?" Mab asked, her features darkening.

"I don't think the whole thing is corrupt. I think there are still ignis and captains and even Princeps we can trust. But at this point, we have no way of knowing how far Enrique's reach goes. He clearly has some sleeper agents in the Sanctum." Max looked at Quin.

"Cyprian," Quin said, and Max nodded.

"Cypra-who?" Ander asked.

"Cyprian Ursus. He was the ignis who attacked Quin at the raid," Max said.

It did not escape Quin's attention that Mab let out a small sound of anger at this announcement. Quin looked over at her, trying to understand what that meant, but she was looking down at her food rather than at him.

"We think he killed Micah. But we're not sure how." It still bothered Quin. He was sure it had something to do with what Cyprian had said to Micah, they just had no proof.

"So, you can't trust anyone. Everyone might be corrupt. Which means you're going to rush headfirst into a battle against countless other ignis. Just the four of you?" Ander looked between them. "Over my dead body."

"Ander ... " Max started.

"No." Ander's voice was firm, unrelenting. "If you four are going, then Mab and I are coming too."

"*What?*" Max's voice was high-pitched in surprise.

Quin's gut tightened in dread and refusal. "No. We don't take untrained civilians into the field with us."

Mab snorted. "Untrained."

Ander rolled his eyes. "Do you have any idea how old we are?"

Quin didn't. Not exactly. He had an inkling, but he hadn't actually looked at the years either of them were born.

"What does that have to do with anything?" Max asked.

"Life experience, darling. Mab and I have trained with many martial arts masters. And while I don't like breaking a sweat, my mother insisted I learn to defend myself since my grandfather kept trying to kill me."

"And since humans like to try and light me on fire, Andy and I figured I should learn too." Mab plucked up her mug and took a defiant sip.

"We've trained together for hundreds of years. And that only intensified after the whole Enrique fiasco."

"Still ... " Max's face pinched with dread.

"*Plus,*" Ander continued, "there's also this little thing

called *my magic*, and Mab's got her wail. So . . . we're coming with you." He reached over to take Mab's hand, and she squeezed back.

They were a united front. And Quin hated it. There was an impenetrable feeling to them when they paired up. Fighting it was just as futile as separating the twins. Despite how Mab's wail was meant for protection not for battle and her body was that of a human, he might not get a say in whether she came or not.

Max looked over at him and signed, "I don't like this."

"Me either," Quin signed quickly.

"Stop talking so we can't understand you. It's rude," Ander grumbled.

"Test?" Max asked, ignoring Ander.

Quin nodded and signed back, "Test."

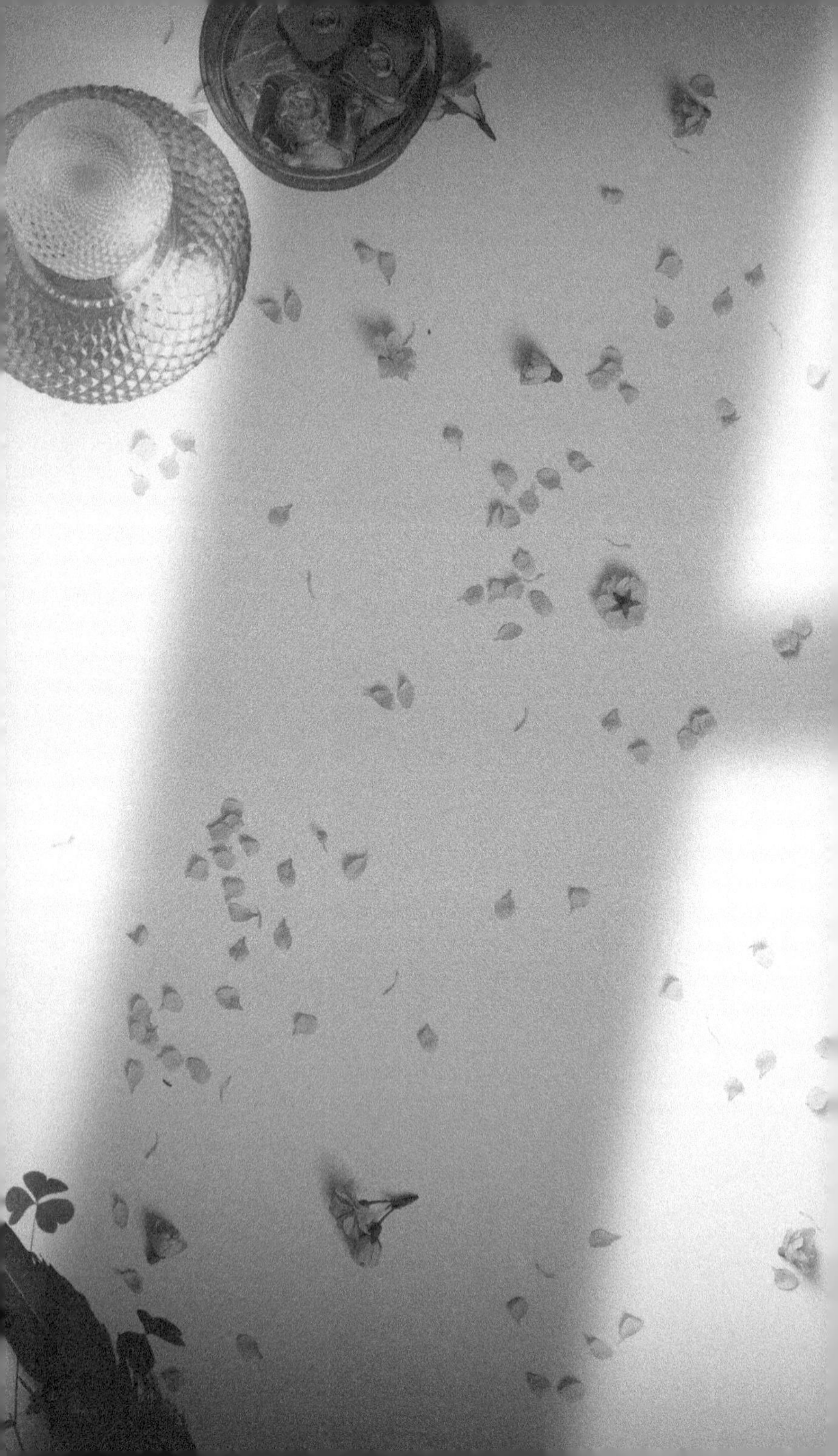

Chapter 42
Mab

Mab almost—*almost*—felt bad for the embarrassing beatdown she knew was about to occur. But not *too* bad, because Quin had used the word "untrained" with his whole chest like he and Max knew half the shit she and Ander had been through. And that just wouldn't do.

So she resolved to show him.

Max and Quin thought they were putting her and Ander to the test, through their paces, so to speak. But Mab knew differently. She could see the competitive gleam in her best friend's eyes.

"Wanna make bets on how long it takes us to bring them to their knees?" Ander cooed, his eyes sparkling.

"Not really. You have an unfair advantage," Mab huffed, tightening the bandana she'd used to keep her curls out of her face.

"Oh, come on, Mabbers. What's the harm in a little wager? You know ... to make it more fun!" He bounced on his toes, clearly a little too excited at the idea of fighting his fiancé. Not that Mab could blame him, really; the same feeling buzzed under her skin, bubbled in her chest. Both of them had spent most of their lives being underestimated, and while there were advantages to that, it was always hilarious when they got to show people just how wrong they were. And the thought of showing off to their soulmates? Well ... Mab could see the appeal.

"The harm is, I know I'd lose." Mab crossed her arms over her chest. "And I don't like to lose."

Ander chuckled beside her, stretching his arm over his chest in a motion that she knew was purely for show. "You're right, my darling, you are a terrible loser. I hope Quin isn't. That would make things very difficult for the both of you."

"Guess we'll find out." Mab rolled out her shoulders and stretched her neck from one side to the other.

The room they were using for their little "test" was Ander's dining room, but it had been cleared of all furniture, and mats were placed on the floor to protect them from injuring themselves. It actually looked almost as official as some of the training rooms Mab was used to.

While Mab and Ander stood on one side of the mats, Quin and Max stood on the other, but neither of them looked very comfortable with what was about to happen. *Both still so sure they're going to best us, I see.* She smirked to herself.

"What's taking so long?" Nash asked, off to another side where he and Nox were splitting a big bucket of popcorn. Mab wondered if Ander had snapped it in or if they'd found it somewhere in the kitchen. It did add to the dramatic flair of everything, so chances were, it had probably been Ander.

"Intimidation is half the battle, young one. Watch and learn." Ander stretched his other arm, but the smile hadn't slipped from his face yet. It wouldn't be long before it did, Mab knew him well enough to know that. He was all charm and frivolity right now, but soon enough, he'd be down to business, and Max would be in trouble.

"Just get on with it, Andy. The sooner this is over with, the longer they'll have to soothe their wounded egos."

"Fine. Fine. You're never any fun, Mabberella." Ander flapped his hand at her and made his way onto the mat, where Max was waiting, the smile still in place. Max wasn't in trouble . . . *yet.*

Max sank into a fighting stance, his hands at his sides, weight evenly distributed. It was a good stance, she'd acknowledge that. Exactly the stance any master would recommend a fighter of his build to start in. But Ander wasn't a newbie fighter, and he knew what worked for him, so he stayed standing tall, his posture loose and relaxed. Waiting. He'd let his opponent make the first move; that's what they'd both been taught. Because they were smaller, they needed to let an attacker build momentum that they could then use against them.

Max struck fast, faster than any normie could, but not fast enough. He lunged, and Ander snapped away, appearing behind him in a moment.

"Over here, darling," Ander cooed, landing a soft kick to the back of Max's knee and making his leg give out under him. "That's a point for me, I think."

Max whirled around, his leg flying out to swipe at Ander's ankles. Ander's grin widened as he leapt into the air, just above the swipe, and landed a blow of his own to Max's shoulder, knocking him off his center of gravity for a moment before Max could recover.

"Two."

"Stop playing with your food, Andy," Mab scoffed, rolling her eyes.

"I'm just giving him the chance to make a good

showing." Ander shrugged, dodging another well-placed blow by grabbing Max's wrist and spinning behind him to land a light chop to his shoulder. "Three."

Mab clicked her tongue.

"Shall we go to ten?" Ander asked, side-stepping another blow, his movements sly and graceful, like he was dancing. And the longer they went, the more serious Max's movements seemed to get. He hadn't been expecting Ander to actually put up a fight, but Mab would wager he was enjoying this far more than he let on. His lips were ticked up in a smile, even as his jaw clenched, his limbs going looser as this became more dance than fight.

"Don't get so cocky yet, baby." Max chuckled and rolled out of a hold onto his feet. "We're just getting started."

"Boo! Stop going easy on him!" Nash crowed from the sidelines.

"Who are you talking to?" Nox asked, tilting her head. "Ander or Max?"

Nash shrugged.

Mab shook her head and turned back to the fight. Ander hadn't even broken a sweat yet, but there was a nice flush about his cheeks, the smile crawling ever farther up his face. He was enjoying himself. Way too much, honestly, for what they were trying to achieve here.

Max landed a blow to Ander's sternum, making him stagger backward, and used the way he was off balance to knock him to the ground. "One," Max said, a grin on his face.

Ander blew him a kiss from the floor.

"This isn't about *flirting*, Andy."

"Maybe we shouldn't have let them go first," Quin murmured, suddenly at her side, and Mab let out a short, sharp laugh.

"Maybe not. They could be at this a while, knowing Ander." Mab tilted her head, wincing a little when Max tried to grab for Ander and bring him down to the mat. He went down, of course, of his own volition because he wanted to be under his fiancé—Mab knew him well enough to know that—and it looked like Max might have a good hold on him, his hands tight on Ander's wrists. But Ander was a slippery little devil, she knew that from experience.

"Three," Ander conceded with a breathless little laugh. Then he looped his leg around Max's waist and rolled them until Ander could swoop easily to his feet and press the heel of his foot onto Max's chest.

Max patted his ankle affectionately, and Mab had to look away for a moment because these two idiots had definitely gotten away from the original point. If Max were taking this seriously, he'd grab Ander by the ankle and—

Max did just that, throwing Ander across the mat in a move that would have hurt anyone less flexible, less ready to duck into the momentum and roll to their feet.

"Four," Max stood, settling into his stance again.

They fell into a grapple. Ander didn't have the upper hand in terms of power in combat this close, but he did have a tendency to be a tricky little bitch. He leaned in closer, let Max think he had him. Let Max put more of his weight into the hold as if he would push Ander to the ground with brute strength alone. Then Ander did what Ander did best: he slipped out of it, dropped to the floor, used Max's weight against him, and flung him onto his back on the mat with a hard *thud*.

"I think that's seven, sweetheart. Shall we call it?" Ander sing-songed, delighted, as he rolled to his feet. "I believe I've made my point." He held his hand out to Max to help him up, and Max grabbed it, yanking him back down and rolling to get Ander under him again. Ander squawked, but didn't let Max pin him. Instead he used the momentum to roll them over, bracketing his knees on either side of Max's hips, and taking hold of his wrists before dipping down to press a kiss to Max's lips. "Eight to four, sweetie. What do ya say?"

"Fine." Max huffed, dropping his head down onto the mat. "You can come. But the jury's still out on Mab."

Ander snickered lightly and rolled to his feet, helping Max up as he went. "Honestly, I feel sort of sorry for you, Quin." He tutted lightly. "I was playing nice. Mab has a mean streak." He patted Quin's shoulder on the way past him to get some water.

"I'm not mean! I just don't like to lose, is all." Mab moved into the center of the mat, bouncing a little to test the give and acclimate herself to a new surface. It'd been a while since she had to fight on something that gave like this. And honestly, she didn't love it. Hard floors were easier to maneuver on, easier to keep your footing on. This she was likely to slip and slide across. Not ideal. But she'd sort it out.

"You can't snap yourself all over the place," Quin warned, like he thought that would make a difference in this sort of thing. She almost thought *maybe* he was trying to let her save face and step down. Like there was a snowball's chance in normie hell that she'd do that. She was *not* going to let her brother, her soon-to-be brother-in-law, her soulmate, and their family go to war while she sat at home doing what? Nursing a cocktail? Doing *needlepoint*? No way.

"I'm aware of that fact, thank you." And if the words had a little more bite to them than necessary, so be it. Mab was just psyching herself up. She was decent at sparring, but she always fought better when there was a little bit of fury lighting her movements. "All right, birdbrain, pick your weapon and let's go."

He shifted a little, looking distinctly uncomfortable with what was about to happen. "Bo."

"Andy!" Mab called and held out her hands, waiting and ready. He snapped, and two bo staffs appeared, one in each hand. She tossed one toward Quin and settled into her stance. It had been a while since she'd used an actual weapon, but what was that saying about riding a bike? Yeah, this was nothing at *all* like riding a bike. And Quin was good, she recognized that on sight.

He took her first strike with ease, his brow still pinched in the middle. She wondered what it would take to get him to take her seriously. He was clearly holding back, letting her advance on him and only reacting defensively. It was maddening. She wanted him to put up a real fight! To put her to the test! None of this dancing around and placating her. Letting her back him into a corner that she knew he could easily get himself out of.

Her strikes became harder, more determined, and just as she let him think they were getting into a rhythm, she dropped, borrowing a move from Max—although, honestly, she'd been using it since before he'd even been forged—and swept Quin's legs with the staff.

He only had a moment to react. He didn't stumble, just sidestepped the blow. But it was enough, she saw it, to make him realize that perhaps he should stop pussyfooting around.

"Are you ready to really try now?" Mab asked, rising to her feet. "Or are you going to keep being a condescending ass about this? Because I've got to say, Quinny Bear, I'm over it." She tapped her staff lightly against her foot, and her grin sharpened when he settled into a real fighting stance.

Good. Let him give her the ability to honestly show him what she had.

His next series of strikes came hard and fast, but Mab blocked every one. Their feet danced across the mat as they dodged and parried. They were all moves right out of a training manual. Boring. Predictable. The only difference was the speed and veracity at which he struck. She let him advance on her. Let him go on the attack, looking for the openings in his guard, the places where she could fight back. He was bigger, stronger than she was. But that made him slower too. Made it harder for him to spin on a dime.

She could use that. Coupled with the fact that he wasn't protecting his middle, like an absolute dumbass.

The next swipe of his staff went high, and Mab ducked, thwacking him hard on the ribs as she slid under his arm to come up behind him. He started to turn, to follow her movement, but she swiped at his legs again, this time successfully, and he went down. Hard.

There was a whoop from the direction of the twins, but Mab didn't have time for that. She kicked his staff away from him, dropping onto his chest with her bo braced over his throat, pressing down just hard enough to get her point across.

"You leave yourself too open, soldier boy." She leaned down to whisper close to his face, just for him to hear, and smirked, only panting a little from their match. "You're not afraid to die, and you should be."

Quin's brows rose in question.

"You've got too much to live for to not be afraid." She patted his cheek lightly, then pushed herself to her feet in one swift motion. "So. Do I pass muster? Or should I start screaming and bust everyone's eardrums?"

"Uh ... no ... no need for that." Quin scrubbed at the

back of his neck. There was a light flush to his cheeks from the activity. It was unbearably attractive. Mab wanted to grab him by his cheeks and kiss him. Which was . . . well, that was a thought, wasn't it?

She shook herself and spun on her heel lest she do something foolish. "Right, then. I guess we're ready to start planning, aren't we?"

"Yup! Planning!" Max grinned widely at her. "And lunch, I think."

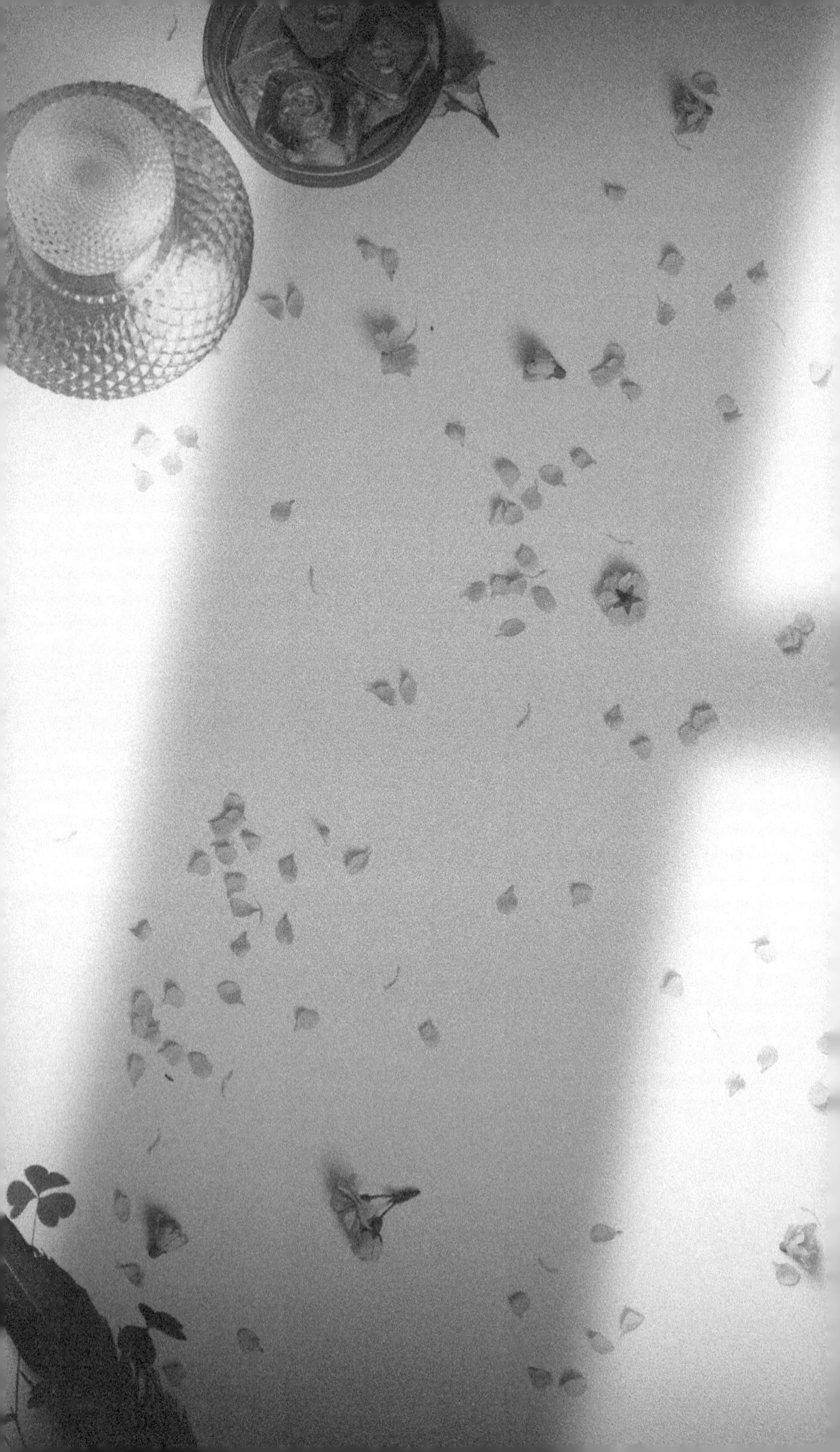

Chapter 43
Quin

Quin's heart still pounded away in his chest. Not from exertion. It would have required a lot more fighting for him to be breathless. No, this was all to do with Mab pinning him to the floor and leaning down so close.

He wished his father was here right now so that he could talk to him about this. Ask if it was normal to react to the person every time they were around.

Maybe something was wrong with him.

"Well, if we're going to face off with Enrique again, we're going to need some more *dues somnum*," Ander stated. "While you guys figure out what our attack plan is, I'm going to brew another batch. I think I have enough of all the ingredients left." He leaned in to kiss Max quickly.

"And I'll make us lunch," Mab offered.

"Just don't get in my way." Ander slanted a look at her.

"You don't get in *my* way," she said as she headed into the kitchen.

"It's my kitchen," Ander retorted.

Quin's eyes followed them, mainly because he liked seeing Mab with him. She was lighter when she was with

Ander than she was with anyone else. Quin suddenly had an overwhelming desire for Mab to look and feel like that when she was with *him*. Like he would be a safe port for her to harbor through the storms in her life.

A sharp jab in his side brought Quin back to himself, and he looked at Max, who was eyeing him questioningly.

"Q . . . I've said your name three times. What's going on?"

Quin cleared his throat and turned away to head into the living room where the whiteboard was still set up. "Nothing."

Max looked from him to the kitchen and back again. "That didn't look like nothing. Do you—"

"*Nothing*," he growled. It wasn't something he was ready to talk about. Whether it was Max or not. Everything was too new, too uncertain. Talking about it to their papa had been difficult enough; he didn't want to try explaining this to his brother. Or risk the twins overhearing. They would *never* let up.

Thankfully, his brother seemed to realize he was pushing Quin on a topic he wasn't comfortable discussing, so he let it go.

"Okay, where do you want us to start, boss?" Nash asked, opening up his laptop as he plopped down onto the couch with the computer on the coffee table in front of him.

"We need a printout of the compound layout so we can start discussing our best means of getting in and out." Max stood with his hands on his hips and his wings spread slightly behind him like an avenging angel.

He really was the best of any of them. The one most in this for all the right reasons. Max just wanted to protect good people and take bad people off the streets. He didn't have a secret well of anger inside of him that came from a world of hurt and torment. A well that made him question his motives sometimes. Not like Quin did.

"Comin' right up!" Nash chirped.

Quin moved to the printer to be ready for the photos as they were spat out.

"Nox, do you have access to any blueprints of the compound?" Max asked.

"Oh Maxxy, what do you think we spent all that time doing?" Nox taunted. "On their way to you, Quin."

He nodded, not bothering to speak. They all knew he was there and ready. As the printer began to spit out paper, he collected the sheets and started taping them up on the board.

Once the compound and its blueprints were pieced together on the whiteboard, the twins joined Quin and Max before it.

"So," Nox started. "We believe this large building here is being used as the barracks." She tapped on the largest building in the north-eastern corner. "As you can see from the blueprints, it's broken up into plenty of smaller rooms and potentially some communal sleeping areas."

Max stepped in and scrawled "barracks" over it in red marker.

"From what we can tell," Nash continued for them, "this one holds what is likely a mess hall and training areas." He tapped on both rooms in the center of the building.

Max marked those two areas in red as well.

"Any idea where Orcus may be?" Quin asked.

"This middle building also has smaller rooms that look like they could be used as offices." Nash's finger dragged along a hallway that was off of the possible training room and circled three smaller rooms. "But the other building here"—he tapped the most narrow building on the western side—"seems to have apartments."

Max and Quin both leaned in to take a look. He was right. There did appear to be apartments. Sinks, ovens, and bathrooms were noted on the blueprint in each separate space.

"Well . . . Enrique's going to take his own private quarters, right?" Max looked over at Quin.

"He's not going to share a bunk," Quin muttered.

"Then I vote we start looking in this building." Max tapped on the narrow one.

"And if anyone sees us?" Quin asked.

"We pretend we belong there." Max grinned.

"When are we going to leave?" Nox asked.

"Going under the cover of night is our best chance of going unseen. Even if that is when they're the most active," Quin suggested, and Max nodded in agreement.

"Ahhh night, when all the best things happen." Nash smirked.

Ander portalled them about half a mile from the compound, which he complained about. Apparently, the muse did not believe in walking. Something Quin wasn't exactly surprised to learn, since Ander happened to teleport himself everywhere.

But after studying a map of the surrounding area, Max and Nox had settled on a location they believed to be the safest to portal into and would give them the ability to sneak up on the compound with tree coverage.

Nox had walked Ander thoroughly through its location

and shown him as many satellite photos as she could to give him a proper heading, then the six of them stepped through the portal together.

They tucked themselves into the tree line that surrounded the compound, waiting to see if there were guards patrolling. They didn't want to be seen by a lookout and have this entire operation go belly-up because they weren't careful. This was dangerous enough without that complication.

Quin hated that Mab and Ander were there.

Sure, they had proven they could fight. Ander had his magic. Mab had her wail. But none of it made him feel any better. Quin had been fighting for his life since before he could remember. There had been a weapon in his hand since he was strong enough to hold it up, and he had lived every day with the knowledge that he could die at any minute.

None of that changed when he came into the Schields home; only now he had a little more to lose than just his life.

But Mab and Ander didn't live like that. Mab belonged behind her bar mixing martinis and Tequila Sunrises, not crouching behind a tree at his side.

"We're not getting a heat signature," Nox whispered from where she and Nash had set up a little command center there in the woods.

Nash was bent down on one knee, pointing the thermal imager toward the compound.

"What do you mean you're not getting a heat signature? In Enrique's building?" Max hissed.

"None." Nash looked over at them. "At all."

Quin frowned. That made no sense.

"Q, are your comms working?" Max asked.

Quin lifted his wrist to speak into it. "Yes."

Max looked over at him. "You and Mab take the south end, see if you can get into the building. Ander and I will take the north end. Check every room as you go, and we'll meet in the center. If there's no one in there, we'll move on to the main building."

Quin nodded. "Will do." He looked at Mab. "Guess you're with me." His words were clipped. He didn't mean to sound that way. But he hated that she was here. Hated that he was walking her into potential danger.

"Lead the way, Tweety."

Quin lifted a brow, and Mab just lifted one back at him. So he simply grunted and headed out. "Keep behind me," he ordered. He wanted her tucked behind his wings for as long as he could manage to keep her back there. If she was going to come with him, he was going to shield her.

Except, as Quin ran across the open area of the compound, heading to the southern tip of the building, Mab didn't stay behind him, she hurried up to run by his side. He shot her a glare, and she simply glared back.

"I'm not hiding behind you."

"Shh," he hissed as they came up to the building. Nox and Nash weren't seeing bodies inside, but that didn't mean Orcus hadn't managed to put a spell on the base to keep them hidden.

The first door they came to was locked, but it took no effort for him to crush the handle in his grip and knock the rest of the mechanism out. Pushing the door lightly so that it swung open, he heard Mab mutter behind him, "Show-off."

Quin looked back at her and nodded inside.

He pulled the small black flashlight from his hip and switched it on with his thumb, then held it up before him to show him the way. In his other hand, he pulled out his bo, preparing to fight anyone he might come across.

The first door swung open without any issue, and as they stepped inside, sweeping the flashlight around, they found it was indeed an apartment. Sparsely furnished. Smelling a little stale. And empty.

So was the next apartment, and the one after that.

As they exited the third, Max and Ander were waiting for them.

"Nothing?" Max asked.

"Nothing," Quin seconded.

"Okay, we're going to have to hurry from this building over to the main one. We don't want to be spotted by someone from the barracks." Max peered out a window toward the building they had to get to.

Eighty yards separated them from where they needed to end up safely.

"How about I do us all a favor and snap us over there?" Ander asked.

Max looked at Quin quickly, as if checking to see if there was anything he could think of that would make this a problem.

There wasn't. It was quick, effective, and would prevent them from being spotted. Quin nodded at his brother.

"Okay. Thanks, babe." Max grinned at Ander and pulled him in close.

Quin wanted to remind him there was no time for cuddling until he remembered that teleporting required proximity.

He stepped close to Ander and found Mab in front of him suddenly, her white fro of curls tickling at his chin and her fresh soapy scent invading his nostrils. His heart beat faster, and suddenly, he felt the desperate need to drink something, or at the very least swallow.

There were hands pulling him closer—whether it was

Max or Ander, Quin didn't know. But he put his arms out as well, wrapping them around the bodies before him, and held on while he was teleported via muse magic.

It made his ears pop and his eyes dry.

Quin drove a knuckle into his ear, trying to take away the aching, plugged sensation. He frowned and really wished he'd been able to just fly across the yard.

However, they were now just outside the doors of the main building. Doors that swung open easily at Max's touch. No locks, no resistance.

Together, the four of them stepped into the building. It was dark and silent. Which wasn't usual for an operation that was supposed to be primarily operating at night. Unless they still operated during the day and simply restricted outdoor activities until the sun went down.

"There should have been security at the very least," Quin said out loud, finishing his thought, although the others had no way of knowing where his thoughts had been.

"Nox, are you positive there were heat signatures here prior to today?" Max said into his comms.

"Yes! There were hundreds." Nox was irritated at the doubt. "I don't know where they've gone, Max, they were there last night."

Max looked at Quin. "Let's get into the office. I think if we head down this hall"—he pointed ahead of them—"we'll bypass the training spaces and get to the back hall where we thought they would be."

Quin nodded quickly and pressed his hand to Mab's back. He felt the need to keep her close. "Let's go." He pressed lightly and was grateful when Mab moved along with him.

Their steps were hurried as they moved down the hall. They stopped long enough to peer into the training space to verify that was, in fact, what it was and that it was also empty, then they headed to the back of the building.

The hallway was narrow, clearly not made for large ignis with an even larger wingspan, so they moved into single-file. The building was dark except for the glow of emergency exit signs pointing out the direction of egress providing just enough light to give them an eerie view of where they were going.

The quiet over the premises seemed vast, causing every slight sound to echo. Quin's neck tightened with tension, and his shoulders bunched beneath the weight of the anxiousness he carried with him. Apprehension swept over his skin, making his heart beat a little faster and his eyes dart to every darkened corner they passed. Nothing about this was right.

The first office they opened was empty. Nothing but storage for weapons. The second one, which had been the largest on the floor plan, was not. There was a wooden desk in the middle of big floor-to-ceiling windows that looked out over the woods. And all over the two walls on either end were pictures, floor plans, and maps.

Quin walked up to the wall on the left and swept his flashlight over it. At first, none of it made sense. Then he stopped at a photo of the Roman sanctuary from the outside. There were two guards posted at the entrance.

As he moved his flashlight up, he saw another photo of the inside of the main hall of the Rome-Olympia sanctuary. Quin knew it because when an ignis was sworn into service by the Sanctum, it happened in Rome. The Princeps heard their vows and officially accepted each new ignis into the Sanctum before assigning them to their district.

Beside him, Max cursed. "I know what this is," he whispered.

Quin looked at him and saw what Max was staring at. A detailed blueprint of the sanctuary in Rome.

"He's going to attack them, isn't he?" Quin rasped.

Max stared over at him. "I think he's already there."

They all jumped as Max's phone went off. He pulled it from his pocket to silence it but stopped when he saw the name on the screen. "It's Georgie . . . She's on night security training this week."

Quin met his worried eyes as Max answered the phone and hit Speaker. "Georgie?"

"Max!" Quin had never heard his little sister sound frightened before. "You have to get here!" She whispered her words, rushing through them.

"Georgie, what's going on?" Max frowned.

"Galeo . . . he . . . Gods, Max. He wants to go after the Princeps. He kept spewing on about taking control of our race and no longer bowing down to the Royal Triad. He's either locked up or killed anyone who wouldn't go along with him."

Was Galeo suggesting an insurrection against Indra, Hades, and Poseidon?

"Where are you right now?" Quin growled, his stomach turning to dread while his heart filled with fury.

Galeo.

The manipulative, lying bastard.

In the darkness, Ander cursed loudly, foul language a thirteen-year-old should not be hearing. But that was beside the point.

"I'm hidden in the armory. Me and Titus ran for it when it all went down."

"Do they know you're there?" Max asked.

"I don't think so. But I don't know for how long. He's

got ignis with him, Max. He's going to find us eventually." She was trying to be brave, but her voice trembled.

Quin wanted to pull Galeo apart piece by piece. That angry, traumatized part of him he kept buried deep reared its ugly head. Their baby sister was in trouble, and for what? Greed?

"Stay put. Stay hidden. And if they find you, don't fight. We're on our way, Pinky. Just stay safe." Max frowned down at the phone.

"Hurry," Georgie begged, then the line went dead.

Max and Quin stared at each other in the darkness of the room.

"We have no idea what we're walking into," Quin said.

"No," Max agreed.

"We have no idea who's sided with him and who hasn't."

"I know," he agreed once again.

"Ander." Quin looked at his future brother-in-law. "Can you get us to the sanctuary?" Ander nodded and stepped forward, holding out his hands. Quin looked at Max.

Max straightened and took Ander's hand. "Let's go save our baby sister."

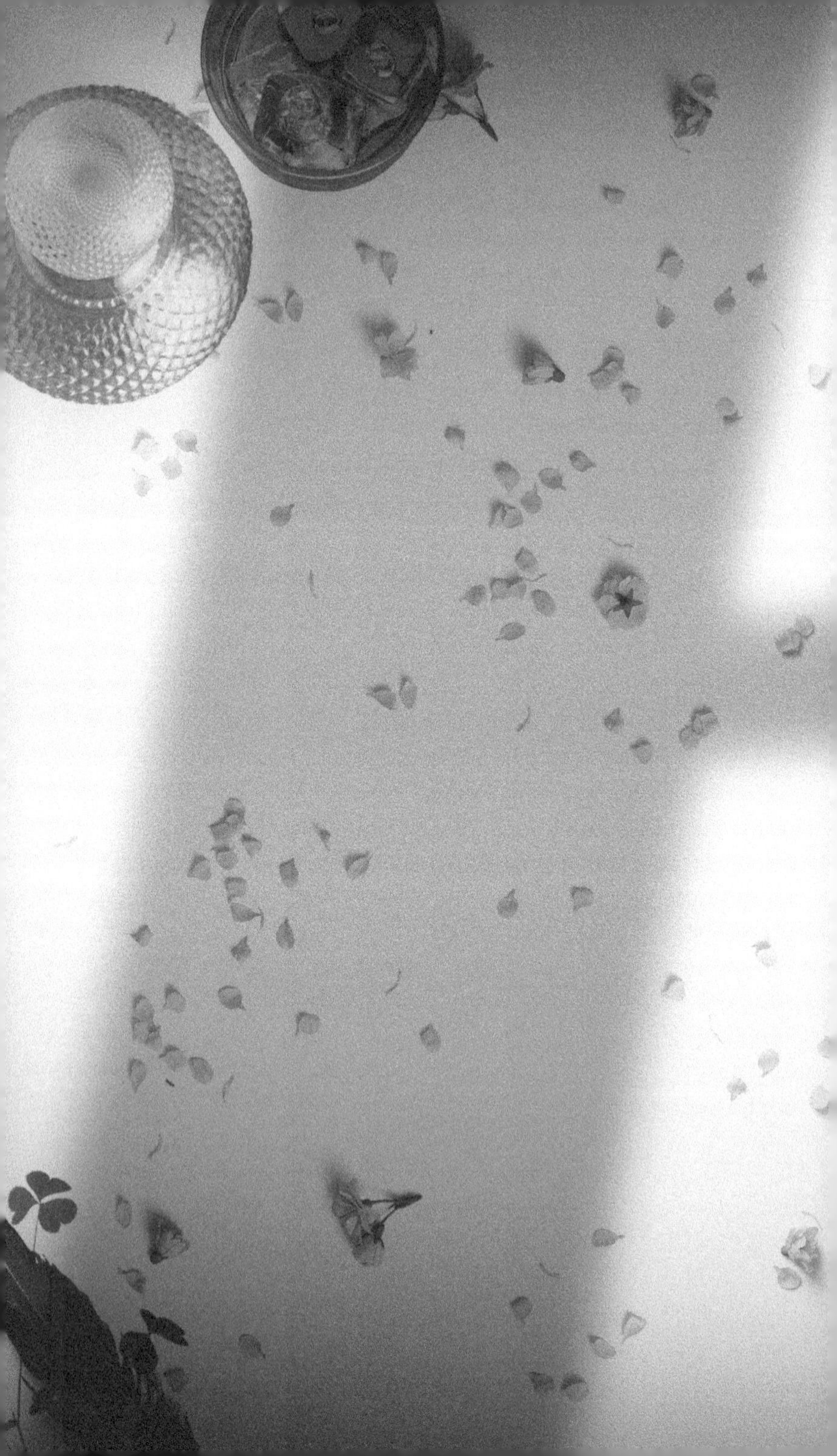

Chapter 44
Max

Max's heart was beating hard in his chest, rabbit-quick and twice as unsteady.

This wasn't supposed to happen. This was *never* supposed to happen. Georgie was too young to even be out in the field. The sanctuary was supposed to be just that: a *sanctuary*. A safe place for all of them. The ignis were never supposed to turn on one another. Their allegiance was always meant to be to the Princeps. To the mission. To their king.

All of that had been turned on its head now.

Georgie was in danger.

The sanctuary was a battle ground.

And his own commander was leading the charge against their people.

It didn't make sense. None of it made sense. Bile crawled up his throat the longer he thought about it.

This wasn't supposed to happen.

"They'll probably have the doors sealed to prevent anyone else from getting in," Quin murmured softly as they all appeared in an alley around the corner from the gate to the sanctuary.

"No." Max shook his head, something inside of him settling now that they were so close to the fight. "Galeo wants us there." He didn't know how he knew it, but he didn't think it was by chance that Georgie had wound up on patrol duty the exact night all of this shit went down. Galeo had held a grudge against the Schields for years now; he'd want them there. Especially knowing that Max and Quin were grounded and thus not at their best.

"You think—" Quin started, but Max didn't even let him finish the question.

"I think this is the perfect opportunity for Galeo to take out a family he's hated since day one." Max tightened his hands at his sides, his nails digging into the palms. "That means he'll be gunning for us." He looked around their small group. Quin. Nox and Nash. Mab. And Ander. "All of us."

He didn't want to scare them, but they had to know what they were walking into with this. It wouldn't help any of them to not be prepared. To not realize that each and every one of them had a giant target painted on their backs, courtesy of Galeo.

There was a collective nod.

"So, are we just going in the front door, or should I make a little magic?" Ander asked, waggling his fingers.

"Can you get us all into the Schields command center at once?" Max rubbed at his jaw in thought. That would give them the element of surprise, and Ander was more intimately familiar with that space than anywhere else, besides the holding cells. He did *not* want to pop up in the holding cells, not right now.

"The most I can manage is four at a time." Ander

frowned, brushing a hand through his hair. Max could tell that he was disappointed in himself, that Ander thought he was letting them down. But he wasn't. He never could. He'd already done far more than Max ever expected of him for a battle that wasn't really his own.

"Then you and I will go first. I need to make sure it's still empty. Then you'll come back for the others." There was obvious displeasure painted on everyone's faces at the order. Especially Quin. "Stay with them," he said, his gaze fixed on Quin's. "Make sure no one sneaks up on them while I'm in there. Ander will be right back."

Then he grabbed Ander's hand, and Ander didn't wait another second to snap them into the command center at the heart of the Miami-Feugo sanctuary. It was eerily quiet and empty. Nothing left behind by Galeo's cleansing of the Schields family. That made Max's job easier. He needed a safe place for his people to enter, and Galeo had unintentionally provided that for them.

"Remind me to thank him," Max muttered to himself, making his way over to the door to peek out into the hall. Also empty, for the moment. No telling how long that would last.

"Thank who, darling?" Ander tilted his head curiously.

"No one." Max shook his head. "Go get everyone. I'll keep watch here to make sure you all have a safe place to land."

Ander nodded, blew him a kiss, and disappeared. Max moved over to the door again to stand sentry, even if he knew it wouldn't be long for everyone to join him. A moment later, the command center was full of his family again, as it was always supposed to be, and he ignored the little pang that went through him at the thought.

"All right, we're splitting up from here. Our priority is

getting Georgie out. Anything else we accomplish here is a bonus, am I clear?" A wrinkle formed between his brows as he waited for someone to disagree, but no one did. "Good. When she called, she was in the armory. Mab and Ander, I want you to start there. It's down that hallway." He pointed. "If you find her, you snap her home and come back for the rest of us right away."

"Babe ... " Ander frowned.

"No arguments. You snap my baby sister home, then you come back." Max met his eyes and waited for Ander to nod before continuing. "Quin and Nox, you're heading down to the holding cells. Georgie said that Galeo locked up any ignis who didn't agree with him down there. If we want allies to go with us to Rome, our best bet is the ones he has locked up. Same as with Georgie: get down there, get them out."

"Yes, sir," Nox and Quin said in unison.

"Good. That leaves you with me, Nash. We're going to take the offices." Nash moved to his side, and Max gave him a curt nod of approval. "Keep in contact. Stay alert. If something goes wrong, radio in. We're not playing around here, and I'm getting all of you out of this. Clear?"

Another collective nod.

Then Max took a deep breath, his eyes a little warm when he said, "I love you all." Turning on his heel for the door, Max motioned everyone out into the hall beyond. From there, they split off.

He and Nash headed toward the right, deeper into where the command centers and the offices of the upper-level ignis were. The daggers in his hand felt heavier than normal as they swept into the first emptied command center. This one, unlike theirs, had not been uninhabited when the siege began. There was glittering ignis blood on the floor and a screen with a hole in it on the wall.

"Anything?" Max asked from where he watched the door. He didn't know what he had been hoping to find. Maybe that his baby sister had tucked herself away in the room nearest their official command center to make herself easier to find. Life was never that simple, and battle was even more complicated.

"Max," Nash said softly. "There's a pile of ashes back here."

"We need to keep moving." He couldn't think about that, not right now. He just had to pray to the gods that none of the ashes they found were his family. He didn't think he could lose any of them. They meant too much to him. And he'd already failed them enough.

Nash nodded, settling in at his side again. They made their way quickly down the hall, checking room after empty room. More piles of ashes. More signs of destruction. So many lost. So much gone to waste. And all for what? What was Galeo hoping to achieve in this?

The first ignis they came across were closer to the officers' offices, and they were carrying heavy stacks of paperwork, books, and journals. Things that Galeo had obviously decided were important enough to take with them.

Max dropped into a crouch and held up a wing to indicate that Nash should stop. Then he held up two fingers to let Nash know how many there were, and signed the word "ignis."

Nash nodded, his bright eyes narrowing as he pulled something from one of the many pockets on his legs—because apparently the twins had decided the best assault gear was cargo pants. And Max thought maybe they were onto something as the sound of metal rolling across the floor filled the air, and a second later, a smoke bomb exploded in the small round atrium all of the officers' doors led off of.

The ignis were on high alert immediately, and more came out to see what the commotion was about. Their wings flapped to try to dispel the smoke, but they weren't quite quick enough, and whatever mixture Nash had put into the smoke bomb was too heavy to disperse that easily.

Max slid across the floor, using his daggers to slice at the tendons in their legs and bring them to their knees. Making them easier targets for Nash, who ran up behind him, a taser in his hand.

Dodging the swing of a wing, Max ducked and rolled across the floor before popping up out of reach of one ignis' sword. It embedded itself into the wall just where his head had been a moment before. The ignis hissed and spat, cursing. But his eyes were on Max and no one else, so busy thinking Max was the real threat that he left himself open to Nash, who tasered him and dropped him to the floor with the others.

"Do we have a way to restrain them for the time being?" Max asked, brushing his hair out of his face and leaning into the first office on the right to make sure no more were coming.

"On it already, big bro." Nash held up what looked to be a handful of zip ties, but they were made of iron wire. Then he set to work hog tying them all. "Good thing I got practice on Dad's ranch."

"Yes. I'm sure this is exactly what Dad envisioned when you guys were watching all those cowboy movies together." Max huffed, but he couldn't help feeling a little giddy at the conversation. It was probably the panic talking, really. But it was nice to be with Nash, who didn't take things too seriously, even life-or-death situations. It eased some of the tension. "It doesn't look like they have anyone holed up here. They were just clearing out the files and logs."

"Why do you think they were bothering? Most of the important shit is digital."

"Not everything." Max shook his head. "All the oracle records are on paper. Remember?" He ducked into another office and frowned at the sight of another pile of ash, this one in the seat of a chair.

"Celaeno," Nash sighed. "I always liked her."

"Yeah. Me too." Max frowned, then stopped abruptly. "Someone's phone is vibrating." He tilted his head to the side to listen better and stepped out into the atrium again. "It's coming from Galeo's office."

"Are we gonna, like . . . answer it?" Nash nudged the office door open a little farther with his toe, and it creaked on the hinges.

"No." Max shook his head. "But it wouldn't hurt to see if we can find anything in there that'll help us with all this. Right?"

"You think Galeo left his dastardly plans on his desk?" Nash scoffed, disbelieving, but it didn't stop him from striding right over to said desk to start digging.

The phone was on the corner, and Max watched it, a frown on his face. Who would be calling Galeo? Why? Was it Enrique calling to give more orders? Maybe he'd leave a message? But he wouldn't that be stupid.

It started ringing again, the sound so much louder now that there wasn't a wall between them. And before Max could stop him, Nash reached out and answered it, putting it on speaker.

"Well, well, well," a deep, lyrical voice said into the silence that followed. "If it isn't Ander's little pet."

Max ground his teeth together but didn't say anything. He held up a hand at Nash to keep him silent as well.

"That's all right," Enrique said, sounding amused. "I don't need the brat to say anything."

Nash puffed up, his cheeks filling with air like he was about to scream.

"That's right, little boy. Throw a tantrum," Enrique snickered. "Prove me right."

"What do you want, Orcus?" Max asked as he grabbed Nash's wrist and gave it a firm squeeze. An order to not play Enrique's games. "And how did you know—"

"That you were in there?" Enrique clicked his tongue. "Please, Galeo's given me access to all the cameras in that little sanctuary of yours. For instance, my princeling and that banshee of his are about to walk right into an ambush ... Won't *that* be fun?"

Max tightened his jaw, the muscle ticking. Mab and Ander would be fine. They had each other. They had their magic. And they were both trained fighters. They would be fine. "You didn't answer my first question."

"What do I want? Yes, I heard you." Enrique snorted, and Max could just imagine him rolling his eyes. "Well, for starts, I'll have your fucking wings mounted on my wall as a trophy, Schields. But that's just the beginning." He laughed, soft and dark. "Then, I'm going to take ... *everything*." He sighed the last word the way one did when the thought brought them great pleasure. "You can try to stop me if you like. I'll see you in Rome, angel."

Then the call went silent.

"We have to get to Mab and Ander," Max said, not missing a single beat as he swept from the room, Nash at his side.

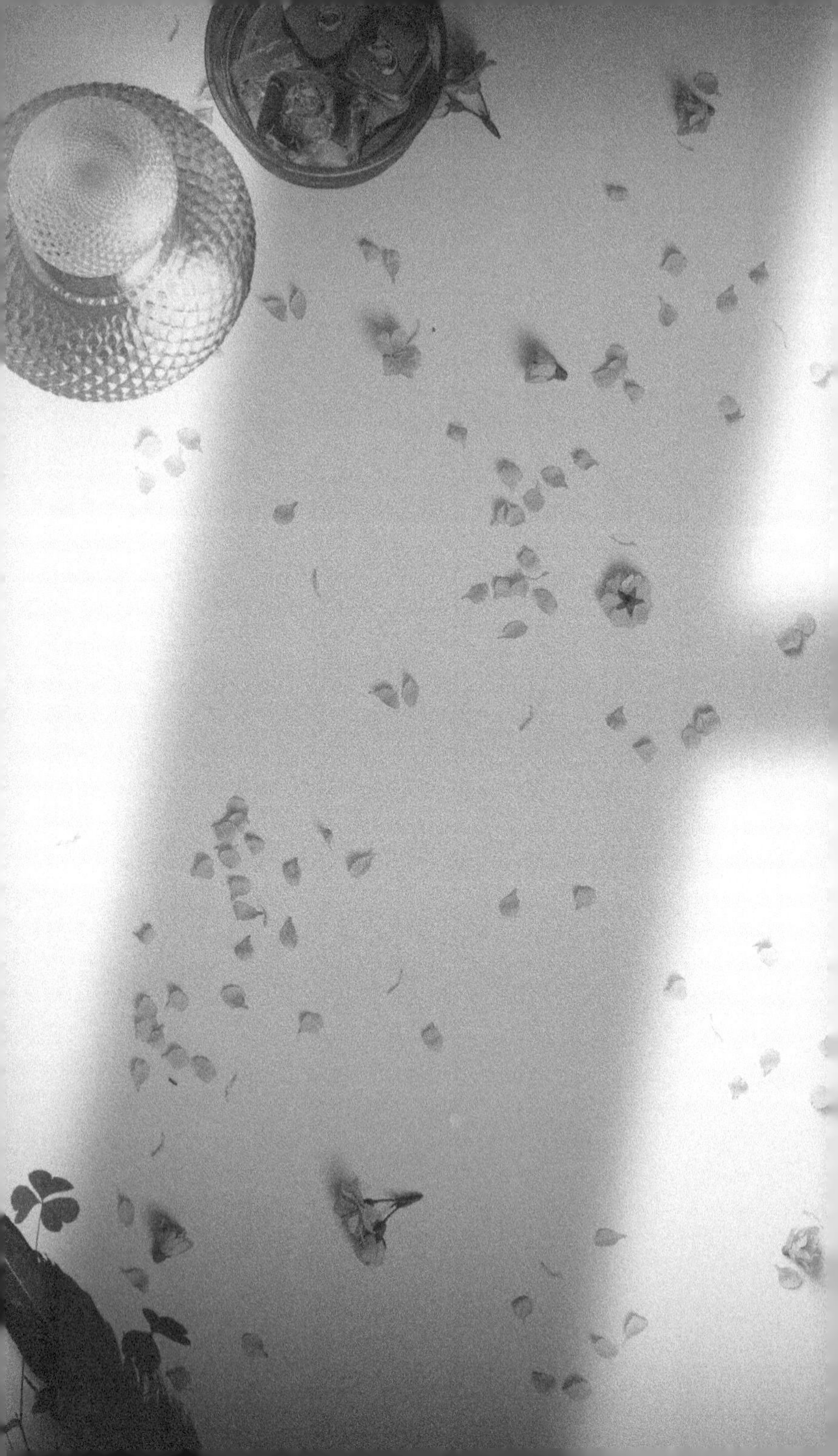

Chapter 45
Quin

Quin didn't let himself think about anyone else. He couldn't think about Max and Nash off in another area of the sanctuary possibly facing off with Galeo and his crew. Couldn't think of them surrounded by the enemy and not able to fight their way out. He most definitely could not think about Mab and Ander on their way to the armory.

They would be fine.

Everyone would be fine.

"How many do you think will be in there?" Nox whispered as they hurried down the hall, ducking past doorways and trying to keep quiet on their feet.

"Probably a lot. So we have to be careful." He looked back at her. "Do you have a weapon on you?"

She held up a taser, a wide grin on her face. "Kind of hoping I get to use it."

He shook his head a little, but as he faced forward once more, a little smirk tipped the corners of his lips.

There was no one guarding the doorways into the holding cells, but there was a pile of ashes scattered in front of the doors, like someone had stepped in them, possibly slipped. His stomach rolled at the sight. Who had that been? Whose body had fallen lifeless to the floor and lain there long enough that it could disintegrate into ash? Had it been friend or foe?

He didn't want to step in it, to disrespect one of his comrades in such a way, but it was impossible to get to the keypad without doing so.

Quin took a wide step, clearing as much of the ash as he could, and pressed his keycard to unlock the door. Nothing happened. He tried it again. It beeped, but the locks didn't click open.

"They've canceled your access." Nox stepped up beside him and shouldered him out of the way. "Let me."

Quin shuffled to the side, turning to the hall to keep an eye out while Nox did her work. "Hurry."

"I'm going as fast as I can." She pulled the dagger from the holster strapped around his thigh, and Quin's brows shot up as he watched her.

Nox used the tip of the dagger to pry the front panel off the keypad, which clattered to the floor, exposing all the wires. Quin hissed as the noise echoed in the silent hall.

"Are you trying to give us away?"

She shot him a look. "I need both hands." Nox shoved the dagger back at him, which he took before she could stab him with it, then she pulled pliers from one of her many pockets.

As she worked on the keypad, stripping wires and connecting them elsewhere, Quin shifted on his feet, his hands clenching and unclenching around his bo staff. He hated waiting. They were too exposed. Standing out in the open, with no cover, where anyone could spot them.

"Hurry up, Nox," he growled.

"I *am* hurrying!" she hissed.

Of Hope & Blight

He shouldn't push her, but the urgency was starting to set in.

The sound of the locks clicking open preceded a happy little, "Yes!"

Quin moved around her and carefully pushed the doors open, his bo poised and ready for an attack. As he stepped into the room, three ignis turned to him. They were not ignis that he recognized, which made Quin wonder if these were reinforcements from Orcus.

"Hey! Who are you?" one of them asked.

"Quin!" A voice shouted his name, and Quin turned in its direction, spotting Georgie, her face pressed against the bars and her pink wings flapping in anxiety.

"We're coming," he called back, then raced toward the first ignis, his bo staff crossed over his body before him.

The ignis had just enough time to draw his sword and swing it down at Quin, who blocked it with his staff, deflecting it to the side. He sidestepped through his guard and drove the end of his staff up into the ignis' chin. His opponent's teeth snapped together hard enough to chip them, and his head flung back.

As the ignis dropped to his knees, Quin jabbed him hard in the temple with his staff, just for good measure.

Out of the corner of his eye, Quin saw Nox run in, drop down to slide beneath the second ignis' sweeping sword, and kick at his ankles. It only made him lift off the ground with his broad wingspan, but Nox was still able to press her taser to his calf, which had him spasming in the air and crashing to the floor.

"Yes! That'a girl, Nox!" Georgie cheered from the cells.

Nox appeared to have her situation under control, so Quin raced toward the last threat, who held two daggers up before him. "Come for me, baby bird," the ignis cooed, his lips twisted in a dark smirk.

Quin glared at him as he readjusted his handhold on the bo staff. "Sure," was all he said, and he stepped forward, swinging the staff toward the ignis' head.

He knew that the other ignis would block and parry; he would have been a fool if he didn't. That was fine. Quin wanted to see how he handled the blades in his hands anyway. He was good and managed to deflect Quin's bo with one dagger and slice at his forearm with the other, sending a spray of blood through the air, but Quin was better.

"Get him, Quin!" Georgie yelled.

He moved fast, attacking the ignis with hits from all sides, forcing him to spin on his feet, protect his back and his front. Quin couldn't fly, couldn't use his wings to lift him into the air for a higher strike, but that was okay. He was used to fighting beings that were bigger and taller than him.

Used to being at the disadvantage.

All of the swift attacks forced the ignis to leap into the air, wings extending to give him the extra lift and also the added push downward for a harder strike. It was what Quin had been hoping for.

He lashed out not at the ignis' body but at his extended wing, smashing his bo down on the tip of it.

Their wings were highly sensitive, and even minor hits directly to the arm bone could cause near-blinding pain. The ignis roared, recoiling his wings into himself. As he went into an instinctive protective stance, Quin took the opportunity to strike again, this time at his knees.

He went down, dropping to the floor. Quin struck him once more, forcing him onto his back, where he was able to pin him to the floor by the weight of his staff pressed against his sternum.

Quin sought out Nox and found that she had already bound her ignis and was moving on to the first one he'd taken down. "Once you're done there, this guy could use some too."

"On it," Nox chirped.

Quin looked down at the ignis he had trapped on the floor. "Are you one of Orcus' minions?"

"Who?" The ignis lifted a brow.

Quin snarled, irritation coiling his muscles tight. "Enrique. Do you work for Enrique."

"Who?" he echoed again.

Quin glared.

"What is this guy, an owl?" Nox grumbled.

"Ground him," Quin ordered, the words short and cold.

The ignis' brows went up. "What?"

Nox glanced at Quin. "You sure?"

"They'll grow back, if the prisons don't keep them clipped, anyway."

The ignis began to struggle, trying to keep his wing out of their reach. Quin moved to stand on the forearm of his gray wing, holding it down.

The ignis howled. "Don't you dare!"

"Why? Won't be any good to the god of punishment if you can't fly for him?" Quin snapped.

Nox accepted the dagger Quin held out to her and grabbed a handful of gray primary feathers. She brought the dagger up to them and had just started to cut when the ignis shouted, "Stop! Stop! It's Orcus! He's—"

"Brutus, by the gate of Acheron, shut up!"

Nox froze, waiting to see how this was going to play out.

"Don't listen to your buddy, Brutus," Quin growled.

"We're going to ground you unless you speak. I want to know what Orcus plans to do once they've taken the Roman sanctuary."

Brutus looked from his counterpart to Nox and back up to Quin, dread filling his eyes. "He's—"

"*According to his sin shall a man be punished!*" the other ignis shouted, his eyes wild and his voice tense.

Hearing the words, Brutus froze, and his entire demeanor changed. Instead of desperation, there was calm. Quin frowned, watching him, and opened his mouth to speak, but Brutus bit down on something in his mouth, then he was gurgling, foam streaming from his parted lips as his eyes rolled back in his head. Within seconds, he was dead.

"What. The. *Hell*?" Nox rasped.

Quin knew those words. Had heard them before played over and over again on a surveillance tape.

"Go get Georgie and the others out of the cells," Quin ordered Nox. "If you're lucky, the keys will still be at the station. If not … "

"I'll work some magic." She nodded and ran off to check the guard station.

"You okay, Pinky?" Quin called out to his little sister as he removed his staff from the dead ignis and headed for the other one.

"Yeah, I'm okay. We've got some injured in here, though."

Quin glanced over at the cells and the other ignis inside. There weren't as many as he would have liked to have seen. Which meant either many had died in the initial battle or more had turned and followed Galeo than they hoped.

He stopped before the ignis Nox had taken down. "What has Galeo promised everyone here?"

The ignis simply smirked. "You're not getting anything out of me."

"Maybe not, but your part in all of this is over." Quin pointed at the ignis that Nox was busy letting out of the cells. "We're taking back the sanctuary. You're done."

The ignis just grinned broader. "You're a mindless minion. Fighting for a god who doesn't care if you live or die. Who's the real loser here? I die because it's my choice. What choices do *you* make?"

Before Quin could move, the ignis had chomped down on the hidden capsule in his tooth and followed the path of his cohort. His body shook, ravaged by the poison, then he slumped to the floor, foam pooling around his cheek.

Quin took a quick step to the side, and a small pink force collided with his body. He wrapped his arm around Georgie as she hugged his middle tightly, her cheek pressed to his chest.

"I knew you'd come for me," she said.

"We will *always* come for you," Quin vowed, dipping his head to kiss the top of hers. He looked over her head to Nox and the other ignis. "Grab what weapons you can. We're taking back this sanctuary."

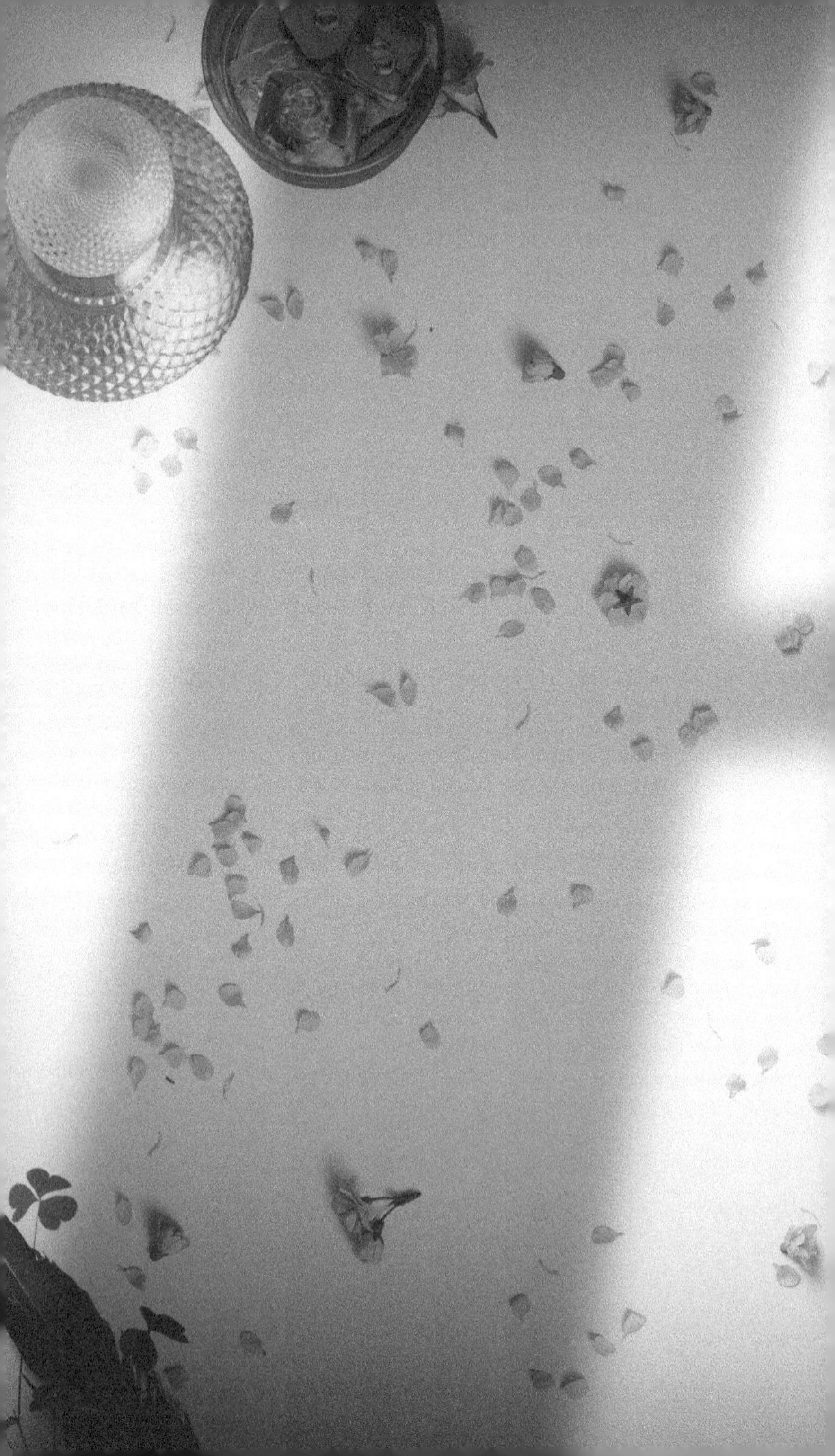

Chapter 46
Ander

They had been pointed in the right direction and left to their own devices. Ander wasn't sure how smart of an idea that was, but his love had given him a mission, and he was going to do whatever he could to get Max's snarky little sister out of there safely.

"Do you have any idea where we're heading?" Mab hissed.

"No." He stopped and peeked around a corner. Seeing that the coast was clear, he darted out into the next corridor and hurried down it, wishing that he had picked boots that didn't squeak on the floor so much.

"Well, this is just flipping fantastic," Mab was grumbling behind him.

Ander stopped, causing her to collide with him, then he spun to face her. "Look, we'll just start opening doors, okay?"

Mab rolled her eyes but nodded.

Ander stepped up to the first door on his left while Mab went to the right side of the hall. Taking a deep breath, he wrenched the door open, his hand extended in preparation.

The room was empty, just some computers, a large screen displaying white fuzz, and two piles of ash.

His stomach turned into a pit of acid.

How long did it take for an ignis to turn into a pile of ash? He had heard of it but never seen it. Ikari had still been a body when Enrique hauled Ander out of the dungeons of Acheron.

Unable to think about what those piles meant, Ander closed the door, casting a quick glance at Mab, and moved on to the next door. When he opened this one, an unfamiliar ignis glanced up from a computer, a confused look on his face at the sight of the horned half-muse before his eyes darkened.

"You're not supposed to be here." He began to rise, but Ander lifted his hand and sent a wave of energy toward him, which threw the ignis through the air.

His body slammed into the large screen on the wall, and sparks flew as the sickening crunch of skull on hard material echoed through the room.

Ander stepped back out of the room and found Mab at his side. "What happened?" she gasped.

"Baddie." He pushed her away from the door, and they hurried together to the last one.

Inside was most certainly the armory. Weapons lay scattered around. Obviously there had been a fight in here as some tried to get weapons while others stopped them.

But there was no Georgie.

"Shit." Ander took another look around the room, checking all the cabinets and behind any stands to see if she had tucked herself away. "Shit. Shit. Shit."

He whirled around again, desperate for a flash of pink. She had to be here somewhere. Ander couldn't fail at this. Couldn't tell Max he hadn't been able to find his little sister.

"Come on, Andy. She's gotta be here somewhere. We'll keep checking doors." Mab picked up a bo staff for herself and twirled it in the air.

Ander sighed, trying to calm the racing of his heart.

"You're right. Let's go."

He didn't bother with any of the weapons. While he could have used them, his magic had always been his best chance at survival.

Ander took Mab's hand, and together, they ran down the hall, carefully sneaking around another corner and skirting around a pile of ashes scattered in the hallway. Gods . . . how many ignis had Galeo killed?

How many of his own kind had he so heartlessly cut down? And *why*? He was clearly a part of Enrique's schemes, but what had the god offered Galeo to make him turn on his own kind? What did he hope to achieve under the reign of a madman like Enrique?

The third hall was much shorter, but there was a big set of double doors at the end. Ander's skin tingled, and a sixth sense told him he was going to find something terrible beyond them.

"I think we have to go in there," he whispered.

Mab nodded beside him. "You ready?"

"As I'll ever be, toots." He winked at her, and she shook her head, but a little smirk caught at her lips.

"Gods, this is a terrible idea."

Ander laughed. "I know."

But that was their friendship. Full of awful ideas but doing it together anyway.

They raced up to the door, and Ander, knowing that it was better to make a big distraction than to come in meek like a mouse, crossed both arms before him, then swept out with a large blast of magic.

The doors flew open, smashing off of their hinges and crashing to the floor. The room was large, filled with a giant wall of screens and several rows of computers. This was obviously their main command center, where they had been able to prepare for and launch a full-scale attack when needed. On the screens, there was footage from inside the Roman sanctuary. Camera feeds attached to ignis who were hunting down, capturing, and killing any Roman ignis who stood in their way.

The ignis inside the command center stopped what they were doing and turned to look at them. One of them was Galeo, hovering over the shoulder of several ignis who were busy working on computers.

"What the hell are you doing here?" Galeo snapped, his face creased with a disgusted sneer as he realized who it was.

He looked terrible. Several feathers were missing from his wings, and even his hair seemed to be falling out in chunks. There were brown spots forming on his cheeks that looked like age or decay. The sight of it made Ander grin broadly, knowing his curse was the cause.

"Here to tell you, honey, you look downright awful. An uncontrollable molting hitting you right now?" Ander asked.

Galeo opened his mouth to respond, then paused, eyes narrowing. "How did you know that?"

Ander smirked and lifted his fingers to wiggle them. "You took my Max's flight, so I doled it right back to you. You're cursed, and you won't stop degrading until you make it up to him."

The ignis hissed and pointed to the five other ignis in the room. "Take him down. Don't kill him, but make him wish you had."

As the ignis all stood up, two of whom Ander recognized as the ones who had been dealing with Mab's case, Ander held his hands out, palms up. Not in surrender but in preparation.

Why were there *five* of them?

"And you, little banshee, give up now before I have to hurt you," Galeo called out.

Ander cast Mab a quick glance, but she barely spared him a look. She was glaring at Galeo.

He didn't have a chance to make sure she was going to be okay. The first two ignis were upon him, and as their swords swept down, Ander snapped himself quickly out of their reach. Except that this placed him in the midst of the other three.

A fist swung toward his face, which he managed to duck, but then a knee shot up and clipped him in the jaw. Ander's body twisted, and he fell to the floor. He caught himself on his palms, elbows and shoulders aching from the impact. As another grabbed his arm and a third his ankle, Ander forced himself to concentrate through the pain.

He wouldn't go down like this.

He snapped his fingers and appeared across the room, able to push himself up onto his feet and square off with them once more. Twirling his hand, a mace covered in blunt knots appeared in his clutches. It was a medieval weapon but one that he loved. This one was from his own collection and had belonged to a Slavic ruler once upon a time. It felt lucky.

Going on the offensive, Ander snapped his fingers again, appearing behind the first ignis, who he quickly bludgeoned with the mace. The ignis grunted and went down. He snapped again and showed up behind the ignis farthest from him.

This time he was ready for Ander and swung back with his wing. It was like being hit by a shield, and Ander flew backward, but curled his body into a roll, popping up on his feet. He was breathless but once more ready to fight.

They all rushed him at the same time, and Ander snapped quickly, showing up behind one, landing a blow with the mace, and snapping quickly to another spot to strike out with the weapon once more.

His body ached, not from the blows but from the excessive use of magic. Ripping his form from one location and thrusting it into another over and over again. But it kept him out of reach of the ignis. Let him wound them before they had a chance to turn on him.

Except as he came out of another snap, preparing to strike again, one of them had clearly picked up on the pattern of Ander's appearances and disappearances. He wrapped his arms around Ander's body and grabbed his wrists. Before Ander could react, the ignis slid his hands up and over Ander's, curling his fingers into fists and holding them tight so that he couldn't use them or his magic at all.

He was a massive ignis, possibly the largest Ander had ever seen. No matter how he struggled, Ander could not break out of his hold, and without the use of his hands, his magic was nearly useless. Fortunately, he was half-muse, and for them, magic was woven through art.

Ander started humming, even as the other ignis surrounded him. A punch was landed to his abdomen, which made the air leave his lungs, and his humming was broken for a moment. Gasping, he lifted his head proudly.

"Boys," he wheezed. "Is that any way to handle a prince?"

His head swung to the side as another landed a punch, splitting his lip and spraying blood. Ander forced a smile onto his lips anyway, despite the pain and the taste of copper.

"Thanks, honey." He smirked. "Just the incentive I needed." Ander started singing at the top of his lungs. Singing of hurricanes and twisters. Of raging winds and cyclones. The air around them shifted, the hair on their heads whipping around and the feathers of their wings beginning to ruffle. Then the winds increased until the six of them were entirely encased in a whirlwind.

The force of it knocked them off their feet. Ander was pinned beneath the crushing weight of the large ignis, but thankfully, the hold on his hands released. Ander snapped, and he was outside the small cyclone of air trapping the five ignis inside.

Gasping for the breath that the whirlwind stole, Ander lifted his hands and clapped them together. The cyclone shrank violently, forcing all five ignis to collide. When the wind finally stopped, they were in a pile of wings and limbs, and none of them moved.

Still panting, Ander turned to check on Mab and Galeo.

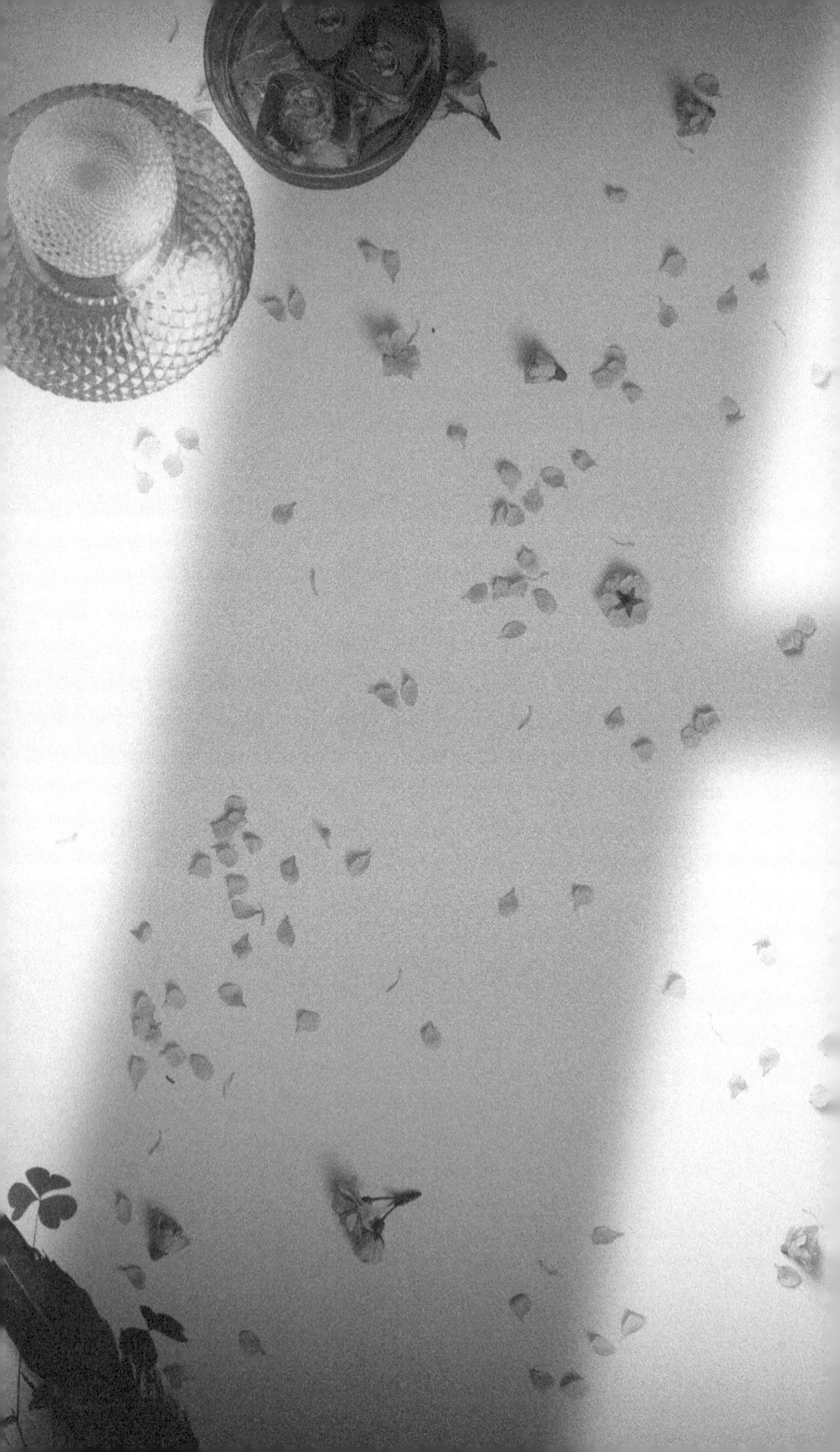

Chapter 47
Mab

"And you, little banshee, give up now before I have to hurt you," Galeo called, a look of sheer arrogance on his face. Like he thought just the threat of violence would be enough to bring her to heel.

"Promises, promises." Mab grinned darkly, spinning the bo in her hand. She couldn't really explain why she'd chosen it; it certainly wasn't the weapon she'd go for normally. But something felt right about going into this battle with something of her soulmate's in hand. A reminder of why she was doing this. Not that she really needed one.

"Fine," Galeo huffed, falling into a fighting stance. "You've left me no choice."

Mab shrugged, unbothered. "This is how I wanted things anyway." She kept her stance upright and loose. She wanted him to underestimate her. To not take her seriously. To be surprised when she felled him and screamed into his face until his ears and eyes bled.

Galeo lurched toward her in the tight space, a sword suddenly in his hand, and she blocked the strike with her bo, hands spread wide along the length of it to halt the downward swing of the sword. He was stronger than her, larger than her. But that was all right. She could work around that, she thought, even as she ground her teeth against the strain of holding off this initial blow.

"Why bother?" he asked, genuinely curious as he ground the sword down on her, moving to his full height so he could put the force of his body weight behind it.

Mab ducked and spun away, knocking one of the wheely chairs into him to give her room to recover. She hadn't expected him to come at her so hard right out of the gate. She thought maybe he'd toy with her a little first. That's what big guys like him always did. They got overconfident, thought this was a game that they were going to win. But then ... Galeo wasn't some normie shithead at the bar. He was a trained warrior.

"Why bother with what?" she countered, not really caring but hoping that the conversation would keep him distracted enough that she could figure out a way to combat his blows. He clearly wasn't willing to give her any time to study his style to find a weakness in it. All she knew was that he was using brute strength to his advantage. So she'd have to be quicker, more flexible. And he fought the way Quin had, leaving himself open because he was sure no one would dare slip past his guard, and even if they did, he wasn't afraid of getting hurt. Foolish.

"With all this." He waved his sword around him in a way that seemed to be all-encompassing and kicked the chair out of the way as he advanced on her again. "This isn't your fight. You aren't with an ignis. Why put yourself in danger for them?"

Mab tilted her head, her grip tightening on the bo in her hands, anger coursing through her. So that was it, then? He couldn't see why an inanimi would want to help simply because it was the right thing to do? Idiot. She could use that too, though; he didn't understand her motivations, he didn't understand the anger that simmered through her blood at the reminder of what he'd ordered done to Quin and Max. Grounded. Their beautiful wings clipped, unable to fly, and all at the hands of this simple bastard.

"It's the right thing to do," she grunted, side-stepping another blow of the sword. It was such a cumbersome weapon, and something about his movements told her he wasn't used to using it the way that Max was. Maybe because he spent so much time behind a desk these days. She could use that too.

Galeo snorted, then growled as she landed a blow to his open middle. It didn't do much, but it proved she could hit him, and that's all she wanted right now. "No. This is personal for you. Why?"

"None of your fucking *business*." Mab snapped, swiping for his legs and snarling when he leaped into the air, out of her way.

The next strike of his sword was sloppy, his grip on the hilt loose, either from annoyance that she wasn't giving him an answer or that she hadn't fallen under his first strike. It didn't matter. It left her the moment she needed to knock the weapon from his hands. Which wouldn't make him less of a danger to her—she recognized that—but at least he would have to get closer to hurt her. The sword clattered across the floor.

"Is this because I framed you for the death of the fury?" Galeo smirked, pulling a dagger from somewhere to twirl between his fingers. Lazy and arrogant.

"What?" Mab's grip on the bo faltered, confusion making her stutter. "That was *you*?"

It gave him the opening he needed to grab her by the

throat and slam her against the wall, her head bounced so hard, it made her ears ring. "Of course it was me. I found their pack, enticed one of the young ones out with meat, and used a handy little deafening tool we possess." Galeo laughed, furious and manic. "Who else would it have been?"

"I thought . . . Enrique." She sucked down another breath before he could tighten his hold enough to cut off her air flow. She'd need air in her lungs to use her wail, and as hard as it was to think past the realization that she'd been set up by this absolute prick who had then used her as a weapon against the people she cared about, it was all instinct to keep enough air in reserve to use her wail.

Galeo scoffed. "As if he'd waste his time on someone so worthless. You were just a distraction, *banshee*. Just a way to keep the Schields from looking too closely while we launched our attack on the Princeps."

This was all a game to Enrique. He was just moving them like pieces on a board, and she'd been used against the people she'd cared for by this . . . by this . . . this unjust, manipulative sack of *shit*. Not even seen as enough of a *threat* to be worthy Enrique's direct involvement in getting her out of the way. And Mab was tired of it.

"Why?" she asked, the sound a croak. It didn't make sense. The ignis were meant to protect, to be honorable. Why align themselves with someone like Enrique? "Why help him?"

"Because he gave me what I wanted." Galeo shrugged. "I'd rather serve Enrique than stay under the thumb of that moron, Indra."

Mab raised a brow, goading him on. It would be better if he monologued a little bit, let her know his plans. Then she could use them against him. Still, the sound of his voice grated, and she had to grit her teeth to keep herself under control.

"And look what happened," Galeo jeered, leaning in closer. The cold press of his dagger scraped down the side of her face. As if that scared her. Like she hadn't disfigured *herself* once upon a time. "I gave the Schields just enough rope to hang themselves, and they walked right into it. Let me ground them. Idiots."

"You fucking bastard," Mab snarled, her eyes narrowing. "That's my *family* you're talking about." She sucked in another big breath, then she screamed, the wail ripping from her forcefully enough that she felt it claw at her throat, tasted blood on her tongue. But it didn't matter. None of that mattered. Because she was going to fucking *kill* him.

The force of it sent Galeo flying back, slamming into the opposite wall of the room hard enough that cracks formed. He blinked, stunned. But Mab left him no room to fight back. She grabbed the dagger he'd dropped and plunged it into his wing, ripping through the soft membrane under the feathers to draw a scream from his lips.

"You stripped my *soulmate* of his best defense, and now I'm going to fucking end you," Mab hissed, pulling the dagger out the bottom end of his wing, and slashing across his cheek on her way to the other. He was trying to fight her. Landing glancing blows in his struggle to buck her off. Enough that she was sure there would be bruises. Let him try and get her off. She was determined now. Her legs tightened their hold around his waist and refused to let him push her away as she dragged the dagger through his other wing.

"Your . . . your *soulmate*?" he managed right before he started screaming again.

Mab leaned down again to press her face in close to Galeo's as she whispered, "Quintus Schields." The name snapped something inside of her into place. The bond, she realized distantly, as the ache in her chest that had lived there for days finally dissipated. Then she pulled the dagger away, opened her mouth, sucked in another deep breath, filling her lungs with enough air to end a person immediately, and—

"Mab." Ander grabbed her shoulder, his fingers tight enough to make her pause. "Leave him."

"You heard what he did, Ander," she snarled, bracing the dagger against Galeo's throat, close enough to draw glittering blood from beneath the skin. He needed to die. He'd hurt everyone Mab cared about. Her soulmate. His brother. Her family. Ander. He deserved this and so much worse. "He doesn't deserve the chance to—"

"And he won't get it." Ander nodded toward the feathers that had sloughed away onto the floor, leaving behind a bald patch. "Let him decay, *slowly*. That's what he deserves."

"Fine. But I'm taking these before I do." Mab twisted and cut through Galeo's primaries, so close to the quill that she almost had the whole feather in her hand. Then she turned and repeated the action on the other side. "Rip them out if you want, but by the time they go to grow back, Ander's curse will have made it impossible."

She took Ander's hand and let him haul her to her feet, a vindictive smile on her face as she threw the discarded feathers onto Galeo's chest. "I'd suggest staying far away from the Schields family from now on. Lest you piss us off again."

"Ander, Mab, are you there?" Max's voice came through the comms, his words a little strained. "Are you okay?"

"We're good," Ander answered, his hands moving to brush hair away from his face and snap his fingers so bindings appeared on all of the ignis to prevent any further attacks against them. Max was going to be furious when he saw the state Ander was in, but that was an issue for later.

"You sure?" There was worry in Max's voice.

"We've got it taken care of," Mab assured him.

"We've got Georgie," Max said. "We'll meet you at the front door. Do you need help getting there?"

"Nope, we can manage." Ander looked over at Mab as he spoke. "Ready to go home, darling?" he asked her.

"You know this isn't over," Mab warned, taking his hand and letting him lead her out into the hall.

"No. You're right. But at least everyone is safe . . . for the moment."

Mab gave his hand a squeeze, knowing full well he was thinking exactly what she was.

How long would that be true?

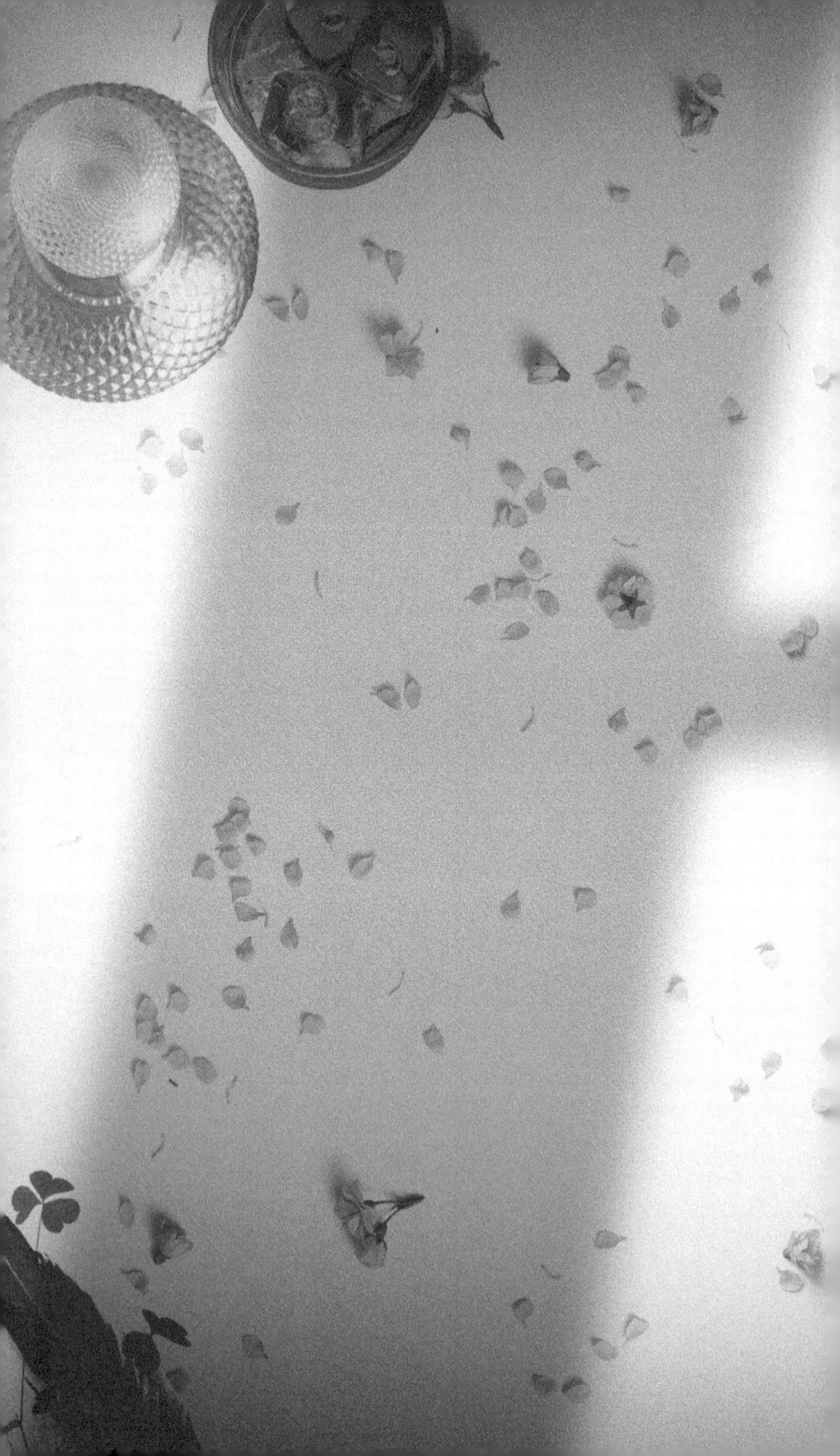

Chapter 48
Quin

They gathered in the lobby of the Sanctum.

Once Galeo and his followers were locked away in the holding cells, everyone who remained seemed to find each other.

Max had gone immediately to Ander's side at the first sight of him and was now fussing over his busted up face, and Quin was left with the twins and Georgie. Except his attention wasn't on his younger siblings but the bruises along Mab's throat. Had Galeo done that to her? Wrapped his strong ignis hands around her slender, fragile neck and tried to crush the life out of her?

A surge of deep anger rose up inside of Quin. His fingers trembled at his sides with the force of it. It was hard to breathe, the anger constricting his chest and making his heart hammer viciously against his sternum.

"What do you think our chances are?"

Quin jumped, startled by Max's voice. He hadn't realized his brother had left Ander and come to him.

Ander and Mab moved away from them and together were examining the group of surviving ignis, assessing each wound, binding, and treating what they could. While their core group was relatively whole, the ignis who'd fought back against Galeo's insurrection had not been so lucky.

"We don't have nearly enough, Max. Half of the ones who *can* fight will need to remain here to guard and protect the sanctuary. We can't leave the mortals completely unprotected."

"I know, but Rome is under siege as we speak. We have to do something."

They shared a look. Quin wanted to fight back. Didn't want Enrique to win after everything that had happened. "But what can we do?" They weren't even *whole*.

"We find someone in Rome who can tell us what is going on and where we can join the fight." There was a deep furrow in Max's brows. Even he didn't believe what he was saying.

Ander stepped away from the ignis he had been working on and joined them. "What's the plan?" He looked between Max and Quin.

"Max wants us to join the fight. Wherever and whatever that might be." Quin growled. Because this wasn't going to work. Mab and Ander were hurt, just as they'd feared. Their Miami numbers had been decreased by more than half, and of the ones who remained, most were injured and unable to fight. And while the rest of their family had walked out of the battle unscathed, would that be the case in Rome?

What had taken place here in Feugo was nothing compared to what awaited them in Rome.

Quin turned away from Max, finding a blank space on the wall to glare at, concentrating all his rage on that spot so that he didn't spew the upset inside him.

"It's what we have to do," Max argued.

Quin spun back around to finally release his doubts and anger, but Ander was already speaking.

"There are ten of us." He frowned deeply. "The rest can't fight, and I can't heal them and still have enough magic in me to be of any use in Rome." He looked around their group. "I'm going to contact my mother."

"What?" Max asked, surprised.

"I'm going to contact my mother, as well as Indra. This is his fight after all. If Rome falls and Enrique has control of all the ignis, Olympia is just through the portal and the first place he's going. He wants it all."

Ander had a point. Just because the Princeps were at battle in Rome didn't mean that it was only the ignis who had to protect them.

Max nodded. "Okay. And while you do that, we're going to work with Nash and Nox to see if we can get in contact with anyone in Rome and find out what's actually happening there."

Ander leaned in to kiss Max, and Quin looked away, giving them a moment of privacy. His eyes drifted to Mab, who was wiping her hands on a towel as she finished with the last injury. She turned then, and their eyes met across the room. Heat blossomed in his cheeks, and Quin had to look away.

Quin didn't know what was happening with Mab. She was igniting extreme emotions in him that he'd never experienced before. He hated the uncertainty inside him, and hated even more that he didn't know how she felt. He'd never had to try and figure out if someone was interested in him before. And now was not the time. Now, Quin had to focus on taking down the angry god trying to destroy their entire justice system. And somehow keep them from all dying in the process.

"Nash, go see if you can get into the computers at the first command center. Nox, call Dad and tell him to come and get Georgie," Max said, falling back into the role of leader.

"What?" Georgie squawked from where she sat perched on the reception desk. "I'm going with you to Rome. I can help with this fight."

"No!" Quin wasn't surprised when Max, Nash, and Nox all joined him in telling their little sister no. What did surprise him, however, was that Mab and Ander had said it as well.

Georgie stared at the six adults all glaring her down with varying degrees of sternness.

"Oh, come on, how can not *one* of you be on my side?" She crossed her arms.

"Because you still react like that when you're told no." Quin pointed at her arms, indicating her sulk.

She huffed. "I can do this."

Max stepped up to her. "There will be plenty of fights when you're old enough, but for now, you have to go home so the rest of us can fight and not be worried about you the whole time. Plus, someone needs to look after Tavi and Papa, right?"

Georgie sighed but nodded. "Fine. I'll go home."

Max leaned in to kiss her forehead. "Thanks, Pinky. Nox, see that she gets there, then join us in the command center."

"Sure thing, boss." Nox held her hand out to their little sister. "Come on, Dad's already on his way."

As Quin turned to follow Max, he stopped beside Mab. "I don't know if you know any inanimi who might want to help us . . . but we could likely use all the help we can get."

Mab nodded. "I'll call some people. Ander and I have a few friends who wouldn't mind seeing Enrique go down."

Quin nodded, his eyes falling once more to take in the bruises along her throat. "Are you okay?" His fingers itched to reach out and gently brush her skin. Make sure that she was indeed all in one piece.

Her own hand raised to brush along her throat. "Yeah, I'm fine. It'll take more than an angry ignis to stop me."

"Yeah ... I suppose it will." At least he hoped so. There were about to be many more angry ignis where they were headed.

"Now go." She nodded her head in the direction of where Max and Nash had disappeared. "You've got plans to make, and I've got inanimi to call."

Quin didn't say anything, just headed after his brothers. Mab was right. He didn't have time to stand around and check on her. But he wanted to. He needed to. There was an ache in his chest that he couldn't explain, and it wanted him around Mab. Wanted him to stay by her side and make sure she was all right. That ache inside of him didn't care about the war raging on in Rome right now. Didn't care that his entire way of life was being threatened.

It just wanted him with her.

Quin had to agree with it. At least partly.

He walked through the doors and into the hall that led to their command centers. Nash and Max were set up at Luca's station.

"Who do we know in Rome?" Max was asking Nash.

"Spurius, Claudia," Quin said, moving up beside them.

"Antonius," Nash offered.

"Antonius," Max muttered. "He's with their tech team, same as you, right?" he asked Nash.

Nash nodded. "Yeah."

"Which means he might be at a computer right now." Quin understood what Max was angling at.

Nash was already furiously typing on his keyboard. "Let me see if I can get him. 'Feugo attacked. Back under control. Want to help Rome. Need update on situation,'" he muttered for their benefit as he typed up the message and sent it off.

It was the longest ten seconds of Quin's life while they waited, then Nash's screen was flooded with camera feeds from all over the Roman sanctuary.

Fighting in the armory. Fighting in the mess hall. Fighting outside the main Presiding Hall, where the Princeps convened to make their final proclamations. It was also where every ignis was sworn into service once they came of age and completed training.

Orcus was at the forefront of that fight. Battling through the ignis like a bulldozer.

"Gods ... " Nash rasped.

"Yeah, gods. That's the problem." Max pointed to several different screens, where some of Orcus' godly counterparts had clearly joined in the fight.

"I hope Ander made lots of powder," Quin grumbled.

This was worse than they had expected. Rome was barely holding their formations. It wouldn't be long before Orcus would have command of the entire sanctuary.

"We have to get there. Now." Max's voice was stern, his eyes filled with concern and a desperation to help as his deep-seated need to protect rose to the surface.

Mab and Ander entered the command center at the same time.

"My mother is readying her army, and so is Indra. Mum will meet us at the gates of Helicon. Apparently, there is a portal we can use from there to get to Rome.

Indra will meet us outside of Rome." Ander's hair was a mess, like he had been running his fingers through it frantically.

"Okay, that's good. That'll help. Indra means more gods, Queen Aemiliana means more magic." Max stood straighter, some of the crazed look in his eyes from before dissipating. He was starting to believe that they had a chance to win this thing.

Quin wished he could say the same for himself. Doubt weighed heavily on his shoulders, and a dark, ominous sensation of doom seemed to shadow the corners of his mind.

"And I've got a group of minotaurs, a band of gorgons, and some fairy folk willing to join in," Mab announced, holding her chin aloft, pride and accomplishment shining in the depths of her warm brown eyes. She looked regal. Quin wondered if she knew that. That there was a quality about the way she held herself that came off like a queen about to go to battle.

"Dad's got Georgie!" Nox burst in. "I think it's killing him not to come, but he realizes someone has to keep Georgie from sneaking off and Tavi soothed."

Nash snorted. "Yeah, and that's not gonna be Papa." Quin smacked him on the back of the head. "What?" He rubbed at the spot. "We all know it's the truth."

"Thank you, Nox." Max shook his head and moved on. "We have visual on Rome. By the time we arrive, Enrique will likely have taken possession of the sanctuary. Whether he'll leave the Princeps alive . . . I don't know. But we'll be fighting to take it back, not keep it out of his reach. So be prepared."

Everyone nodded.

"Let's suit up," Quin said, looking around at them. "We

need proper tactical gear and weapons. That means you two as well." He pointed at Mab and Ander.

Ander made a face. "I don't think I need full—" His words cut off as Quin narrowed his gaze at him.

"At least something better than skinny jeans and suede boots, baby," Max implored.

"Fine. Fine. I'll borrow some cargos." He made a face.

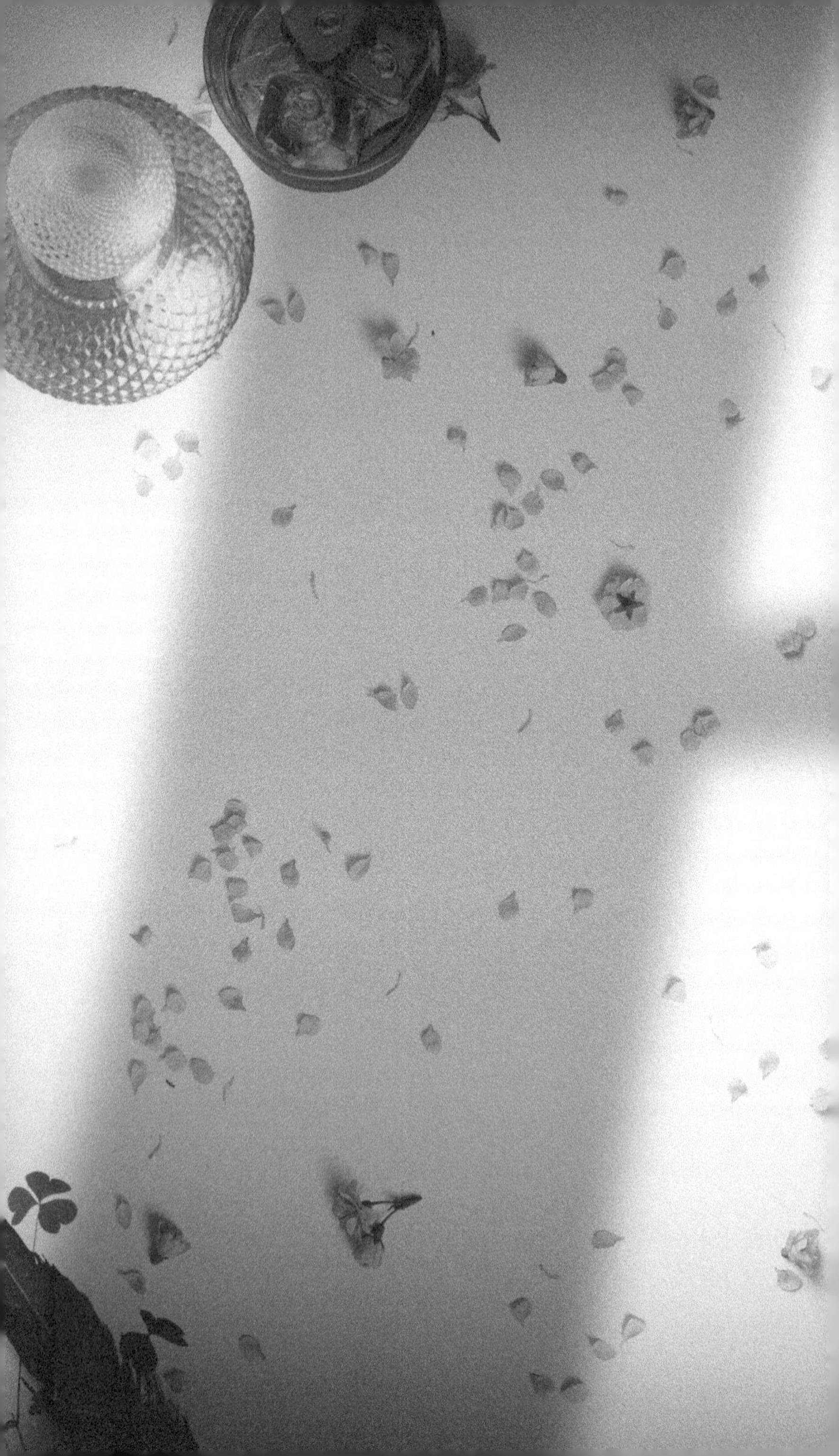

Chapter 49
Mab

This was far from the first war Mab had been in. Humans were always fighting each other over this spot of land or that resource. But it was the first one where her life was truly in danger. The first one where she had a family at her back. And there was something . . . different about that. Something she didn't think she liked very much. There were too many people she loved in danger. Too many of them possibly about to lose their lives. And all for a fight that should never have happened. All because someone got greedy.

"Oh, come on, Andy, we used to rock cargos all the time." Mab nudged him lightly, giving him a grin.

"Yes. In the '90s." Ander's mouth twisted in disgust. "That was before my fiancé was even born."

"If it helps, they still look hot." She grabbed a dagger to tuck into the holster on her thigh. It fit oddly over the cargo pants, but she wasn't going into another fight without a blade on her. Even if the bo had been handy for medium-range fighting, she needed something for if someone got too close again. Not that she was going to let that happen. If she could keep everyone away from their little group via wail, she'd scream herself hoarse.

"You shouldn't lie to people right before they go into battle, Mabbers, that's rude," Ander huffed, packing another of Nash's powder bombs into his pockets.

"The etiquette teachers I had as a kid never once said anything about battle situations." Mab shrugged, grinning. "Toss me one of those."

Ander raised a brow but threw the powder bomb to her, and she packed it into her pants along with the wire zip tie restraints the twins had been using, a flash bomb or two, and some throwing stars. She hadn't used throwing stars in at least fifty years, but maybe that part of fighting *was* like riding a bike. She could hope so, anyway.

She twirled a karambit around her finger, and Quin caught her eye again.

They hadn't spoken much since they won back the Miami sanctuary, but Mab could feel something lingering between them. Like they were being forced apart by the battle when all either of them wanted was to be close together. Two magnets held apart by a child's hand. Or maybe that feeling was all one-sided ...

Even if it was, she couldn't deny the tug in her chest threatening to draw her closer. The itch under her skin that made her want to stay at his side so she could look after him, protect him. She knew he didn't need her to. He was a warrior in his own right, fully capable of taking care of himself. But what if he got hurt? What if something bad happened and she wasn't there? The thought sent her stomach to her feet. Her hand tightened around the blade, the grip digging into her palm painfully.

Then there was a soft touch on her shoulder, and she turned to find Ander close behind her, like he'd read her thoughts. He hadn't, but they'd been in sync for so many years now, it was hard for him not to read her distress and know the cause of it. "Have you told him?"

Mab scoffed, tucking the karambit away. "Yeah. Sure. On the singular date we went on, that he didn't even realize was a date. Right in front of his daughter. That's a thing I did."

"Mab," Ander said, a note of chiding in his voice. "He should know before . . ."

He didn't have to finish that sentence; she knew what he meant. Quin should know they were bound before he went into what might be their final battle. Quin should know he was her soulmate, and she loved him, before he gave up his life to a fight that never should have been. The question was, would it make him a sharper fighter or would it make him sloppy? Would letting him know right before cloud his mind too much? Or would it give him the something to live for she'd recognized he so sorely needed? In the end, it didn't matter because . . .

"Now isn't the time, Ander. And even if it were, I'm not ready." She didn't know that she ever *would* be ready. Because she knew what this would be for him, and it wasn't fair to him to do that. To stuff him into one more cage. To shackle him all over again. To clip his wings. She couldn't do that to him. He was a bird, and birds were meant to fly.

"Mab," Ander sighed. It was amazing how he could say her name a dozen times in the span of a couple of minutes and every one would sound different based on his tone. She'd lived as a member of his family for hundreds of years now, and she was sure she still hadn't heard all of the ways he could say *Mab*.

"There will be time after." Even if she had to make that time herself. Even if she had to glue herself to his side to make sure Quin made it out of this thing alive. There would be time after. There had to be. There was no other option.

Ander gave her shoulder a squeeze, and she waited a moment for him to say her name again with a note of disapproval in his voice, but it never came. Maybe because he was in the same place she was: not wanting to acknowledge what could go wrong with all of this. Neither of them could think about the possibility that there *wouldn't* be time after, because if they did, they'd surely grab every Schields within arm's reach and cart them back to Helicon where they could keep them safe.

"There will be time after," she repeated, more to convince herself than to convince him. Because there wasn't any other option. If there wasn't time after, then she'd ... She didn't know what she'd do. She didn't want to think about it.

"Of course," Ander said, his voice soft. Then he handed her another powder bomb, pressed a kiss to her cheek, and pulled away with a murmured, "Come on. Our boys are waiting."

She nodded and followed him back over to where the rest of the Schields family was armed to the hilt and just waiting for the portal to open. Her phone buzzed in her pocket, and upon reading the message, her smile turned sharp. "Our local reinforcements are here. Andy, let them in."

A portal opened between the sanctuary and the street outside, and a small group of inanimi trudged in. Some from Inferno. Some from their time traveling. Some they'd known for hundreds of years. Alfie and Tommy were leading the circus fae, their eyes gleaming at the prospect of a fight.

"A pleasure to be under your command once again,

Lady Duchan." Alfie gave a sweeping bow that made Mab roll her eyes.

"You were never under my command, Alfie." Mab clicked her tongue. "You were my sergeant, and I was a bloody nurse."

"And yet ... " He laughed lightly, standing up straight again. "We both know who was in charge."

Mab couldn't help the little flush that heated her cheeks at the reminder. She'd never particularly liked war, but she'd been good at it for a time. Good at planning out a raid that would get their people in and out and back home safe with minimal casualties. It came with the territory of being so old.

"As always," Tommy said, joining in on the gentle teasing of old friends, "we defer to our elders."

"I'm not that much older than you! Stop it!" Mab huffed. Gods, she hated fairies. But then they were laughing, and the tension that had been building up from before burst like a bubble. Things seemed more possible now. Like it was more likely that there would be time after everything for her to talk to Quin. To explain to him that, just because they were arrow-bound, it didn't mean he was chained to her. He could go his own way if that's what he wanted. She'd just ... she'd just deal.

"Are you ready?" a soft voice asked from behind her, and when she turned, she found Quin waiting, his dark brows lifted in question. His expression was something she couldn't parse. She couldn't tell if he was disapproving of her closeness with Tommy and Alfie or if there was something else going on. And they didn't really have time for her to sort it out.

"Yeah. Let's go."

He nodded, then they all turned to where Ander was

standing at Max's side at the front of the small group. There were maybe twenty of them, twenty-five at most. Not nearly enough to take on Enrique and his army. But they'd put a dent in his forces, Mab knew that from experience. Understood how a small collection of truly angry and dedicated fighters could turn the tide of a battle. Plus, they had magic.

Quin stayed at her side as they headed through the portal into Helicon, where they'd meet Aemiliana, then head through the portal there to Rome. Hopefully, with Aemiliana and Indra's forces, they'd have enough people to really give Enrique the fight he deserved. And Mab would be able to keep her own close enough to her that she could keep them safe.

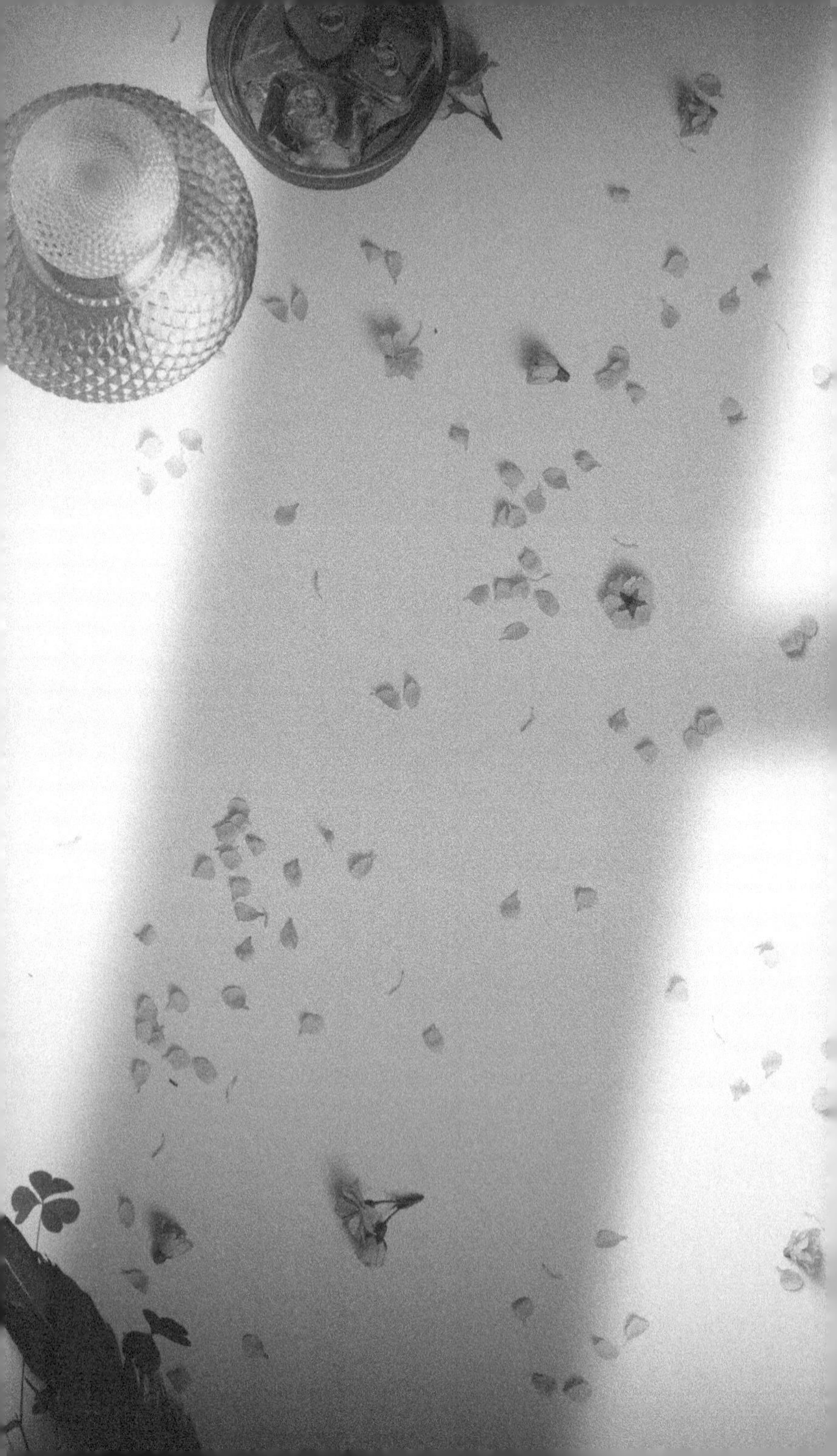

Chapter 50
Quin

Queen Aemiliana showed up with a full-sized army that would have been impressive on a normal day but was even more so because of how desperately they needed it. And because this wasn't actually the muses' fight.

Quin was also able to see why Ander had made a fuss about the cargo pants. The Heliconian armor was beautiful. Intricately handcrafted gold chest plates, stained and etched leather bindings and vambraces, and finely woven linen shirts and slacks beneath that looked breathable as well as easy to move in. Each soldier held a spear in their hands and had a sword strapped to their side. It definitely made their own tactical gear seem mundane and trifling.

Ander moved up to hug his mother, quickly flashing her his engagement ring, and drew Max to his side.

"I don't think anyone ever taught us about the Helicon army," Quin said at last. Mab quirked a brow at him.

"No?"

"No. I knew they had one, but I didn't expect the beings known for the creation of music, dance and art to be so . . . "

"Intimidating?" Mab asked.

"Yes."

"Have you *spoken* to Aemiliana?" Mab laughed. "She's absolutely intimidating. Plus . . . many would say there are a lot of similarities between fighting and dancing."

"Nah . . . pretty sure that's sex and dancing," Nash butted in. Quin smacked him lightly on the head, not enjoying the tonal shift of their conversation or his having butted into a moment when he was able to speak to Mab. "Whaaaaat? It's the truth!" He rubbed his head as he walked back over to where Nox was busy talking to a tall minotaur Quin recognized as the bouncer from Inferno.

"Let's move out!" Max called.

Quin looked over at Mab, and she nodded. "Yeah, I'm ready," she said, seeing the question on his face before he even had a chance to ask it.

It made him smile a little. An ease was beginning to grow in their interactions, and there was something comforting in that knowledge.

A part of him wanted to reach out and take her hand. But he balled his own into fists to keep himself from doing something so weird and strange that would have her asking where his head was at.

As a large formation, they moved through the portal that led from outside Helicon to Rome. It didn't lead directly into the Roman sanctuary, for safety purposes. But there was a portal point about half a mile away.

There, with his own army of gods and ignis, waited King Indra.

The sight of them was as comforting as it was terrifying. The armor on their chests and shoulders gleamed in the early morning sunlight, the red bristles on top of their helmets a stark contrast against the blue sky.

"Shiiiiit," Nash rasped. "Indra brought backup."

Quin cut him a glance but decided not to say anything. He was right, after all. It was impressive.

Quin fell into step with Max, and together, he, Ander, Mab, and Aemiliana met Indra where he stood. The king of the gods nodded to all of them and smiled fondly at Queen Aemiliana.

"Aemiliana!" Indra boomed. "It's been months. Who would have thought this would be how we met up again instead of over a glass of wine."

The queen of Helicon curtsied a little in deference to him. "We've got more important things to be concerned with right now than missed wine, Indra."

Quin's brows lifted. Was Queen Aemiliana scolding the king of the gods? It would seem Ander had come by his audacity naturally.

Indra laughed, dark and deep, then looked at Max and Quin. "Tell me what the situation is."

It was like a switch was flipped, and suddenly, the king was all seriousness.

Max cleared his throat. "Well, Your Hi—"

"Indra," the king cut in. "We're in battle. Don't bother with formality right now. Plus, a little birdy told me you're about to marry our dear Ander here. That makes us practically family."

"U-um . . . of course. Your—Indra." Max straightened his shoulders. "Orcus spent the last few days amassing his full ignis army in Texas. We went to collect him, but the army had already moved out. At the same time Orcus moved on Rome, Captain Galeo moved on the Feugo City sanctuary."

Indra's face hardened. "How far has Orcus' army gotten?"

"Before we left, they had fully infiltrated the sanctuary,

and Orcus was surrounding the Princeps in the Presiding Hall. We fully anticipate that he's managed to take it by now," Quin said.

"Do you have contacts on the inside?" Indra looked between them.

"We lost contact with our one tech about twenty minutes ago. If he's been taken as well, there likely isn't any part of the sanctuary they're not in," Nox stepped up to fill in.

"Do you have a plan?" Indra asked, staring Max down.

"Not exactly ..."

Indra lifted his brow. "Speak, boy."

"Well, I think it makes sense for us to surround the sanctuary. Attack from different directions since we now have two armies," Max began, then looked at Quin.

Quin nodded. "Keep them distracted and focused on the larger teams."

Max grinned at him, and Quin could see that it pleased his brother that he was catching on to his thought process. "Exactly. If Orcus' army is busy trying to keep the Olympia and Helicon armies out, then our smaller crew can sneak in with less resistance and possibly get to Orcus before too much damage is done."

"It could work." Indra nodded. "What say you, Aemiliana?"

The queen had been silent, contemplating their words. "I think it could work. We'll take the western side, come in over the drawbridge."

"Then I will send my army to the east and split my ignis troops to north and south." He looked at Max and Quin once more. "You two fly your—"

"They can't fly," Ander said, his words biting and filled with loathing.

"What do you mean they can't fly?" Indra looked puzzled.

"We've been grounded." Quin stated it calmly and without emotion. Because he didn't want to think about that moment in the grounding room when he had been strapped down on his knees and his flight taken from him.

"You've been *grounded*? By whom?" Indra growled.

"Galeo. Because we went against his orders and were looking into finding Orcus." Max's face was hard.

"We'll find another way in besides flying." Quin knew they would. They were too stubborn to be held back from where they needed to be. "There's a side gate. We'll take that."

"It's made to be impenetrable from the outside," Max said, frowning.

"We have acrobats," Mab piped up.

Everyone turned to look at her, but she didn't shrink under their combined attention. That calm, cool air was about her again. Her confidence always carried her through each situation.

"What?" Indra asked.

"We have the fae circus with us. We have acrobats. If they create a ladder with their bodies, we can get over the outside wall and inside. If they take a few beings with them, we can take the gate and let the rest of our team in," Mab explained.

Quin's brows lifted, a warm sensation filling his chest at the ridiculous yet brilliant idea.

"That could actually work," he told her. Pride blossomed inside him, swelling until a little grin tugged at his lips.

"Of course it could work, Big Bird. Don't you know I'm

amazing?" She smiled at him, and he grinned back, a little in awe.

"Okay, then I suppose we have our positions." Indra grasped the hilt of his sword, which hung in the scabbard at his side.

"I have extra comms!" Nash trumpeted from behind Max and pushed his way into the group. "If we want to orchestrate a proper attack, you'll need to be in contact." He held a set out to Max and then to Indra. "The two of you will be in direct contact." Next, he handed a set to Ander and Queen Aemiliana. "And the two of you will be in contact. Max, Ander, try to stay close to each other so you can pass information back and forth."

Ander reached out and took Max's hand. "I think we can do that."

Indra fit the comms piece into his ear and attached the mic. "Get in position, but wait until Aemiliana and I have given the signal before you attack. You'll want the attention fully on us before you go in."

Max nodded. "Will do, sir."

Ander moved to hug his mother quickly, and Mab did the same. Then the queen of Helicon left them, heading back to her people to lead her army through the streets of Rome and take the sanctuary from the west.

"Should we get our people?" Quin asked Max.

"Yeah, let's get moving, we've got a bit of a hike."

"Nox, where are we going?" Quin called out to his sister.

Nox appeared at their side, pulling out a map of Rome. "Nash, come here." Her twin came over, turning his back to her so that Nox could lay out the map. "So, here is where we are." She tapped the street they were on. "And this is where the sanctuary is." She tapped it. "The gate you want to go in is along this side."

Max and Quin leaned in around her. "So if we take this street, go left here, we have a fairly straight shot to it," Quin mused.

Max studied the path Quin had marked out and murmured. "I agree." He turned back to their group and waved them over. "Let's move out."

Their trek through the city was quick and quiet. Ander put a glamour over them, so they went unseen by the early morning tourists and Roman citizens opening their shops and heading to their jobs.

As they approached the sanctuary, its tall walls and towers came into view. It looked like a large cathedral made of brick and stone. High gothic-style windows showed nothing of what was happening inside its walls. Around it was a ten-foot brick wall, blocking it off from the city.

Max stopped them at the edge of a tall building, and together, they looked around at the side gate they wanted to go through. There were four guards posted outside of it.

"Pontius, Dido, and Fallux." Max waved over the only ignis who had been in fit enough shape to come with them and hadn't needed to remain behind to keep a presence in Miami. "I need you three to fly in and distract those guards. Pull them away so that we can get in and over the wall."

"Can do, Maximus." Pontius nodded.

"Once you've got them contained, join us inside. *If* you can do so safely." Max looked between them.

"We'll see you inside." Dido stretched out her hand to shake Max's. "Be safe in there."

The three of them launched into the air, and a pang of sorrow coursed through Quin. They shouldn't have to send in others to do this. He and Max should have been able to take out those guards on their own. It was frustrating having to rely on others for things he had always been able to do.

The three ignis swooped down from high above, dive-bombing the four guards Enrique had posted outside. The attack caught them by surprise, and they were able to knock the guards to the ground. However, they weren't so easily kept down.

Pontius leaped into the air, and Dido and Fallux followed. Though he couldn't hear what they were saying, Quin could tell Fallux and Dido were taunting them, until the guards flew after them, leaving the gate unattended.

"We have clearance to mount the wall. Are you in position?" Max spoke into the comms, waiting for Indra to respond.

Quin watched him, waiting. Max nodded. But before he could say anything, a loud explosion rumbled through the air from the other side of the sanctuary.

"I take it that's our sign?" Quin asked.

"Let's go!" Max shouted.

They crossed the street quickly, heading straight for the gate. Once at the wall, Quin took up the position of lookout as the fae acrobats Mab had brought with them began to climb onto each other's shoulders until the one at the top was able to scale the wall. Max climbed up the bodies and was dropped over the other side. Ander followed him.

Quin kept watching the street and eyeing the skies, making sure they weren't about to be surprised by Enrique's guards. He hated not being on the other side with Max.

From beyond the wall, they could hear a number of grunts and a hard *thump*, like someone's head going into the wall.

Then there was silence, until the lock clicked, and the

gate swung open. Max, looking a little ruffled but grinning, stood on the other side.

"Inside, now!" He waved everyone in.

Quin waited until their team was on the inside, eyes darting up and down the street to make sure no one caught sight of them, then he followed last, shutting the gate behind him.

The unconscious forms of two ignis lay crumpled on the ground.

"Having fun?" Quin asked Max.

"You know it." Max winked and lifted his wrist to his mouth. "We're inside the walls. About to head into the sanctuary itself."

Max had barely finished when four more ignis dropped in on them from the sky. They wore pitch black and dark gold, Orcus' colors. One of the minotaurs, the bouncer Quin recognized earlier, dove at the first ignis, his horns scraping off the ignis' chest plate with barely a scratch but knocking him back.

Ander appeared suddenly behind the second, while Mab threw herself at him from the front.

Seeing this, Quin raced forward, blocking the downward strike of the third ignis, who was attempting to cleave Mab's head off in a sneak attack. Quin growled and smashed his bo into the ignis' knee. He grunted in pain and thrust at him with his sword.

Spinning out of the way, Quin expanded his wings, using them to keep himself upright. He blocked another thrust of the sword, parrying it away and driving his bo staff into the ignis' groin. He dropped to his knees, looking ill.

Quin raised his bo up into the air, then in a sweeping arc, smashed it into the side of the ignis' head. Blood sprayed, and the ignis fell face-first into the dirt.

Nox was suddenly at his side, a metal zip tie pulled from her pocket, and she knelt down to bind the ignis' arms behind his back, conveniently trapping his wings by his arms as well.

"Thanks," Quin muttered.

"No prob, big bro." She grinned.

They proceeded across the courtyard and through the small door on their end of the building.

Awaiting them on the other side was an alcove off the main lobby. In the lobby, which they had no choice but to exit into, was a small band of Orcus' soldiers. And beyond, a large double staircase led into the upper wings of the sanctuary.

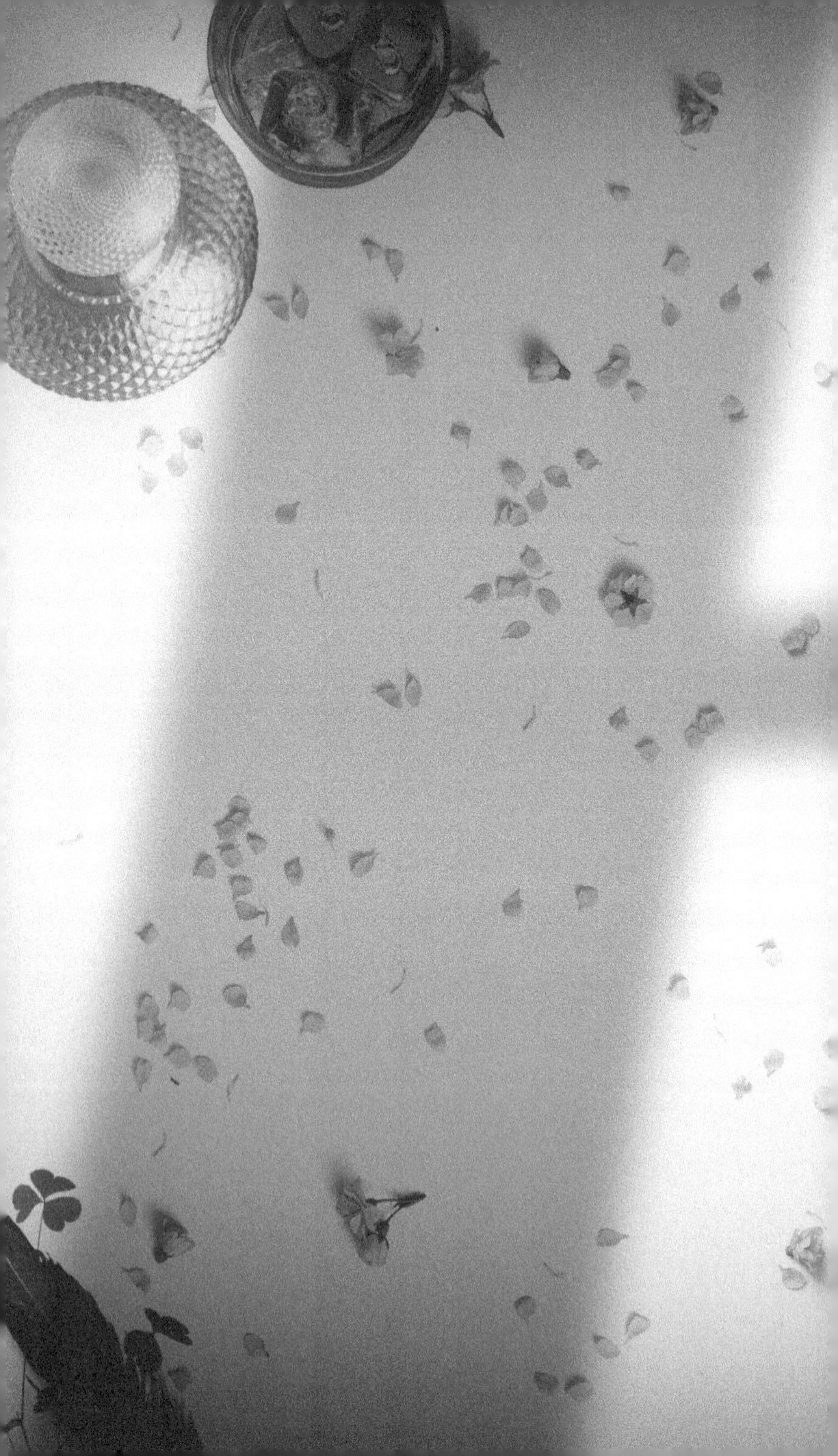

Chapter 51
Mab

Mab hadn't been in a real battle since WWII, and it was nothing like this. That had been all machine guns and tanks, normies and their oversized firearms. This was something else entirely. Although no less deadly, even for the fact that they were utilizing archaic weaponry. An ignis didn't need a machine gun to kill someone; they had enough power behind their swings without modern engineering. Add in the fire they could conjure on a whim, and you had killing machines that could rival any tank.

The stairs up ahead were going to pose a problem for any of them who couldn't fly. It gave those they were fighting against the chance to surround them and the higher ground. But there wasn't really anywhere to go but up, was there?

"Stay together," Max ordered, nodding his head toward one of the staircases.

Mab didn't know how long that was going to be possible. Eventually, they'd have to split their forces, but for now, she supposed, staying together was their best option.

Especially since they thought they knew where Enrique was holed up. That would hopefully cut search times down, but Mab didn't like not being certain.

"Do you think we can get one of them to talk?" Mab asked as she moved toward an ignis blocking their way. The ignis swung forward with his sword, the full force of his strike slicing downward. Foolish opening move, if you asked Mab. Left your head wide open.

She ducked under the blow, leaving her own back open, and cut through the side of the ignis' head so he choked, growled, and dropped his sword to clutch at the place where she'd cut through his cheek, leaving behind a gaping hole that showed his teeth, trying to hold everything in place.

"You stupid little *bitch!*" he snarled, fire igniting from shoulder to wrist as he reached out to grab her by the arm. His touch seared her skin, and she shrieked.

Mab saw someone move toward them, trying to help, but she was quicker. Sucking in a breath, she opened her mouth and screamed, the wail even louder than the one that she had released on Galeo. The ignis fell a second later, his eyes open, unseeing, his ears bleeding. She wasn't sure if he was still breathing, and she didn't care.

"Talk about what?" Ander asked, continuing their conversation as if nothing had happened and placing a hand on her burned arm to soothe away most of the blisters.

"Where that fucker is. The twins got us his location an hour ago, but maybe he moved, and I'll bet my favorite set of wrenches that he's crawled into a hole somewhere that's going to be a bitch to get into." She blocked a strike from an ignis coming up behind Ander with her bo. "We should ask."

"Fair point," Nox called, a bright smile on her face. She looked a little manic at this point. Mab was beginning to think all the Schields were a bunch of adrenaline junkies. Even Quin looked a little livelier than usual.

"I'll ask!" Nash volunteered, his bloody blade slicing through the arm of an ignis attacking his sister, forcing the ignis to drop their weapon and retreat lest Nash cut them to ribbons. He pulled a wire zip tie from his pants pocket and started wrestling the ignis to the ground with the help of his sister. It was a sight to behold, honestly, these two little normies bringing down a fierce bird of prey with nothing more than determination and rage.

"Impressive," Ander murmured beside her, perfectly echoing her own thoughts.

Then another ignis came their way, and they were forced apart by a blow from their sword. It was honestly amazing how many ignis used swords. Like, did none of them think of trying anything else? And why were the Schields more flexible in their weapon choices? Must have been a consequence of their upbringing.

They spun on Ander, leaving their back open to Mab, and she was fully ready to take advantage of that until movement caught her attention out of the corner of her eye, and she wheeled around to find another ignis striking for Quin's back. She had just enough time to put herself bodily in the way, taking the blow to her bo with a grunt and knocking her back into him. It jerked her shoulder, but she used the momentum and the opening not seeing her coming had provided to swipe her blade across the ignis' sword arm, cutting through muscle and tendon.

"Jeez, these things are sharp," she muttered to herself, lifting her bo to block another strike. "Remind me when we're done, I need to get my set sharpened."

"Your set?" Quin asked, looking at her over his shoulder.

She smirked at him, spinning the karambit around her finger before adjusting her grip again and landing a kick to the stomach of the ignis to give herself *some* breathing room —not much, but some. "You okay over here, big guy?"

"Yeah. All good." But he smiled a little like maybe he was grateful for her checking in. Mab didn't know what the hell that meant, and she didn't have time to ask because a moment later, a wing thwacked her in the face.

"Sonuva—" she hissed, wiping blood from a cut on her temple and blocking another swinging sword, this time going for her middle. Cute. Like she hadn't just used that tactic herself.

"Switch," Quin muttered, not taking his eyes off of the ignis in front of him, who he had already disarmed and was now fighting in close-range combat, making her easier prey.

Mab hummed her agreement, and in one quick, coordinated movement that almost felt like a dance step, they swapped places, leaving Mab facing off against a smaller female ignis. "You know, normally, I think I'd be offended that you gave me the weaker opponent."

But that wasn't true, and she knew it. The ignis in front of her was smaller but faster. And as Mab turned her attention more fully toward the female, the ignis leaped into the air to get the upper hand.

"Oh, fuck off. I'm calling foul play!" Mab hissed, tucking the karambit into the sheath in her pants and pulling out a throwing star.

"Ha! *Fowl* play!" Nox shouted from across the little atrium where she and Nash were binding every ignis the rest of them managed to take down.

Quin huffed behind her, a sound that might have been a laugh, and Mab's heart soared.

"You good back there, soldier boy?" Mab asked, spinning the throwing star around her finger and adjusting her stance. The ignis hadn't launched at her yet, was still trying to understand what kind of opponent Mab was. She was being more cautious than any of the ignis Mab had faced so far, which was annoying, but she could understand it. After all, she was in the same position, wasn't she?

"Just focus on your own battle, Mabbers. Jeez!" Ander shouted from wherever he was.

Mab felt more than saw the attention of the twins swivel her way, but she ignored it because a moment later, the ignis dove for her and grabbed ahold of her hair. Pain shot through her scalp, burning down her neck and spine, and something nicked her ear, cutting a thin line along her jaw and cheek. A dagger, maybe. "Mother—" she choked and chucked the star at the ignis, clipping the side of her wing and drawing a harsh cry.

"Chick fight!" Nash cheered from the sidelines.

"I think I hate your brother," Mab grumbled to Quin through her teeth as she reached for the blade at her side again to slice through the arm holding her hair in a death grip, wrenching her neck back, and threatening to lift her into the air by her curls alone.

A second later she jammed the point of the curved blade into the ignis' forearm, blood spirting and coloring her white hair pink, but it had the desired effect. She let go, and Mab was able to grab onto the ignis' injured arm and rip her from the air. Mab didn't have the same upper-body strength the ignis did, but she was definitely more determined and more annoyed. So, after some struggling, she managed to knock the ignis' head against the floor, leaving her dazed, and pull out a set of ties to bind her.

When she was done, there was a hand waiting to help her to her feet. "You all right?" Quin asked, and Mab smiled at him, letting him tug her up.

"Peachy keen." Mab winked at him, and he huffed another laugh, then went off to check in with Max as they started the trek up the stairs.

"Okay, but . . . what the hell is that about?" Nash asked suddenly at her side. He had a busted lip and a bruise forming on his jaw, but otherwise, he looked relatively unharmed. Impressive for a normie, but Mab kind of wanted him and Nox to train with her and Ander some more. To make sure they were as safe as their ignis siblings. That was a thought for later.

"What is what about?" Mab brushed her hands through her hair and frowned when her fingers got stuck in blood-clumped curls. "Gross. So gross."

"You two." Nash pointed between Mab and Quin. "You've been, like . . ."

"You're adorable," Nox finished for her brother.

"Right. You keep checking in with each other." Nash nodded in agreement.

"We're just curious. When are you going to get together already?"

"You're nosey, is what you are," Mab said, brushing past them to get back to Max, Ander, and Quin, ignoring the faint flush crawling up her neck.

"I'm calling it," she heard Nox say from behind her, "they're the next to get engaged."

"I give it a month," Nash agreed.

Mab shook her head. She didn't have time to spare a thought for the twins and their antics. They were likely just teasing her; they didn't mean anything by it. They didn't know how close to the truth they were. Or how close to home they were hitting. And she wasn't going to engage with that gentle ribbing, not when she knew for a fact none of it was true.

"How are the others doing?" she asked Max and Ander, taking a moment to catch her breath and bandage up the cuts along her arms and face. Gods, if this was her new reality, being bonded to a warrior, she needed to get back into shape. She couldn't afford to be a weakness for him. Never again.

Max held up one finger as he listened to something over the earpiece, then smiled a little. "Indra and Aemiliana have made good progress in surrounding the compound. Indra has the first floor clear at the rear of the building. He'll be following us up to the second as we infiltrate further."

"There's been no sign of Enrique yet." Ander frowned.

"Did you expect there to be?" Mab scoffed. "He's a weasel, he's going to hide as long as he can to save his skin."

"Either way," Max said, leading the charge up the stairs, which were mysteriously vacant of more forces. That didn't bode well for them. It meant they'd be faced with a much larger army once they reached wherever Enrique was. "We know where he's at. He hasn't left the Presiding Hall."

"There's enough space there for him to have at least a force of fifty." Quin frowned, looking back at their own small contingent of fighters. There weren't enough of them for that, Mab knew it, even when half of them weren't sporting injuries.

"Alfie," Mab called back to the fae who was helping his partner bandage a wound on his arm. "Head back. See what reinforcements you can get us from Indra and Aemiliana. If they have anyone to spare, we need them, and fast."

"Aye-aye, captain!" He gave a little salute, then he

turned and broke off into a run much too quick for any normie, his shape blurring.

"Tommy, you're in charge of the wounded. Everyone else, come this way." Mab turned back to Max and nodded, then they started up toward the landing at the top of the stairs just as Pontius, Dido, and Fallux rejoined their group.

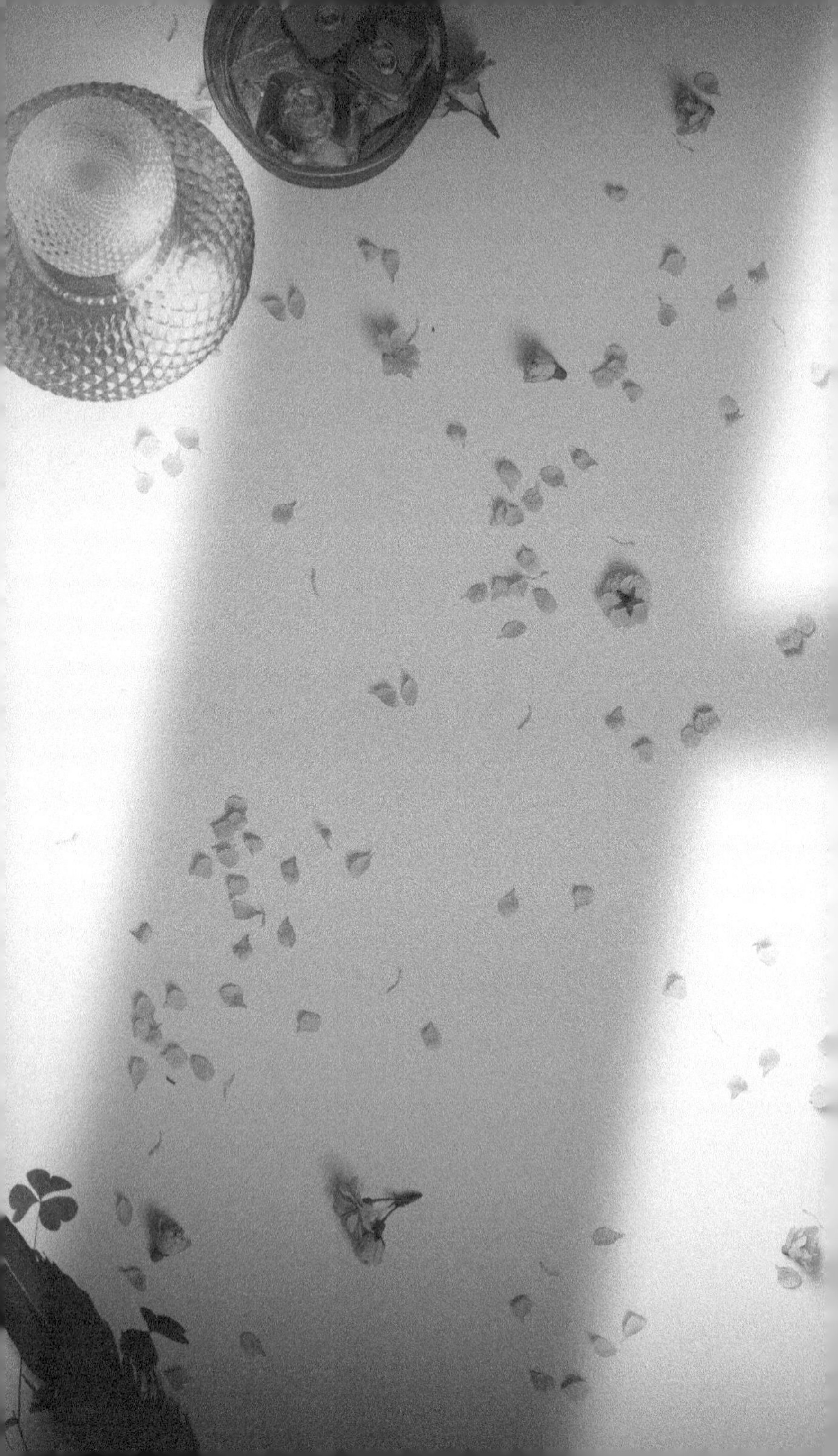

Chapter 52
Ander

Somehow, they were all still whole. Mab had tried to burn herself alive again—they really needed to discuss her habit of always finding the flame—and the others bore numerous cuts, bruises, and scrapes, but somehow, they had made it this far and were still alive.

Ander had a large gash down his back where an ignis had taken the cheap shot and tried to literally stab him in the back. Thankfully, Max had seen it and pulled Ander out of the way just in time for only the tip of the sword to cut through his black T-shirt and the flesh of his back.

If it scarred . . . he and Enrique were going to have words.

Ander had his eyes on Max as he hurried up the large staircase leading to the second level. Behind him, Mab shouted commands to the fae. The upper level was empty and quiet—until it wasn't.

Just as Max reached the top steps, a new wave of ignis seemed to come out of everywhere. They swept from the halls and flooded the top floor. Several leaped over the balcony and dropped down on their group below.

As the wave of the ignis broke, three beings in togas appeared behind them. A tall, dark-skinned male with a shaved head, broad shoulders, and muscular chest. A tall, slender female with strength evident in the way she carried herself and a sour look on her face that had never faded as long as Ander had known her. And the third, a slightly shorter male, lean and wiry. The look on his face chilled Ander to the core. Scowling, disdainful, condescending.

Sorkis, Louba, and Sophocles.

Sophocles was Enrique's right-hand man, the other two his lovers. The polyamorous triad were meant to have been friends for Ander but had really only been another way for Enrique to control him. To watch every step he made and make sure he didn't step out of line.

Max rushed them, heading straight for the gods without hesitation. Ander gasped but was too late to stop him. Sorkis stepped up to meet him, his large hands stopping the swing of Max's sword, holding it midair. Max's wings spread wide, attempting to give himself more leverage, but it wasn't enough against the god.

They grappled, Max pushing forward as fire ignited along the blade. Sorkis planted his feet, then the god gave a strong shove and sent Max flying backward, over the railing and toward the floor.

"Max!" Ander shouted, waving his hand to soften Max's fall as he hit the floor.

"I'm okay," he groaned.

Ander looked back to the main landing. Sorkis stood at the top step, towering over them all. He put his hand into his opposite fist and squeezed.

"Well, if it isn't the Prince of Helicon come to finally receive his punishment."

"My punishment?" Ander called up to him.

Sophocles came to stand beside him, staring down his long, aristocratic nose at Ander. "Yes, for betraying Orcus."

Ander scoffed. "I betrayed Orcus?"

"Yes." Sophocles narrowed his eyes. "Not understanding your place in his life and leaving him to one hundred years of torment."

Ander laughed, extending his hand to swirl it before him. "Yes, Sophocles, *that* was the issue." He thrust his hand forward, sending a wave of energy toward the slender god.

Sophocles flew back, into Sorkis and Louba, who caught him.

The god righted himself, then with a snarl, threw himself down the stairs at Ander. It knocked him off his feet, and they tumbled down the stairs, smashing into marble edges and stone banisters.

Above them, Quin and Max raced up the stairs to face off with Louba and Sorkis, their sword and bo blazing with fire. Ander barely had a moment to spare them a look before he was forced onto his back by Sophocles, his fist coming down to connect hard with Ander's chin. It smashed his head back into the stone floor beneath him.

Ander's vision swam, but he managed to move his head out of the way of the next hit and snap himself out from under Sophocles. The god snarled at him, rising to his knees.

"You're going to have to fight harder than that if you want to take me out," Ander snipped, remembering all the moments in Acheron when Sophocles had looked down on him. Made snide comments to Enrique about him. Undermined him in any way possible.

As Sophocles started to stand, Ander kicked forward as hard as he could, catching the god in the side of his head.

His body arched, toppling backward. A feeling of satisfaction washed through Ander at the sight of the asshole sliding across the stone floor.

Beyond, Nox was pinned to the floor by an ignis, her taser just out of reach. Seeing it, Ander sent out a blast of power that drove the ignis into the wall. Nox hopped up, grabbed her taser, and jammed it into the ignis' side. His entire body spasmed uncontrollably until he collapsed. Nox sent Ander a thumbs-up before grabbing the ignis' discarded sword and squaring off with the next one approaching her.

Above on the stairs, Quin had Louba pressed back over the railing of the stairs, doing his best to force her over, the blaze of his bo catching her robes on fire. Except Louba drove her knee up into his abdomen and rolled them both over the edge. They landed with a hard *thud*, sparks of fire and ash scattering in the air, Quin on his back and Louba on top, her dagger poised to come down into him.

"Ruin!" Sophocles growled, striding forward, golden blood trailing down his jaw from the corner of his mouth.

Ander pulled one of the powder bombs out of his pocket and threw it to the ground. It exploded, sending a wave of *dues somnum* into the air. Another powder bomb went off on the stairs, thrown by Mab.

Sophocles coughed, a large amount of the powder going into his lungs, then he swept out at the air, trying to clear what was around him.

"What is this?!" he yelled.

"Just a little trick I had up my sleeve." Ander launched himself at Sophocles then, causing him to take several steps back. He kneed him in the abdomen, making the god double over. Also effectively making him inhale more of the powder.

Sophocles choked on the powder and staggered sideways, his hands sparking. He swept them out and around him causing a strong wind that drove the powder away from him.

But it was too late. His eyes sagged, and his hands searched for something to help keep him propped up. Ander took the opportunity presented to him. Drawing his arm back, he threw a punch, putting his whole body into it. Sophocles' head swung harshly to the side, fresh gold blood spurted from his lips, and a dark bruise formed on his cheek as he dropped, eyes rolling back in his head.

Ander didn't leave himself enough time to gloat, though he wanted to. Instead, he snapped himself up to the second floor, appearing just behind Sorkis. The god, starting to stagger a little from the powder but not enough yet to take him down, grabbed ahold of Max and threw him across the room.

Max spread his wings to help catch himself a little, but he still tumbled to the floor and rolled.

"Don't touch my fiancé!" Ander shouted. Using his magic, he pulled Sorkis off his feet. The god spun in the air, and his own blast of power sent Ander reeling backward. He hit the wall, all the oxygen forced out of his lungs as he sagged down to the floor.

Sorkis staggered toward him, a growl on his lips. "Who do you think you are, *princeling*?" He spat Enrique's pet name for him like it was a curse.

Before he could reach Ander, however, Max leaped on his back, one arm around his neck while he pulled back on it tightly, pressing into his throat, the other hand pressed to the side of his face, fire licking over his skin and hair. Sorkis screamed and shook frantically, trying to dislodge Max.

Ander climbed to his feet and rushed them both. He

thrust up with the palm of his hand directly into Sorkis's chin, and it drove his head back. Gold blood trickled from the corner of his lips where he bit his tongue.

Max kept his arm around his throat until Sorkis finally dropped to his knees. When he let go, the god fell face-first into the tile before him, face smoking and sizzling from Max's fire.

Ander panted and looked over at Max. "You okay?" he asked.

Max nodded, rolling his shoulders and wiping the back of his hand across his lips. "Yeah. You?"

Ander shifted his head back and forth. "Achy, but hey. I'm still standing." He looked down at Sorkis. "Better than he can say."

Max smirked and held his hand out to Ander, helping him step over the unconscious god.

"Did you make him bleed?" Max asked, looking down at Sorkis.

"Yeah . . . I told you *dues somnum* makes them weak."

A shrill wail filled the air, making both of them wince and cover their ears. As they rushed to the stairs, they saw Mab and Quin squaring off with Louba. She clearly hadn't ingested enough of the powder to knock her out. But Mab had forced her back with the wail, hands over her ears as she tried to get away from it. Mab kept moving closer to her, not letting her escape.

Risking his ears, Ander pulled another bomb out of his pocket and dropped it over the balcony. As the powder exploded into the air around Louba and Mab, the god wobbled on her feet and suddenly collapsed.

Blessed silence filled the air, except for the ignis that were still battling their inanimi friends.

"We have the upper landing," Max said into his comms,

letting Indra know. "We'll see you in there soon." He looked over at Ander. "Indra says they're headed this way from the other end of the building."

"Good to hear." Ander raised his wrist to his mouth. "Mum, we're on the second level. About to approach the Presiding Hall."

"Be careful, my son." Ander could hear the clang of swords over her comms. "We're holding the outside. A number of forces surrounded us as we took the drawbridge."

"Be safe," he said to her.

"I'll find you when this is over."

Ander looked at Max. "We won't be able to count on the Helicon army just yet, too many forces outside."

"We'll deal." Max looked down over the lower level. "Q! Nox! Nash! Mab! Upstairs, let's go!"

They'd made it to the second floor, but they still had to get to the Presiding Hall and hope Enrique was still inside.

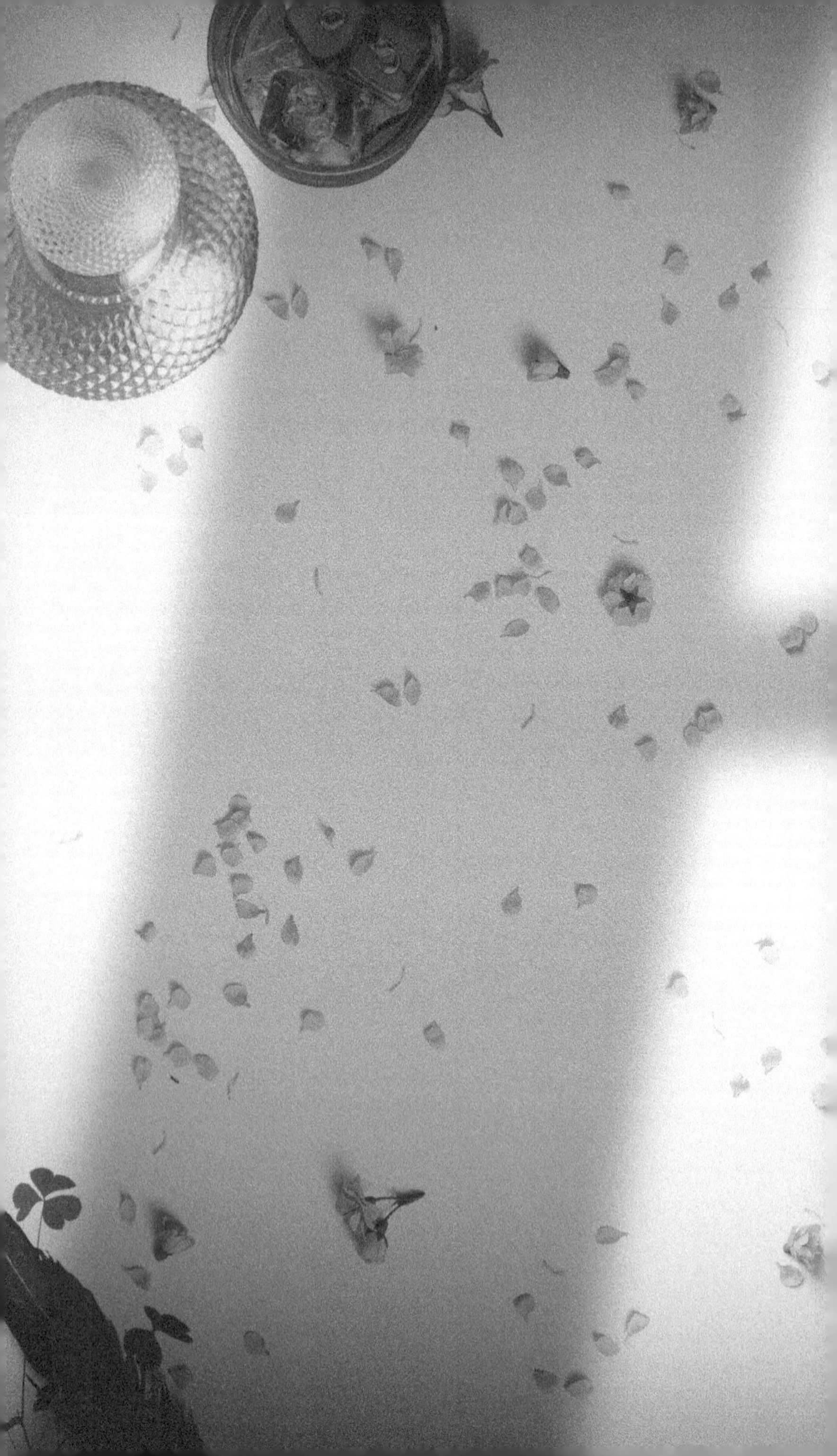

Chapter 53
Max

Their forces were flagging, Max could see it. Exhaustion hung heavy around their shoulders, and there was no end in sight, not yet. But Max had faith. How could he not? He'd seen what those around him could do. He watched his forces take down gods and a tidal wave of ignis. They made it so far with just this small contingent of soldiers, and yes, they'd lost some along the way to injury, but they were still going.

They could do this.

He'd never been more sure of anything in his life—aside from proposing to Ander, that had felt like instinct. They could do this. They could bring Enrique to his fucking *knees*. And with such a small, undisciplined force? Well, being underestimated was always a bonus. Let Enrique be so confident in his victory that he got sloppy. Let him see them as no more than ants to be crushed. It would be *worth* it when they felled him.

"Nox and Nash," he called as they approached the Presiding Hall, fighting through what was left of Sophocles' forces. There weren't many of them. The rest must have been holed up in the hall with Enrique. Likely put there to keep him safe. Coward.

"Yeah, boss?" they asked at the same time, even though they were on opposite sides of the fight, zip-tying any ignis that was taken down and left alive.

"I need eyes in there." He pointed to the big double doors into the hall. If that's where Enrique was, they needed to know what the numbers looked like. "See what you can do."

"Aye-aye!" Nash gave a lazy salute and climbed to his feet, already pulling a phone out of his pocket and joining his sister out of the way of the fight where they could work.

"Ander." Max moved to his side and pulled him in close, twirling them out of the way of the desperate downward strike of a sword. The blade nicked his wing in the process. He hissed, fluttering it a little in an effort to shake away the pain and the now-loose feathers. It did nothing, but Max was accustomed to pain. He could handle it. "I need you to do me a favor, love."

"Anything." Ander panted, pressing into his chest and rising onto his toes to brush a quick kiss to Max's lips before he spun to blast the approaching ignis with his magic. It wasn't the time nor the place for kisses, but Max wasn't going to chide him for it. They should both be taking comfort where it was offered in a situation such as this.

"Talk to your mother. See if there is a way she can block someone from opening a portal. I'm going to ask Indra the same thing." He spun them again, smiling a little when Ander sent a blast of magic over his shoulder to force another ignis away from them and toward Mab, who was waiting with a feral grin splitting her face. "Enrique is cocky now, but I don't doubt that when he's sure he'll lose, he'll try to get away."

"Aren't there protections on this compound to keep people from portalling in and out?"

"There were. But who knows what shape those wards are in." He cradled Ander's head in his hand, pulling him into another quick kiss, glad to have this moment before the final battle. Being able to hold Ander close, make sure he was in one piece, and kiss him was all Max ever wanted. To keep him safe and remind him every day that he was cared for. Once all of this was done, he'd spend the rest of his life devoted to that pursuit. If Ander wanted him to clip his wings and leave the Sanctum, he would, all he had to do was say the word. They just had to finish off Enrique first.

"Good point." Ander moved on his toes to hurl another bit of magic at an approaching ignis before tapping the comm in his ear as Max curled his wings protectively around Ander's back to act as a shield.

Upon relaying the message to Indra, Max received a laugh in response. "Child's play, Maximus. Next time, contact me with something difficult." Then the comms cut out , and Max was left to the silence of the moment with Ander, guarded by his wings. Their breathing was loud with the sounds of battle muffled by his feathers. And for a second, it was almost like they were in their own little world. Almost like none of this was happening. The world didn't exist. It was just them. Pity that couldn't last, but Max would take what he could get.

"I love you, do you know that?" Max asked, brushing his nose against Ander's cheek, a soft murmur of contentment settling into his chest. "So much, it absolutely astounds me."

"I did know that." Ander nodded. There was this teasing little grin on his lips that Max wanted to taste on his own. "But you haven't told me in the last five minutes, so I feel it bears repeating."

"Oh, it definitely does." Max laughed a little and leaned down to put thought into action. Ander's smile tasted like his favorite strawberry lip gloss, the sweat from their battle, and *Ander*. Max's beautiful, wonderful, perfect Ander. Gods, he had gotten lucky. The universe and The Fates had smiled down upon him and given him everything he could ever dream of in a person and then some, without him even having to ask. He wondered briefly if Aemiliana could help him send The Fates a thank you card, but that thought was quickly overshadowed by Ander pressing impossibly closer.

When they pulled back, Max was more breathless than he'd been throughout the entire fight. But he was so happy, it felt like his entire body was humming.

"Come along." Ander held out his hand. "We have an evil ex-boyfriend to kill. Care to join me?"

"I thought you'd never ask." Max laughed and grabbed onto his hand, unfurling his wings to return them to the battle. While they'd had their moment, the rest of the group had taken care of the small contingent of ignis left outside the hall.

Mab and Quin were just finishing zip-tying the last couple.

"So kind of you to join us," Mab groused.

"Sorry, we were talking tactics." Ander flapped his wrist loftily, and Max choked back a little laugh when Mab rolled her eyes.

"Sure you were."

"Nox. Nash. What do you have for me?" Max asked. It was likely better not to engage with Mab's irritation; it would only get her and Ander bickering more, and they didn't really have time for that at the moment. Although it probably would ease some of the tension.

"Heat signatures, a fuck-ton of them." Nash turned his

phone around so that Max could see what they were looking at.

"Mostly ignis, by our estimation. We think"—Nox zoomed in on the image to show a dark red dot in the back—"this is Enrique."

"But it's hard to tell with so many ignis lighting up the place. For all we know, there are inanimi mixed in too." Nash scrubbed at his face, wincing when the movement rubbed against his bruised jaw.

"I don't like going in blind," Quin muttered.

"None of us do," Nox agreed. "But we're not being given much choice."

"Either way, that's too many." Max sighed, looking back at their meager forces. They had started with close to twenty-five, but they were down to fifteen or so now. And all of them were injured and tired. "We need a way to clear out a chunk of them to even make this viable."

"I've got an idea," Mab said, waving her hand a little. "Let me go in and use my wail."

"You can use it on that scale?" Max frowned. He'd never heard of a banshee doing anything like that before. Their wail was not meant for these kinds of situations, usually reserved for self-defense. At least that was his understanding. But then, banshee and sirens tended to keep to themselves. They cloistered themselves away on their island and didn't generally interact with most other people, much less come to the mortal realm. So maybe what he'd learned about Mab's kind growing up was wrong.

"I mean, I'm not really supposed to. I don't think." Mab shrugged. There was a trail of blood crawling down the side of her face from where someone had landed a blow to her temple hard enough to break the skin and another from a thin cut on her jaw. She was probably concussed, and Max was going to send her into more fighting. But what other choice did he have? They needed all the advantages they could get.

"But?" Nox prompted, her eyes wide with curiosity. Which would have been adorable in any other situation.

"But it can be done." Mab lifted a hand to brush away the blood, smearing it across her skin and wincing when the movement no doubt irritated the injuries. "It means I won't be able to use it again for a little while. It'll tear my throat up enough that I might not even be able to talk much. But if I can level some of his forces and give us a fighting chance?"

She already sounded a little hoarse from all the times she'd used her wail thus far, and Max was going to ask her to do it again? Not ask. She was volunteering. Mab was here because she was one of them. Because she wanted to see Enrique brought down as much as the rest of them. Max had to remember that. Had to remember not to belittle any of the others and their contributions. It was hard to override his ignis training sometimes, after so many years of his teachers drilling it into his head that ignis were the best fighters, the warriors created for the king of the gods himself. Clearly that wasn't true, as he'd watched every one of those around him bring down ignis. Maybe it was just a matter of wanting it more.

"All right." Max nodded. "But you're not going in alone."

Mab snorted. "Anyone I take in with me might wind up deaf. It's safer if you all stay outside while I do this."

"You're *not* going in alone," Quin repeated, his hand tight around his bo staff. As far as Max knew, Mab hadn't told Quin about their soulmate bond yet. But Max could see the way things had changed for Quin in respect to Mab. He wasn't willing to let her get hurt. He wasn't willing to lose her. Even if he didn't know what those feelings meant yet. It made Max want to smile, to pull his brother aside and chat with him, to tell him that it was okay to love someone. But they didn't have time for that.

"Ander, can you fashion him some magic ear plugs?" Max turned to him. He knew full well there was no stopping Quin. He wanted to go in with Mab and have her back? He was going to do it, damn the consequences. But that didn't mean Max shouldn't give him the most protection he possibly could.

"Not from thin air. Do you have anything I can use to create them?" Ander looked distinctly uncomfortable with this conversation, and Max wondered if it was because he didn't want Mab to do this either. Without her wail, she would be down one seriously powerful defense. But she'd shown herself to be an extremely competent fighter. Max had faith she'd be all right.

"Oh! What about these?" Nash pulled out a set of earphones dangling from a long cord.

"Why do you have those?" Nox asked, her brows raised.

"I like to listen to tunes sometimes when I spar, figured this wouldn't be any different." Nash shrugged. "And look, they came in handy!" he crowed as Ander snatched up the earphones and started to work his magic over them, humming and singing to himself.

"Yes, yes. Don't break your arm patting yourself on the back." Despite the snide tone, Nox patted Nash's back like one might a very good puppy, and Max could just imagine Nash wagging his tail. "I'll tell Licia you came through in a pinch today."

"Yes!" Nash threw his fist into the air in victory.

"All right. Give them a test run." Ander held the earphones up to Quin, who took them and situated them in his ears, tucking the cord down the front of his shirt so it would be out of the way.

He tilted his head this way and that for a moment as Nash and Nox clapped and hollered in front of him. Then he signed, "Can't hear a thing. Let's get this done," and turned his attention back to the door.

Mab frowned. "What'd he say?"

"He said he's good to go," Nash translated. "Good luck!"

"Have fun storming the castle!" Nox waved.

"Do you think it'll work?"

They both broke out laughing, and Max rolled his eyes.

"Can they take anything seriously for more than an hour?" Ander asked, his arms tight around his middle as he watched the doors shut behind his sister.

"No. They can't." Max shook his head.

A moment later, Mab's wail pierced the silence, the sound so loud, it left Max's ears ringing and his stomach roiling with nausea. It lasted for much longer than he thought it would, making it impossible to hear afterward, but when Quin flung the doors open again, there were bodies littering the floor, and the remaining ignis had taken a collective step back. Mab was holding her throat, a little bit of blood trickling from her mouth as she panted, but otherwise, both of them seemed okay.

"Let's move!" Max called, and their small contingent entered the room just as the next wave of ignis crashed down upon Mab and Quin.

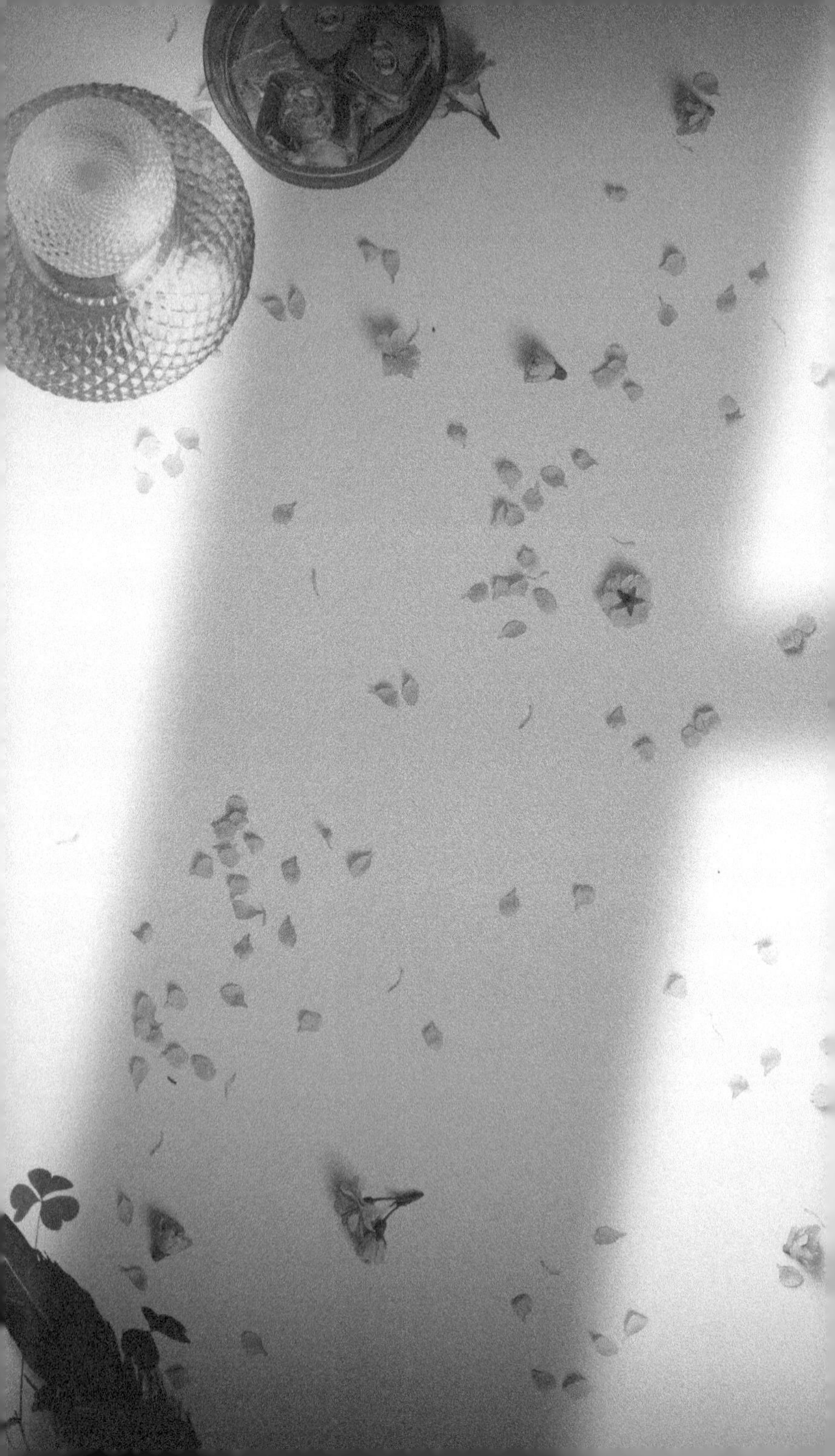

Chapter 54
Mab

Mab's throat was on *fire*.

It wasn't the first time she'd overused her wail, but it was the first time she'd pushed herself to her absolute limits. She was sure if she tried to speak now, any words that left her lips would be a croak, a wheeze, a cough. They would burn the whole way up, and she'd regret even trying.

But it was worth it to see how many had fallen. To know that she was giving them a fighting chance. It wasn't much. Not nearly enough in the grand scope of things. But it was something. She turned to look at Quin pulling the earbuds from his ears, the taste of blood on her tongue, and grinned at him. She was sure her teeth were pink with it, based on the look of concern on his face.

"Are you okay?" he asked, his hands moving in the signs along with his words.

Mab nodded, even as she tried to get enough saliva together to swallow right, and when she finally did, it burned the whole way down. She winced. Nothing a cup of tea with some honey couldn't cure, but there would be time for that later.

Quin opened the doors behind them, and Max and the others filed in, weapons at the ready, just as the next line of Enrique's soldiers marched into battle. Mab pulled her own weapons from the pockets of her pants and spun to face the oncoming horde. Now that she was looking, she was able to better appreciate the drama of the scene Enrique had set.

The Presiding Hall was gilded and beautiful.

Underneath the bloody bodies of the ignis she'd felled with her wail was a marble floor inlaid with veins of gold that perfectly mirrored the blood of the ignis themselves. Pillars were spaced every few feet, cut from the same stone, reminiscent of the grand receiving hall Indra himself had in his palace. And between those pillars was what looked like wallpaper, though it was hard to tell from a distance, with a golden feathered pattern. Light streamed in from large windows that showed nothing but clear blue sky from this angle. Arguably, it was beautiful in any other setting. But there was something gaudy about the extravagance too. Something grotesque about this being the place where the ignis were shackled to their duty for the rest of their immortal lives, making it more of a spectacle.

Mab hoped this room fucking *burned* by the time they were done.

Turning back, she saw that Quin was already fighting against another ignis, the earbud cord still hanging around his neck as he ducked and swiped with his bo, all movements carefully calculated and elegant, like dancing. Gods, he was beautiful like this. He was beautiful any time, really, but like this, he looked every inch the avenging angel. His black wings fluttered out behind him, helping him keep balance and warding off attacks. Flames danced along the metal of his bo, reflecting warmly in his eyes.

Mab only had a moment to pick her jaw up off the floor,

then she was in the thick of it herself. The first sweep of a sword almost got her. In fact, she thought she saw a couple pieces of white hair gather on the floor as she ducked just under it. Why they kept trying to behead her, she didn't know! It wasn't like she was a *gorgon*!

But it left the ignis' lower half open enough for her to cut at their legs, forcing them back and away from her to avoid her nicking a major artery. With a deep breath that burned all the way down, Mab rose to her feet, grateful for the space she was provided to go on the defensive once more.

They circled each other, sizing one another up as the battle raged on around them. It was curious: most of the ignis they'd encountered so far had come at them swords blazing, but this new wave approached Mab with more caution. Maybe it was because of how many of them she'd taken down with her wail. They were wary of her now. Unsure if she could use it again. Good. She wanted them afraid of her. It might keep them off her back a bit more. Although, how long until they realized she'd used her one great wail and now her voice was completely useless?

Or until they decided it made her more of a target than a threat? Probably not more than a few minutes. That's all she had, if she knew anything about fighters who thought themselves infallible. Maybe less. She'd have to see how many she could take down with her weapons and speed alone before that happened.

Movement caught her eye from the side, and she turned to see two more ignis forming a little circle around her.

Not as long as I'd hoped, then. She sighed. Fuck. This was not going to end well for her. She was good at one-on-one fighting, but she'd never been particularly adept at numbers, even though she'd trained for decades to be better at it. There was something about dividing her attention that just didn't work for her in this situation. Give her a crowded bar with five different people ordering drinks, three more flirting with her, and at least one broken glass, and she was fine. But that wasn't a fight-or-flight scenario.

Ander had always been better at dealing with groups. And she'd gotten so used to having him at her back in times like these, she almost caught herself looking for him over her shoulder. He was with Max. She knew that. They'd stick close together now that Enrique was just a few yards away. Which left Mab on her—

One of the circling ignis fell to the floor, clutching their broken wing, hissing and spitting, and Quin stepped up behind her, his back to hers.

"You okay over here?" he asked, voice soft. Always soft. Always checking in. Gods, they'd been fighting for what felt like hours at this point—but had, in reality, probably not been more than an hour—and through all of it, Quin had had her back. He checked in. He looked after her. He didn't even know he was her soulmate, but he gave a shit about her. Which was strange. Yet, maybe some part of him knew.

Instead of answering and risking further damage to her voice box when she needed to be resting it, she shrugged. She had definitely been better, but at least she wasn't alone anymore. And she'd take that above being surrounded by the enemy and caged in like she'd felt a moment ago. With Quin's back close enough to her own that she could feel the heat of his skin under his feathers, Mab settled into her stance.

They attacked. All six of them at once. Swords raised high, each blazing with the flames of an ignis. Hot enough to cauterize any wounds, but Mab didn't really want to find out. She ducked the first swipe, kicked out a leg at the middle ignis, then caught the next with her bo. It clanked loudly, making her ears ring. The ignis' strength greatly outmatched her own, but she slid away, smooth as water. Not fast enough though. Not nearly fast enough. The third ignis to her left clipped her in the shoulder with a blow that did cauterize.

She opened her mouth to scream, but no sound came out. Her voice box was still too damaged from the wail. And that was a mistake, she realized all at once. It exposed her weakness. Fuck.

Quin was at her side in seconds, fighting the remaining ignis off with swift, death-dealing blows, the end of his bo connecting with temples and crushing in skulls. Then he was fussing over her wound, already pulling bandages from somewhere. Likely the endless pockets on his cargo pants. It hurt like hell to press gauze against the burn, but it was better than getting dust in it, she supposed. Or it being ripped open further. Still, some aloe wouldn't go amiss.

"You didn't tell me you wouldn't be able to talk *at all* after," he hissed at her, his bright eyes narrowed in frustration. Like she'd kept that from him because she was being a pain in the ass, not because she knew it would be enough for the others to tell her not to do it. She didn't bother to remind him that she had said it *might* do that. Because, in truth, she'd said it in such an offhand way that they probably hadn't even put any credit to it, when she'd known exactly what it would do.

She shrugged, patting his hand lightly in comfort.

He curled his wings more around them, protecting her from anymore attacks while he finished tying off the bandage.

"That was stupid," Quin told her, but it sounded like he meant something else. Gods, she really wished she could dig around in his brain and figure out all the things he wasn't saying to her. The hidden depths were making her batty. Why couldn't he just say what he meant? Why did he have to keep skirting around whatever he was feeling?

She wanted to grab his face in her hands and scream at him.

She wanted to grab his face in her hands and kiss him.

Actually. That wasn't such a bad idea.

When he finally finished, he was about to pull back and return to the fight. Mab grabbed his hand and gave it a little squeeze. Then she lifted her hand, signed the word "sorry" with her uninjured arm, and grabbed his face by both cheeks. He jerked a little, confused, but Mab didn't give him time to pull away before she moved onto her toes and pressed her lips to his.

There wasn't any real heat behind it. There was too much else going on.

But it felt like she was asking a question with the kiss.

What does this mean? What do you want from me? Do you even care?

It was close-mouthed, mostly just pressure. She didn't want him to have to taste the blood that still coated her tongue from her wail. And when she pulled back, she could hardly meet his eyes because that wasn't . . . He hadn't reciprocated at all. He hadn't wanted that. And she was such a selfish bitch taking it from him when they were in the heat of things.

So she spun on her heel and dove right back into fighting, switching her karambit to her left arm to avoid messing up her injury even further with the excessive movement.

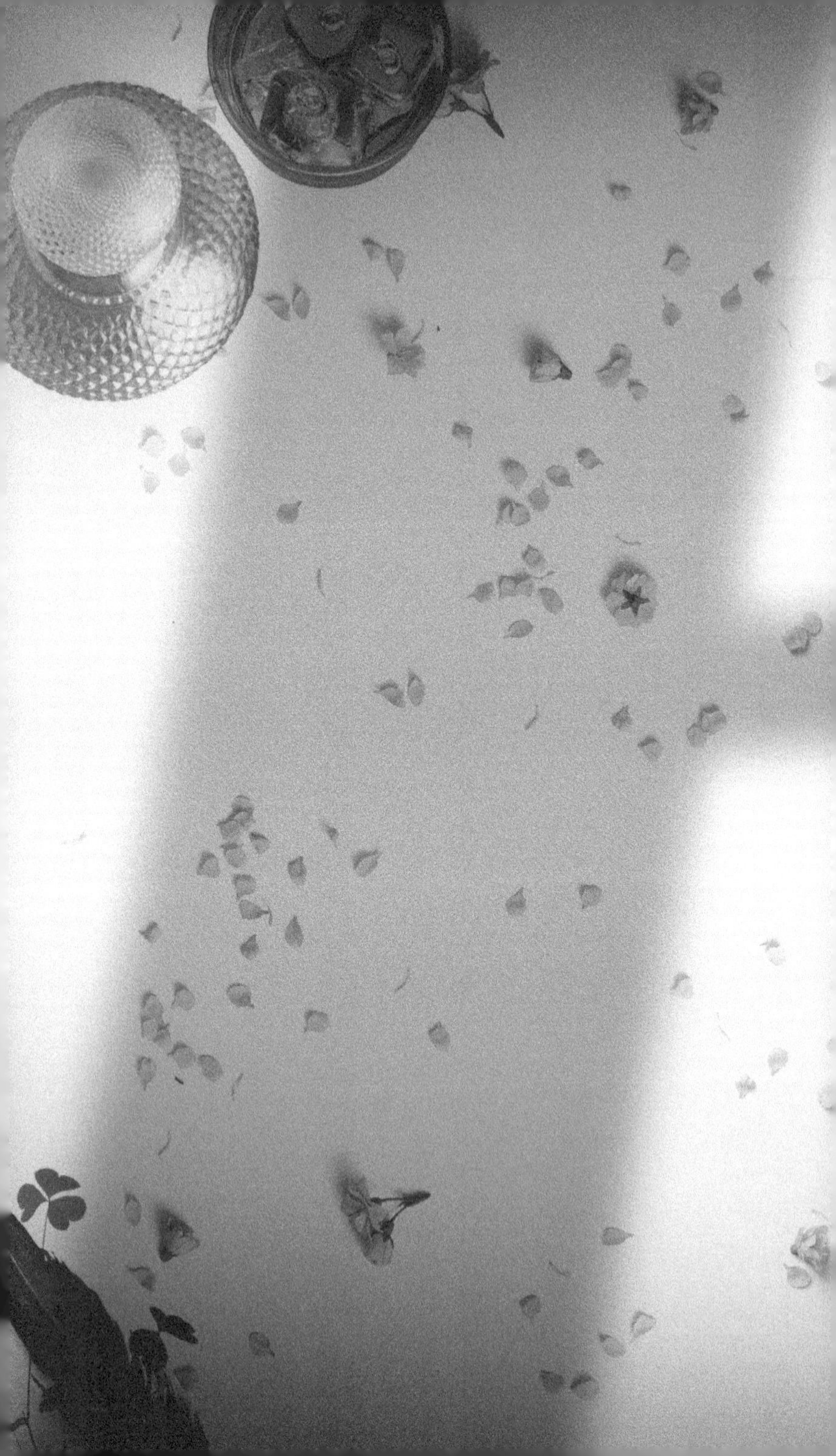

Chapter 55
Quin

Quin's mind was blank. Mab pulled away from him before he could even react, then she was fighting once more. His eyes followed her. He wanted to ask what that had meant. But she wasn't looking at him. She couldn't even speak right now.

Reflexes alone were what caught the sword swinging toward him. Quin turned, blocking it with his bo, sliding the metal staff down the blade hard enough to smash the fingers holding the hilt. The ignis didn't release his sword, but he took a step back, and that one retreat was all Quin needed.

He stepped into his guard, drove his staff down on top of the ignis' foot, breaking the bones there, then thrust it up into his chin, snapping his head back and making him take yet another step away. The ignis wasn't guarding himself at all now, Quin was moving too fast, and he took advantage of that.

With a snap of his bo, the sword went flying out of the ignis' hands, and Quin grabbed the dagger from his thigh and drove it up into the ignis' ribs, twisting. He groaned and stumbled back, his hands flying to the gushing wound Quin left in his side.

He was finished.

Quin sought Mab out again. She was fighting, holding her own, but her movements were slowing. She and Ander were well trained, but not well conditioned. They didn't fight every day, training until their muscles screamed and they couldn't breathe anymore. Not like the ignis did.

Had she meant that kiss? Is that what all her handsomes and the day at the beach totaled up to? Did Mab have feelings for him? This was neither the time nor the place. But he needed to know if she was feeling the same draw toward him as he felt toward her. If every cell in her body longed to be with him. If she wanted to wrap her arms around Quin and hold him as badly as he wanted to hold her.

He never wanted to hold anyone.

A shadow fell over the floor in front of him, and he snapped out of his daze. Now was not the time. He could ponder the world of attraction and love after all of this was over.

Quin spread his wings and used the momentum of flapping them to push him back quickly and out of the way of the ignis who'd been attempting to drop in on him. It was just enough to keep booted feet from taking him out but not fast enough to prevent the dagger that jabbed into his side.

He snapped his bo into place just as the blade entered his flesh, knocking the hand away so the blade wasn't able to go too deep but not fast enough to prevent it from sinking in a couple of inches.

Quin hissed in pain but forced his arms up, lifting the bo staff before him. He could feel the warm trickle of blood drip down his hip, but he wasn't going to bleed to death just yet. What he could die from, though, was the ignis approaching him and the second swooping in from above.

He hated that his wings were useless beyond a little stabilization. Hated that he couldn't launch himself into the air and turn this into flying combat.

The ignis who'd stabbed him thrust forward once again, the blade angling for his throat. Quin blocked it easily enough, teeth gritting as the wound in his side protested the movement. But he shoved back at the ignis to force him to retreat.

His opponent held his ground, pulled out a second dagger, and forced Quin to parry that away while taking his own step back, directly into the path of the ignis who'd landed behind him. She swung her sword. Quin ducked to protect his head. It clipped the edge of his wing, getting lodged in the forearm bone buried beneath feathers.

Quin howled but twisted, pulling his wing free, and ducked into a roll. When he came back up, he was facing off with both the ignis, giving him a better chance to fight them. He was never going to win if he kept playing defense. It left them the ability to force him back until they had him truly cornered.

Which left going on the offense.

Quin angled his bo across his torso and ran toward them, jumping into the air and spreading his wings to give him better leverage. His back muscles strained, having to work harder to make up for the missing primaries that threw him off balance, but it was enough to give him the height he needed so both of them were forced to block.

He thrust the sword of the male out of the way, then did the same for the female. This gave him enough space and speed to hit hard at the male's side. The crunch of breaking ribs could be heard over the battle, and his cry of pain sounded out not too long after.

The female turned to block as he swung back in her direction, but Quin slid the bo down her blade and crushed it into her instep, then smashed it over her fist, forcing her to drop her sword, and twisted it to smack the opposite end into her jaw. Another *crunch* hit his ears, and the female went down.

The male growled and rushed him, but Quin crouched a little, parried his blade to the left, and smashed his bo into the male's knee. The male buckled under the force of it, and Quin drove his elbow hard into his temple. His eyes rolled back, and he slumped to the ground.

Quin rose, panting, and pressed a hand to his side. It was bleeding harder. All the activity had opened it up more, but he wasn't in danger of dying.

Unlike Ander, who had somehow ended up facing off with Orcus in the middle of the room. The god seemed to tower over Ander even though there wasn't that much height difference between them.

Ander lifted his hand to throw a blast of power at the god, which made him slide across the marble on his heels. But the god kept upright, and in return threw a ball of fire in Ander's direction.

It caught the half-muse in the abdomen and sent him skidding across the floor.

Orcus wound his arm back up, ready to throw another, and from the corner of his eyes, Quin saw Mab pull away from her fight, ready to run between them.

She was going to throw herself in the path of the fire. Take the next hit for Ander. Likely die.

Quin acted without thought, every instinct inside him taking over. He ran for Mab. His arm looped around her waist and pulled her up and off the floor to swing her back out of the way, his wings wrapped protectively around her.

She struggled, making garbled, scratching sounds that were probably an attempt at an angry scream. Quin only tightened his hold and turned in time to see Max leap into Orcus' path instead, shoving his arm up so that the fireball went wide, colliding with one of the pillars and making it explode.

The old structure trembled and echoed from the force of it.

What happened next happened so fast, Quin could barely comprehend it.

Max and Orcus were in a fist fight, grappling for control. Max swung at Orcus, catching him in the jaw. The god growled angrily and shoved Max, his eyes blazing with fury. Max leaped at him again, his sword drawn. He took a swipe at Orcus with the blade, but suddenly, Orcus pulled his own sword seemingly from thin air.

They parried back and forth, Max forcing Orcus back, Orcus then getting the upper hand and forcing Max to retreat a couple of steps.

Their blades zinged through the air, clashing with the ring of metal on metal. The rest of the fighting in the room stopped, everyone zeroing in on what was happening between the god and the white-winged ignis.

The devil and the angel.

Max finally gained ground. He parried fast enough that he was inside Orcus' guard and forced him back.

But then a small blast of power from Orcus' hand caught Max on the chin, causing him to stumble. Orcus swung quickly with his blade, slicing through Max's side and up into his left wing, severing a large chunk of it from his body. White feathers filled the air, worse than the spray of blood, blocking everything from view.

Someone screamed Max's name.

Max was on his knees.

His hand at his side.

Orcus took the final blow, thrusting his sword deep into Max's chest.

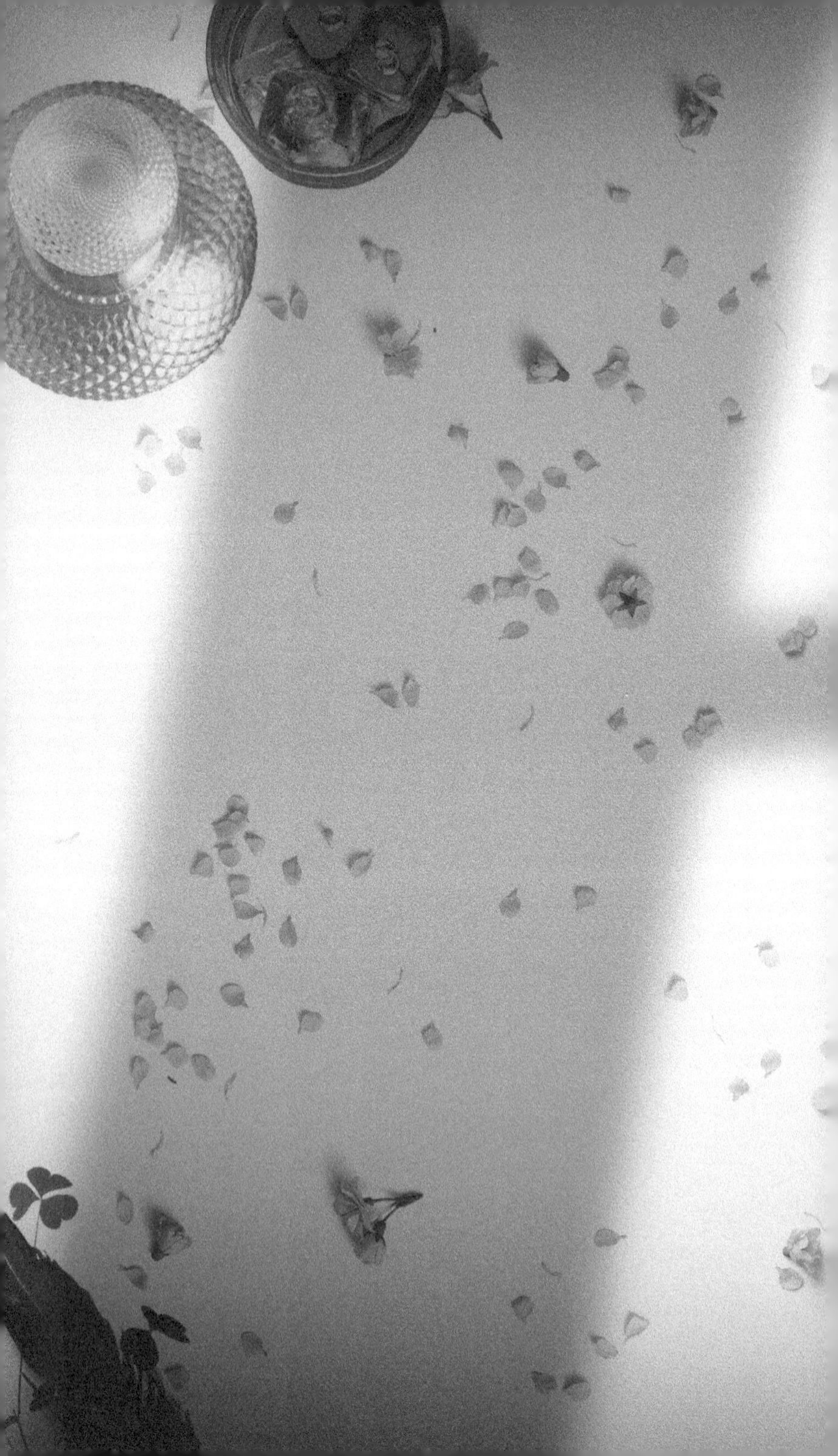

Chapter 56
Max

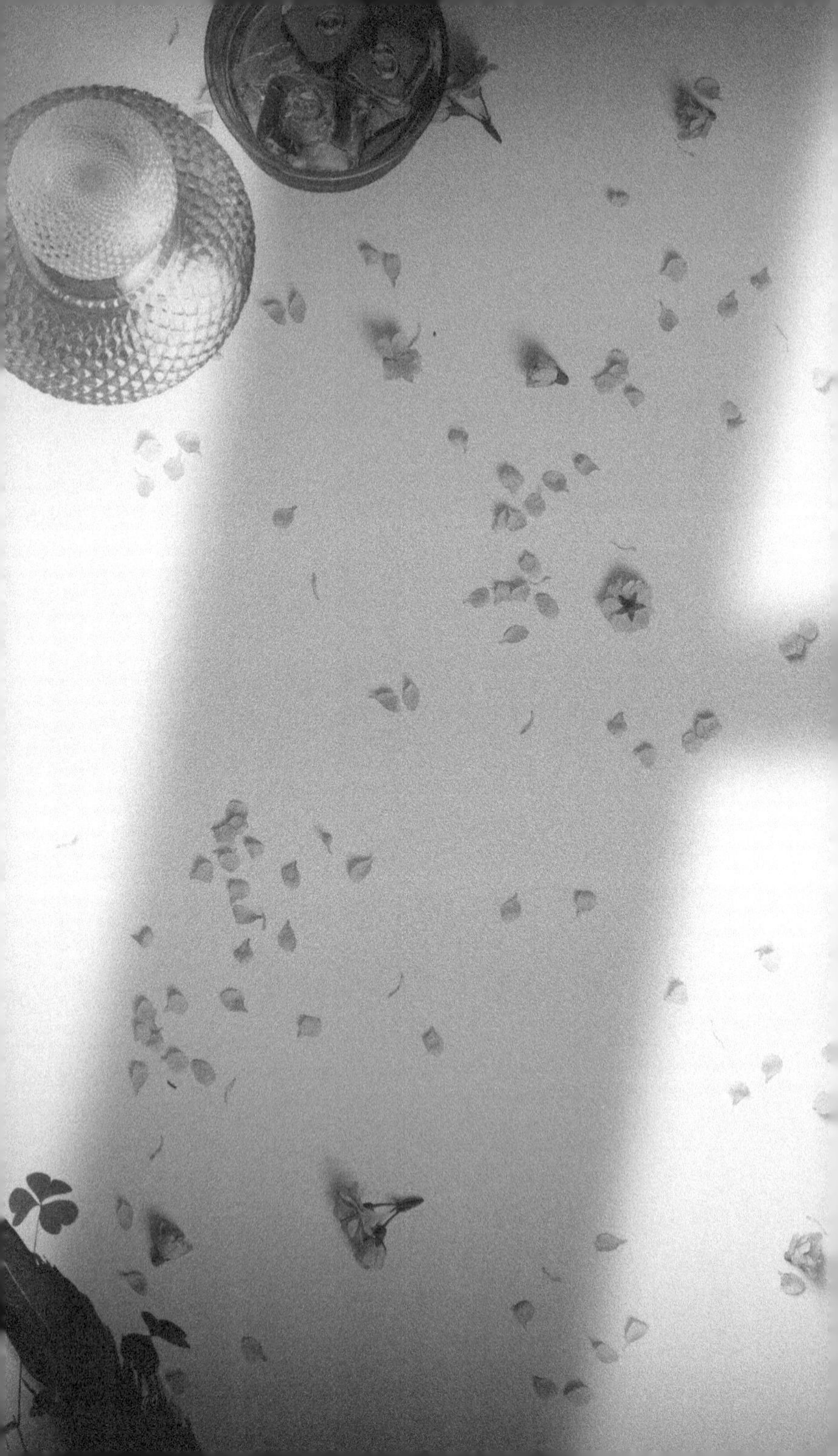

Chapter 57
Ander

Ander's world came to a crashing halt. He didn't hear the horrifying sounds of battle around him. Didn't hear the screams of pain or sadness. It was like he was under a bowl beneath the ocean, with only the sound of his own heart thumping in his ears and a faint ringing that wouldn't go away.

A sharp, excruciating pain pierced through him, tearing his heart in two. His hand rose to press against his breastbone, and he gasped against the agony of it.

He staggered to his feet, something halfway between a sob and a gasp catching in his throat, unable to escape past the ball of misery lodged deep inside him.

Ander didn't feel the singed edges of his clothing still lightly burning or the seared flesh of his chest. He only felt the agony of something inside him shattering into pieces. Tearing through his soul, mind, and body like crystal shards exploding.

He stumbled over a body, caught himself, and scrambled to Max's side.

His beautiful angel stared up at the ceiling, a glassy emptiness filling his hazel eyes.

"Max! Maximus!" His name tore at his throat, ripped from him in desperation as he pulled Max's bleeding and broken body into his lap. "Max please. Please, Max. Don't leave me." Ander pressed his hand to his cheek, turning his face to him. He was cold. So cold. It wasn't right.

Ander pressed a shaking hand to the large wound on his chest, forcing healing magic into him. Searching for even a single string of life to tug on, to pull desperately back into being.

The heat went in, and nothing responded.

"Max *please*!" Ander screamed, shaking him. "Baby, please. Look at me. Look at me. Sweetheart. No. Nononono . . . " He wailed, his body arched over Max as the weight of his pain bowed him low. Ander wrapped his arms tightly around Max's shoulders and pulled him in against his chest, rocking quickly, trying to soothe an ache that was forming so deep inside him, it was a chasm that could never be filled.

"Sweetheart, please. Don't leave me." This couldn't be happening. Not this. Anything but this. Ander would wake up soon from this terrible nightmare and realize that the battle was over and he had been hallucinating this whole time.

Max's body began to feel lighter, and Ander loosened his arms just in time to see his beloved's face one last time before his body disintegrated into ash and sparks, leaving Ander with nothing but dark soot covering his hands and torso.

"*No!*" It was a scream that came from his gut, ripping through him in a wave of agony and disbelief.

And above him, Enrique laughed. A deep, booming

sound that shook his body and made his eyes light up with satisfaction.

"Did you think you would win?" Enrique asked, gloating. "Did you think you could interfere in my plans so many times and never suffer the consequences?"

Ander looked up from the ashes covering his palms, all that was left of his soulmate. His eyes met Enrique's, and everything came back. Every angry word. Every oppressive thought. Every terrible, horrible thing Ander ever witnessed the god do or had done to him.

The pain inside him was matched only by the rage. A rage that had built for over a hundred years. It had only waited for one last spark to set it off entirely.

"Come for me, princeling. Let's end this once and for all." Enrique smirked and opened his arms wide.

He didn't fear Ander. He'd hurt him plenty of times in their relationship. Trapped him. Broken him. Beat him down until there was barely anything left. And now he had taken Ander's soulmate. Severed the ties between them with the strike of a sword.

Enrique wasn't afraid. But he should have been. Ander had nothing left to lose.

Ander's hands lifted from his sides, fire starting to burn in his palms. He laughed a manic laugh as his tears flowed freely down his face. He tipped his head back and let the rage and agony engulf him, erase any and every other thought until all that was inside him was the pain and the fury.

As he rose to his feet, Ander screamed. A primal scream filled with everything that he was feeling. And as he did, the flames spread to his entire body. Ander was nothing but the fire. It licked over his lips, twisted in his hair, curled around his arms and torso like a wicked lover.

Something changed in Enrique's eyes, the gleeful assurance fading just a tick. But Ander didn't wait, didn't let him stop to rethink what he was doing, and walked into Enrique's arms. He wrapped his own around his waist, pulling the god up against him, pressing his cheek to Enrique's so he could whisper in his ear, even as the god began to writhe and scream in agony.

"I will take you down with me," Ander breathed into him, flames licking his tongue and lapping at Enrique's lobe.

Ander watched the flesh burn and blacken, then seem to melt. Clutched tighter as Enrique fought to break free. Fought to get away from the flames. Fought to escape the agony of his death.

But the all-consuming grief in Ander was like a cage of iron. There was no escape. There was no breaking free.

Ander held him until only jerks and wheezes came from Enrique. Held him until any movement stopped. Held on until the form of the god began to shrink and shrivel into a husk of emptiness. Like a log that had burned down to its core.

Then he let go. Watched the god's blackened form hit the floor and shatter into wasted pieces of nothing. With it went the flames and the fury.

Ander returned to himself, smoke and steam rising from his shoulders and somehow still intact clothes as the flames disappeared.

He turned back to where Max had been and dropped to his knees. Shaking hands drifted through the ash, pulling the remnants of his love into a small pile.

The tears were gone, the fire having burned them all away.

All that remained was a hollow emptiness and the deep

ache that began at his core and wafted out on wave upon wave of endless pain.

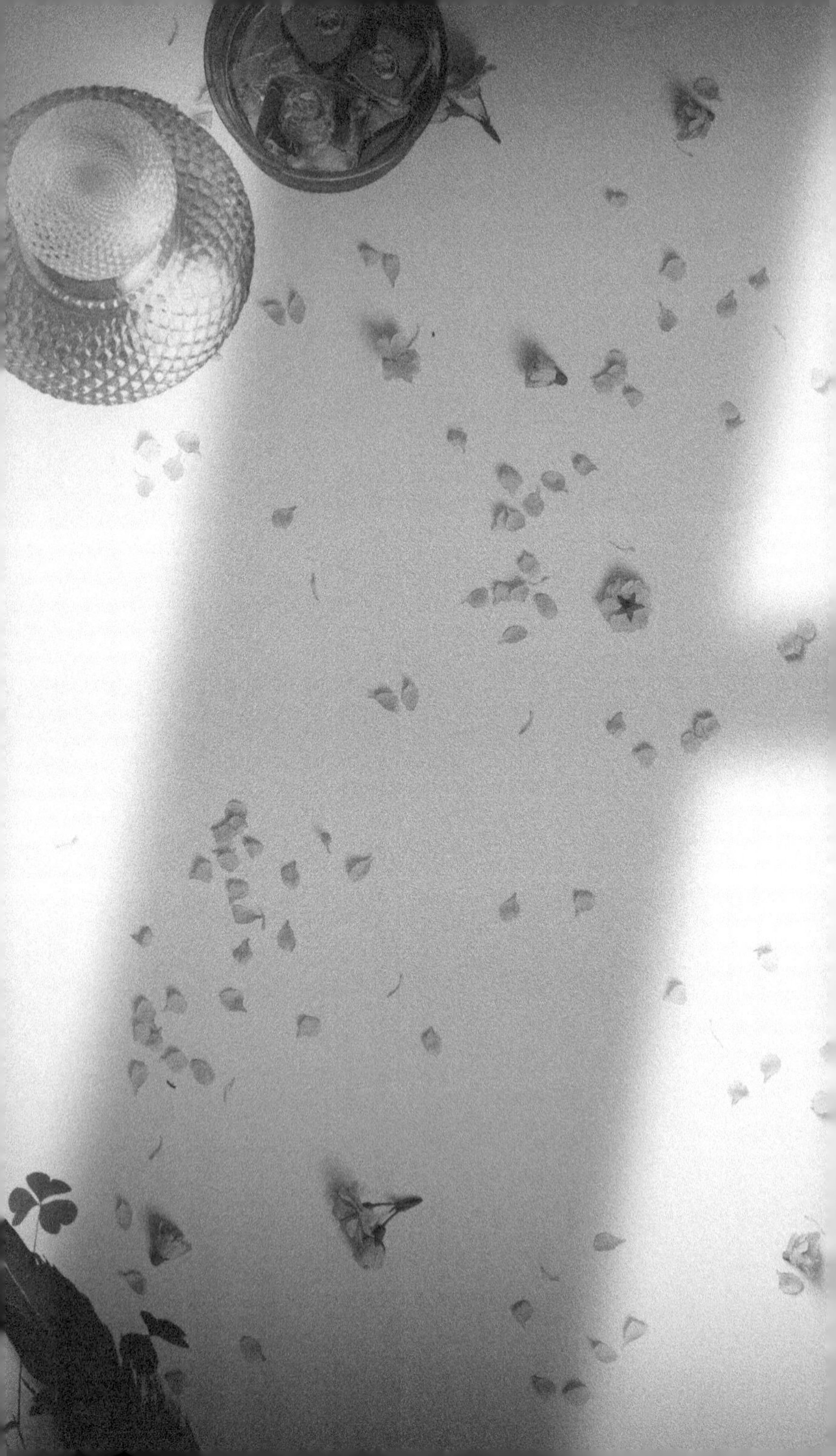

Chapter 58
Mab

Mab lifted her hand to rub at her eyes, scrubbing away the dust from the battle and hopefully the image in front of her. This couldn't be. It just *couldn't*.

But there it was just the same, she realized when her eyes opened again. Through the feathers and the dust, Ander Ruin, his face a mask of anguish so raw, it cut her to the bone, burning alive.

Enrique. Blood dripping from his hands. White feathers and viscera clumped on the polished metal of his sword, a crazed look in his eyes, a vicious victory Mab had thought she'd *avoided*.

She'd seen this before, centuries ago. But she'd stopped it. Hadn't she?

A scream. The final wail of a heart breaking ripped from Ander's throat as the flames burned hotter, turned from red to blue, staring not at Enrique but at the place where Max had been and was no longer. She'd thought that, in the vision, she couldn't see what he was looking at because of the brightness of the flame, but that wasn't true.

She couldn't see what he was looking at because the person he was searching for was *gone*.

Her eyes burned with tears that made the whole battle swim before her, Mab pushed out of Quin's hold. She had to get to Ander. She had to bring him out of his own head before he did something he couldn't take back. Before he left her entirely. Quin seemed as stunned by what was happening as she was, because he let her go, if just for the moment. Let her stumble forward on legs made of jelly across the broken, uneven marble streaked with ignis blood.

She had to stop him. It didn't matter what happened to her. She had to bring Ander back to himself before he burned himself out. Quin must have regained his senses because he scooped her up again, his big black wings curling around them both protectively, keeping her from advancing.

She struggled. Fought. Scratched. Kicked. Punched. Did everything but scream because what was the use in screaming now that Max was dead? Now that Ander would be left hollowed out and empty? The tears burned her cheeks, slid through grime and blood. She didn't stop struggling. Didn't stop telling Quin without words to put her fucking *down*. To let her go and do the thing she was always meant to do, the thing she'd been trying to do for the last hundred and fifty years! Ever since that day on the cliffs.

Stop her vision from becoming a reality.

She had failed him. She had failed all of them. She knew this was going to happen, and she hadn't been able to stop it. She hadn't been able to protect Ander. The one thing she was good at, the one thing she'd always vowed to do. She was a useless sack of shit for not seeing this coming.

And gradually, she stopped struggling. Silent, shaking

sobs pressed into Quin's neck, his shoulders, smearing the blood and the dirt from battle all over her face like war paint. Only the war was over. And she had *lost*.

Frustrated.

Devastated.

Furious.

Broken.

She was all of these things, and yet she was none of them because she'd failed at the one thing she'd been trying to do for over a century.

Stop the prophecy from coming true.

Save Ander Ruin.

Mab knew when it was all over because Quin finally let her go. Her feet touched the ground, and she was running across the slippery floor, heedless of the bodies in her way and the blood. Not caring at all about the fact that they were still surrounded by enemies on all sides. She'd throw herself on a blade if it would make this right for him.

The flames fizzled and sputtered just as she dropped down onto her knees beside Ander and pulled him into her chest. Her throat was still wrecked from her wail, but she could manage a harsh whispered, "I'm sorry."

I'm so sorry. I'm sorry. I'm sorry. Sorrysorrysorrysorry.

How could she have let this happen? How could she not have seen the differences between the scene in Acheron and her vision? Their clothes had been all wrong. There had been no white feathers on Enrique's sword. The floors were the wrong fucking color, for gods' sake, and she'd thought she'd defied fate. She'd thought she'd saved Ander from the destiny that was written for him in stone.

Arrogant. Prideful. Stupid. Bitch.

She rocked them, her fingers brushing through his hair, never giving up on the chant of apologies that scraped her throat raw. This wasn't right. It wasn't fair. Ander and Max had only just found each other. They'd been thrust together by the soulmate bond. Made for one another. Their love crafted by destiny herself. And then The Fates had ripped it away. How was that right? How was that fair? It wasn't! It wasn't! *It wasn't!*

A wall off to her left collapsed, and Mab curled her body more tightly around Ander to protect him from the rubble. When the dust settled, and Mab blinked, she found Indra standing in the big hole he'd obviously blasted in the wall. "I am here!"

Mab growled, the sound more a vibration than anything else. How fucking *dare* he.

"Uh . . . " Indra paused, his nose wrinkled a little as he surveyed what was left of the battle scene. Then he made his way over to where Mab was still curled protectively around Ander. Ander, who hadn't moved. Ander, who hadn't made a sound. Ander, who was just staring forward like there was nothing at all behind his eyes. "Mab, what happened?"

She knew it was going to tear her voice up for weeks to come. She knew she'd have to drink tea non-stop and avoid alcohol. She knew she wouldn't be talking for days. But it was worth it to snap her head around, narrow her eyes, and hiss in a whispered snarl, "You're too *late*." Her lips peeled back from her teeth. Vicious and biting. "You're here too late. Where *were* you, Indra? This was your fight! Where were you?"

Indra frowned, his beautiful face going distressed, though she wasn't sure if it was because of how soft her voice was or if it was the words themselves. "I was on my way. I was—"

"You weren't here." She curled more tightly around

Ander, pressing his face into her shoulder. The next words were ripped from her throat, and she tasted blood on her tongue again. "This whole thing is because you didn't do what I fucking *begged* you to a century and a half ago. All of this could have been avoided if you'd executed Enrique the last time he hurt Ander. But no. A hundred years of punishment would be enough, you told me. I knew it wouldn't be. I knew he'd just grow angrier, and more spiteful. You"—she pointed at Indra, her voice cracking—"are a *useless* god."

"Mab," Indra said, his tone a warning, but she was done. She was done with gods and prophecies and fate. She was done with all of it.

"Fuck off, Indra," she hissed, snapping her jaws in a vicious snarl when it looked like he might try to take Ander from her. "Consider yourself uninvited. Don't darken our doorstep ever again. And stay away from Ander."

With that, she ducked her head back to Ander and pressed her face into his hair, ignoring anything else Indra had to say to her. Ander was still breathing. But the shaking hadn't stopped yet. Would it ever? Would she ever be able to make this okay for him?

No. Probably not.

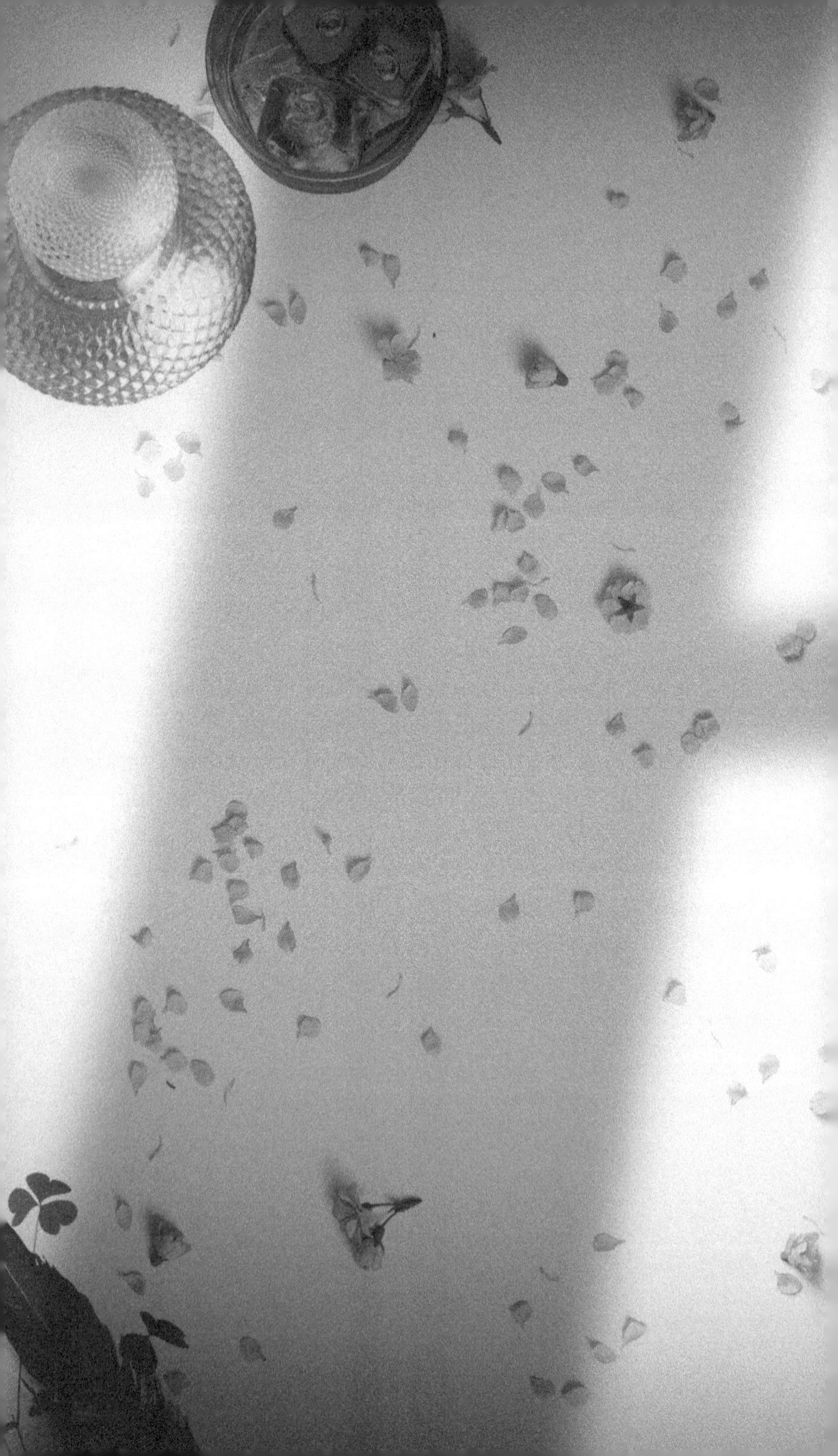

Chapter 59
Quin

Quin managed to hold Mab back from the flames. To keep her from burning herself alive on the fire that fully engulfed Ander. But after that, his mind shut down.

He released her as she pushed against him, letting her run to Ander to pull him into her arms. And his stomach lurched as the ashes that had once been Max wafted up into the air. They caught the light around them, sparkling in the sunlight that shone in from the large gothic windows on the eastern side of the room.

It couldn't be possible. One moment, Max had been there. His brother. His confidant. And the next, he was gone, bursting into a million little specks of ash and sparks.

Gone. His essence returning to the primordial fires they had all been crafted in. Not his soul. Ignis didn't have souls. But the fiery essence that had created them all. That flowed through their veins and heated them from the inside. They were all a part of the primordial fire, and when their immortal life ended, they returned to it.

Quin couldn't breathe.

There was a weight crushing down on his chest that kept each breath short and desperate.

He finally tore his eyes away from Mab and Ander and the gray pile of ash and sought out the twins. Nox and Nash clung to each other, their faces smeared in grime and blood. Their hands empty of any weapons as they filled with each other's clothing.

Their visible pain brought him back to himself. Made Quin force more oxygen into his lungs, breathing in deeply through his nose and slowly out through his mouth. He couldn't fall apart. Max wasn't here to be the one that held them all together.

Max wasn't here.

Max was gone.

It was a fresh wound, lancing through his chest and making his insides ache.

Ignis weren't supposed to be able to love. But what did you call this feeling inside him if it wasn't love? This pain did not come from a mere acquaintance. This pain came from true loss.

Quin stepped over to the twins and pulled them both into him. Their sobs came fresh as they turned into him, burying their faces into his shoulders and clinging to the fabric of his shirt just below his wings.

He held them because that was all he could do. There were no words for what had just happened. No way to explain it away.

Quin barely acknowledged that King Indra was there now, his army collecting the rest of Orcus' group, binding them and chaining them together. Beyond, where the dais stood, the two Princeps who were still alive were being freed from Orcus' chains. They rubbed at their wrists and shook out their wings.

They hadn't seen Orcus coming either. Had been able to do nothing against his onslaught.

No one had done anything. If they'd only stopped him in the beginning, locked him back up sooner, *executed* him for his treason ...

Max would still be alive.

But Quin hadn't done anything either.

He should have told Max they needed to wait. Shouldn't have come in here with Mab to take down the first wave of soldiers. They had been too cocky. Too sure of their abilities after making it this far.

None of them had stopped to think, to reason. To suggest they wait for Indra or Aemiliana to arrive.

Quin should have.

He should have forced them to wait. To make them stand guard at the doors until reinforcements arrived.

Max would still be alive.

His brother and sister wouldn't be sobbing into his shirt. He wouldn't have to go home and break the news to his parents and his baby sister that Max was never coming home. That they hadn't gotten a chance to say goodbye.

They'd been too full of themselves. Too sure that good was going to triumph over evil because that was the way the world was *supposed* to work.

But in reality, it wasn't how the world worked. Awful things happened all the time. Truly terrible things were allowed to take place. Hurting people. *Breaking* people.

The world was dark. Life was cruel. And The Fates did not care who they tore apart for their plans to unfold.

"What are we going to do?" Nox asked, hiccupping through her tears. She stared up at him, her eyes begging him to have a solution.

"I don't know." He spoke honestly. "Do you have an

empty canister?" he asked, struggling to keep his voice from shaking but failing.

"I do," Nash whispered, pulling an empty metal canister from his pocket. Something they used to collect evidence. It was no bigger than the palm of his hand, only three inches in diameter and two high. But it would work.

Quin took it from him and pulled away. Instantly, the twins folded back into each other's arms.

They were lucky they had each other. The other half of themselves was still here. There was comfort in that for them.

The shoulder Quin had leaned on was gone. His solace in the dark, taken away. He had done nothing to protect the beloved brother that had brought him from a cocoon of silence into the world of the living.

Slow, careful steps carried Quin over to where Mab and Ander still kneeled, Mab curled around Ander in a protective manner. She looked like she was ready to knife anyone who came for them.

He made sure to approach from her front so that she saw him coming. She began to curl up more, as if she were readying to attack or fight him off of Ander. He held up a hand to her to let her know she was okay.

Then he kneeled, opening the canister, and gently scooped some of the ashes into the bottom of it. He couldn't just go back to his parents and tell them Max was gone. He couldn't go home and leave them with nothing of their son. The first youngling they'd brought into their home. The one who made them parents to begin with.

When the canister was filled, Quin pressed the small, metal lid back on top of it.

It didn't seem right, or feasible that it was his brother's

ashes inside. That all that was left of Max's brightness, his kindness, and his love was a pile of dust.

"I failed him." It was raspy and so quiet, Quin could barely make it out.

But he lifted his head to look at Mab, who was staring back at him, her brown eyes tear-filled and aching.

"So did I."

Quin didn't need to specify that he meant Max. She knew. Knew that he was also aching over the loss of his brother. Over the way he'd failed to protect him. Failed to be there fighting at his side as his partner.

They stared at each other. A whole world between them.

There was a pull inside him that still drew him to her. A pull that wanted him to wrap his arms around her shoulders and keep her safe from all that was plaguing her.

But he couldn't save her from this. The damage had been done. Quin didn't know how to bridge the gap or even if he wanted to. If she wanted to.

Max was gone. Ander was broken.

And Mab and Quin were on either side of a vast divide of pain and tears.

They had all failed. There was no winner of this battle.

There was only what came after.

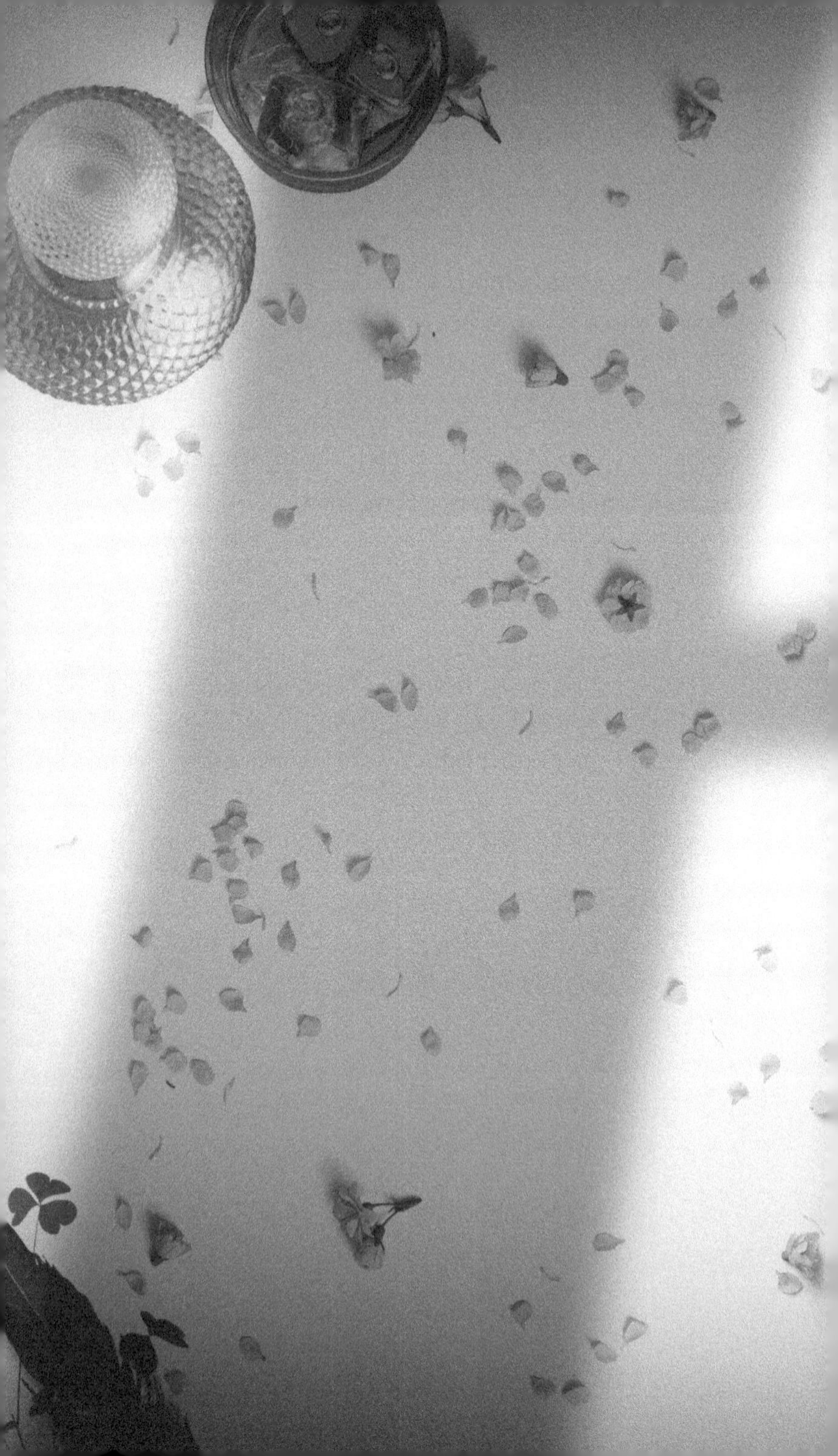

Epilogue
The Ghost

There was a man in a condo with a view of the ocean.

There was a man with a little white dog.

There was a man with horns and dark hair.

There was a man with all of those things who had not moved in what seemed like hours, but perhaps it had been days; it was hard for the little ghost fire to understand time with the way that they blinked in and out of existence sometimes.

The little ghost fire did not know the man's name or how they were connected, but they were drawn to him over and over again. Every time they blinked from existence and managed to gather their essence again, they wound up floating back to him. Lingering in the corners of the rooms where he sat, staring listlessly.

The little ghost fire didn't know why they were there or who they had been before, but they knew that they weren't meant to stay. There was a call like a mermaid always in the back of their mind, a not-so-gentle reminder that they didn't belong in this place. Not anymore. Begging and pleading for them to return to the eternal flame of their kind. Insisting that they abandon this life. But they couldn't. They were still tied to this place, to this man. They didn't think they'd have it any other way.

There was a man with horns and dark hair, who cried sometimes. Who said a name into the stillness of his condo with a view of the ocean, as if by saying the name, he could bring that person back.

The little ghost fire would try to reach for him sometimes. Would float close to him and try to nuzzle themselves against his cheek. Ultimately, they always went right through him. Because they were not really there. They were just a little ghost fire. Just a half-remembered life that they couldn't seem to let go of.

But the ghost would keep trying. Their flame would flicker, burn out, and reignite over and over again if it meant they could come back to the sad man in the condo that echoed with silence. They wouldn't return to the fire, not so long as this man needed them.

Did he need them?

Why did they think he needed them?

It didn't matter.

The little golden flame wasn't going anywhere.

Acknowledgments

We are so thankful to have gotten a chance to continue the Sanctuary of the Lost. This series embodies values we both hold dear: the importance of found families, and acceptance/celebration of personal differences that make us all unique. While Of Love and Ruin was a tale for the cinnamon rolls out there, Of Hope and Blight is for the introverts. Those who enjoy their own personal space more than any other, people watching from a distance, intimate settings with close friends, and speaking only when there is something important to say.

Mab and Quin are the steady, silent players on the side who always remain loyal, show up for you even when they'd rather be somewhere else, and will absolutely go down with you in your sinking ship. We want to thank every reader who excitedly commented on their hope of seeing more of them and showed so much love for both when they were only side characters to Ander and Max's love. Thank you for your patience in their slow burning love story, and we promise you there is more to come.

Thank you so much to our beta readers. As always, your love of the characters and desire to see the book become the best that it can be is appreciated and felt. Where would we be without you?

To Meg, our glorious, fearless editor, you polish our work to perfection! And your comments in the notes fuels our muse for the third and final book.

Lastly, we wish you all happy reading, and hope to see you all for Sanctuary of the Lost Book 3; Of Blight and Ruin.

XOXO
 Lou & Christis

About Christis Christie

Christis Christie was born and raised in a small town in New Brunswick, Canada where she spent most of her time either reading someone else's book, or dreaming of writing her own. Her favourite thing to dive into is an epic fantasy, or anything else magical and wondrous that really allows her imagination to take her away.

She now lives on the East Coast in Halifax, Nova Scotia where she works as an event designer, putting her interior decorating degree to wonderful use. Whenever she's not busy magically transforming venues for her clients, Christis is working on her own writing, playing with her mischievous cat, Robert, or attending local CPL football matches with her partner.

One day, she hopes to visit Costa Rica, to sleep with the sloths.

Also By Christis Christie

Spun Gold: A Rumpelstiltskin Origin Story

Reaping Book One: Epheus

Sanctuary of the Lost
  Of Loyalties and Wreckage
  Of Love and Ruin
  Of Hope and Blight

Anthologies
  Cirque de vol Mystique
  Something in the Shadows: A Halloween Anthology
  Emporium of Superstition - An Old Wives' Tale Anthology

Co-Authored with Elle Beaumont:
  The Dragon's Bride
  Seeds of Sorrow (Immortal Realms Book 1)
  Tides of Torment (Immortal Realms Book 2)
  Wages of War (Immortal Realms Book 3)

About Lou Wilham

Born and raised in a small town near the Chesapeake Bay, Lou Wilham grew up on a steady diet of fiction, arts and crafts, and Old Bay. After years of absorbing everything there was to absorb of fiction, fantasy, and sci-fi she's left with a serious writing/drawing habit that just won't quit. These days, she spends much of her time writing, drawing, and chasing a very short Basset Hound named Sherlock.

When not, daydreaming up new characters to write and draw she can be found crocheting, making cute bookmarks, and binge-watching whatever happens to catch her eye.

For more information visit
www.LouInProgress.com
Follow Lou on social media!

facebook.com/LouWilham
instagram.com/lou.wilham

Also By Lou Wilham

The Witches of Moondale
The Hex Next Door
The Ghost of Hexes Past
Home is Where the Hex Is

The Hunters of Ironport
Overkill
Fresh Kill

Sanctuary of the Lost
Of Loyalties and Wreckage
Of Love and Ruin
Of Hope & Blight

Benvolio & Mercutio Turn Back Time

The Heir To Moondust
The Prince of Starlight
The Prince of Daybreak
The Crown of Night
The Kings of Dusk & Dawn

Completed Series
    The Tales of the Sea Trilogy
    Villainous Heroics
    The Clockwork Chronicles
    The Curse Collection

More Books You'll Love

If you enjoyed this story, please consider leaving a review.

Then check out more books from Midnight Tide Publishing!

Of Flames and Curses by Whitney L. Spradling

Do fairies exist?

This is the question Lainey asks herself after her sister's brutal murder in Central Park. Armed with her sister's diary and the mysterious entries within, Lainey's quest for answers leads her to Phoenix, a surly but handsome fae.

The answer to Lainey's question reveals a truth that will change everything she thought she knew about herself and the world she lives in. A sacrifice must be made to break a curse that locked the gate between the human and faerie realms.

Leaving the only world she has known, Lainey finds

herself surrounded by evil queens, curses, and magical creatures. Together, Lainey and Phoenix must find a way to break the curse that doesn't result in Lainey's death—like her sister's.

Do fairies exist? The answer will change Lainey's life in ways she never imagined.

Available Now

Maiden of the Hollow Path by Shar Khan

Something dark has shaped the Marizad Palace and pulled Shahina Rukhezzi from exile. After spending eight years amongst the dwarven regime, the Paragon and Fifth Raja to the Lotus Throne has returned. A curse has touched the royal family, leaving the Great and Immortal Maharaj to stray upon his death bed.

In the seaport city of Stonegrave, Crogan Takahashi stands as the King of Lords. He rules over the War Table in a place forsaken and left to rot. With magicks that run rampant through his veins, he finds himself at the mercy of Shahina who searches for answers he's not willing to give so easily.

Yet as her presence pulls dark entities from their resting place in the Northern Province, Crogan learns there are things worse than death. As an ancient evil struggles to take the throne, he realizes Shahina might not be as bad as she seems.

Or so he thinks.

Available Soon

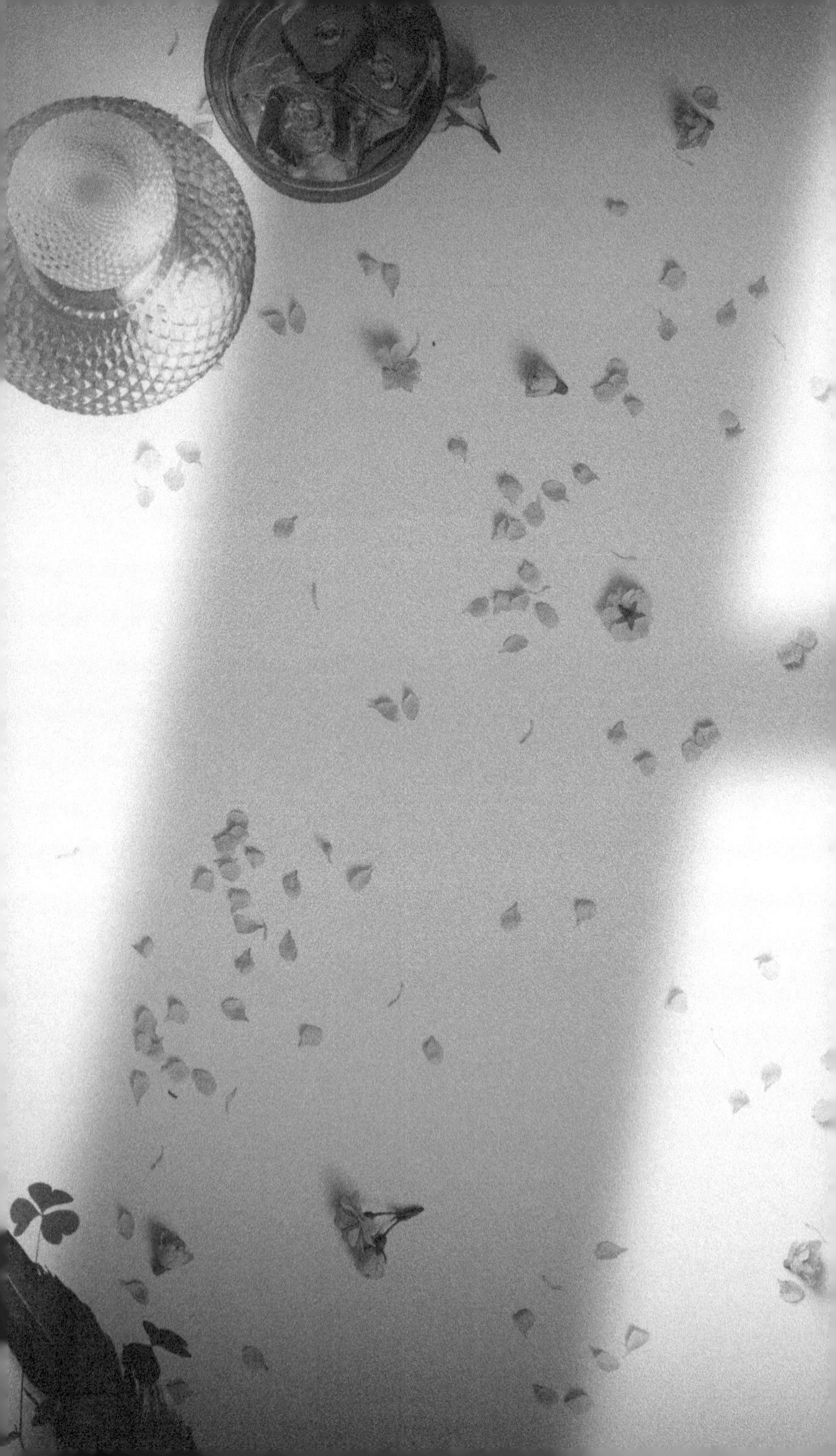

Dead Rockstar by Lillah Lawson

Stormy Spooner is at her wits' end. Careening towards bitter after a nasty divorce, she sometimes wonders what her life is becoming.

After unearthing a cryptic set of lines from a dusty album cover, Stormy tries the impossible: to resurrect Phillip Deville, enigmatic former frontman of the Bloomer Demons. Stormy's love for her favorite dead rockstar knows no bounds…but it was all supposed to be a joke.

When she answers a knock on her door the next day and finds herself face to face with the dark-haired rock god of her every teenage fantasy, her entire world is turned upside down.

Turns out, she's awakened more than just Philip, and Stormy will have to do battle against a cast of strange characters to keep herself and her new undead boyfriend safe.

Available May 15, 2024

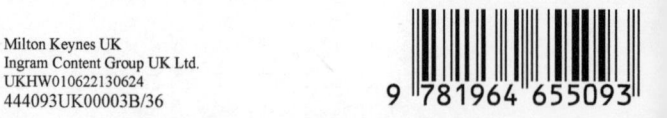

Milton Keynes UK
Ingram Content Group UK Ltd.
UKHW010622130624
444093UK00003B/36